UNTIL GREG

PULSETUNES ROCK GODS SERIES

K.L. SHANDWICK

Copyright © K. L. Shandwick 2023

The author has asserted their moral right under the Copyright, Designs and Patents Act, 1988, to be identified as the author of this work.

All Rights reserved. No part of this publication may be reproduced, copied, stored in a retrieval system, or transmitted, in any form or by any means, without the prior written consent of the copyright holder, nor be otherwise circulated in any form of binding or cover other than that in which it is published and without a similar condition being imposed on the subsequent purchaser.

This ebook is a work of fiction, Names, places, characters, band names and incidents are the product of the author's imagination or names are used within the fictitious setting. Any resemblance to actual person's living or dead. Band names or locales are entirely coincidental.

DEDICATION

this book is dedicated to the unsung heroes
of any rock band
- Bass players

"None of us wanted to be the bass player. In our minds he was the fat guy who always played at the back" ~ Paul McCartney

PROLOGUE

GREG

"Excuse me, my name is Annie, and my girlfriend Lou-Ellen, over there, bet me five hundred dollars that I wouldn't walk up to a hot young guy and ask him for a kiss."

I eyed the embarrassed, mature, redhead with the gorgeous crystal blue eyes and fantastic smile, and I figured, why not?

Although the dress she wore was tacky and she was quite a bit older than me, she had obviously taken care of herself. She was exactly my type—big tits, small waist, firm ass. She was a knockout.

Smiling, I slung my arm around her waist, and as I drew her body toward me, she wobbled on her feet.

Annie was petite, slightly drunk and her breathing grew faster as I took her in my arms. Her muscles tensed as I held her firmly, yet she had somehow fit perfectly against me. Staring down at her, I bit back another smile when I saw how petrified she looked. Glancing over at her friend that had dared her to ask, I flashed her a wicked grin.

"Are you really down for this?" I queried when I gazed back down into her beautiful, worried eyes.

"It's a bit late to back out now," she replied, a little less boldly than her playful tone when she'd first sidled up to me.

As her posture was still rigid, I found myself stroking her back in a soothing gesture as I gave her what I had hoped was a more reassuring smile. "Guess what?" I asked, whispering into her ear, so only she could hear. A shiver ran through her that made her knees buckle. I pulled her tighter to my chest and as I steadied her, she swallowed nervously, but determinedly held my gaze. "You just won yourself half a grand."

I chuckled when her breath hitched, and I guessed that she hadn't believed I'd say yes. Then, as I wanted to give her friend a show for losing that five hundred bucks, I crashed my mouth down on Annie's.

My initial reaction was that it was like kissing a dead fish. Annie's mouth was open more from surprise than to give me access, and there was no sign of tongue.

However, the moment mine found hers my body woke up as if I'd thrown a burning match into a box filled with fireworks.

Her body sagged against mine and a soft moan escaped her lungs. My dick swelled as I felt her give herself over to me, and when another soft moan of pleasure rolled from her tongue to mine, desire sparked within me.

Tentatively, her hands moved up my back until her fingertips reached the nape of my neck and she ran them gently along my hairline. A moment later, her nails scrapped over the back of my scalp as she surrendered to the pure passion of our kiss.

Since I'd been in the band and had sex on a very regular basis, my cock seldom grew hard from a kiss. In fact, kissing wasn't high on my to-do list these days. I was cautiously unsure of where those groupies' mouths had been before me. That said, the moment Annie kissed me back, my dick responded to her.

A little perturbed by my body's reaction to her, I pulled back, stared at her, then dropped my hands from her waist. Annie stepped back, eyes wide in shock. She looked deliciously flushed, and slightly out of breath as she struggled to hold my gaze.

Raising her fingertips to her swollen lips, I could see by the lust I had sparked within her eyes that it had been some time since she'd been kissed passionately by any man. Then, for some strange reason, I felt oddly responsible for putting that attractively dazed look on her face.

"Oh, my fucking God," Lou-Ellen blurted out, breaking the stunned-into-silence moment that had been passing between us. "Look at you! Annie McGillvary, you should be paying me five hundred bucks for challenging you to do that."

For a long moment, Annie stood motionless, blinking rapidly, still pink in the face, as she tried to come to terms with what she had done. Eventually, she sucked in a sharp breath and shook her head. "Wow."

"You're welcome," I replied, chuckling, but feeling confused by the instant connection I'd felt between us during the kiss.

She slapped her palm on her forehead as her eyes instantly brimmed with tears. Then, she made several attempts at clearing her throat before I realized she was distressed. "I wasn't expecting that."

"Hey," I said softly, my smile falling from my face as I cupped her chin and raised her face to look at me. My heart stalled when I saw how upset she'd become, and I second guessed myself about what her expectation had been when she'd propositioned me. "What's the deal? You got what you asked for."

"It's nothing, I'm sorry," she muttered, laughing nervously even though she was barely holding it together. Then, as if something spooked her, she pushed past me and headed toward the bar restrooms.

Folding my arms, my eyes instantly narrowed as I glared at

Lou-Ellen, believing I'd missed something. "Not had that reaction to kissing someone before."

She threw her head back, laughing. "Oh, don't mind Annie. She'll be fine. It's about damn time she got back on that horse. I'm glad you pushed through and took her up on her dare.

"I knew what she was doing, picking the hottest guy in the room without a date. She expected you to laugh and decline. "My guess is she's just a tad overwhelmed. I mean, you're most likely the first guy she's kissed since her husband passed away nine years ago."

"Fuck," I muttered angrily as I ran a hand over my head. "I'm going to check up on her." My widowed mother instantly came to mind. It had been around fourteen years since my dad had died, and she still grieved her loss. Shoving past a puzzled-looking Lou-Ellen, I made my way to the restrooms to find Annie.

"Wow, you're Greg Booker," a cute, little brunette mumbled, smiling coyly as she twiddled a curl around her finger. If I'd met her at any other moment, I'd likely have given her the time of day, but my focus was on the distressed woman in the bathroom, that I'd clearly upset.

"Thanks for the ID check, baby. For a minute there, I was wondering who I was," I replied sarcastically as I gently moved her out of the way, and stepped inside the restroom. Once I'd closed the door, it drowned out the music and I was pleased to see that there was only one girl in there apart from one person who was behind the only closed stall door in the restroom.

"Can you give us a minute?" I asked the girl who stood staring at me, obviously starstruck. "Baby?" I asked like a question, prompting her again.

"Su-sure, Greg," she mumbled, nodding like she knew me. It still freaked me out that random people I'd never met knew me by name. As she began walking toward me, I moved to the side, opened the restroom door, and she left without saying anything else.

I tapped lightly on the stall door. "Annie?" I asked softly.

When I got no reply, I wondered for a second if it even was Annie behind the door. *What the fuck are you doing Greg?* An image of a potential story in a tabloid newspaper flashed through my mind, its headline carrying a story about me hanging around women's restrooms.

I turned, almost ready to get the hell out of there when a woman's small voice replied, "God, I'm sorry."

"Annie?" I questioned.

"What are you doing in here?" she asked, sounding alarmed.

"Do you think you could get your ass out of there? I've learned from Korry's experience in our band that it doesn't take much for the wrong kind of story to circulate in the press." The bolt on the door clicked and she stepped out, her red-rimmed eyes making it apparent what she'd been doing in the stall. In that moment she struck me as vulnerable, and my heart clenched to think I'd made her cry.

"Jesus, Mary and Joseph, am I that bad at kissing that I reduce a beautiful woman to tears?" I teased, making light of the situation.

"The kiss ..." she shrugged as she glanced up at me through watery eyes and swiped roughly at her nose with some toilet tissue.

"Personally, I thought it was pretty incredible," I remarked, sounding serious and cutting her off. "But it's obvious from your tear-stained face that we weren't experiencing the same thing." I flashed her a small smile and her lips curved in one of her own.

"It's just ..." she shrugged, lost for words and I thought she was going to cry again.

"I know, your friend told me," I muttered, sparing her the ordeal of talking to me about her loss. "It's okay, I get it. If I'd known the circumstances, I'd still have given you that kiss because … well, you're gorgeous. But perhaps it would have been a peck on the cheek."

"You don't need to flatter me to take the edge off of my stupid reaction," she insisted.

"Oh, is that what you think I'm doing? I'm not one for saying something I don't mean. It's a waste of my breath. Annie, you're an extremely attractive woman, and those eyes," I groaned. "I could stare at them all day."

Looking instantly flustered, she turned, stepped back into the restroom cubicle, and threw the damp tissue into the toilet. After flushing it, she then wandered over to a sink. "What would a bad boy like you want with an old woman like me?" she asked as she began to wash her hands.

I laughed at her assessment of me as a bad boy. "Plenty," I replied. "And you're not old, you're mature. I love mature women … maybe because I'm not … mature," I said, laughing again.

Annie stopped washing her hands. "Did you just tell me that you're immature?"

I chuckled. "I have cultivated that reputation," I confessed, smiling. "But, whatever, people can say what they want. I know what I am, and I'm completely at peace in my skin." Her eyes narrowed like she was reassessing her opinion of me. "So, what would you say if I asked you to join me for a drink. Since we've exchanged saliva, I think it only right that I buy you a drink at the very least."

"You shouldn't feel guilty, and you don't need to buy me a drink."

"I know … and I don't feel guilty for kissing you. I do feel a little responsible for how I reacted when your friend set up that dare. Besides, I wouldn't waste money on someone I wasn't invested in. And I certainly wouldn't give away free alcohol, my friends would vouch for that. I can be a bit wayward, but I never do anything that I don't want to."

Annie huffed out a breath, and for a moment I thought she was going to decline. Then, she shrugged, and a small smile played on her lips. "Oh, what the hell. If I can use your excuse, everyone has the right to get a little wayward in Vegas. Come on, you can buy me a bourbon on the rocks."

PROLOGUE

ANNIE

*S*tartled awake by the sound of an unfamiliar male voice talking in a strange accent, I instantly froze. A streak of fear coursed through my veins as I lay trying to comprehend what the speaker was saying during the rapid monologue. As there were pauses, it occurred to me that he was on the phone.

My heartbeat thrummed against my ribcage as I tried to reflect through the haze, until the pounding headache lodged at the base of my skull grew more intense.

Vegas. I'm in Las Vegas, I suddenly remembered, relieved for this small recollection that brought about a brief respite. *Is Lou-Ellen here with me as well? What the hell is a man doing in my hotel room?*

"Lou-Ellen?" I mouthed because nothing came out when I moved my mouth and spoke.

My body felt heavy and too fatigued to try harder. It then occurred to me that I was naked beneath a cotton sheet that covered my frame from my chest to my toes.

Another streak of fear initially stopped me from looking to see where the voice was coming from. Then, I became frustrated because I couldn't sufficiently tune into his tone, and so I couldn't understand what he was saying. This was more due to how quickly he spoke, the constant sound of blood rushing through my ears and how sluggish my thought processes were.

Gingerly, I slid a hand across the bed to check that I was there alone, then was relieved on the one hand to know that I was, and desperately embarrassed on the other because it meant I might have been in bed with some unknown man.

Holy shit? Was I kidnapped and drugged? Is this one of those date rape cases like I'd seen in TV documentaries?

I cracked an eye open very briefly and saw instantly that I wasn't in my hotel room. For a few moments I lay trying to formulate a plan for my escape, wondering if my purse was nearby, or if I could create a chance to call reception from the hotel room phone to summon help.

Peeking through mostly closed eyes, I glanced around the unfamiliar room. Then, my heart stopped for a beat. A jolt of electricity left a sour, metallic taste in my mouth from the shock, the moment I recognized the gorgeous, young, tattooed man pacing the floor in front of me.

Then, a memory of the most incredibly passionate kiss I'd had since my husband died, made my core pulse.

Humiliation overwhelmed me as I wracked my brain for flashbacks of what we'd done in the bed I was laid in. When nothing came to mind, a suffocating feeling of distress left me struggling to breathe.

It was strange because my memories around our kiss became crystal clear, at how gentle and kind he'd been when I'd gotten upset.

Straining for recollection, I vaguely remembered him introducing me to his friends. Then more memories of my heart feeling lighter than it had in years as we drank and danced in the bar.

After that, my mind was blank, and I could remember nothing at all from then onward.

Quietly, I lay observing him strutting back and forth at the bottom of the hotel bed, padding around naked with one hand over his lean, muscular chest. He was chatting in a playful tone on his cell phone like he didn't have a care in the world.

Fuck, how did I get here ... and what the heck did we do?

I didn't feel sore and prayed that this meant we hadn't had sex because I had no recollection of this. Had I been sober, there was no way I'd ever have agreed to such an act, especially with a man so young.

"All right, I'll speak to you next weekend," I heard him say in a singsong, cheerful tone as he concluded the call. Then, I had my first full frontal glimpse of his delicious, athletic build as he wondered up my side of the bed and lifted the receiver on the hotel room phone.

"Hello, could I order some breakfast to be brought up to my suite?" he asked. There was a slight pause before he said, "Right then, could I get some scrambled eggs, bacon, tomatoes and mushrooms ... are your sausages pork, beef or chicken?" he asked, planting his ass on the bed only inches from me. "Pork ... four of everything and some brown bread toast, oh can I get some white as well? I'm not sure what my wife likes, and I'll take some beans and grits. Coffee and orange juice to drink, and bananas ... and pancakes." He chuckled. "Ah, well, you could say we worked up a bit of an appetite for this morning."

Wife? Whether it was because I was fully alert by then or he was talking to someone American, the speed of his conversation suddenly sounded slower, allowing me to process his words, and I figured he sounded Irish.

After he hung up, the mattress decompressed when he stood up again. Relief washed through my body when I thought he had stepped away.

"Are you intending on lying there sleeping all day?" he asked.

I squinted through the same cracked-open eyes around the room again, thinking perhaps there was someone else with us that I'd missed, then I realized he was talking to me.

"What the hell am I doing here?" I asked gruffly. Once I opened my eyes and took in his naked frame again, I was instantly mortified. My heart pounded in my chest, at us both being naked and we were alone.

Alarm registered in his bulged eyes, and his jaw dropped for a second before he recovered. "Ah, you're joking, right?" he asked, grinning and wagging a finger playfully toward me.

"Am I? Exactly what would I be joking about?"

His smile faltered before he grinned wider. "Oh, you're good, you almost had me there."

Struggling to sit up, I carefully tried to protect my modesty by tucking the bed sheet under my arms. Staring pointedly toward him with a racing heart, I shook my head. "Look, this isn't a joke," I muttered, acutely aware of the panic in my tone. "You need to help me out because I have no idea how I got here, or even where I am."

"You remember nothing? Or are you trying to back out now because we did the deed and that makes all that we did legal now?" he questioned, frowning.

"Makes what legal?" My spine straightened in distrust.

"You, being my wife—Mrs. Booker. It took us no time at all to consummate our marriage," he explained, nodding toward my hand. I glanced down to it and saw a ring with a huge stone that I guessed was zirconia. I laughed. "I might live in the sticks, but that doesn't make me stupid."

"Whatever the hell that means," he replied, looking puzzled. "If you want to back out of it now, we'd need to get an annulment because I'm not down with divorce," he replied.

"How much do you want?" I asked, wondering if I had been duped and he somehow knew I had money. I considered how stupid I was for making such a monumental fuck-up on my first vacation in many years.

"How much do I want?" he asked, snickering. "Getting married was your idea. When you asked me last night, I was drunk. Even so, I suggested holding off for a proper wedding in a chapel. You were the one that challenged me that it was now or never when you suggested that little chapel down the strip."

"Wedding? I asked you to marry me?" I shrieked. "Are you fucking insane? How old are you?"

"Twenty-eight," he told me, looking proud of that fact. Like he figured that was plenty old enough.

"Jesus, I have kids older than you," I stated, and I immediately felt dizzy. "I would never ask anyone to marry me."

"Well, you asked me in front of a whole pub full of people," he replied, grinning proudly. "Got down on one knee and said nothing would make you happier than to be Mrs. Greg Booker."

"I've never heard anything so ridiculous, like I'd ever do that. Besides, you can't just get married … even in Vegas." Relief flooded my body when I thought about this and let out a long sigh in relief. My muscles instantly relaxed when my remark sank in.

"Yup that's true. That's why we headed to the Clark County Marriage place to get one."

"That's it, I'm calling bullshit. Put some clothes on, you've had your fun. Where's Lou-Ellen? This is a sick joke, and it needs to stop now." I heaved ragged breaths to try to maintain some calm.

"Oh, it's no joke, darlin'. See for yourself," he muttered and handed me the paperwork that said I was his wife. I stared at the document and recognized my signature before I stared in stunned silence toward him. "If you still don't believe me, check this out."

Picking up his cell phone, he opened the picture gallery and sure enough, there we were, standing at an alter in a wedding chapel, kissing. It was a selfie he'd taken, and I was dumbfounded.

"Our marriage is as serious as it gets. You can thank your

friend, Lou-Ellen for your new husband. She placed a ten grand bet on us that we wouldn't go through with it. She disappeared from the proceedings, but we're legally hitched."

"This is un-freaking believable. I mean, if we were that drunk, surely the pastor should take some responsibility for this fiasco." *We must have been completely inebriated.* "How the hell did we manage to get a license?"

"Bernadette helped us," he remarked sheepishly.

I studied Greg carefully, and decided he didn't have the remotest possibility of fitting into my world … or me in his. Granted, he was one of the hottest men I'd ever seen, but with his tattoos and almost shaved head, he looked far more suited to a motorcycle club, than coping with a cattle drive on the prairies. "You're a kid … you can't be tied … and who the fuck is Bernadette?"

"She's our band's PA," he said proudly with a smile.

"Band's PA? Are you freaking kidding me? This has got to be the biggest cliché ever. This has the hallmark of insanity about it. It's laughable. Are you seriously telling me, I got so drunk that I married a guy in a band?"

"Wait," he said, looking offended. "You really don't know who I am?" he inquired, like he was offended.

"Well, you already said your name is Greg Booker. Apart from that, no. And I couldn't give a flying fuck if you're King Kong. You … and me … we really can't be married," I said, wagging my finger between us. "My boys are going to go nuts when they hear about this." I shook my head, thinking that Greg was cocky because he couldn't believe that I hadn't heard of him and his two-bit band before.

"You're in cahoots with Lou-Ellen, aren't you? Has she put you up to this? What I want to know is, are you some kind of mail-order groom from Ireland?" I rambled, suddenly suspicious. "Why would a gorgeous, young musician want to marry me—unless it was for visa status or a cut of my money."

"Your money?" he asked, then scoffed indignantly before he wandered toward me with his bare cock directly at my eye line. I almost gave myself whiplash turning away from him, mortified by the close, personal view of his impressive cock.

Focusing on the bathroom door, I inhaled deeply lured by the smell of clean man and citrus shower gel. It was obviously from this that he had recently showered, and my core pulsed in reaction to the sexy, fresh scent of him closely behind me. I swallowed roughly when I allowed myself to turn back to look up at his face.

"You're not honestly going to sit there and tell me you don't recognize me?" Greg persisted, looking perplexed. "I figured that's why you sought me out for that kiss. I thought you'd think I'd be unfazed by your request."

"How would I? I've never seen you before. Now would you please put some clothes on? It's embarrassing and you're making me feel vulnerable sitting here like this. How am I supposed to have a serious conversation with you, while you're standing there naked."

"Is that right? Because you sure as shit weren't shy last night, when you palmed my dick through my jeans in front of everyone and told them my dick was yours."

I covered my face with my hands, groaned into them and wanted to die. A wave of guilt and sadness overwhelmed me because I had never touched another man until then, and when I made that choice, it should have been a highly significant act with someone who meant something to me. "Please ... just ..."

"All right, you win," he muttered. "Do you want to grab a shower? I already had one. Breakfast will be here soon," he informed me. Turning, he slipped his legs into his jeans, pulled them over his ass and turned, fastening his zipper.

"A shower would be good," I mumbled, still shaken, and

confused by the whole incident. "Can you turn to face the window until I get out of bed?"

"For God's sake, we're married," he grumbled under his breath as I quickly scooted off the bed and grabbed the stupid dress that had been yet another of Lou-Ellen's bets. Snatching my purse off the floor, I darted into the bathroom.

The moment I bolted the door, I fished out my cell phone. Seeing that it only had ten percent battery left and twenty-seven text messages, I quickly called Lou-Ellen.

"Where the hell have you been? I was ready to file a missing person's report. I thought you'd been kidnapped," she blurted, sounding anxious after answering on the first ring.

"You're fucking dead when I get a hold of you," I muttered. "Tell me this isn't real," I pleaded.

"What isn't real? What's happened? Where are you?"

"With my naked, tattooed husband," I snapped. "Apparently, I got married during the night. You owe me ten grand by the way."

Lou-Ellen sucked in a breath, then began laughing. "What? Nonsense! You can't be married," she declared. "Annie McGillvary, you are a bad liar."

"I am married, at least that's what it says on the marriage license he showed me," I said dryly. My chest tightened in panic at the potential consequences of that, the moment I spoke those words out loud.

"Marriage license? Someone's yanking your chain, Annie. It's got to be some kind of scam," Lou-Ellen replied in disbelief.

"Nope, it looks authentic enough and now I'm in some hotel bathroom, with this stupid leopard print dress scrunched in my hand, and I've got no idea where I am or what to do." A wave of panic threatened to grip me, and my chest tightened further. "I married a guy I don't even know, one who looks younger than some of my boys. Good grief, can you imagine how they'll react?" I asked, fighting back hysteria.

Lou-Ellen chuckled nervously. "Alright, you had me going there for a minute," she said.

"That's what he said, when I admitted I couldn't remember anything. But this most definitely isn't a joke," I snapped, hearing another bout of rising anxiety in my tone.

"It must be. One minute we were having fun in the bar, then I left to go to the restroom. At that point you were dancing on the table with his bandmate and his girl was impersonating Cher.

"I couldn't have been gone more than five minutes. Then, when I came back, the barman told me you'd all gone off in an Uber. I must say I was horrified that you left me and gone off with him and his friends, Annie. I've been frantically texting you ever since and you didn't reply."

"My boys are going to go crazy," I groaned, sounding defeated. Catching sight of my disheveled image in the mirror made me almost lose it, when another wave of panic set in. "I don't even know this guy at all," I hissed, quietly. "For the glory of all that's holy, what am I going to do? And I don't need to spell out that there's no prenuptial agreement. Some friend you turned out to be," I hissed, frustrated that she wasn't in front of me.

"I'm not taking all the blame, Annie. I didn't pour all that alcohol down your throat. In fact, I don't suppose you remember, but at one point I told you to stop downing shots like you were a teenager." There was a long pause before I heard her sigh. "Listen, there's got to be a way out of this. I mean you didn't have sex with him, or anything, did you?"

I fell silent again because I hadn't thought so, but I couldn't remember.

"Oh, Annie," she remarked, getting the wrong idea about my silence. "Tell me, it was great at least. There's no way that guy looks and acts like he does, and has no idea what to do with his dick," she mumbled, as she tried to inject some light into my dire situation.

"Alexander always said you were a bad influence, and I defended you. Now look at what's happened," I said, reaching for some toilet tissue as the tears began to flow again. "I don't remember a thing. But I'm almost certain we didn't because he's packing... if you know what I mean."

"Then you'd definitely know if you had sex," she mumbled. "Look, it's not the end of the world. I mean, you can always get divorced."

"No, I can't. You know how much my faith means to me." My reply was instant and resolute, but the reality of this was devastating at the same time.

"What is he saying? From the sounds of things, he's not panicking like you are. He's the same faith, I believe. I vaguely remember him talking about a brother who is a priest."

"A priest? Is he? How the hell can you remember everything, while I remember nothing?"

"Maybe because I wasn't losing at those drinking games y'all were playing. I know I said let's go to Las Vegas and let our hair down before we're too old to enjoy it, but I didn't mean for you to go off the rails, Annie."

"Yeah, and look how that turned out," I tutted.

"Anyway, on the bright side, from the way most of the women in the bar were flocking around your new husband, I'd say you got yourself quite the catch. Someone mentioned he was in a famous band so I looked him up to see if I could find a clue on how to find you."

"You did what?"

"I Googled him. Greg Booker—aka your new husband, he's the replacement bass player of a legendary band. Not knowing who he was beforehand, has made me realize how sheltered ranch life is. His band is called Screaming Shadows. It would appear you inadvertently snagged yourself the last remaining unattached guy among them."

Lou-Ellen gave me another nervous chuckle but this time, I hadn't missed the rising alarm in her voice.

"What the heck am I going to do?" I cried, sounding helpless. "What a mess. It's something I would half-expect my Buck would do, just to get on my last nerve." Buck was my youngest and the most wayward of all my boys. The kid had my heart roasted on more than one occasion since he'd turned eighteen. "How do I explain this away to my children?"

"They're not children anymore, Annie," she reminded me.

"No? What about Angel. She's my seventeen-year-old baby girl. What kind of example have I set for her?"

"Annie your children adore you. They love you. I'm sure they'll be supportive of you … once they get over the initial shock," she reasoned, trying to play down what I'd done.

What she said, did nothing to console me. There was a time in my life when I'd thought nothing could faze me. It was a time when I believed that Alexander and I were invincible. Then, my beautiful husband was suddenly snuffed out on a straight stretch of Texan highway. The authorities concluded that he'd probably fallen asleep at the wheel.

Since then, I'd never so much as looked at another man … until last night. My children were used to me being on my own, and despite one suitor that came calling, I'd remained true to my late husband.

"Oh, yeah? And how do you think that conversation is going to go? 'Hey, Mom, how was your weekend away?' How do you suggest I answer that?" I eventually piped up. "Oh, you know … it was mostly uneventful, apart from the night I got blind drunk, and married a rock star. But it's exciting, right? Kids I want you to meet your new stepdaddy, Greg Booker."

"Yeah, you've got a point. But I think Buck and Angel will be fine … I mean two out of four isn't all that bad," Lou-Ellen suggested, knowing all too well, Wayne and Ashley would likely have fits.

"Well, I fully expect the other two to stage an intervention. If I end up being detained for my mental health, make sure you find out where I am because I'll be expecting a visit."

CHAPTER 1

GREG

The morning after I'd married Annie was the most disappointed I've ever been in myself. This time, I was the asshole everyone thought I was, and I'd really let myself down.

Despite leaving her behind, my heart belonged to a girl back home. And even though we were no longer together, she still owned it. Even after leading a hedonistic lifestyle with too many women to count, no one had ever measured up to Eliza.

Sometimes I wondered why I had allowed myself to sink to the level of depravity that I had, and the reason I came back to each time was that if I couldn't have Eliza, I couldn't imagine ever committing myself to one woman again.

So, why earlier that day, when my mind had been filled with nostalgic reflections on the anniversary of our breakup, had I done something completely ridiculous as marrying a stranger?

Sure, I'd felt low, seeing everyone else in the band finding their soulmate and believing mine had let me go, but it made no sense … I'd made no sense by acting in such a bat-shit crazy, reckless way and it was the latest in a series of impulsive decisions. The worst one I've made to date.

Of course, Annie and I were three-sheets-to-the-wind drunk, but it was the weed that drove me to do it. I wasn't so out of it that I hadn't known what I was doing, it was more that the longer-term consequences of that night didn't kick in.

What else could I do after seeing the marriage certificate lying on the nightstand except to make light of the situation. But after seeing Annie's reaction when she first awoke, I realized she genuinely had no recollection of the night before. Then a whole heap of negative implications for me about us being naked in bed together came to mind.

The last thing I'd needed was to be marked as some kind of predator, preying on some innocent widow, but thankfully a few things were clear in my mind from after we'd gotten back to my room. We had both been so drunk we'd climbed into bed and passed out. I was certain I hadn't touched her.

My get out of jail free card was that I had a legal certificate, a perfectly good explanation for us being in bed together, otherwise with her memory loss, things could have gotten tricky.

I consoled myself that she was the one who had asked me, and if anyone should have felt aggrieved, it should have been me. No point in apportioning blame, we should both have known better.

On reflection, Lou-Ellen was to blame for setting that stupid bet to begin with. However, that didn't excuse the fact that Annie and I were adults. We'd made a stupid error during our night of excess.

Now we had a clusterfuck to deal with but from my perspective, it wasn't the end of the world. However, from Annie's guilt-ridden, horrified reaction, I'd put my money on Annie never accepting a dare or a bet from her loud-mouthed friend ever again.

Somehow, we stumbled through the last two nights in Vegas, with Annie following my lead, agreeing with whatever I'd said to the band, even to the point of saying we'd consummated the marriage, although there was no truth in that.

I barely knew anything about her, yet I was proud that Annie had held her own with the boys in the band when the barrage of questions came hurtling toward us. Bedtime was the only exception to us spending time together because she went back to her hotel and stayed with Lou-Ellen, while I slept alone.

Raff, the guy charged with my personal protection that night was livid with me. The incident likely wouldn't have happened, had he not taken ill. To be fair, Raff had called Bodhi, who hadn't answered his phone, resulting in a huge argument about more security for us guys being needed.

I felt ashamed for putting myself first and not considering the consequences of ditching a guy that was paid to stick with me like glue. So, I lied. I told Bodhi that Raff had tried to stop me, but I was determined to go through with it.

Since I'd been with Screaming Shadows, I'll admit, I'd behaved like a clown. Yet until that night, Raff had always been there to de-escalate whatever situation I'd found myself in, and he'd prevented me from going too far.

After Vegas, Annie, and I both agreed to let the dust settle before we tried to deal with the fall out. So, we went our separate ways, me leaving with the band that first week to promote Screaming Shadows' up-coming album, while she flew back to Kentucky.

Every night after I left my bandmates, I called Annie and talked as we plotted a way forward. Initially, we'd discussed trying to get a secret annulment, but I figured that the press might catch on. Annie was mindful of her children finding out like that. Therefore, we arranged that I would go to her place, and we'd tell them together before seeking the annulment.

Miraculously, our wedding still hadn't made the news, thanks mainly to me being the least notable member of Screaming Shadows to the press, and my call to Rolling Stone about Korry and Bernadette being the newlyweds.

This threw the paparazzi off the scent about our wedding as they were looking for their names not ours. Personally, the whole charade hadn't affected me as deeply as it had Annie.

The one thing that had gotten in the way during our discussions was our mutual religious beliefs. My brother was a priest in the Catholic church and Annie had been brought up with a strong religious background.

From my point of view, I'd foregone most of the morals from my faith since I discovered women. But I'd also been brought up to believe how I acted with girls while single, was different to how I would worship a wife.

Annie cried when she explained that in her first marriage, she and her husband had practiced abstinence until they wed. I joked with her that we'd also followed that rule because we'd never had sex either.

I had one reason for not rushing into the annulment with Annie. It was due to a mantra my father had taught me during his time here on Earth. It was something I still said to myself at the start of each day.

Mistakes—are actions that teach me life's lessons or experiences in disguise. Some will test me more than others, but I must trust that everything happens for a reason.

Learn from the good to stop me from panicking my way out of any situation, and possibly getting into something worse. Don't be afraid to say what's on your mind. However, only speak your truth and never share your message with a barbed tongue.

To this day that mantra still holds weight with me, and because I continued to be devastated by my father's untimely death at the age of 45, I swore to live each day as it came. And as if it were my last.

CHAPTER 2

GREG

"You're actually going to stay married to her?" Levi asked, sounding incredulous as I slid my favorite bass guitar back into the soft case, and handed it to the roadie.

As I stood, I realized how near he was to me and faced him toe to toe. Of course, I wasn't, but I loved to fuck with Levi. "Yeah, I am. I'm going up to Kentucky this afternoon … meeting her kids tonight."

"Fuck me, do you think that's wise? I mean, they're hardly kids. Isn't one older than you?" he asked, his brow furrowed in concern.

"True … two of the boys are actually, Wayne and Ashley," I informed him. "I don't see it as being a problem."

"Maybe you should think about this, Greg. I mean, what have you gotten yourself into?"

"You should be the last one to judge," I replied, sounding indignant given Levi's checkered history with women. Even though Annie and I agreed an annulment was the way to go, it was none of Levi's business. "Who knows, Annie might be the best thing that's ever happened to me."

"I'm not judging you, merely expressing a concern. It's not as if this marriage was thought out. You were stoned. I mean, Annie's not exactly who you'd have chosen to live your life with otherwise, is she? Jesus, you don't know the woman. How is her life in some Podunk ranch in the middle of bumfuck Kentucky going to gel with what you do for a living?" he suggested, running a hand through his hair in frustration.

"Look, I'm not discussing this with you anymore. If my personal life doesn't interfere with my performance in the band, it shouldn't be an issue."

"What isn't an issue?" Jude asked as he wandered over and stood beside Levi.

"His marriage to Annie," Levi muttered, giving me a dark, puzzled look.

"What about it? Isn't that for him to work out?" Jude asked, his careful gaze darting between us.

"That's what I said. I get you wanting to protect me … or maybe it's protecting the band's image, I don't know …" I trailed off.

"It's not about the band's image," Levi said gently but sounded insistent all the same. "It's out of concern for you. You should at least get legal to do a background check."

"I know all I need to from talking to her. We've done nothing but talk this past week. Christ, it feels like I know more about her life, than I do about my own family."

"That's positive," Jude remarked. "So do you have plans to see her again yet?"

"I'm going to Kentucky this weekend. We're going to talk to her kids."

"How did they react?" Jude asked, folding his arms and studying me more intently through narrowed eyes.

"They don't know yet," I replied sheepishly.

"Goddamnit," Levi muttered, aghast. "You're going to faceoff with some rough and tumble cowboys ... and tell them you married their mom?"

"Yeah," I said flatly.

Levi flashed a worried look toward Jude that said *help me out here*. "And how do you think that'll go down? Is anyone going with you? No, Raff needs to go with you," he corrected.

"This conversation is over, Levi. Raff isn't coming to Annie's house with me ... not for this. My life outside of the band is just that ... mine. I've never passed comment on how you live. What I do with mine is up to me." My chest tightened as frustration weighed my heart down, so I turned on my heel, and walked away.

"Greg, wait ... you need to lighten up," Jude reprimanded Levi. "We gave you space when you needed it, remember? Let him sort his own shit out."

A text arrived from Annie, immediately wiping my bad mood.

Annie: What time do you arrive? I'll meet you at the airport.

Me: Touchdown is 5:45 p.m. So 6:00 ish?

Annie: We are doing the right thing, right?

Me: It'll be fine. If not, I'll make it all good.

Annie: I only wish I had your confidence.

Me: I have enough for the both of us. Don't worry. All will okay.

Annie: There are going to be bumps.

Me: Baby I walk out on stage in front of 60k people some nights. A few cowboys and a schoolgirl don't give me sleepless nights.

Annie: Then don't say I didn't warn you.

Me: Consider me warned. See you soon. X

"What's with the frown?" Deakon asked as I wandered into the dressing room to grab my bag and shit.

"Levi's drowning me with his negativity," I confessed.

"Levi needs to chill. I must admit that I'm surprised he's protective of you in this scenario. It's usually the chicks he's concerned about."

I shrugged. "Who knows why. Maybe he thinks I'll get beaten up by her boys or something."

Deakon chuckled and raised a brow. "Bro, he could be right about that. Cowboys are famous for slugging out their problems first and asking questions later."

"Well, all the arse-whippings in the world won't change that Annie is married to me."

"That's it, you tell them, Daddy," Deakon teased, chuckling.

I laughed. "I can't say I'm not amused by the fact that I'm stepdad to a bunch of hairy-arsed wranglers." I sighed, then gave him a more serious look. "Fuck, I really did it this time, huh?"

"The fuck you did," Deakon said in support. "It'll get sorted … just do what you do, and it'll work itself out."

I nodded. "Agreed."

Deakon snickered. "Talking about wranglers, you'd best buy a couple of pairs of Wrangler jeans, if you're going to look the part."

We both laughed. "Thanks for the humor. I needed that after the heavy vibe from Levi."

"Fuck Levi. I love him to bits, but he gets fiercely protective. You need to just do you in this situation."

I shrugged on my jacket and grabbed my overnight bag. "Oh, don't you worry, I will. I just want to get this weekend over with so that I can tell my own mother.

"Once I do, I'll need to be ready for the fallout of not giving her grandkids and a million and one irritating questions after that. Fingers crossed I'll have the right answers after my visit to Annie."

"Dude, maybe Levi's got a point. I mean apart from the age thing, there's the sex …" he trailed off, his lips twisting as if to say, someone middle aged won't be as adventurous as a younger person.

"That's the one thing I really do need to figure out," I murmured so no one else heard. I had disclosed to Deakon and Korry we hadn't consummated the marriage.

"What if …"
"Not going there, Deak."

CHAPTER 3

ANNIE

"Mom, did something happen when you were in Vegas?" My first born was tough on the outside, and highly intuitive on the inside. I swear that man could smell trouble long before it happened.

"What? Why are you asking that?" I asked, frowning, and hoping my face was sufficiently schooled so as not to give up my secret just yet.

"You've been different since you came back ... not ... present," he decided.

"Not present?" I scoffed. "Who has been feeding y'all every night since?"

"That's not what I mean, and you know it."

I grabbed the keys to my truck and headed toward the front of the house. It was still two hours until Greg's plane landed, but I wanted to be anywhere else than under the scrutiny of my son.

"Wayne, I don't have time for these cryptic conversations," I said avoiding his concerns. Lying would only come back to add to the hurt he'd feel once I'd picked Greg up and brought him back to the ranch.

"Mom," he called out, but I closed the front door behind me and hastily made it to my truck. Driving down the road leading from the ranch, I saw Wayne standing with his hands above his head, clutching the entrance beam to the porch in my rear-view mirror.

Seeing him standing there watching after me, sent another wave of guilt coursing through me.

What the hell am I doing? It was the same question that I had been chanting in my head after every conversation with my stranger-husband Greg. Don't get me wrong, I felt he was always mindful of the situation on my end, as it was me who had the burden of how my children were going to react.

In the short time I had been trying to get to know Greg, I'd found him light-hearted and amusing. But there were still three facts about this situation that I couldn't get past. Number one, why he'd agreed to the bet in the first place. Two, why he felt the need to humor a middle-aged woman who had been a stranger to him. And three, how ridiculously attractive I found him despite him being much younger.

I loved the way he usually shrugged off any negative concerns I had, and appeared as if he had no concept of the inconvenience this had caused.

Today hadn't been the first time Wayne had questioned me. So, on the one hand I was relieved that the time had come for Greg and me to face this situation head on. On the other, I was terrified my boys would never hold me in the same high regard as they did now.

During the previous few weeks, there were several times that I'd fought back the urge to blurt out what a fool I'd been. But now, as I drove to the airport and the wait was over, I was relieved Greg would be there to support me.

As I arrived in Lexington at the Blue Grass Airport, I eyed the dashboard clock in my truck, and saw that there was still over an hour before Greg's plane landed. Nerves in my belly unexpectedly fluttered at the thought he was on his way until I told my belly I had no business having those at my age.

Next thing, I found myself checking my appearance in the mirror, then shook my head. It had been years since I'd cared what I looked like to other people, let alone a man. Unless I was attending a charity gala, a wedding, Buck's high school graduation or visits to Angel's school's open house evenings, I'd never been seen out of jeans and an assortment of plaid shirts or simple T-shirts.

"You're being ridiculous, Annie McGillvary," I mumbled, sternly scolding myself. Cutting the engine, I climbed out, locked up my truck and headed into the airport.

"Hey, Annie, I thought it was you. It's great to see you. For a while there I had begun to think someone had kidnapped you in Las Vegas," Lonnie Miskell said, interrupting my thoughts.

Guilt immediately washed over me at the sound of a familiar voice. I'd been sitting at the table in the coffee bar for around fifty minutes when Lonnie, another ranch owner and close friend of my late husband, stopped by.

My heart almost leapt out of my mouth at being found there in that situation by him. Lonnie was that one person above anyone else outside of my family that I had dreaded facing since Las Vegas.

Apart from my children, he had been on my mind since the moment I'd found out I had married. He was one of the last people I'd wanted to know. Knowing Lonnie had always had feelings for me only compounded my guilt.

Right from the moment I'd heard about Alexander's accident, Lonnie had been there for me. Nothing had ever been too much trouble for him. He was always the first to volunteer his men to help during cattle drives, and he had been a faithful listening ear and trusted companion to me at events for many years.

We were as close as two people could be, and had I ever been on the market for a second husband, Lonnie would probably have been my first pick.

"H-hi, Lonnie, what are you doing here?" I asked hesitantly. I immediately wished I'd asked him a different question because I knew I'd opened a line of conversation for him to ask me the same. My eyes searched the arrivals board for the time and figured I didn't have all that long to wait for Greg to appear on the concourse.

"Just a second, let me grab a coffee really quick," he replied, holding up his hand to stop me, before heading over to the counter.

My mind was blank when I tried to come up with some other reason why Greg would be coming to Kentucky. As I did this, I observed Lonnie as he gave his order.

Taking a deep breath to calm myself, I studied the ruggedly handsome man I'd known all my married life. A fresh knot of dread grew in my stomach. What Lonnie didn't know was that I'd been avoiding him since Vegas, and now he was walking back toward me.

"Right, where were we?" he asked, flashing me that familiar, warm smile that normally brightened my day. My heart sunk to the pit of my stomach when I saw his trusting face, observing me with interest.

"Where have you been?" I asked, taking the lead, and encouraging Lonnie to talk about himself, rather than him question me.

"Just flew in from St. Louis, went to visit my sister. You?"

Shit. I glanced at my wristwatch and back to Lonnie.

"What? What is it?" he asked, as alarm flashed through his eyes.

I knew immediately he'd read the panic in mine. For a long

minute I stared at him, or it had felt longer in any case because he didn't prompt me again. "Sorry, Lonnie," was all I managed.

"Sorry? What's the matter?"

I stared again at the man who had been my rock for years and knew I couldn't lie ... not to him of all people.

"I did something really stupid," I confessed.

"Stupid? Annie, I've never known you to do anything stupid in your life," he assured me.

"Then I've definitely been saving all my moves up for this one," I replied, feeling tears burn at the back of my throat.

"I'm sure it's not as grave as it seems," he offered in his usual calming, nothing-can-be-that-bad, tone. "Go on, tell me. I'm sure you'll feel better once you do."

His response was typical of the man who always wanted to shelter me from the stresses of being a widowed woman with four kids, running a large ranch.

"I'm afraid it's worse than even you could imagine," I said, shaking my head. I felt a smirk on my lips mentally mocking me. "During my trip to Vegas ..." I took in a deep breath and the pause felt dramatic, even to me. "I married a rock star."

Lonnie laughed—hard. If he'd said the same to me, I'd likely have reacted the same way. I glanced down at my coffee cup and began turning it around under my fingers.

It took him at least twenty seconds to see that I wasn't laughing along with him, then his wide grin instantly vanished. "Annie! Jesus Christ, Annie! You're serious."

I nodded. "He'll be here any minute. His plane has probably landed by now," I informed him and briefly glanced up at the arrivals board again, to see that it had.

Watching my longtime friend's expression change from disbelief to confusion, then horror, until eventually, hurt and anger warred for dominance in his eyes. His nonverbal reaction broke my heart. Lonnie had been an amazing friend, and I'd trampled all over his feelings.

"I … I have no words," Lonnie confessed, his face pale from shock.

"Me neither … nor ones that will make any of this untrue. Greg's coming back to the ranch today, and we're going to tell my kids together."

"You're not actually going to continue with this," he stated, his tone sharper than I'd ever heard it before.

I shrugged before shaking my head. "Of course not, but he's offered to come explain to everyone before the tabloids get hold of the story."

Out of the corner of my eye, I saw a commotion and realized the man at the epicenter of the huddle was the gorgeous rock star I'd been chatting to on Facetime for most of the past week. Breaking free of the group, Greg had a girl on either side of him as he came directly into view.

Butterflies fluttered in my chest despite the situation, and as his eyes caught mine in their sight, an easy smile spread on his lips. Excusing himself from the girls, he began striding toward me.

As Greg grew nearer, Lonnie stared up at me from his seat. "You've got to be fucking joking, Annie. That boy striding toward us is your husband?"

"Told you …" I muttered, giving Lonnie a constipated smile.

"I believe you. Now, I know you've gone crazy," he protested.

"Not as crazy as my boys are going to react," I replied. I barely managed a shaky smile as Greg reached me, took my head in his hands, and pressed a small kiss to my lips.

"There you are, wife," Greg said, playfully without regard to the man standing beside me. Then he glanced around him to ensure no one had heard his remark before opening his arms wide and grinning down at me. "Annie, you're looking as beautiful as ever."

Embarrassed, I glanced toward Lonnie again whose eyes held a mixture of bewilderment and disbelief. It struck me that's exactly how I felt about Greg being married to me.

"Who's this, your brother?" Greg asked, flashing a small smile at Lonnie.

Lonnie looked incensed and it was in this moment that I considered an immediate annulment might be the only viable option.

CHAPTER 4

GREG

"Fuck me, is your place in the middle of nowhere?" I asked after we'd been traveling for about half an hour. For the previous ten minutes we hadn't passed one house, car or anything, and I then understood why Annie hadn't known who I was when we'd met.

"I can see why none of your kids are married. Where's all the people? Neighbors?"

Annie managed a nervous laugh. "We do have neighbors, they're about an hour's ride over that ridge up there."

"Bejesus, that's a long way to go for a cup of sugar if you run out. So when will we get to your place?" I asked, admiring the view that was rolling plains on both sides of the road.

"We're on the ranch now, didn't you notice the archway when I drove through it?"

"Nope, guess I was distracted by the view," I mumbled. "I was just thinking that the grass isn't as green as it is in Ireland."

She chuckled. "We get extremes in weather sometimes. It's been unseasonably hot this past month or so. The land is parched."

"The ranch looks pretty big since we've been driving for so long."

"Fletcher Ranch it's a little over three thousand acres. It's been in my family for five generations."

"I can't comprehend what three thousand acres looks like, but it sounds like a lot."

"It's a pretty large size," Annie replied, leaving me none the wiser.

"So, you gave your kids a heads up I was coming?"

"No", she replied, stealing a guilty look at me before staring at the road again.

"How do you know they'll be around then?"

"Oh, they'll be around. You can't run a place this size without all hands in use."

"Right, so you said you have cows?" I muttered for something to say.

"We're not talking about cattle, Greg," she admonished. "Can we rehearse what we're going to say?"

"We already did that on Facetime. Look, when it comes down to it, I'll tell them."

"That's what I'm afraid of. This needs to be handled ... delicately."

"And I'll do that, but I'll be firm at the same time ... remind them who's the daddy now."

Annie's nervous eyes almost bugged out of her head, and she almost drove us off the road. "Greg—"

"I'm kidding. Jesus, don't take life so seriously."

"This might be amusing to you, but this is my life. The life I had to fight hard to hold together for my children after Alexander died."

"You're right," I agreed as a substantial, old stone house came into view. "Oh, jeez, tell me that isn't yours," I muttered because it smacked of wealth on a whole other level than anything us guys in the band had.

"It's mine ... or ours rather, given I didn't sign a prenuptial agreement," she said, sounding nervous again.

"I don't want your money. I had no idea you had money when I married you. The irony is that Levi was harping on at me because I didn't have a prenuptial agreement," I replied, laughing. "Don't worry, it's not mine. I'd have no idea what to do with a cow, apart from eat it."

Annie eyed me, carefully. "You mean that don't you?"

"If you don't lay claim to my favorite bass guitar, or my football program collection from when I was a kid ... or my The Pogues CDs, you got yourself a verbal agreement. Write something up, I'll sign it." Annie's body sagged in relief. "I'm serious, darlin', this is all a bit surreal but life's complicated, right? I'm looking forward to meeting your tough guys and your sweet baby daughter."

"I wish I was as optimistic as you are."

"Really? Well, in that case, I'm hoping you have a decent first aid kit. I promise not to throw the first punch, how's that?"

"Greg, you're not going to fight with my boys," she stated firmly.

"Then best you tell your lads the same, because if they start flinging their weight around, I'm not going to be anyone's punching bag."

The instant I said this, Annie fell silent, and I could see she was having second thoughts about me being there, but as she drew breath to argue with me, a tall, rugged cowboy with a shock of red hair came out of a barn at the side of the house, with a shotgun bent over his forearm.

"Shit, that's Wayne. Let me do the talking until we get into the house, and we'll take it from there."

A text alert came in on my cell phone and I pulled it out of my pocket.

Deakon – I've set up an alert on Facebook for you to mark yourself safe from Fletcher Ranch - Kentucky.

"Fuck me, what is it with people, thinking I can't handle myself?" I mumbled as Annie pulled the hand brake on and turned off the engine.

She turned to look at me. "Promise me that if this talk goes to shit, you'll just come to the truck to leave."

I glanced at the scowling dude staring directly toward me and nodded. "Whatever you need, wifey."

CHAPTER 5

ANNIE

"Where the hell did you go?" Wayne barked, flashing a visibly angry glare toward me. He shot Greg a dark look before his gaze swung back to me. "Is this the reason you rode out of here like your ass was on fire? He looks like a scrawny waif. Y'all didn't agree on anything yet, did you?" he asked, tipping his chin toward Greg. "Didn't I say that any new hires are to go through me."

I almost laughed that he thought Greg was a wrangler, but my eldest son wouldn't have seen the funny side of his mistake. Wayne had a volatile temper, and the one I was most worried about since he had an extremely short fuse.

"He's not a ranch hand," I replied nervously, thankful that at least Wayne hadn't appeared to recognize who Greg was either.

"No shit," Wayne muttered as his eyes raked the length of Greg and settled on his extremely short hair. An awkward silence ensued between us.

Needing to do something, I waved my arm toward the house and began walking, silently directing Greg to walk with me.

Wayne immediately began walking behind us. Nervously, I

stopped and turned to face him. Seeing his narrow-eyed, scrutinizing gaze made my heart thunder in my chest. I swallowed roughly and nodded toward the stables and garages. "Would you find Buck and Angel please. I'll call Ashley and we'll meet in the great room."

"Not until you tell me who this is and what he's doing here?" my son insisted, sounding more agitated. Suspicion and aggression were Wayne's default positions. Usually, I would have cut him some slack but not at that moment, despite him having good cause to be brisk.

Since the age of twenty-one, Wayne had been the man of the house. He had stepped up and taken over the day-to-day running of the place the moment his father passed. Even though Alex wasn't hands on, he had still managed the day-to-day running of the place with Wayne until his death.

"The sooner you do as your ma asks, the sooner you'll find out," Greg responded assertively.

The muscle on Wayne's jaw ticked like he was about to lose it. However, after assessing Greg through narrowed eyes, he must have read a warning because he dropped back down from the porch steps at the front of the house.

Turning, he slowly headed toward our large garages, but he glanced over his shoulder several times while I watched him and the last time he turned his head straight, once he kicked up dirt with his battered cowboy boot, it confirmed how furious he was.

Buck came out of the garage, faced Wayne, and listened for a few beats. He then glanced over toward the house, gave me a wave, and then went back inside.

When my youngest son wasn't taking care of copious amounts of paperwork for the ranch, Buck could always be found tinkering with the classic car his father had left him.

"God, I feel sick," I said, at the thought of facing my kids. My anxiety had never been worse, and the moment I was inside the front door, I bent over and inhaled deeply through my nose.

"Hey, it's all good. You can do this." A deep crease was etched between his brows in concern. Stepping forward, he tugged me upright, wrapped his arms around me, and held me in a tight embrace.

Instantly my eyes met his and for a moment I breathed him in. His cologne smelled so enticing that I forgot about my concerns. He flashed me a disarming smile and I leaned into him, to bask in the warmth and safety of his embrace.

After a few moments, he leaned back just enough to look at me. "All better?" he asked, holding my gaze as he began to rub my back.

I nodded, wondering again why a man, who had women falling over themselves for him, would want to take the time to consider my feelings. Then he unexpectedly dropped his head and pressed a small kiss to my lips.

"Come on. Let's get you seated before your family come inside," he commanded as my lips buzzed from the brief, intimate contact and butterflies coursed through my body in response. I glanced up and considered whether he'd kissed me out of pity, or if it was an absentminded gesture that had meant nothing to him.

I then remembered he had been considerate from the start. However, consideration for my feelings wouldn't protect Greg if Wayne were to go ballistic when he learned why Greg had come.

"Mom," Angel called from the hallway before coming into view in the great room. My beautiful daughter's long, blonde hair flowed freely, aided by the air from the ceiling fans in the room. She cast an eye in Greg's direction and immediately threw herself at him.

"Oh. My. God," she blurted, bouncing on her toes with excitement the moment she saw Greg. "Is this the birthday surprise you were hinting at?" she gushed, instantly wrapping her arms around Greg's neck. "I was ecstatic when the others picked you for the band. You were the hottest looking applicant, and the best bass guitarist by far," she muttered, flashing a beaming smile at my secret husband like he'd hung the moon just for her.

"Would you stop harping on about your birthday, it isn't for three weeks yet," Buck admonished as he came into the great room in oily coveralls, munching on a hard, green apple.

"Get those coveralls off. How many times must I tell you," I ordered, feeling my face go red because I had raised my voice. I figured I looked every inch the middle-aged housewife and mother in that moment. The thought depressed me when I took in how vibrant and youthful Greg looked in comparison.

"And your hands are filthy, it's a wonder you don't poison yourself," Angel added.

"Will y'all stop fussing, I ain't dead, am I? What happened to us being responsible for ourselves? That's what you said when we were leaving for college," Buck replied, then turned his focus on Greg. "Hey, are you that dude from Screaming Shadows? The one that replaced the 'stoner'?".

"That would be me," Greg confirmed, smiling, as he took a seat.

"Love those tats you got there," Buck praised nodding at Greg's athletically built arms. "Did you get them here in the US?"

Greg eyed his arms and smiled proudly at Buck. Seeing them both having a normal conversation almost freaked me out because they didn't look all that far off in age. "Nah, I got them back in Ireland."

"What're you doing here? Berea is the last place I'd have expected a rock star to turn up. Are you lost? Don't tell me, did your car break down in town and my mom came to the rescue? It wouldn't be the first time she picked up a stray and brought him home. What did we tell you about giving strangers a ride and bringing them back here? One of these days we'll wake up to find us all murdered in our beds."

Greg chuckled at Buck's comment, but it only embarrassed me more. "Greg's not a murderer," I replied confidently.

Greg gave me a slow smile and winked. Then for some reason, my heart fluttered uncontrollably for a few seconds in response.

"And you know this how?" Ashley, my serious, veterinarian son challenged as he entered the room, obviously having heard the previous conversation.

Ashley sat on the edge of the armchair nearest the door and pulled Angel down onto the seat beside him. "Jelly, that calf might come around midnight … if you want to take over the birthing," he informed her. Angel's eyes lit up the moment he informed her of this and smiled widely. "Under my supervision mind you. If I tell you to bail, you must get out of the way."

"Yay. Oh, I promise," Angel replied excitedly. The pure glee in his sister's eyes warmed my heart. But it also reminded me that she was due to graduate shortly and would be going away to college. I'd miss her terribly, but she was fulfilling her dream to follow in Ashley's footsteps by studying veterinary sciences.

"All right, less of the excitement in here. Y'all got chores after this. Just because someone is interrupting us, doesn't make all the animal feeds go away," Wayne stated, asserting his authority again.

I felt relieved when no one answered him back because I could sense he was about ready to burst with frustration. I had given them no warning about Greg's unexpected visit, and seeing how agitated Wayne had become the moment I came home had filled me with more dread about disclosing the news Greg and I had to share.

"Okay, so we're all here," I remarked, nervously. "Obviously Angel and Buck know who Greg is, Ashley?"

Ashley shook his head as he studied Greg while he chewed his bottom lip.

"Right, well I met Greg when I was in Las Vegas with Lou-Ellen."

Greg eyed me carefully, and obviously saw how anxious I was because he rose from his seat, came over, and sat down beside me. As his arm brushed mine, it instantly anchored me.

"And his band have agreed to play at my eighteenth birthday?" Angel blurted, after I'd gotten distracted by Greg.

"Jesus, Angel, shut the fuck up or we'll never get to bed tonight. Some of us have been up since sunrise," Wayne snapped, losing the little patience he had. "The dude obviously isn't here for you."

"Maybe it would be better if I did this," Greg suggested, placing his hand over mine and squeezing it gently.

"Sure, there might be less interruptions," Ashley agreed, taking the decision out of my hands.

CHAPTER 6

GREG

Clearing my throat, I flashed a quick smile toward Annie and clapped my hands together. "First of all, thanks for inviting me to your awesome ranch, Annie. I'm in awe. I mean, the scenery is magnificent. I had no idea how beautiful Kentucky was," I said softly. Turning my attention to her grown up children, I shared a small, confident smile with them. "And thanks for having me, guys." Everyone smiled back pleasantly, apart from Wayne.

"I get that you're all wondering what the hell your ma is doing with me, right?" Each of them nodded, except Wayne, who blew out a breath like I was wasting his time.

"It's a wee bit embarrassing, but allow me to fill you in. Your beautiful, awesome mother and I met in Las Vegas a few weeks ago. And … you could say that we really hit it off."

I rubbed my hands, pretending I was nervous to tell them what we'd done. But if I'd been honest, I'd done plenty of crazy shit in my life, and marrying Annie was just the biggest blowback in a long line from some of the impulsive decisions I'd made in my life.

Wayne scoffed and glared at his mother like no one could find her interesting. But I did, and the vulnerability on her beautiful, nervous face, made Annie more interesting to me by the minute.

"Listen, there's no easy way say this other than to put it all out there for you guys. Then your mother and I can deal with the fallout," I suggested. "You know the saying, what happens in Vegas stays in Vegas?"

"You better not be going to tell us you fucked our mom," Wayne bellowed, immediately jumping to his feet with hands balled into fists. By the instant deep red color in his cheeks, I figured he was fixing to beat me.

"Sit the fuck down, Hulk, and show your mother some respect," I barked back, quietly eyeing the exits while trying to conjure up a speedy plan as to how I could save my arse if he turned on me.

For a moment Wayne looked stunned that I'd dared to call him out and for some reason this made him wary. Glancing toward his siblings, I figured he was expecting backup.

Initially, I thought the others might have been too stunned by his outburst when they didn't respond. Then, it struck me that he wasn't used to not getting their immediate agreement.

"Now wait a goddamn minute," Wayne protested, stepping into my space. Rising from my seat, I stood almost chest to chest with him, which only irritated him further. "Get out of my fucking house," he said through gritted teeth as he pointed toward the door.

The moment he tried to intimidate me was the moment my brave Irish warrior gene kicked in.

If he thinks his threatening cowboy routine is going to work on me, he has another thing coming.

Growing up in Ireland, I'd survived many drunken fights at closing time in pubs back home. I wasn't fazed by taking a punch or two. Plus, I had a fiery temper as well, I just controlled it better.

My build might not have made me the biggest guy in the room, but Wayne wouldn't have been the first to misjudge my ability to defend myself. I may have looked lean, but I was strong and I had a passive brother to protect growing up, I could more than handle myself.

"I had hoped we could do this in a civil manner, but you're making it neigh on impossible," I stated to Wayne in a flat tone.

"Don't you dare tell me what I can and can't say in my own home," he countered as he rolled his shoulders and eyed his mother with suspicion again. As he had a good few inches on me, I figured he thought his height and bulk gave him superiority over me. However, in my experience, the bigger they were, the harder they fell.

"Don't you mean your mother's house?" I challenged, squinting to study his immediate reaction.

"Listen, you annoying little shit. I have no idea why she even entertained bringing you here. But I'm telling you, you're not staying."

I glanced down at Annie who worriedly bit her lip and could barely look back at me. Her demeanor made me wonder if she was afraid of her son. Not wishing to add to her fears, I shook my head and decided to pull the proverbial rug out from under Wayne's feet.

"You know what?" I asked, reaching for Annie and pulling her to her feet. I side-stepped Wayne and placed Annie beside her daughter. "I'm sorry, darlin', but with you being a classy lady, I naturally assumed your offspring would be as refined as you. I figure, in Wayne's case, I thought wrong."

Wayne drew a breath as Angel snickered, and I held up my hand to stop any more arguing.

"I came here on a short visit today, out of respect for all of you, and most of all for your mother," I said, addressing everyone in the room. "Seems Annie and I aren't being given the same respect in return from you, Wayne.

"So, instead of telling you all in a calm manner, what we

wanted to say, I guess I'm just going to throw it out there. Throwing fits and making threats isn't the way ahead. Neither is trying to rule the house with an iron fist because what I won't accept for one minute is you disrespecting my wife."

Wayne's angry and confused expression instantly turned to total confusion. Then, if it had been possible for a human being to explode into tiny pieces, I'm sure Wayne would have achieved it. But instead, his snarled lips and scrunched up features, along with his reddened face and neck gave away how angry he felt. As anger turned to horror, his jaw dropped open and he forgot to breathe for a few beats.

Then, he sucked in a breath so hard that he began to cough. "What the hell are you talking about—your wife," he scoffed. "I've heard it all now."

"Yeah, you have ... son," I replied, deliberately asserting my position within his family for now. If I hadn't been pissed, I'd have laughed.

"Huh?" Ashley huffed, clearly as stunned as everyone else. "Wife? Now wait a minute ..." he argued and started to rise to his feet.

"Are you saying my stepdad's a rock star?" Angel cut in, unable to hide her excitement and completely riding roughshod over her older brothers' protests. "Are you my stepdad, Greg? Gee, this is incredible ... a dream come true."

"Shut up, Angel, are you out of your mind?" Wayne seethed. Angel instantly clamped her mouth shut but wriggled from side to side in her seat in excitement. "Y'all need to get a fucking grip here ... do you know what this means?" he screamed as he connected the dots and recognized how difficult life could get for him.

"It means we get free tickets to gigs," Buck chipped in, completely unaffected at all by the news. "Mom deserves someone to take care of her. Way to go, Mom, bagging yourself a rock star boytoy."

"Are you two for real?" Wayne challenged, pulling at strands of his hair. "Can't you see what this means? This guy here is muscling in on what's ours, and y'all are just going to accept him? This is insanity ... Ash?" he said, turning to the brother closest in age for support.

Annie stared at me in horror, and even though I was kind of enjoying putting Wayne back in his box, I felt a smidge bad for blurting our news out the way I had. However, as I couldn't put the water back in the faucet, I pulled Annie closer and put my arm around her waist.

Turning to face the others, I pleaded with my eyes not to make this hard on their ma. "Listen, I'm sorry. The last thing we wanted was for our news to come out like this. We wanted to sit down with all of you and try to have a civil conversation."

"Civil? Why in Hell's name did you get married?" Ashley asked in disbelief. "I've heard lust makes people do crazy, irrational stuff but—"

"There was no lust involved," I quickly stated, holding my hands up to take heat out of the conversation. "Just a bad batch of whiskey," I told all of them quietly. "One minute I'd invited your mom and her friend to join a few of us for drinks, and the next thing I knew, Annie and I were married.

"Apparently, the strength of the bourbon was off and it was much more potent than anyone knew," I said, dropping in a white lie to save Annie's reputation. "Your mother has no recollection of the wedding at all, and it's patchy at best for me."

"So, it was an accident?" Ashley asked. "But how? I mean didn't you need paperwork or anything?"

"How the hell can you have an accidental wedding?" Wayne said, scoffing again. "He's lying to help her save face."

"She's not 'Her', she is your mother, and you'll speak to her with respect," I demanded, pointing a finger at the floor.

"Or?" Wayne muttered cockily.

"You're free to go find a job on another ranch." Annie gasped and began to shake her head toward me, until I squeezed her waist. She met my gaze and the pleading look I gave her said trust me. "I came here out of respect for Annie and for all of you … to man-up as it were and tell you all face-to-face what had happened. I felt it was the least I could do. And to answer your question, Ashley, yes you do need paperwork. It was unfortunate that my bandmate's girlfriend who was with us at the time, is also our overly efficient personal assistant. I demanded that she arrange the license while we were all drunk."

"Jeez, Mom," Ashley muttered staring at her, still stunned by the news.

"I know," Annie replied helplessly, looking mortified.

"It's been a week since this happened, so you weren't all that concerned about her or us or you'd have been here already," Wayne muttered, angrily.

"I had work obligations I needed to fulfil. Annie understood that. My schedule opened this afternoon. I've got a couple of days off now, so I came straight from my band's last appointment to talk with all of you."

"So, you thought you'd move in and take over?" Wayne ground out.

"As there is no prenuptial in place, I suppose I could do that … if I had a mind to," I mumbled, pausing to let that sink in. The sadist within me had wanted to let Wayne mull over what it would feel like to lose his control on the ranch.

"This … this is …" I watched him struggle for a suitable comeback until it became uncomfortable for Annie. I glanced down at her, and she pleaded with hurt in her eyes.

"Look, I'm not interested in owning this ranch or anything else your mother has," I disclosed, putting Wayne out of his misery. "I already told your ma to get her lawyers to put something in writing to that effect and I'll sign it. Anything Annie wants. Like I said, I came here out of respect for this lady because we didn't want news of our marriage to get into the public domain without all of you being prepared. That's also why we didn't file for an immediate annulment.

"It had been my intention to come here and stay a day or two until we sorted out the paperwork."

"You're not staying married?" Ashley asked.

"No, we're not staying married, but I'm being mindful of how your ma wants to do this. And for your information, Wayne, I prefer older women." That wasn't strictly true, I didn't have a preference one way or another.

"Had our circumstances been different, I would have been proud to have Annie as my wife. Your ma is a beautiful woman," I said, stepping away from Annie and allowing her space between us. "Oh, and for the record, your ma didn't have sex with me. So, let's try to have a do-over, Wayne. You can begin by apologizing to your mother."

After that, the rest of the evening went smoothly, although Annie and I were kept busy with Angel until Annie cooked. Then we had our one and only family dinner together.

Sitting there in this wholesome family kitchen with Annie and her family felt like I'd entered the twilight zone. The conversation about cows, animal feed deliveries and farm equipment repairs was so far removed from any topics in my life, I just couldn't join in.

Once dinner was over, Annie went to help Wayne in the barn while I got roped in to chatting with Angel and her two friends, who were also fans of Screaming Shadows on Facetime. I felt it was the least I could do since I wasn't going to be her stepdad for long, so long as she didn't tell them I had married their mother.

Thankfully, Ash and Buck appeared to take me being there in their strides as each of them headed out for their date plans for the night.

CHAPTER 7

GREG

"So, how did it go?" Deakon asked eagerly the moment he answered my call.

"From my perspective great, from Annie's it was a regular shit-show," I surmised, chuckling as I sat rocking in a rocking chair on Annie's porch.

"What happened?"

"Her eldest wanted to break my back, tie my balls in a sock and throw them as far as his arm would let him."

"That well, huh?" Deakon commiserated, laughing. "You're still breathing though so it couldn't have been that bad."

"The others appeared to take it better than I thought they would. Obviously, I blamed it on the booze, which was a half-truth, but I hinted at a chemical imbalance. That way, Annie's reputation stays intact."

"Good call, you're not as stupid as you let people think you are."

"Not stupid at all … just fucking impulsive at the wrong times," I grumbled.

"Yeah, and I thought that stunt you pulled jumping from Korry's bedroom window in Italy was freaky," Deakon recalled.

"But that turned out fine in the end, and so will this. I just got to give Annie a little support. It's a religious thing you probably wouldn't understand. I'm going to call my brother for guidance."

"Better than calling Levi, I suppose," Deakon joked.

I laughed. "Poor guy will be wondering if I'm still alive. He painted Kentucky like the wild west. Although I must say, when Wayne greeted us with a shotgun over his arm, my arsehole sealed watertight."

Deakon snorted. "I'd have enjoyed watching that."

"What my asshole turning in on itself?" I asked, grimacing.

"Nah, the dude with the shotgun. You're a brave guy, going to face three burly wranglers protective of their mom."

"Again, I never really gave it much thought. However, I'm thinking the alpha in Annie's pack needs taking down a peg or two."

"Just get the hell out of there. Sadie, Beth and I want to go clubbing. We could all do with a night out." Beth, Levi's half-sister, lived in Miami, and had become a good friend of ours.

"You know what? I had a call from Flynn Docherty a few days back … you know he has ancestors back in the old country?"

"Oh yeah he mentioned that once, but I didn't know he was talking to you."

"Yeah, my brother helped him track down some relatives in parish records or something. Anyway … he mentioned they were coming to Miami next week sometime. I'll give him a call and get his exact dates. Sadie would get on well with Valerie."

"Yeah, not sure how Sadie would deal with Flynn's bass player, Lexy, from RedA' though. She's a fucking handful. Did I tell you the first time I met her she put her hand down the back of my jeans, grabbed my ass and yanked our hips together?" Deakon muttered. "I made the mistake of telling Sadie about that one night."

I laughed. "Can we not mention anything about getting laid.

I'm sure my cock has ears right now. It's been weeks since I've seen any action. I'm trying to be …"

"Faithful? In a mock marriage?" Deakon suggested, tutting his disapproval.

"If you'd been brought up in my household about fidelity in marriage, you'd get it."

"All right, but take care of yourself, we don't want you going blind."

I smiled. "You're a pill, Deak. Thanks for humoring me. I needed a bit of light relief after all the testosterone that's been oozing from Wayne's pores."

I WAS SITTING ALONE on the back porch, nursing a tumbler of malt whiskey I'd found in the kitchen when Annie came back from the barn.

"Angel gone up to bed?" she asked, while her nervous eyes glanced around the empty porch, like Angel might have been hiding somewhere.

"Yeah, worn out from all the fangirling," I joked.

"Thanks for taking over today. At first, I was horrified you were making things worse, but you handled Wayne really well," Annie admitted.

"I hate to break it to you, but your firstborn is a bully," I said, nodding toward him carrying a hay bale into a barn in the distance.

Annie shook her head. "He's an old head on young shoulders. He bore the brunt of all the work here after Alexander passed away."

"How come? I didn't know your guy worked the ranch. I thought you said he had a business in Texas?"

"Oh, Alex didn't do manual work. That didn't stop him from pushing my boys to have the skills required to support the ranch. My husband felt supporting Wayne to take responsibility as foreman would teach him how to handle the ranch when the time came for him to inherit this place."

"There are three other kids, Annie."

"I know, but Wayne's not as … gifted as the others. They all want to do their own thing eventually. Although with Buck … that boy will be the death of me." She chuckled and shook her head. "Try not to be so hard on Wayne. He feels he has a lot to prove.

"His younger brothers have lived bigger lives than him already. They have master's degrees and in Ash's case a doctorate, and it looks like Angel is heading that way too. Wayne has grafted hard from the moment he was old enough to help. And he's worked the ranch full time from the moment he received his high school diploma on his second attempt."

"Doesn't mean he's stupid, it just means he doesn't know how to pass exams," I suggested.

"And you'd know this?" Annie said with a raised brow.

"You're looking at a MENSA member since I was twelve. All brains and no common sense my ma says."

"MENSA?! Wow," Annie muttered, impressed.

"Yeah, it's no sweat for me to figure out logical sequences, patterns, work out formulas and all that shit. Since I was a small kid, I could spout facts and figures until the cows came home, if you'll pardon the pun since you raise bovine.

"I was rubbish at tests in school though. It just never occurred to me to say what they wanted because the answers were so simple, I figured there must be a catch somewhere."

"Hm, sounds a bit like Wayne. That boy can discuss the intricacies of soil composition, then work out smart farming solutions for the land in the cattle's best interest that would make your eyes cross."

"He sounds capable all right. It sounds to me he has an inferiority complex around his siblings."

"Maybe," Annie agreed. "I have noticed that he lacks confidence in conversation, so he mostly tries to dominate others, or he excuses himself for some reason."

My cell phone rang, and I saw Bernadette's name flash on my screen.

"I just need to take this," I said, gesturing toward my cell phone. "Hey, Bernadette, everything okay?"

"The word is out about you and Annie. I just had a call from the public relations team. It would appear someone sent a picture of you both at the airport and overheard a conversation you had."

My chest tightened then relaxed the moment I remembered that Korry and Bernadette were with us, and since they subsequently got married, Annie and I being there could be excused away.

"Some investigative journalist did some digging and got your marriage license details."

"Shit, now what?" I said, asking myself the question aloud rather than directing it toward Bernadette.

"Raff's on his way to you. From what the PR team are saying, Annie's place is tucked away, so it might take the press some time to find you."

After a quick call to my brother, we were relieved that we hadn't broken either of our faith's beliefs. Once he explained that Annie didn't have capacity to consent to the wedding, we knew we could file for an annulment without offending our church.

Then Annie, and I both agreed we had to file for an annulment straight away.

Bernadette lined up an attorney to handle the paperwork for us so once I gave her the nod, all we'd had to do was print off the forms, sign the statements—which Ashley and Buck witnessed— then Ashley scanned them back to her.

That same evening, our PR team lined up an exclusive interview to a sympathetic reporter by Zoom. And as the reporter was a fan, he passed the article off as a crazy rock star doing a normal rock star thing.

Afterward, I explained to Wayne and the others that we'd already filed to have the wedding annulled. I then discussed with Wayne about supporting and respecting his mother, and from that moment his attitude appeared more cordial toward me.

Raff arrived in the dead of night to take me home the following morning. It felt a bit weird leaving Annie, yet I barely knew her. The parting was strange because I sensed she liked me, but she was far better suited to the guy at the airport than me.

To be frank, I think she was glad to see the back of me because the look of fear on her face that she might have to face me again said she'd rather forget the whole embarrassing event.

Nevertheless, I left her by saying that she had my number, and if she wanted to meet up at any time, I'd be more than happy to see her.

"Well, that's over, you're a free agent again," Raff reminded me as I buckled myself into my plane seat.

"Thank fuck," I muttered, flashing him a sheepish smile. "I blame you ... if you hadn't gotten the runs, and left me to my own devices, none of that would have happened."

"Not fair," he grumbled. "My asshole was on fire that night," he replied, grimacing.

I chuckled. "Oh, well, don't be in a rush to get married. It's not all it's cracked up to be."

Raff laughed. "Grab some shut eye, you look exhausted."

"I am. I've had a narrow escape," I joked before I settled back in my seat. "Going to take a nap."

"Yeah, and me too. At least I'll know you can't go anywhere else without me ... for a few hours at least."

THE ANNULMENT CAME through a few days later, although it barely had time to register with me before the band's busy schedule took over.

To be honest, I just wanted to forget the whole sorry episode and hope that in future, my impulsive nature gave my brain enough warning to flag things of such magnitude and prevented me from making such a potentially catastrophic decision again.

Before I could put it behind me never to be mentioned again, Floyd McDade back in Ireland grilled me for every detail. Floyd and I had been friends since childhood. We'd been through hell together and knew me better than anyone. Instead of seeing the funny side, he berated me for being so stupid.

"Sure, I always said that impulsive streak of yours would get you into trouble, but marrying someone on a bet?" he asked as he shook his head. "Maybe your ma was right, and you'll never learn."

"Trust me. Going to Kentucky was a lesson. I mean, seeing her grown children with better beards than I could grow in my lifetime was a wake-up call. I looked like a kid beside her eldest son."

Deakon knocked on my bedroom door. "Got any spare jacks for the amp downstairs?"

"Sure. When did you get here?" I asked as I untangled the wire he was looking for.

"About twenty minutes ago. Can I borrow this?" he asked, wrapping it around his thumb and elbow as he wandered back toward the door. "Who are you talking to?"

"Floyd, we're on Facetime," I muttered, turning the screen so they could see one another.

"Hey, dude," Deakon beamed. "When are you coming stateside again?" he asked, interrupting our conversation.

"Maybe the month after next? Just waiting to have my holiday approved from work," Floyd replied.

"Sounds good. We'll make sure to meet up. I'll let you get back to your conversation," Deakon mumbled, casting his eyes toward me.

"Oh, you remembered Floyd's *my* friend?" I joked.

"And so am I," Deakon countered. "Or is there a new rule that you can only hang with one friend at a time?"

I laughed. "It's been a while since I had a threesome," I teased.

"In your dreams," Deakon replied playfully as he left the room.

Turning the screen back around to see Floyd's face, I said, "A day out with Deakon sounds pretty great, right?"

Floyd tapped his chin. "Erm, let me think? A boring weekend in the local pub … chance of a fist fight at closing … not me personally, spectating of course … or a trip to Miami to hang with a bunch of rock stars? Can I check my calendar and get back to you?"

I laughed as I glanced at the time.

"Shit. I need to run. I've got a couple of local radio interviews on the hook, on the debacle of the annulment. Our PA will be here in a minute to run through things with me."

"Right. Remember, no more shit decisions. I worry about you sometimes."

"Me? You're the big logger working in the forest. There's more chance of you getting injured than me."

"Nah, not me. You know I never do anything that isn't deliberate."

"I'm not worried about you. I'm more concerned with the people surrounding you. They're not all as diligent as you are," I remarked with genuine concern. Not everyone was as careful as Floyd in the workplace.

"Nothing's going to happen to me … got it?" he insisted.

"See that it doesn't," I demanded. "Okay, I'm out. Peace, light and all power to big breasted women," I joked before I dropped the call.

"You know what I think? I don't know that you've ever gotten over Floyd's sister," Deakon suggested once I met him downstairs to wait for Bernadette.

I shrugged. "That's the truth," I agreed. "Don't ask me to explain why no one has measured up. The girl broke my heart and I've never recovered. The moment I try to talk about her I get an ache in my chest."

"You need to try harder to find someone new," Deakon advised.

"Believe me, I've tried to forget her. It doesn't work," I confessed.

"It doesn't help that your best friend is her brother," Deakon suggested.

"Floyd and I agreed a long time ago not to talk about her."

"You're never tempted to ask what she's doing?"

"Oh, all the time ... every time I talk to him, but I don't."

"That's fucked up," Deakon mused.

"Agreed. She's a damaged girl ... way more than Sadie. Lizzie had a difficult childhood. It's made her as stubborn as fuck ... she doesn't see things the way most girls do. All that said, Lizzie was worth it. Getting behind that hard outer shell wasn't easy, but the moment she allowed herself to be vulnerable around me, I fell hard. And she's still the only girl I've ever met that's left a lasting impression."

"Damn, you've lived in the US for a long time now. There must have been a few women you've thought maybe this one could—"

"No," I said sharply, cutting him off. "No one can hold a candle to my Lizzie."

"Hundreds of women and not one of them has made you change how you feel?"

My heart squeezed so tightly in my chest it stung, because I didn't have to think about my answer. "Not even a little," I replied grimly. "Apart from fucking them, I feel numb about other women. I can't muster up any interest to get to know them better."

"You've hit a rocky patch, dude. Since your annulment, I think you've been partying even harder than usual. You've been drinking heavier as well."

Deakon wasn't wrong. That was until a few days ago when I'd given Raff the slip and had woken up in a strange hotel room the following morning with three party girls in my bed. There wasn't a condom in sight, and try as I might, I had no memory of what I'd been doing.

The shame I felt in asking Bernadette to arrange an STD screening outside my routine one, gave me enough pause to think that it might be time that I took my behavior in hand.

It could be awesome being single, living a carefree existence, if I was making conscious decisions. But it was quite another, now I was taking risks with potentially lasting consequences that I couldn't even remember. I tracked my mind back to where my problems appeared to escalate, and I decided to swear myself off smoking weed.

As the band were all assembling for a meeting, Levi sat flicking through the TV channels as the elevator door to the penthouse opened. Jude, Bodhi, Bernadette and Korry came into the apartment. Bernadette casually slipped a manilla envelope into my lap as she wandered over to the coffee pot.

A sense of dread immediately washed over me, and my heart pounded as I slid the slip of paper out from it and slowly unfolded it. Then, relief instantly ran through me as my eyes were drawn to a column with the word negative against each test performed.

Although I'd been given a clean bill of health, it was the first time the potential implications of the results stating otherwise sank in. I'd had a lucky escape, which made me vow even more to drink less and make wiser decisions in future.

CHAPTER 8

GREG

Bernadette sat next to me and gave me a gentle bump in acknowledgement of my clean results. Then, she reached into her oversized bag, pulled her tablet out, and called everyone to order.

"Before we discuss your interview answers from the PR team for everyone individually, I just want to talk to Greg about something else."

For a moment I thought I was in for somewhat of a lecture about ditching security and living recklessly, but the moment she smiled reassuringly toward me, I figured it wasn't that.

"We just had a call from Lori Sinclair's people asking if you'd escort her to the Oscars," she remarked excitedly.

"Me?" I asked, slapping my hand on my chest in surprise. "Why? Who's Lori Sinclair? I've never heard of her."

"Well, she knows who you are. She's asked her public relations team to reach out."

"Damn, does she need glasses?" Korry teased.

We got invites to stuff all the time, but not usually for something like this. "I don't want to go to an award ceremony with a chick that can't get a date. She must be hard up when she needs to get her team to find her a date."

"Jesus, sometimes I really do think you guys live under a rock. You're seriously telling me you don't know who the hottest, young actress in Hollywood is right now?"

I shrugged. "Why would I? Most of the time I don't know what day of the week it is we're so busy," I countered honestly.

"Lori's the leading lady in the biggest grossing, box office movie of all time as of now."

I sat up straighter. "She is? Then why would she need me? Surely there would be people lining up to take her."

"She's been too busy focusing on her career to date. She's gorgeous but completely unattached. Look," Bernadette urged, and pulled up Lori's Wikipedia page on her iPad.

The face pouting back at me from the iPad appeared demure and was absolutely stunning. With crystal-clear blue eyes and perfect, even features, Lori's face was framed by sleek, dark brown, edgy, bobbed hair.

"Fuck me, and she doesn't have a date? What's wrong with her?" I questioned, staring at her picture again.

"Like I said, she's too busy to date. It would be great for your image … and that of Screaming Shadows to have your name linked with her."

I stared at the innocent-looking face for a few more seconds before inhaling a breath. "I'm in," I said quickly.

"In for what?" Levi asked like he hadn't been paying attention.

"Lori Sinclair's people have reached out to Greg. She wants him to accompany her to the Oscars."

"Lucky bastard," he muttered, flashing me a wicked grin. "You'd better watch yourself if you tap that one," Levi warned.

"Oh, yeah? Why's that?" I asked, intrigued.

"If she's anything like the parts she plays, the girl's a man-eater."

I glanced back at the sweet face on the iPad and chuckled. "You're joking."

"I'm telling you, those sex scenes she's in … you only need to read the title of the movie to know it's a play on words."

"Huh? What's the name of the movie?" I asked, glancing from Levi to Bernadette.

"Red Velvet Petals," Levi remarked, chuckling.

Bernadette frowned. "What do you mean, I don't get it."

"Good grief, Bernadette. Sometimes I think you prefer to act innocent. You must know what Red Velvet Petals stands for," Levi mumbled as his eyes darted toward her groin. As she looked up, Levi was making a crude gesture with his tongue between a V he'd made with two fingers.

Bernadette's face fired up and she shook her head. "Trust you, Levi Milligan. You're going to be a dirty old man."

"He is a dirty old man," I muttered because Levi had a few years on me.

Levi chuckled. "Happily guilty," he agreed unabashedly. "Anyway, you should go. The rest of us will get to live vicariously through you, since we've all got partners. I'm dying for you to spill the beans on her."

"Alright. Tell Sinclair's people I said yes," I agreed, throwing my hands up in surrender. "What have I got to lose?"

"I'd say your virginity but that would be a lie," Levi joked. "Bernadette, make sure you wait until the end of the day tomorrow to tell them. We want them to think Greg has options. We want Lori to be grateful when she meets our bandmate."

I laughed. "I do have options … but it looks like I'm off to the Oscars."

ONCE I HAD AGREED to fly to Los Angeles for Lori's big day, every minute of my schedule had been accounted for. Had I known they'd booked me to fly commercial, I'd have asked that someone assist me to board ahead of the other passengers.

Not because I wanted special treatment, but rather to avoid the crush that had occurred at the airport check-in once I'd gotten spotted by some overeager fans.

Raff was pissed at the lack of regard from Lori's team and complained that had this been our team bringing Lori to our neck of the woods, Bernadette would have ensured Lori's privacy would have come first.

Then again, not everyone's PA was as forward thinking and risk management savvy as our fabulous Bernadette.

The one good thing about the flight though was that my seat was at the back row in first class and the toilets were at the front. This meant there was far less disturbance from people wanting to talk to me.

The moment my feet touched the ground in LA, I was whisked off to my plush suite at Le Petit Ermitage Hotel, with Raff having the suite interconnected with mine.

The hotel choice surprised me because it was much less in your face than I imagined someone nominated for an Oscar would choose. Nevertheless, it was opulent with gold, beige and white rooms, an intimate rooftop bar, al fresco dining, and it even had an outdoor cinema.

Less than fifteen minutes after I arrived, a pretty masseuse turned up to give me a full body massage. This treatment was gratefully received after hours of sitting on a plane. Afterward, I felt like a wet noodle, but showered before the rest of the pampering began.

After the barber, stylist, and manicurist were done with me, I still looked mostly like me, but felt drained from being made 'Oscar' ready.

"Man, you smell ... fragrant," Raff muttered, chuckling and wafting his hand in front of his nose as I dressed in the rented tuxedo. I smirked as I sauntered over to the mirror.

"Don't I scrub up well?" I admitted as I stared at the now stranger in the mirror. I'd come a long way from the shoulder length hair, baggy jeans and busted up sneakers I used to wear back in my busking days.

"Right. Let's have at it," I said, snapping out of my trance-like stare at the shiny version of myself in the mirror. "When and where am I meeting this woman? It's fucking rude that she hasn't called me herself."

"Her people will be in touch any minute. Just smile and play nice. Think of the positive publicity," Raff urged.

"Did Donnie or Bernadette tell you to say that to me?"

Raff chuckled. "No ... all me."

I studied him for a few seconds and concluded he was telling me the truth. "What if I get starstruck?" I muttered as Raff glanced at me in the mirror.

He scoffed. "Seriously? You still get starstruck? I didn't think you had a hero-worshiping nerve in your body."

"Of course I do. I mean if any of the Marvel's guys are there? I'll probably piss my tuxedo, quote one of their famous lines back at them or make an arse of myself."

Raff laughed. "No, you won't. You're not here to rubberneck at the celebrities. Besides once you get to check out Lori's rack, I doubt your eyes will be anywhere but her tits."

"Oh, man," I said, smiling. "Sexy?"

"You seriously didn't google her after all that stuff Levi said about her?"

"No, I figured I'd wait until I saw her. I didn't want to hype myself up with pictures. Photoshop can do wonders for people. I'd rather let my gut react once I see her."

"Okay ... Deakon and Korry are so on the money when they say you're a little bit loco."

I grinned. "Only when it matters," I replied, giving him a demonic stare with wide eyes. He laughed. "Right. I've had enough. Get Bernadette on the phone and tell her to tell Ms. Sinclair if she doesn't get her arse into gear and introduce herself soon, I'm bailing."

"You wouldn't dare," Raff warned.

My brow hitched over one eye. "Wanna bet?"

CHAPTER 9

GREG

It's a wonder I didn't drown in my own drool once I finally met Lori Sinclair. From the Wikipedia image Bernadette had shown me, I'd seen her pretty face, but the moment I took in the full effect of the pint-sized, silver screen goddess, she stole my breath away.

As she sashayed toward me in a black satin gown, I became aware that my mouth was suddenly dry and my jaw was gaping, so I closed my mouth and fashioned it into a self-aware smile.

Nowhere in my thoughts had I expected her to be all of 4'10", with an hourglass figure that could have given Dolly Parton a run for her money. Levi wasn't lying, Lori Sinclair was the complete package.

Then we were moving fast, being ushered to our transport. I didn't get time to collect my thoughts as she climbed into the back of the limousine, and could only admire her sexy, bony spine in her incredible, low, backless dress. Then, my tongue almost fell out of my mouth once my gaze dropped to take in how perfect her ass looked as the fabric of her dress clung to it like a second skin.

"Hi, Greg," she said, sticking out a hand once we were seated side by side with our seatbelts on. Every inch of Lori looked and smelled alluring, as expensive creams and perfumes mingled with her natural scent.

"Hey," I replied, a little tongue-tied and distracted by the pint-sized bundle of sexiness sitting next to me. She was mesmerizing to look at, impossible to ignore, and I could see instantly why she'd gotten the leading lady role in the movie.

"Thank you for agreeing to do this," she said, placing a hand on my thigh like we were intimate friends. "If I had to go to this with a stranger, I figured it should be someone I was dying to meet."

"I'm flattered," I said, smiling.

She smiled and this morphed into a wry one of regret. "I'm sorry you were left to your own devices for most of the day. You know how these things go. One interview after another, quick changes of outfit for something else. I've barely had a minute's peace today."

"Ah, never having had an Oscar nomination, I wouldn't know this," I said dryly. "If I'm honest, I was starting to think I was a chump, being wheeled out at the last minute, for your pleasure."

Lori laughed. "You ... a chump? Never," she said, placing a hand over her cleavage, blocking my incredible downward view of it. "This is the highlight of my day. When they asked who I'd like to be my plus one, I didn't hesitate on asking for you. To be honest, I thought it was an extremely long shot, and never thought for one moment you'd say yes."

"I almost didn't. I'm embarrassed to say, I'd never heard of you before our PA came with your request," I admitted sheepishly. "This business is strange, the requests we get from perfect strangers who seem to know everything about us is ... fucking weird."

"Exactly," she said, unfazed by my remarks. She turned into me in her seat, gave me a cute grin and brushed the lapel of my jacket. For a moment she openly objectified me then let out a wistful sigh.

"Jesus, I've always thought you were smoking hot, but having you here in the flesh, dressed in this James Bond look has taken your sex appeal to a whole other level."

"Why, thank you, ma'am," I joked, feeling a little self-conscious from the scrutiny of a woman for once.

"It's quite the thrill, knowing you appear all smart and respectable on the outside right now, yet you have that dirty, dangerous reputation that women are automatically drawn to. Not to mention that ripped, tattooed body you're hiding beneath those threads," she disclosed, patting a hand against my chest again. She groaned as her eyes rolled to her hairline. "I'm sorry for perusing you like this. Do you mind?" She didn't appear in the least bit sorry with her raised brow and the salacious smile she wore.

Playing along, I slumped further down the seat and did that man-spread thing. "Have at it, objectify away," I teased, laughing. "It'll make up for that male stylist pawing my junk more than once, while he obsessed about which side I 'wore my package on.'"

"So ..." she glanced down to my lap and her eyes widened, "to the right then," she muttered before she bit her lip and her gaze rose to meet mine again. If I'd expected Lori to blush, I was dead wrong.

"Indeed," I replied. She chuckled at my response and wasn't in the least bit fazed by my gesture.

I grinned because she licked her lips when she realized I was sporting a semi. "I get the feeling that tonight might be a little less tedious than I thought it might be," I suggested.

Raff cleared his throat, reminding us, he and her security guy were with us and I grinned over at him. Ever the professional his face was schooled in a serious expression. I took his hint and steered our conversation in a more general direction, by asking her about the R-rated movie she'd starred in.

Obviously, Raff had given me a brief account about Lori, from a handout Bernadette had passed on to him, giving me the movie title, she had been nominated for. The information also stated that her lead role had been opposite Hollywood's newest, leading heartthrob, Shaun Valdez.

Shortly afterward, our ride arrived at the venue. As we stepped out a roar of appreciation went up from the crowd. We both waved as we were ushered along the red carpet, pausing occasionally to give the crowd photo opportunities. Then, once inside the theater, it was like waiting in line with peers of Lori's that appeared to be a who's who of A-list actors in Hollywood.

The moment it was our turn, we stood in front of the media board. Immediately the noise of cameras clicking became deafening as we stood side by side.

Turning my head, I noticed Lori's tiny frame made my 5'11" appear much taller, so I dipped slightly and wrapped my arm around her waist.

"Lori, over here ... Greg this way," a crowd of photographers called out as they tried to capture the best pictures. Lori was smart and glanced adoringly toward me, so that from wherever an image was taken it increased the chances that someone would capture the perfect shot.

Turning, I gazed down at her, and she muttered through her smile. "We can go now." I grinned at her professionalism, stepped away from her, and she slipped her hand into mine.

"Is this something your fans need to know about?" An entertainment network reporter suggested, thrusting the mic into Lori's face. Protecting Lori from the reporter getting too close, I put my hand up and pushed the mic back a little.

"Lori and I are great friends," I replied, glancing down at Lori, who dutifully nodded, smiling warmly like we'd known one another for years.

"Come on, Greg, comment for us, I'm sure everyone at home is dying to know."

Lori grinned and shrugged her shoulders. "All I can say, is I'm one lucky girl. I'm thrilled that Greg had a window in his tight schedule to escort me tonight."

"It's my pleasure, princess," I responded, grinning. Winking, I drew her closer and gave them something to talk about when I pressed a kiss to her hairline. "Now, if you'll excuse us," I said, leading Lori away from the over-excited reporter.

"Wow, did you catch that PDA folks?" she gushed breathily. "Sounds to me like Lori Sinclair is one lucky girl all round. An Oscar nomination and Greg, the last, single hunk from Screaming Shadows waiting in the wings. That's the stuff dreams are made of, right?" she asked before we were out of earshot.

"Well, that's my night made," I said, grinning widely.

"Excuse me?" Lori asked, glancing up, amused.

"Little, ragtag, Greg Booker from Dublin being likened to an Oscar prize."

Lori laughed. "If I had to choose between you and the Oscar, it would be a tough choice."

I laughed. "I can see why you've been nominated, you're one hell of an actress."

"Who's acting?" She let out another guttural groan like she had earlier. "Dude, you have no idea ..." She left her thought unsaid as she fanned herself and shook her head. "Why is it men think women can't be as confident as men when it comes to their sexuality?"

"Are you hitting on me?" I asked playfully, with a raised brow. The sexual chemistry between us was off the charts, and I already believed my chances of fucking Lori Sinclair were a dead certainty.

"Win the Oscar or not, either way I'm either going to need someone to distract me ... or someone to celebrate with."

"That's a very philosophical approach you're taking ... and I'd just like to say, I'm one hell of a multipurpose date," I said jokingly with a thicker Irish accent than I had already. "And to be sure, I'll be more than happy to fill the shoes of whichever guy you need me to be."

I only realized we were still holding hands when she pulled her hand from mine and placed both of hers against my chest.

"So, shall we go see if you're going to be celebrating or commiserating with me?" she asked, nodding her head toward the seats.

"After you, princess."

NEVER IN MY wildest dreams did I ever think I'd be sitting in the front row of the Oscars. My heart thumped in my chest as I passed by many faces that I'd only ever previously seen in the movies over the years.

"Dude," Jason Momoa gushed as he stood from his seat and patted me on the back. "I saw you in front of the media board but by the time I got through that cattle herding, you'd vanished. "Congratulations on the nomination, Lori. You get my vote. What does a guy need to do to be your next leading man?" he asked, winking.

"Sorry, dude," he said to me, before turning to Lori. "But those scenes were fucking hot, baby." He glanced back at me again and gave me a wolfish grin. "Joking, Greg. What would she want with me when she's got a guy with fingers as skilled as yours."

I laughed and glanced toward Lori, expecting her to look embarrassed, but she chuckled.

"I was just about to pose that question myself," she said, laughing.

"Damn, I'm having the same dirty thoughts as Lori Sinclair," Jason remarked playfully. "Seriously though, bro, Screaming Shadows picked the right guy to replace that dick bass player they had … Joe … whatever." He held his fist out. I took in the metalwear on his fingers before we fist-bumped.

"Loved you in *Aquaman and The Lost Kingdom*. You were awesome," I said, then chuckled because I sounded like I was about twelve.

"Thanks, dude." He beamed. "Hey, are we both fanboying?"

"Erm. Hello, tonight is supposed to be about me," Lori muttered, pretending to pout.

"Princess, I'll get to you. And when I do there won't be any doubts where my attention will be," I replied in a flirty, husky tone.

"Ah, the smooth-talking Irishman with the quick wit and the silver tongue," Jason teased.

"Yeah, I'm kind of banking on that tongue," Lori said, pretending to mumble to herself.

"Jesus, princess, we're not going to make it through the Oscar ceremony at this rate."

Lori cleared her throat. "Right, we'd better get to our seats, or the show will be starting without us."

"Later," Jason mumbled, fist-bumped me again and retook his seat.

"We'd better tone it down or we won't make the afterparty," Lori admonished, patting my chest. She turned to address Jason again. "You're coming to my party, right?" Lori inquired.

"Of course, catch you there," he replied, grinning.

Lori and I were led to our seats beside her leading man, the director and crew before the show began. For a few moments I forgot I was famous, and I sat there in awe. Everywhere I looked there were famous faces that were familiar to me, people I'd only ever known as the characters they'd played, than as the real people behind them.

Then the star-studded event was in full swing, with accolade after accolade handed out to screenwriters, directors, composers, producers and cinematographers for each category, until it came to the best female lead which Lori had been nominated for.

As each nominee was announced a small clip of their performance was shown on the screen behind the presenters. It wasn't until Lori's scene was aired that I realized just how seductive her acting was. Like I imagine ninety percent of the men in the room were, I sat there open-mouthed, instantly turned on by the raw sexual energy that emanated from the screen.

I shouldn't have been surprised because much like my first impressions of Lori, her commanding stage presence was mesmerizing and completely believable.

"I was wondering where they were going to edit a shot that was family friendly enough to show," Lori muttered, cupping her mouth with one hand to prevent anyone from lipreading what she said.

I immediately figured if this was the family-friendly part of the movie, I couldn't wait to see the rest.

The clip was a shower scene, Lori's character lathering herself up, delivering a fast-paced dialogue about her cheating to her male counterpart who was leaning against the partially steamed up glass on the other side. His body strategically maintained her decency from her hips to her collarbone.

The director had focused on beads of water running down Lori's tan legs before the shot panned away to focus on the guy's hands curling into fists as he took her in. It was a hot 'you can look but you can't touch' scene.

Another rapturous round of applause rang out before the tension rose and Lori's name was announced.

"Yes!" I exclaimed, jumping to my feet and clapping so hard and ecstatically proud for her, yet the girl hadn't even been on my radar a day before.

I grabbed her, kissed her cheek and she beamed up at me, not even a little bit shocked they had called out her name. Spinning away from me, she moved elegantly up the few steps to the stage and received the coveted statue from the presenter.

The whole auditorium was on their feet cheering for her. For a moment she stared out at the faces before humbly clutching her award to her chest. Lori stepped up to the podium and looked demure as she held her Oscar in both hands.

She began by thanking the director, casting director, the money men for backing the project, and the crew for all their hard work during filming. Then she turned her attention to the guy sitting one over from me, the leading male actor, Shaun Valdez.

"Obviously, roles like *Red Velvet Petals* has its challenges. For me, it meant spending ninety percent of my time naked, writhing shamelessly against Shaun's codpiece." A ripple of laughter ran through the audience. Lori brazenly wiggled her brows and grinned. "However, having a natural sexual chemistry with my leading man, made the role much less daunting than it had when I first read for the part, and dare I say fun? It also helped that Shaun is hot as hell."

"I'll pay you later," Shaun called out. I glanced along the row and saw the woman with him was much older, and I guessed it could have been his mother. Although, I'd married a much older woman recently, so I was hardly the best judge of that.

Another peel of laughter settled before Lori's eyes landed on me. "Last but not least, I'd like to thank my date for coming all the way from Florida to help me celebrate this incredible award. Thanks Greg, I owe you one," she mumbled into the mic and smiled. Everyone applauded and without further fanfare, she held her Oscar in the air and made her way off the stage.

"Can you believe this?" she asked, staring down at the gold statue, sounding breathless and beaming from her moment on the stage. It was the reaction she should have had the whole time, but like the true professional she was she'd held it together until she had a semi-private moment.

"Congratulations," I mumbled, as I bent over, slung my arm around her shoulder and pulled her in for a side hug.

She turned her face and pressed a kiss to my lips, pulled back and grinned again. "PG version of what I hope will happen later," she mumbled, coyly.

If I'd had any doubts that she wanted to fuck me, that was my green light right there. Personally, I couldn't wait to get started. I'd met plenty of forthright girls in my time with the band, but Lori left me breathless by her upfront confidence.

"Is that a promise?" I asked quietly.

"I think it's a certainty," she whispered into my ear.

"Are we done here already?" I teased in a seductive tone.

Lori shivered, and as I pulled back to see her face, her pretty blue eyes glittered with lust. "Just got to get through the afterparty, then ... fireworks," she explained with a salacious smile.

Her comment made me instantly hard. "Roll on the party," I mumbled, earning a wicked grin from her.

Once the award ceremony ended, we headed over to the Ritz-Carlton where the celebration for her movie continued into the night. It was interesting to see how some celebrities aligned themselves with her in their bid to raise their own profiles.

"Isn't life strange. A year ago, none of these people would even look in my direction, now they're all behaving like we've been friends forever."

I liked the fact she'd seen through them. It was the same in any of the arts. People rose and fell, falling into popularity and when their careers waned, they were no longer part of the 'in crowd'.

Over the years, there had been times when I'd met many disingenuous people who only wanted to introduce themselves in their efforts to be associated with our band. But what I saw during the five hours we ended up staying at her after gig, was a whole event full of people desperately networking on a whole other level.

I'd never heard so many false compliments, and I wondered if they really thought that their whiney, exaggerated tones were believable.

"Can we get out of here yet?" I whispered into her ear as I sidled up behind her and slid my hands around her waist. We'd gotten separated when she was dragged away from me by her agent while I was in mid-conversation with two other A-listers.

"Sure," she gushed. "If you would excuse us," she told the small group of men that had gathered around her, listening intently to her.

I didn't recognize any of them and wondered if they were important behind the scenes people, like movie producers or directors.

"Greg travelled over from Florida this morning," she glanced at her wristwatch, "I mean yesterday morning. Poor baby, you've been up for over twenty-four hours with the time change." Lori turned and patted my chest with a sweet smile on her lips. "Time that we got you to bed."

"We?" one of the men muttered suggestively.

"Greg's bodyguard and mine," she replied sweetly.

"And I'm on a promise," I added, grinning down at her.

She chuckled. "With your bodyguard or mine?" she teased.

"I'm up for a threesome if you want, but with your bodyguard, sweetheart. It would feel a little incestuous to invite mine."

Lori laughed as she glanced toward the group of suits standing around, most with their tongues hanging out at the thought of her having a threesome. "See … this is why you're my favorite rock star. You didn't even blink at my suggestion."

"Well, my ma always told me if I blinked, I'd miss things so …"

"Come on, I just know I'm going to be walking bow legged in a few hours."

My jaw dropped for a second before I recovered. "Oh, you think you'll recover that quickly, huh? Gotta love an optimist."

Taking Lori's hand I turned and nodded toward Raff, who

slapped Lori's security detail on the stomach with the back of his hand. Both men edged their way around the room, and we met them as we broke through the crowd of celebrities milling around.

Mind you, that took almost five minutes since there were more arse-lickers wanting to grab their ten seconds of fame with the Oscar-winning leading lady.

The journey back to our hotel was fraught with sexual tension, with Lori placing a hand over my junk and me with my tongue down her throat. The woman was breathless by the time Raff opened the back door of the transport and we were about to exit onto the street.

Both outside and in the hotel foyer, fans swarmed around, obviously having learned where we were staying.

"Fuck. Is there a back entrance to this place?" I asked, suddenly too warm. I peeled off my jacket and placed it on the seat between us.

"Got it covered, Bruce and I already figured out a plan B in the event this happened." Our transport stopped in an alleyway and Bruce led us through the kitchen to a service lift.

"The place is swarming with fans. Stay inside the elevator until we check the floor out," Raff warned with narrowed eyes. "I rescued your jacket by the way," he muttered, gesturing toward my tux jacket under his arm.

"From the way your guy just demanded you do as he says, I'd say you don't take orders very well."

"I don't ... but isn't that half of my appeal?" I whispered into her ear from behind. I ran a hand down her bare back and traced the two dimples that had been driving me nuts for most of the night.

For a second, I felt her legs go weak before she leaned back against my front and rubbed her tiny arse against my thighs, her back pressing into the bulge in my pants. The pressure was both a brief relief and a tease at the same time.

A few seconds later, Raff came back and gave us the thumbs up.

Once we stepped out of the elevator, I realized the guys had brought us to my suite when Raff opened my door with his key.

"We figured the spotlight would be on Lori tonight, so figured it would be better if you were going to spend time together it should be at your suite. It's easier for us to manage this way."

I frowned because it was Lori's night, and I didn't want to take anything away from her.

"Perfect, although I'll expect you to escort me to my room in the morning. It won't look like the walk of shame if you're with me," she mumbled playfully.

"Who the fuck are you? And where have you been all my life?" I asked, dipping my knees, and scooping her up in her little tight dress.

She grinned but didn't respond to me as I held her to my chest, bride-style and carried her into my suite. "That'll be all, boys. Take the rest of the night off," she called out as I kicked the door closed with my heel.

CHAPTER 10

LORI

*A*s I looked into Greg's eyes, I recognized lustful intent in them. The moment he swept me into his arms and carried me into his suite, my heart almost beat out of my chest. My whole body lit up from the thrill that ran through me as he flashed me a wicked grin.

A night with Greg Booker had been a fantasy of mine since I'd watched his first TV interview after joining the band.

Everything about the guy turned me on. Greg had been the band's wild card. The newbie bass player with a soft Irish accent and a boyish, playful vibe. Yet beneath that first nervous interview, Greg had oozed sex appeal.

Now I was surrounded by the scent of his woodsy cologne, whiskey on his breath and the faint smell of citrus body wash. Greg was everything I loved in a man—lean, toned and tattooed with a glint of dangerous mischief in his eyes. It was his playful, roguish attitude in that interview that had captured my attention.

If I'd expected Greg to rip off my expensive designer dress and take me in frantic throes of passion the moment we were alone, I was mistaken. Part of me felt disappointed until what he did next.

Greg strode over to the nearest chair and sat down, me on his knee. "This night has been one for the books for sure," he remarked as he smoothed my hair down. He gazed into my eyes like he was memorizing them, while he held my head in his hands. "What I want to know is, what you thought you needed me for? Every man in that room wanted you tonight."

"But I only wanted you," I replied honestly.

"Is that so now?" he asked playfully. The amusement in his soft Irish lilt left me weak at the knees. "Feel this," he ordered, dropping his hands to lift one of mine. He placed it over his warm chest, then pressed his palm over mine to hold it in place. Doing as he asked, I splayed my fingers wider, instantly relishing in the warmth of his strong, hard pectoral muscles beneath his white, cotton shirt.

"Are you excited," I asked, surprised that the man who had a reputation for bedding women like he did, could have such a strong reaction toward me. Then, I wondered if his expectations of me would live up to the real deal, since I had a reputation of my own from the movie.

"I am," he said, grinning. "Been waiting all night to get my hands on you," he confessed. "You?" He nodded toward my cleavage trussed up in my elaborate evening wear and suddenly my bravado had gone.

"Is my heart racing? Yes," I said in reply.

He leaned in and whispered, "Do I make you wet?"

I chuckled, a little taken aback by his straight-talking question.

His hands cupped my face as he held my gaze. "You're looking awfully shy all of a sudden," he mumbled, tracing a thumb over my bottom lip.

I nodded. "Weirdly, I am."

Without warning, he wrapped his arms around me again and stood. "Not having any of that. Don't lose that confidence now, darlin', we're just getting started."

As he carried me through the living area to the huge, custom-made bed, the conversation between my publicist, my talent agent and I that had led me to Greg quickly ran through my mind.

"Divas make demands every day. You're an Oscar nominee, you can invite who you want. What's the worst that can happen?" Walter my agent suggested. "Any man would be delighted to escort you to the Oscars."

"I don't want to spend an evening in the company of just anyone. It's supposed to be a memorable night. How can it be so if I spend it with a stranger."

"Okay, let's think of this in another way. Who is your fantasy, celebrity man ... he'd need to be single though," he quickly added.

"My fantasy man?" I asked, confused by the question.

"He wants to know who makes you wet, Lori," my publicist blurted out, mostly to mess with Walter.

"That's just typical of you to lower the tone, Tamara." My publicist grinned because she loved embarrassing Walter. Suddenly he scoffed, and the embarrassed look on his face made me wonder if he still thought it cool to be the agent of the actress who had spent almost four months in character, practically naked.

"It is what you mean though, right? Who do you think about when you're getting yourself off?" Tamara urged, flashing a wicked grin.

"Tamara!" Walter admonished. The poor man looked mortified.

I chuckled again at his reaction. "Alright, I'll bite. Greg Booker."

"Who is he?" Walter asked, blinking because he'd obviously never heard of the man.

Tamara lost it completely this time and bent over laughing. "Great choice," she squeaked out, breathlessly. "From what I've heard through the grapevine, he gives great orgasms."

"No," Walter ground out.

"Oh, come on. The guy is European, he has bags of charisma, and that sexy Irish accent?" she groaned. "Just think of those long, talented fingers," she muttered, getting carried away. She made a crude gesture with two of them and curled them upward.

"Girl, I've about had it with you," Walter admonished again as he gave her a wide-eyed stare. "This is supposed to be a serious conversation. We need someone that's going to raise Lori's profile without outshining her," he muttered sternly.

"Then he's the perfect choice. Greg Booker is the bass player in Screaming Shadows. He has a reputation for being a bit on the wild side and he'd ensure the spotlight stayed on Lori all evening, no matter what else is going on."

I pouted. "If only ... he'd never say yes."

"Baby, he won't, if he isn't asked," my publicist replied philosophically.

"It would be a fun night ..." I mused, trailing off. "But this is all fantasy, the guy probably doesn't even know I exist."

"Then we should rectify that immediately, right Walter?"

"I'd need to research him—do my due diligence and ensure there are no scandals attached to this guy."

"Walter, his brother's a priest. What more do you need to know?" Tamara argued.

"Is it true your brother's a priest?" I blurted out as Greg placed me on my feet beside the bed.

"Fuck. No Tim talk."

"Tim? Is that your brother? So, it's true?" I asked surprised.

"Yeah, but he's the only celibate Booker boy," he muttered as he slowly turned me away from him and moved my hair to one side. Pressing his lips to my skin, he moved slowly down my back, kissing each vertebrae with reverence. At the same time his hands held my hips firmly in place.

"So beautiful," he murmured. "Damn, you smell expensive," he whispered as he rose to his feet. Sliding his hands beneath my dress at both shoulders he slid the straps off, letting the satin material cascade down my body and pool at my feet on the floor.

Then he traced his hands up my sides to my ribs. Lifting me

free from my dress, he kicked it away and set me back down in front of him.

Turning me to face him, he flashed me a slow, wicked smile. "As stunning as that gown is, you look much better without it," he murmured.

"I think you have me at a disadvantage, Greg Booker," I suggested, feeling a little shy despite my previous confidence.

"Is that so?" he replied in that same playful tone that only made what was happening even more intoxicating.

Greg's hungry eyes shone in approval as he took another opportunity to observe my lavender-colored lingerie.

Taking a step back from me, his gaze pinned to mine, he began unbuckling his belt.

"Fair warning to you, rock stars don't wear underwear," he muttered, smiling.

"No?" I asked as his pants dropped to his ankles and his cock poked free from his shirt, I realized what he meant. "Yum, come here," I said, tipping my chin toward his button-down shirt.

"Look at you, getting all demanding. We haven't even kissed yet —not if you discount that peck on the lips you gave me once they announced you'd won the Oscar."

"There's a lot more of me on display right now than there is of you. I want the full, naked effect," I mumbled, raking my eyes down his body again. I hesitated when it came to his cock.

"Ah, I'm not one to boast, but I'm quite a big boy for my height, right?" he said seriously. The humor in his tone made me smile. "I see it's put a smile on your face already, and it's not even inside you yet."

"Cocky," I muttered.

"Call him what you want," he teased again as he sexily untied his bow tie, opened the top three buttons of his shirt and dragged his shirt over his head.

"Turn and face the bed," he ordered.

As I did this, I heard him utter a cuss as he took off his shoes and stepped out of his pants.

My breath hitched when he unexpectedly grabbed both of my wrists and tied them behind my back. "Gotta love bow ties," he remarked, chuckling. "Do you trust me, princess?" he asked, bending forward to gauge my reaction.

"Yes," I said, both loving that he'd given me that corny nickname and the buzz of his dominating tone.

Placing a hand in front of me, he bent my body in the middle and pushed me forward onto the bed. My ass was stuck in the air because I was still standing on the floor in my heels.

"Fuck, your arse is a peach," he complimented before he gave it a sharp slap. The noise from the contact between his palm and my ass echoed around the room. "Sounds perfect as well," he added, chuckling. "Did you know purple was my favorite color of lingerie on a woman?"

"No. I didn't pick this out," I said, answering truthfully because his question took me by surprise.

"Well, whoever chose it did their research. I fucking adore all shades of purple, lace, black hold ups and stilettos. It's my favorite combination."

"Did you bring me here to fuck me or give me a fashion critique?" I grumbled sarcastically. Leaning over me, he laughed, and the low, rumbly tone made my core pulse with need.

My breathing had become shallow and faster as I anticipated the moment that he'd touch me sensually.

<Slap> Greg spanked my left ass cheek. "Ouch," I yelped and groaned into the mattress as a fresh round of wet heat seeped from my core. Greg chuckled the moment he heard me growl in frustration and proceeded to smooth his palm over the stinging globe of my ass.

Leaning down toward me again from behind, he whispered seductively this time, "You're impatient for me to be inside you, aren't you, princess?" There was a short pause and I almost wondered what was wrong until he exhaled a satisfied sigh. "Dear God, Lori, you should see this pretty red welt of my palm on your arse."

Sliding his hand left to my G-string, he gently tugged it two or three times. "How attached to this G-string are you?" he asked quietly.

"Huh?" I asked, still processing his question when he ripped it clean from my body.

Greg chuckled. "These lingerie companies make it too easy for women to lose their underwear." I turned my head in time to see him holding my G-string to his nose and he inhaled deeply. "I thought you'd smell like Heaven, and I wasn't wrong."

"Heaven, huh …" I mused, my heart fluttering uncontrollably as I became unbelievably turned on by his dirty action.

"I think I'm going to take you in this position at first?" he mused as he tapped his bare cock against my wet core. My ass automatically bucked for greater contact.

"Nice, so you like to be taken from behind," he stated casually. Greg dropped to his knees and pulled my ass back to his face. "Got to prep you a little," he mumbled, before licking, sucking and finger fucking me. It took him less than a minute to make me come.

With my heart thudding in my chest, I collapsed on the bed, still shaking as the heady orgasm he'd given me dialed down.

As I was recovering, I heard the sound of a packet tearing. He spat out a small piece of condom wrapper that fluttered onto the bed beside me.

"Come here," he demanded, lifting me up. Before I drew breath, Greg grabbed me by my hips, his fingers pressing deep into the flesh on my hips as he expertly drew me slowly back on to them.

A sting of a much different kind spread fire through my veins as in one deliberate, steady and unapologetic glide his thick girth burned from my core and radiated outward until he was seated deep inside me.

"Oh, fuck," I muttered through a breath before inhaling deeply through my nose. It took several breaths for me to adjust and feel more comfortable with his size.

"Fuck," he muttered after a long, guttural groan left his throat. "So tight. You, okay, princess?"

"Yeah." I winced as I bit my lip and buried my face into the bed. "I wasn't expecting you to be so ..." I trailed off.

"Big? Thick?" he asked, chuckling. "Let's just say the right brother became the priest. Sorry, princess, you're not the first to be surprised. After all, I'm not the tallest man with the biggest feet."

"Yeah, it discredits that myth," I replied warily although the pain gave way to excitement, and I wanted him to move.

As if he sensed there had been enough time for my body to accept him inside me, he pulled back and gently eased forward again. I was surprised at how slow and gentle he moved, like he was used to women having issues with his size.

Eventually, I relaxed and like all the fantasies I'd ever imagined about the man, Greg rocked my world. Being an experienced, confident lover, he knew exactly what to do to send the tiny shockwaves bursting all over my body again and again, until the thrill of it all exploded in the headiest orgasm of my life.

As my body twitched and jerked rhythmically, Greg continued to ride me, but lifted me upright and held me against his front. One hand circled my throat while the other slid to the bundle of nerves between my seam.

After my orgasm wound down, he pushed me back to the mattress, untied my hands and pulled himself out from me.

"Look at you, so beautiful. I want to see you when you come this time," he muttered softly as he turned me over and stared into my eyes with intent. Grabbing my ankles, he spread my legs, scooted down to kneel on the floor, slid his hands to my hips and dragged my ass to the edge of the bed.

Then, with his face buried between my thighs but his eyes pinned to mine, he explored, lapped, and nipped languishingly at my sex until he made me fall over the edge again.

"There you go, princess. Look at me, I got you," he murmured huskily.

My body spasmed for what felt like a whole minute or more before he climbed back on the bed. Surrounding me, Greg pinned me in place with his elbows and knees. As we went forehead to forehead, his breath became mine. He watched me with a soul-searching stare as our mouths were a mere inch apart. A few seconds passed like that until he closed the space between us and gave me a peck on my lips.

"You good?" he asked, his brow furrowed as he gauged my reaction. My eyes flared wide, and he gave me a devilish smile. "That good?" he suggested when I couldn't find words to express myself in reply for a second or two.

Breathlessly, I lay with my heart resetting to its normal pace. "What the hell was that?" I mumbled, my chest still rising and falling a little quicker than normal.

"You're welcome," he muttered in his cheeky Irish lilt. He flashed me his boyish grin. "But it's my turn now. So, have at it, whenever you're ready, jump aboard," he muttered playfully, lying back on the bed, clasping his hands behind his head, and gesturing at his still stiff length.

"You do know you've broken me?" I questioned in a tired mumble, feeling unable to move.

"Nonsense, girl. That was nothing. If you're going to survive in the world of celebrity you need to build up your stamina," he suggested, hauling my noodle-limp body over his and situating me astride his belly. "Let me look at you," he demanded, sifting his hands through my short hair and holding my head firmly in his hands. "You know, I think you might be the second prettiest girl I've ever seen in my life."

I scoffed indignantly, then pouted. "Only the second?"

"Yeah, but that's not too shabby, since I've known the first since I was a kid."

"Ah, well, I suppose I can live with that," I said, smiling.

"Come here. We've known one another for nearly a whole day, and I've still not kissed you properly."

"Yeah, that would be the next logical step since your mouth has been everywhere else."

Pulling me down toward him, Greg's hot, full lips connected with mine and the moment his tongue breached my mouth, he breathed new fire within me. Despite being exhausted, my body lit up again.

Goosebumps riddled my skin as he lifted me up, placed his still-sheathed cock beneath me and began lowering me gently onto him again. "God … so fucking good," he muttered, pulling my face forward and burying it into his neck.

"Fuck, I'm tired," he admitted, his chest heaving deeply when he finally appeared sated. I chuckled and made to move, but he clamped down on my hips, keeping my body pinned to his chest. Rolling his head to look at me, he gave me a tired smile. "That was fun," he barely moved his lips as he muttered the words. Pulling the condom off he tied it at the top, rolled off the bed and went straight into the bathroom.

Once he'd cleaned up, Greg climbed onto the bed, pulled the comforter over us and perched on an elbow to look down on me.

"You are surprising me," I mumbled.

"I am?" he queried with a raised brow.

"Yeah. I thought you would be getting dressed to leave now."

"Um, this is my hotel suite, remember?" he asked, chuckling.

"Oh, right," I said, feeling stupid. I began to move. "I'll just get—"

"Your arse settled in my bed," he said, finishing my sentence. "I'm tired ... it's been a long day," he said, smiling. "I don't imagine it'll be long before someone comes to wake us. You're bound to be in high demand later this morning. Let's catch some sleep and figure things out later." Scooting me closer against him, Greg wrapped a hand around my waist, slung a leg over mine and pulled my head against his chest. "Night, princess," he muttered.

Lying in the arms of my fantasy man, a tear sprung to my tired eyes. I'd found Greg dominant like I'd suspected, but also unexpectedly caring.

As I lay there, I had a major case of be careful what you wish for. What was supposed to be one night to fulfill a fantasy, left me feeling disappointed that I had to let him go. Something told me, any guy after Greg would have his work cut out to make me feel the way Greg had.

CHAPTER 11

GREG

As I'd predicted, Lori's security detail came to my suite door to rouse her around three hours later. Raff took a fresh outfit her publicist had sent down for her to ensure there was no walk of shame in her 'Oscar' dress.

"Your guy outside said your publicist has wardrobe and makeup staff waiting in your suite. You have an interview in just over an hour," Raff informed her before stepping back into the hallway to wait with her bodyguard.

As Lori climbed out of bed, she winced, flashed me a playful smile and wandered sexily with one foot in front of the other into the bathroom.

"Good grief, I look like a train wreck," she mumbled in the distance.

Personally, I thought she looked adorable with her short, messy bob and that well-fucked, glazed expression on her face.

I moved to the edge of the bed, stood and wandered over to the window. It had been a long twenty-four hours, but it had been worth it. Lori was an incredible girl, and it had been a while since I'd met a girl I wanted to see again.

As I yawned, I stretched my hand above my head and felt a small pair of arms wrap around my bare waist. Lori pressed a kiss to my back, and I turned in her arms to face her.

"Hey," I said, bending to press a kiss to her forehead, then noticed she was dressed in the outfit her bodyguard had brought for her. "Are you leaving?"

She nodded with her lips in an adorable pout.

"I don't know what your plans are, but if you have any time in your schedule and it matches with mine, I'd love to see you again," I confessed.

"You would?" Lori's face lit up as she smiled.

"Don't sound so surprised. I think you're an extremely cool girl."

"Greg Booker thinks I'm cool," she said playfully, with a hand over her chest, like she didn't believe me.

"All joking aside, I'd love to spend more time with you away from the Oscar madness."

Lori frowned. "I'm filming in Athens for four months from next week."

"I love Athens. What would the chances be of getting some time off if I dropped by to see you?"

"You'd do that?" she asked as a knock came at the door again.

"Coming," she called out.

"Absolutely." I took out my cell phone. "Here. Punch in your number." Lori did as I asked, and I called her cell back, then saved her number to my contacts. "There you go. We're promoting our new album right now, so no pressure. I won't have any down time for a week yet so… take your time."

Sliding her hands up my chest, she pressed a kiss to my lips and sighed heavily. As she began to step back, I slapped a hand on her arse, and I pulled her tight to my body. Then I gave her a hard, hungry kiss that I'd hoped would make me difficult to forget.

The knock on the door was more insistent this time before Raff used his keycard to enter. "This guy is going to rupture a blood vessel if you don't come out now."

"I'll be in touch," she said as she reluctantly backed away from me, then headed out the door.

Without waiting for the door to close I swung around to look at the view from my window. Clasping my hands behind my head, I stretched.

"Right, Valentino, get your ass in the shower and put that pecker away. You have orders from Bernadette. She's hired a charter for later this morning to fly us up to San Francisco. The PR team have arranged a couple of last-minute radio interviews and a chat show appearance for you, on the back of the buzz of you being at the Oscars.

"They want to capitalize on your high-profile status to plug the album. It'll save some of the band from coming out West if you get these ones done."

"Damn, they're seriously letting me loose on my own to say whatever I want?"

"Oh, I think Bernadette has sent a set of instructions for your dos and don'ts. You should find those in your email. Deakon's flying to San Fran with Sadie. The PR team split the media interviews between you two."

"Still, after all these years of being practically mute during interviews, I feel like I've finally arrived as a member of the band. I mean they're trusting me to do this."

"Trust?" Raff chuckled. "Since I have my orders to keep you on a very tight leash, I'd say they still think you're a risk."

I was about to protest when my cell vibrated. Taking it out of my pocket I saw the text was from Lori.

Lori: Did I thank you for last night?

I smiled.

Me: More than once.

Lori: I wasn't ready to leave this morning.

Me: I wasn't ready for you to leave. It was fun.

Lori: Were you serious about coming to Athens?

Me: Yes. Get your PA to send over the schedule and I'll try to make it happen.

Lori: I have butterflies at that thought. Would you regard me as clingy if I said that I really like you?

Me: The feeling is mutual. I'm looking forward to seeing where this goes.

"Do I need to guess who has put that smug smile on your face?" Raff asked.

"Lori," I confirmed. I tapped my cell phone against my chin as I figured that despite only having one night with her, I couldn't wait to do it again.

CHAPTER 12

GREG

The following morning, we swapped our hotel rooms for a small, secure, rental house. This was due to Raff taking responsibility for Deakon's and my security once Deakon arrived later that evening.

After this, I did my scheduled radio interviews and the live TV appearance, all of which were successful. By the time we arrived back at the house it was after 5:00 p.m. Fortunately someone had had the foresight to order a warm buffet of finger foods and open sandwiches.

Being seen smiling in the right places, giving time for promotions, and being sociable with strangers sometimes got monotonous. There wasn't a guy in the band that didn't feel like I did after one public appearance too many.

Mostly, I tried to toe the line and follow the rules to keep me safe. But there were times when I needed personal space from being a famous rocker because I felt suffocated by schedules and routines.

I'll admit there had been times when I had just taken off. A day without someone else managing me, usually helped me feel that I wasn't put on this planet for everyone else's pleasure.

So, once I'd found out that my favorite band were playing in a venue near to our rental home, I snagged myself the solitary last-minute ticket that someone had put up for sale.

Savage Hook's lead singer, Koogie Myers, had been my rock idol since I had been twelve years old. In my eyes he was a true rock god in the widest sense of that title. In over fifteen years, there was never a month that went by without seeing him or his band splashed in the tabloids for doing some crazy shit.

"What's the plan for later?" Raff asked me as we sat stuffing ourselves from the buffet.

"No plan," I lied. "I'm Facetiming with Floyd at 6:00 p.m. which is 11:00 p.m. across the pond. After that, I think I'll take a shower, chill out and watch T.V. in bed." I didn't feel one bit guilty for lying to Raff because I needed time on my own.

"Well, in that case, would you mind if I took a few hours off? Deakon's not due to arrive here until around midnight. As usual, I'll be at the end of my cell phone if you need to go anywhere."

I had to bite back my smile because the hardest part of getting time alone to go anywhere, was giving everyone else the slip. "Go, take all the time you need," I replied, like I was doing something nice for him.

Raff finished his sandwich, then headed off to his room to get ready. Forty-five minutes later, he came back through the adjoining door, freshly showered and dressed, like he was the groom at a wedding. He also smelled like he'd been hanging around a cologne counter in a department store with all the scents going on.

"Who's the lucky girl?" I asked, leaning back to take in his tall, fit frame, wearing his dark gray suit, blue shirt and navy silk tie. The outfit had transformed him from the normal, casual guy, stuffing his face less than an hour before, to a billionaire appearance.

He smiled bashfully before he cockily smoothed a hand over his dark, slicked-back hair. Reaching into his breast jacket pocket, he took out his aviator shades and put them on.

"She doesn't have a name yet. But I'll be sure to ask for it," he remarked, grinning.

"Don't do anything I wouldn't do," I said, saying my signature sentence, which gave him permission to do whatever the fuck he wanted, because I usually did.

Raff laughed. "Better grab more condoms in that case."

I chuckled. "That's right, you've got to remember to tie one on. Stay safe. Dude, you could have had me tonight if you'd wanted, dressed like that. Look after that suit, it's got pulling power."

Raff chuckled. "Now I'm worried," he muttered seriously. "I'll be back by the time Deakon gets here," he mumbled.

"Got it."

LEAVING the rental house at 8:10 p.m., I slid into the back seat of the Uber I'd ordered to take me to the gig.

Fortunately, the elderly Asian driver had no clue who I was. My luck held up as I shuffled anonymously along with the heavy crowd, and I entered The Fillmore. Our band's music was nothing like Savage Hook's, so I figured no one would expect someone like me to be there.

My ticket was for on the floor, so I moved down the side and got into my position on the edge of the crowd, near the front of the stage by an exit. My thoughts being that by standing there, once the concert was over, I'd be one of the first to leave.

Arriving quite late, I'd missed the warmup band, and it turned out that my timing was perfect because the lights went down within a couple of minutes of being there.

"Hello, San Fran," Koogie's distinctive husky tone yelled into the mic from somewhere backstage before the MC had even announced the band.

The fans in the venue went berserk the moment they heard him. Then the MC hurriedly cut in to announce the band, sounding flustered.

"Tonight, The Fillmore is pleased to welcome back Savaaaaage Hook."

Another roar went up as the crowd screamed, cheered and stamped their feet. Koogie appeared, strutted toward the mic stand waving his arms above his head, with his jeans still partially undone.

"I'll say it again before I was so rudely interrupted by that faceless prick that cut off my mic. Hello San Fran," he screeched, still holding both arms in the air.

The devoted audience lapped him up and cheered loudly back. Turning to look at the band's drummer, Koogie gave a curt nod. Then the distinctive beat to one of my favorite tunes ever scored by anyone began.

"Light The Night For Me" was a power ballad, written by Koogie about thirty years before. The lyrics were the story of his struggle with alcohol following the birth of his daughter, and the subsequent divorce from the love of his life. It was a number about broken hearts, addiction and a man who chose his dependency for alcohol over the needs of his family.

For the following two hours while the band played, I was lost, swept up in the stories from his life most of the lyrics were about. The man was a genius, a musician true to his roots, and while most of his life had sounded tragic, his soul was steeped in music.

For a second, I froze as a tap on my shoulder only meant one thing. I'd been recognized. Before I'd turned round, a quick scenario played out in my head of how I would keep my head down and ask whoever was there not to make a fuss. People were good for the most part, so I never usually worried about giving my security the slip.

My eyes were chest height to a security marshal wearing an orange vest. "Koogie has asked me to take you backstage."

"Me?" I asked, slapping my hand over my chest. I was completely shocked by my rock god's request.

"You are Greg Booker, right?" he queried, frowning.

"Yeah … but …" I muttered, glancing up to the stage in awe.

"Koogie wants you to go back to the green room," the marshal stated.

"How did …" My heart missed a beat that someone as iconic as him even knew who I was … and that he'd recognized me in a crowd.

I glanced toward the stage, and Koogie was now shirtless, in full swing of one of their oldest songs, engaging the audience in the chorus.

My heart raced excitedly as I followed the marshal below the stage to the hospitality suite set aside for the band.

Once inside there were plenty of people mulling around. I vaguely recognized a plump, middle-aged, woman with buck teeth as she came scooting toward me.

"Greg Booker? Koogie's a huge fan. Caitlin Matthews, Koogie's general dogsbody," she muttered, rolling her eyes to her hairline. "Koogie noticed you in the crowd from the stage before the concert started. We had to make sure it was you, so we had someone walk past you a few times, to check you out. If I'm honest, that baseball cap does nothing to disguise who you are."

I smiled nervously, still reeling that my idol knew who I was. Scanning the faces in the room for anyone familiar, I saw a promotions guy who had worked on one of our tours. Other than him, everyone else were fresh faces to me.

Among them were several beautiful women. Groupies I suspected because none of the band were married. All the guys in the band were notorious for their promiscuous escapades. So, I reckoned if the women weren't groupies, they were high class, hired escorts.

One of them glanced my way and flashed me a coy smile. She lifted the champagne glass she had in her hand in salute. I smiled back because … why not?

Reaching over the table, she lifted another glass of bubbly in her free hand and wandered over to me. "Drink?" she asked in a seductive tone.

I glanced toward the champagne and wrinkled my nose. "Got anything harder?"

"Stick around, honey. Everything gets hard around here once the boys come off that stage."

"And sticky?" I asked, playing along with her crude innuendo.

Leaning closer, she whispered, like she was sharing a secret. "Very sticky," she remarked then licked her lips. "I knew I was going to like you."

"Who are you here with?" I inquired because the tension between us was heating up fast. And I had to be sure I wasn't stepping on anyone's toes.

"Whoever gets in first," she replied with a raised brow.

"That remark could be taken two ways," I replied, grinning.

"It could, or all ways. But that would depend on your personal preference."

I chuckled. "I might need you to clarify what you mean by that last comment. I mean you could be telling me you take it up the arse … or that we could add another person. Then again, your comment, 'whoever gets in first' could be a more innocent statement, and you meant the first man who has asked to spend time with you."

"Do I give off a vibe that I want a date? I mean, I already ate dinner," she stated, smiling wickedly toward me.

"So … my preference … and you're not already lined up with one of the band?" I asked with narrowed, suspicious eyes.

"No one has called dibs for the night, if that's what you mean," she mumbled, stepping closer until her big tits brushed across my T-shirt.

"You're making this too easy for me," I mumbled as lust swarmed in her pretty blue eyes.

Her eyes scanned the room and mine followed her gaze. No one was paying attention to us. My breath hitched as she ran her hand across the front of my pants and palmed my cock. She applied pressure to it, making it harden beneath her fingers.

"Indeed," she remarked, smiling. "Come," she mumbled, sliding her hand from my cock to my wrist. She led me across the room, through a set of swing doors and into a deserted corridor.

The moment we were alone, she shoved me roughly against the wall and grabbed my belt buckle. After quickly undoing it, she unzipped my pants, then held my cock in her hand. As she looked at it, she stroked my length with her other hand, like she was petting a hamster.

She reached up, her mouth next to my ear, and whispered, "Pretty."

Grabbing her by the back of her neck, I forced her down to her knees. "Suck it," I demanded, losing my restraint.

"With pleasure," she muttered seductively. She licked her cherry-red lips and wrapped them around my cock.

"Ohh, Fuck," I muttered as a rush of air left my lungs at how hard that first suck was. "Fuck, baby," I said, gathering her blonde, shoulder length curls and scooping them up in a bun. "Yeah, baby, like that." Squelching, choking sounds came from her throat as she bobbed her mouth up and down my thick cock.

I couldn't help smiling, as I fucked her mouth to the sound of my favorite band still playing live on stage. About a minute afterward she began deep throating my cock. The sensation was too much and as I had no reason to hold back, I held her head in place and came in a series of jerky pulses down her throat.

Releasing her head, she pulled out of my mouth and proceeded to lick my cock clean. "Did you like that?" she asked, stopping briefly to press small kisses to my softening dick.

"Eight out of ten," I replied, careful not to give too much praise for fear she'd cling to me all evening.

"You could always take my number if you think I need more practice," she said suggestively as she climbed back to her feet. Dusting off her knees, she stood tall and smoothed down her black dress. "We'd better get back. They'll be off stage in a minute. That's the encore songs they've been playing," she informed me.

Shrugging off her comment about taking her number, I asked, "Can you point me in the direction of a restroom?"

"Sure, second door on the right at the end of the corridor."

As I tucked myself in and wandered away, I considered how she appeared to know so much, and I prayed she had told me the truth about not being attached to one of the band already.

CHAPTER 13

GREG

Since I've been a member of Screaming Shadows, I'd seen more than my fair share of wild parties. But nothing compared to the end of tour party laid on for Savage Hook.

Koogie himself took me under his wing, insisting that I ride to the party in their band transport. Just as well that they did because security was tight.

We were dropped off at the party house they had rented especially for the event. After being dropped off, we followed the sound of music along a narrow pathway toward the house.

"Jesus Christ," I shrieked much to Koogie and the others' amusement because I almost shit my pants, as a giraffe's head poked over some tall bushes.

As we came to a clearing, I clocked two zebras and the same giraffe meandering on the front lawn. At the same time, I felt the vibration of the bass beat from the music coming up through my feet.

Shouldering the front door open, I followed Koogie in and we were met immediately by a squealing, naked girl.

As she dashed across the hallway, laughing and ducking

around furniture two middle-aged men—who were also naked—chased her. One of the guys knocked over an indoor tree, the dirt from the smashed, ornate pot, spilling about ten feet across the floor.

"For fuck's sake," Koogie shouted.

All three ignored him and looked stoned off their faces with their demonic grins and glassy eyes. Glancing toward the living room in the distance, I saw people sitting around on various couches and chairs. None of them appeared to be chatting, and all of them were women. A small, handbag dog wrestled with the stuffing out of one of the cushions with its teeth, yet no one chastised its behavior.

It was clear from the carnage that had already taken place on the living conditions in the house, that the party had been in full swing for many hours before we'd arrived.

"What the actual fuck, dudes," Koogie bellowed as he kicked off his boots. I snickered when I noticed he had a hole in his sock that his big toe was poking through.

"I'm home," Koogie yelled as he stood, theatrically threw his hands out, and did a three-sixty-degree turn in the foyer. I could barely hear him above the heavy metal music that filtered through from the pool at the back of the house.

No one took any notice of him. Even his bandmates pushed past him, grabbing bottles of liquor that were piled by the front door. As they filed through the hallway and headed straight toward the pool, I watched them stripping out of their clothes on the way.

Koogie slapped my back, drawing my attention back to him. "Come, there are some beauties I want you to meet," he informed me. He wagged his eyebrows suggestively and nudged his head in the direction of the living room I'd observed before.

As we got nearer, I realized that what I thought were people were in fact rubber dolls. Eight of them in all, including various body shapes, races, and sizes. "Come, let me introduce you to my beautiful ladies," Koogie said, grinning.

I chuckled because I thought it was some kind of joke. However, he wandered over to the furthest couch, smiling as he sat down, and put his arm around one of them.

"Well, what do you think?"

"Fuck dolls?" I asked, laughing.

His smile fell from his face. "Companion dolls," he corrected me sternly. "Never address any of my ladies in that derogatory manner. These beauties are sensitive souls, and they've never let me down. They don't want my money, divorce me or sell their sex stories for extra bucks."

"Right," I said, still smiling because I thought I was being punked.

"This is Harmony," he said softly. He gazed lovingly toward her, smoothing down her hair. "You were the first in my little harem, weren't you, my sweetheart?"

I blinked back at him still trying to gauge if Koogie was taking the piss out of me. I kept waiting for him to laugh but he never did.

"Well, don't just stand there. Do they not have manners in Ireland? Harmony, this is my favorite bass player of all time, Greg Booker," he informed the doll. He held Harmony's hand out and nodded for me to shake it.

How I didn't piss myself laughing on the spot, I have no clue. Playing along, I reached forward and hesitantly shook the doll's hand with the tips of my fingers, then wiped them rigorously on my jeans. It made me cringe the moment I considered if he had washed those hands, since the last time he'd used the doll.

"I know I've told you before, but you look fabulous in this dress. It really makes your brown eyes pop," he remarked as he toyed with the material of the doll's dress. "How has your day been? Mine has been as good as it gets." He leaned forward and pressed a kiss to the doll's lips. "I believe both you and Solo will be warming my bed tonight. Looking forward to it, my love," he remarked.

Koogie stood and walked over to another couch where two more dolls were seated.

"Hey, my honeys, you're both looking as voluptuous as ever," he muttered, sitting between them. He slid a hand over one breast before resting it on one of the doll's shoulders. "Brenda here gives the best titty fucks ever, don't you, my clever girl?" he asked the buxom, ebony doll with long black hair. Last night was a pleasure as always. I'm sorry if I wore you out. I'm afraid you bring out the animal in me.

"I hope that soak in the tub you had has made you more comfortable, after of our rigorous night between the sheets." Like he suddenly remembered I was there, he directed his gaze toward me. "Forgive me, Brenda. You probably heard me say to Harmony who this is, but just in case you weren't listening, I'll introduce you again."

At that moment, I'd had an urge to take my cell phone out and capture that shit because I figured no one would ever believe this was happening to me. I know I didn't.

Continuing introductions, Koogie introduced me to each of his dolls, before he expanded on his information to include to which sex act each was best at. Such as, I found out that Alice had the tightest ass, while Anya, the smallest of the dolls, was the best lay.

"Celeste, love, you promised you were going to control Myrtle better," he said, addressing the last doll and nodding toward the angry scrap of dog now fully inside the cushion cover and tugging out the last of the stuffing. "You promised you'd do better at keeping her under control," he scolded.

The doll is in charge of the dog? Jesus—if I was smoking weed, I might understand what's going on better.

While he scolded the doll I glanced around at the others. They gave me the creeps, sitting there, some with their legs crossed, wearing stilettos, some more casually dressed in bare feet.

"Celeste, this is Greg, a rock star buddy of mine," Koogie disclosed.

I stood wondering if I wanted that title as his buddy right then, and considered whether the groupie from earlier had somehow transferred an LSD tab onto my dick, and it had somehow gotten into my blood stream.

"I'm trusting you to show him the time of his life tonight, baby."

Koogie's comment dragged me out of my brief reverie. *What the fuck?*

With a beam of pride on his face, he gestured toward the doll he'd been scolding. "Celeste will take good care of you. She loves me watching while she's being fucked. Don't you, angel?"

Fuck no. Try as I might, I couldn't stop my nose from curling up in distaste. The thought that others might have shared that doll made me feel sick.

"Want to take her for a spin?" he asked, like he was offering a test drive of his favorite, classic car.

"Nah, I'm good," I said, trying to sound nonchalant.

This whole situation is fucked up. Koogie wasn't acting kinky, he was a fucking pervert. He was asking me to fuck a rubber doll while he watched. *Not this side of hell.*

I wasn't in the least bit curious to find out what it would feel like to fuck a silicone doll. There were a lot of shady, unhygienic people around in the music industry and I shuddered to think how many cocks had been through Celeste's holes.

Shaking my head, I frantically wracked my brain as I tried to come up for an excuse, if he'd persisted.

"Trust me, Greg, you don't know what you're missing. If you're concerned, Ms. Celeste has always been sexually responsible. She insists on regular STD screening."

I smiled, and considered that Koogie had just delivered what would probably be the most unique pitch for a silicone doll I'd ever hear in my life.

If I'd been drunk enough and he'd just taken her fresh out of the wrapper, and he hadn't wanted to watch, I'd likely have taken Celeste for a spin. After all, from what I could see of everyone around me, no one would remember what went down at a party like that.

My cell began to ring, and I swear I threw a prayer up in thanks. "Just a sec," I said, pulling my cell out. Once I saw it was Deakon, I felt the tension ease in my chest.

As I swiped to answer, I noticed it was almost 12:30 a.m. "Hey, Deakon," I said cheerfully over the heavy beating vibrations rocking the room.

"Hey. We've just landed. We'll be there in a about ten minutes. Raff sent me a code to enter the gate and the house. Whoa, where the fuck are you?" he asked as I stood with one finger in my ear, trying to hear him.

"Koogie Myer's, it's Savage Hook's end of tour, after party."

"Oh, where is it. We'll join you."

"No!" I replied sharply, making Koogie jump. "I mean, I'll be back in half an hour."

I hung up and gave Koogie the saddest pout I could muster.

"Dude. These fucking bandmates," I muttered, pretending to be pissed. "You'd think I had nothing better to do than dig their arses out of the shit all the time. That was Deakon. He hasn't got a key to the rental place. I need to grab a cab home and let him in."

"Ah, what a bummer," he replied as he bowed his head. "Maybe next time, Celeste," he muttered, appearing as if he was disappointed for the doll. Then I realized that he was disappointed I wouldn't feed his thirst for voyeurism.

"For sure," I said making a mental note to tell Bernadette under no circumstances was she to accept an invite to all things Savage Hook in the future.

I gestured to my cell phone. "I'll just call an Uber and wait by the gates until it arrives. Don't let me hold up your enjoyment. This is meant to be a celebration of your end of tour," I mumbled, like I didn't want to be an inconvenience to him.

"Nah, I think I'll just grab Harmony and Solo and head to bed ... after I've escorted my other ladies to their beds for the night."

"Whatever, I'm sure you know better than me that there is more than one way to party," I muttered, ordering my Uber from the app at the same time. "Don't let me hold you back, it's been an ... experience ... meeting you and the boys. Thanks for having me," I said waving and walking backward, toward the door.

After bolting out of the house, I leaned back against the closed door, and sighed in relief. "What the actual, fuck was that?" I said aloud. My voice was drowned out by the loud decibels from the back of the house.

Shoving myself off the door by the shoulders, I began walking down toward the path. This time, I wasn't at all fazed by two zebras getting it on, in front of the gates. Afterall, they were living creatures for a start.

My cell phone rang again, and I answered. "Dude, I had to go through security, and I think we got cut off." I cut him off again because my Uber arrived. It was another ten minutes before Deakon called again. "I'm here. Where are you now?" he asked. "Never mind, you're here," he said.

Right before he hung up, I heard Raff's voice. "Who are you talking to?"

"I was talking to Greg ... but you're here now ... wait, isn't he supposed to be with you?"

Busted. After my near miss with Koogie and his bevvy of silicone beauties, I figured it might be better if Raff tagged along whenever I wanted to do something.

"WHERE THE HELL HAVE YOU BEEN?" Raff barked the moment I entered the Penthouse.

"Relax. I'm here and in one piece. But I could sure use a drink. I've just had a narrow miss, and think I've been traumatized for life."

"Sit. What the fuck happened?" Raff barked in concern. "Deakon said you were at Koogie Myer's party? Rumor has it, he's into all kinds of weird shit," he added.

"How do you know about Koogie Myer's kinks?" I probed.

"Not all security guys have the same relationships with their principles as we do. I've seen the pictures."

"Pictures? Yikes. Principles?"

"Yeah, the important person we're guarding."

"Right," I muttered. I'd never heard anyone say I was important like that.

"I should kick your ass for lying to me," Raff growled as he flashed me a dark look.

"I'm here and I'm fine. The only people that recognized me at that gig were in the business."

"Anything could have happened to you," Raff ranted, more than a little annoyed. "It's not just you or the band that would suffer either. This is my fucking livelihood," he insisted. "Didn't you learn your lesson after what happened in Las Vegas?"

"I thought so ..." I replied sheepishly. "Look, I was only going to a concert."

"That's the point, Greg. What you were going to do and what happens are always two different things. You might not go looking for trouble, but it nearly always finds you.

"That's the second time you've shafted me ... the third if we count that time in Italy, you dived off Korry's bedroom balcony.

Maybe I need to ask Bodhi not to put me on you because it's obvious you have little respect for the work I do."

"Whoa, Raff. Calm your tits," Deakon said as he tried to placate Raff. "The guy only wanted a night out. He's not the only one that feels he's in prison when someone's watching us night and day. To be honest, I used to feel the same. What he did isn't personal to you. You don't know what it's like for us," Deakon suggested in my defense.

"Don't I? Have you ever considered that we don't go anywhere without you guys most of the time either? We have even less control over our lives than you do. We can't say we're taking a holiday when it suits us. And yeah, there's days when I also want to be left the fuck alone. But I can't do that either.

"The only difference between us is that you're famous and earning a shit ton of money. We're salaried workers, earning a fraction of what you earn to keep you all alive. I'm the one that takes the heat if anything happens to him."

"Fuck, man, I said I'm sorry," I insisted, feeling guilty.

"You did. If I'm that much of a burden to you, perhaps I'd be appreciated more by the guys in Sinamen. Kane Exeter's head of security approached me the other week to ask if I wanted to swap firms."

"You wouldn't leave us, would you?" Deakon asked, sounding panicked at the thought we'd lose him.

"I said no … a flat no. But if this shit continues, it's only a matter of time before he'll get hurt on my watch," Raff said, gesturing his open hand toward me.

"I get it. I'm sorry. I promise it won't happen again," I insisted more sincerely.

"It's going to take a while before I believe that statement, after the way you blatantly lied to me earlier," he disclosed.

"I mean it. I feel like shit for deceiving you now. It'll never happen again."

CHAPTER 14

GREG-THREE WEEKS LATER ~MIAMI

My head pounded from the moment I woke up. It had been a long time since I'd felt sick. I rose and showered and as I still didn't feel one hundred percent, I figured a workout and better hydration might sort me out. However, I felt worse after Raff put me through my two-hour workout in our penthouse gym.

"Hey, Greg," Lori cooed sweetly as I lifted my cell from the mirrored vanity station inside the gym changing room.

"Hi, darlin'," I replied as an instant pang of guilt coursed through me. *Fuck, I forgot to call her.*

"You were calling me about coming over, remember?" she said, sounding unsure.

"I was ... I will. Life hasn't stopped since I saw you."

"So, you're still coming?"

"I said I would, didn't I?" I confirmed.

"When?" she persisted.

"The promotion for the album is almost done. I can let you know later this week."

"Definitely," she replied, sounding relieved. "I thought perhaps you had changed your mind since it's been so long. I ... I just had to confirm either way."

A knot formed in my gut once I detected a nervous tone. "You know how it is when you're not in control of your schedule. I'll admit you haven't been a priority with everything going on. But I meant what I said about visiting. I've been swamped, princess. Look, I just finished two hours in the gym, and I have a band meeting to get to. Can I give you a call later?"

"Sure. I'll let you go. I'm learning lines today… so not on set. Call when you get a minute."

"Catch you later," I said, ending the call.

"Do better, Greg. This one doesn't deserve to be kept waiting. "If you like her, you got to be more attentive," Raff warned.

"You did an awesome job of escorting Lori Sinclair," Bernadette gushed. "You really made a huge splash at the Oscars, Greg. It's been weeks now, and the speculation about you both isn't abating. Is she as nice as she portrays herself in her interviews?"

"Yeah, she's …" I trailed off, remembering the night we spent together.

"Oh, fuck, I think our Greg has a teeny crush on her now," Deakon stated. I bit back a grin, despite feeling off, and shrugged off his remark.

"Did you have fun?" Bernadette asked in all innocence.

"Yeah, did you have *fun*?" Deakon enthused accentuating the word, letting me know his question wasn't as harmless as our PA's.

"Yeah, I didn't think I would, but I had a blast," I replied. I wasn't in the mood to rehash the Oscars again.

"I can't imagine being at one of those events surrounded by so many idols," Bernadette mused.

"Sweetheart, I'm the only idol you need to concern yourself with, and you have 'access all areas pass' to me, every night of the week," Korry joked.

Bernadette blushed and swatted her husband's chest.

"Did you get much sleep?" Deakon asked relentless in his quest to know if we'd slept together. The amusement in his tone let me know he wanted a full disclosure.

"I may be going to Greece next month," I shared, not answering his question, but subliminally letting him know I was interested in her.

"Greece?" both Deakon and Korry muttered in unison.

"Damn she must be good if you're going to fly all the way across Europe for another poke," Deakon suggested. I snickered and shook my head at his crude comment.

"Deakon ... must you?" Bernadette admonished.

"What?" he asked innocently. "I'm just sayin' ..."

Fortunately, Donnie, Levi and Jude wandered into the room together, disrupting the conversation.

"Right, let's get straight to it," Bernadette mumbled as Donnie grabbed a coffee and sat down beside her.

"Is this going to take long?" All I wanted was to go and lie down again.

"So, guys," Donnie began. "The sacrifice of those long promo days you've had has paid off. Greg's stint at the Oscars gave us a boost too. Well done, Greg. As a result of his efforts, the album download numbers are off the charts.

"Guys, your new album is your most successful release ever. We knew it was a great album. But this has been a far greater accomplishment for you all than any of us could have imagined."

"The power of the internet," Deakon declared, "I've been watching the album break target after target you predicted we might reach," he told Donnie.

"Now that the album's release is a hit, I've got something I need to share as well," Jude muttered, immediately changing the tone of the meeting, and commanding the attention of everyone in the room. "Esther's pregnant again."

"Sounds like you're going to need a big motorhome, like Korry and Bernadette's, to house that brood of yours on tour," Deakon suggested.

The guys in the band ribbed Jude some more because he'd been adamant that a wife and family would cramp his style. Funny how that all changed once he fell for Esther.

With a son from a previous relationship, two children by Esther and another on the way, Deakon suggested Jude start wearing condoms again.

"Fuck me, three kids and a major tour coming up next year?" Levi mumbled. "Esther might need to stay home."

"Not happening," Jude muttered, determinedly. "We're going to find a teacher and another nanny. They'll all come with us."

"We'll manage it … right, Bernadette?" Donnie muttered, sounding more optimistic about the tour than we felt after hearing Jude's news.

"I'm sure we'll figure something out," she mumbled as she began typing frantically onto her iPad.

"Congratulations, Jude," Donnie offered.

"Congratulations," the rest of us mumbled.

"Anyway, back to business. Best album yet, guys," Donnie gushed, changing the subject back to work. "I'll admit I was scared when you all took up with your women that they would be distractions. However, after seeing the numbers for this album, I'm thinking y'all should have paired off years ago."

My thoughts turned to Lori after Donnie's comment. I liked her, but the moment I admitted this to myself, an image of Eliza instantly mocked me.

"Nothing like being in love to get those creative juices flowing," Levi responded.

"What's the matter with you, Greg? Where is that exuberant puppy we've all come to know and love when someone shares good news?" Donnie asked.

"Sorry, I'm happy. I've just been feeling off since I woke this morning. Maybe I'm coming down with something."

"A dose of the clap more than likely from how you've been spreading yourself. Since that annulment you've hardly had a night where you haven't been out on the town," Donnie muttered. "Do you need a shot of caffeine, hydration therapy … or alcohol?" he asked.

"Nah, I think maybe I'll cut out and head up for a nap, if that's okay with you guys. I want to feel better by the time we get back to Florida. SunFest will be happening next week, and I want to be at my best for the festival."

"Sure, take off, we're done here. Get Raff to go with him," Donnie instructed Bernadette. She immediately sent off a text.

As the group meeting was winding down anyway, everyone rose to their feet and headed toward the hotel meeting room door. The moment Raff saw me, he pushed off the wall he'd been leaning against and wandered over to me.

"Not feeling well?"

"Nah, I've had this headache and a strange feeling all morning. Now I'm completely exhausted. I'm going to head up to bed and grab a nap for a couple of hours. I don't need a babysitter," I mumbled.

"Orders of the management. I'll see you to your room, and then leave you in peace," he advised me as we walked ahead of the others to the bank of hotel elevators.

"Jesus, I can't take a piss without someone holding my hand. I just want to be left in peace right now."

"How's about we just behave like two guys getting into an elevator going in the same direction."

As spaced out as I felt, I couldn't help but raise a small smile.

Raff was a good guy, easy going, the least alpha male of our security detail, so I guessed I should cut him some slack.

"Deal."

Letting out a quiet chuckle, he gestured for me to step into the elevator first, then pressed his room access card against the keypad to take us up to the floor our rooms were situated on.

True to his word, Raff didn't talk to me again, and hung back as I walked to my room. Once inside, I immediately stripped off my clothes, closed the curtains and slid between the sheets. It barely registered how dark the room was before I fell asleep.

CHAPTER 15

GREG

I woke up, startled by the shrill sound of my cell phone ringing. Briefly, I wondered where I was, before the pain in my head reminded me, I didn't feel well.

Grabbing my cell phone from the nightstand, I squinted at the screen and once I saw it was my brother Tim calling, my chest immediately tightened. In all the time I'd been with Screaming Shadows, he had only ever called me once before, and that was to tell me an auntie had died.

"Hey, Tim, everything okay?" I asked, gruffly.

"Are you alright? You sound a bit husky. Do you have a cold?" he asked instead of his usual greeting.

"I just came to bed for a few hours. I felt rough earlier. I've had this weird sensation since I woke up this morning. I can't explain it, but it's exhausted me. Anyway, that's not why you're calling, is something wrong."

Tim let out a sigh and there was something in his hesitancy that felt ominous.

"It's Floyd," he said quietly.

"Floyd?" My heart stopped for a beat as I bolted upright in my bed. "What's happened?"

"Tire blew on his logging truck ... it was raining and—"

"Is he alive?" I blurted out, interrupting my brother's attempt to explain. My recovering heart raced as I climbed out of bed. I fumbled on the floor for my jeans and when I couldn't find them, I strode to the curtains and tore them apart to let light into the room.

Placing my cell phone between my cheek and my shoulder, I pulled my jeans on.

"Barely. He's in the ICU on life support. I hate to break this to you, but I knew you'd never forgive me if I didn't call to let you know."

Tim's disclosure knocked the wind out of me and for a few seconds I gulped, not able to get enough air. Then, I swallowed down an almost overwhelming lump in my throat. My stomach contents churned from shock while I tried not to lose my mind.

I could barely recall a time in my life when I hadn't known Floyd. He'd been my best friend since first grade. Even though our time together was reduced to a few face-to-face visits a year, to me, a world without him was unimaginable.

My best friend and I were opposites in every way—size, temperament, physicality, and nature, but we were kindred spirits in other ways.

Although I loved my blood brother dearly, Floyd and I were soul brothers. Tim understood that.

"How's Ruth?" I asked of the love of Floyd's life.

"Trying to stay strong for the children. I visited with her this morning at the hospital. We prayed together and she took some comfort from that. Ma's making food and feeding her ma and the kids tonight."

"Tell Ma to use the visa card I gave her and buy whatever they need."

For a long moment neither of us spoke and I guessed my brother was waiting for me to ask the question he knew I'd pose next.

"What about Lizzie? How is she?" At one time, I had expected to marry Floyd's sister. That was until Screaming Shadows happened, and she gave me an ultimatum it was either the band or her. I loved her and would likely have married her by now had she not pushed me into a corner.

"She's broken … as you'd expect … angry at the world again. I thought she had moved on after you but…"

My stomach twisted in knots as I imagined how much Floyd's accident would have affected her.

We hadn't been together for years, but thoughts of Eliza still passed through my mind every day. However, I believed if I'd turned my back on Screaming Shadows offer like she'd wanted me to, I would have grown to resent her.

"Right, I'll be home in the morning," I said decisively. "I need to go make arrangements. I'll call you back once I'm on my way to the airport."

Without waiting for my brother to say goodbye, I hung up and immediately called Bernadette. I put my cell on speaker phone and dropped it onto the bed while I slipped my T-shirt over my head and did up the button on my jeans.

"Hey, Greg, feeling any better," she asked.

"I need a charter or a seat on the first flight out of here to Dublin. My closest friend is on life support, and I need to get home."

"Jeez," Bernadette said, pausing. "I'm so sorry, Greg. Alright, let's not waste time here. Give me some time to sort something out, then I'll call you back."

Again, I cut the call and began throwing stuff in my luggage as my mind wandered to the last time that I saw Floyd. It had been Christmas past, and he'd been in great form.

Since the age of eighteen he'd answered to his nickname of Hulk, because at 6'5", he was bulked and ripped beyond the best body builders I'd ever seen. His physical abilities always appeared superhuman to me.

Floyd worked as a forester doing all the manly stuff, like planting and cutting down trees, moving huge logs and sometimes transporting them for extra money as well.

He was a handsome, humble man, and far better looking than me, with thick, dark brown hair, a long, dark beard, and crystal-clear hazel eyes. At 6'5", he towered above most Irish men, but the wee Irish lassies adored him.

I was almost finished packing when Raff came into my room. "We're going somewhere?" he asked, eyeing my luggage stacked by the door. He'd barely uttered his words when his cell phone rang. "It's Bernadette, just a second," he said, holding a finger up and answering.

As he listened his gaze cut to me, and I sensed she was bringing him up to date. When she'd finished, Raff nodded. "Got it. I'll check in when we touch down." He hung up and glanced toward me. "Guess we're going to Ireland."

I stared at him and choked up for the first time as a wave of emotion swamped me. "Can't talk," I mumbled, unsure that I was strong enough to say what Tim had told me without breaking down.

"No need for explanations, Bernadette's filled me in. Is this everything?" he asked, pointing at my suitcases.

"Yeah," I confirmed as I shrugged myself into my leather jacket.

"Alright, let's get a move on and get to that plane," he replied.

CHAPTER 16

GREG

The overnight flight from to Dublin meant we didn't arrive to the hospital until 9:00 a.m. the following morning. I was shattered and riddled with guilt that I had been so far away, while Floyd lay in such critical condition.

Fortunately, Bernadette had arranged for a rental car to meet us on the tarmac on touchdown. On the way to the hospital, Raff turned on the radio. Dean Lewis was in the middle of his emotional song, "How Do I Say Goodbye" and I almost pushed the radio off the dashboard when I turned it off.

From that point on, I sat staring out of the window, nervously swallowing on repeat while my anticipation grew. The thought of facing my injured best friend brought a mixture of emotions too enormous to single one out.

There was also the added anguish of seeing Eliza again.

During that first month of my journey with Screaming Shadows, I bombarded Eliza with messages as I begged her to see sense. It felt like a mission to me, to get her to reply. Eventually she blocked me— on her cell phone, on social media, and eventually even their family landline number got changed.

At the time, her unwillingness to communicate became a major source of frustration because I'd thought I could win her back. However, after around seven weeks, I sent her a letter pleading for her to at least talk to me.

That time was such a low point for me despite my newfound fame. I was pining for Eliza, homesick for Ireland and missing Floyd, the one person who had always instilled a sense of calm within me. So, after my letter went unanswered I behaved like the asshole that lurked inside me, got blind drunk and fell into the arms of a groupie.

From there I made it my mission in life to get laid, but it was a desperate attempt to forget her … sometimes in the wee small hours of the morning, it still feels that way.

The letter was a turning point for me, and I began to accept that Eliza and me getting back together was never going to happen.

Raff stopped the car and got out, jolting me out of my reverie, I took note of my surroundings. My heart pounded in my chest the moment I realized that we had arrived at the hospital.

Raff moved me quickly from the car and into the hospital entrance where all eyes were on me. For years now, I'd lived with being recognized on sight, but if I could have chosen one time to have gotten my anonymity back this would have been it.

"Just keep your head down and keep walking," Raff advised, steering me to the left of the seating area like he knew exactly where he was going. "Bernadette sent me a floor plan for directions to the intensive care unit. Ward J81 is only a short ride to level two in the elevator."

I felt as if I was on autopilot, as Raff guided me into the lift without allowing anyone to interact with me. Once in the elevator, I read the no cell phone sign and quickly turned mine off. As the lift doors opened the smell of the disinfectant and that distinctly clinical scent registered a sense of fear within me

Instantly my anxiety was on another level, just like it had been in the weeks following my father's death. But I wouldn't allow myself to think for one second I might face a final goodbye with Floyd. The thought of living the rest of my life without his calming, reasoning qualities, terrified me.

Floyd had helped me keep my feet on the ground, and his guidance had always centered me. My heart sped to an uncomfortable rate because I wasn't prepared for him to leave me behind in this world.

"I'll take it from here, Raff. You can wait downstairs."

Raff glanced at the empty corridor except for the two women I knew, then nodded. "I think you're safe here. Text me, when you're ready to come down."

"Greg," Ruth breathed. She rushed toward me, I only had a fleeting glance of Floyd's grief-stricken wife before she snuck her arms around my waist, dropped her head to my chest and sobbed.

"God, Ruth, I'm so sorry," I croaked, my voice breaking as the reality of what we faced struck a mutual chord of distress between us. For many seconds, her body wracked in grief as she continued to cry into my chest.

Desperate to support her without becoming emotional myself, I swallowed down my feelings while Ruth sobbed uncontrollably. By the time she broke contact to look at me, my T-shirt was drenched in her tears.

The way Ruth dissolved in my arms, how she did. It was as if she'd held herself together until I'd gotten there before she let her emotions go.

"I'm so sorry, darlin'," I mumbled, pulling her close to me. I rubbed her back to comfort her. "I'm sorry I wasn't here when it happened."

She lifted her head and I looked into her red-rimmed eyes. "You're here now. That's what matters. Thank you for coming."

"Oh, yeah, the calvary's here. Everything's going to be fine now," Eliza muttered sarcastically as she stepped out of a doorway with two paper cups in her hands.

Hearing the familiar voice instantly set my heart ablaze. My whole body felt the shock as our eyes met. The sudden jolt of electricity momentarily stopped my heart. The sad look that passed from her to me instantly disarmed me. No matter how much I'd told myself I could live without Eliza McDade in my life, my instant reaction to seeing her again warned me that wasn't the case.

My lungs crushed in my chest as the air thickened between us, as a weighty atmosphere of hostility, hate and anger arced from her to me. However, the longer I held her gaze, those negative energy vibes were slowly replaced by softer ones of love and yearning between us.

Eliza had changed in many ways. Instead of the cute, curvy, girl she had been when I left, she had matured into a stunningly beautiful, voluptuous woman. The same shock of wild, copper hair was still waist-length, but tied back neatly in a ponytail, not down and unruly like she knew I loved to see it.

Seeing the changes in her—to see her at all—in fact—felt unreal because I hadn't even seen a photograph of her since I'd left Ireland. After she'd cut me off, I'd made it a point not to stalk her or her friends, and as Floyd knew how hurt I was, he agreed not to discuss her with me.

I must confess, Eliza was still the one person in this world that made me wonder 'if only' about my life. There had been weak moments during that first year when I'd almost packed up and headed home to Ireland. If I had, I doubt I would have stayed in the band. That was how much I missed her. And the stark reality on seeing her again was … I missed her all over again.

My heart pounded harder with want, despite her darkening gaze. Pure hate dulled her usually vibrant eyes as I stared into the same stormy look in her eyes that was present the day I left.

"Hi, Lizzie, it's good to see you," I murmured softly. My instinct was to reach out and wrap my arms around her. I became aware that my hands had clenched into fists. Seeing her gave me an overwhelming feeling of finally coming home, but it felt painful at the same time. I'd been home a few times since I'd lived in Miami, but I'd lost that sense of belonging in one place ... until now.

Ignoring my greeting, Eliza sucked in a breath, then spun away from me on her heel. Eliza placed one of the cups down on an empty chair. She then walked over and sat on the seat opposite from it.

Ruth broke away from me, reeled around and faced her sister-in-law. "Not now, Eliza. This is neither the time, nor the place for your bitter tongue, girl," she scolded.

Eliza slumped further into her chair and stared into her cup. I stole another glance toward her while she wasn't looking.

No matter how mad she was with me, I realized I loved being in the same space as her again, despite the harrowing circumstances.

The acrimonious vibe should have made the atmosphere suppressive, yet I felt as if I was breathing fresh air for the first time in years.

I was there because Eliza's brother Floyd, my closest friend in the world, was fighting for his life somewhere close by. Yet for that few seconds my childhood sweetheart, Eliza McDade was all that I saw.

Even though that angry glare she'd given me could have melted the flesh from my bones, she was the loveliest girl I'd seen in years.

"I'm not bitter, not in the least," she muttered, sounding every bit as sour as Ruth had pegged her to be. A small smile attempted to curve my lips, but I bit it back. I told myself Eliza being angry was better than reconciled acceptance because it meant she still had feelings for me.

"She's right, Lizzie," I murmured as I continued to take her in.

A flashback of her lying quiet and sated by my side, her head on my chest as I sifted my fingers through that mane of silky copper hair came to my mind. I shook the thought away and realized my gaze had pinned her to the spot. "I'm so sorry about Floyd," I said, finding my voice again.

"I bet you are. My brother is about the only member of this family you really care about," she countered cynically.

"That isn't true," I said quietly, sounding flat. I stole a nervous glance toward Ruth because the last thing I wanted was to cause a scene of any kind. Not while the man who meant life itself to us all lay critically ill.

"Mm-hm," Eliza mumbled through closed lips with a raised brow in a gesture that dripped pure sarcasm.

"Shut up, or leave," Ruth snapped, glaring pointedly at her sister-in-law. We both stared back, embarrassed and stunned at Ruth's outburst because she'd never raised her voice to Eliza before.

From what I'd remembered, they were great friends. However, Ruth had every reason to be angry. Listening to Eliza ragging on me wasn't why any of us were there. Nor were our differences a stress that anyone needed.

A nurse in blue scrubs stepped outside of a room and quietly closed the door. "Everything alright out here?"

"Yeah, sorry. Emotions are running a little high," Ruth mumbled, glaring toward Eliza. The nurse studied me with narrowed eyes, and I briefly wondered if she was considering whether I was at the center of the disharmony in the room, or if she was trying to place me.

Either way, it hadn't mattered by then because Ruth had taken control of the situation, despite the dire circumstances she faced. Nevertheless, I felt ashamed that my presence had compounded an already tense situation.

"Look, I should go. I don't want to cause either of you any more distress than there already is. I just want to see Floyd... would that be, okay?" I pleaded, addressing both women.

Eliza finished her coffee, placed her empty paper cup on the chair beside her and folded her arms. Her gorgeous hazel eyes that had once shone with adoration whenever she looked at me, held nothing but hatred and suspicion.

Eliza was the girl I had loved since I was fourteen, the girl at nineteen I had thought would one day be my wife. I had even allowed myself to envisage us having children and growing old together. All of which had been possible until the universe played me a this or that dilemma by being chosen to play bass guitar with Screaming Shadows.

As silence stretched between us, I studied her pretty face again, and despite her puffy eyelids and washed-out look of grief, my heart wept because I'd lost her.

"Floyd would want that," she muttered quietly before she turned her head away from me again. My heart sank because she could hardly bear to look at me while I couldn't drag my gaze from her.

"Come, I'll take you to him," Ruth advised as she grabbed my hand.

The moment she held my hand tension rose in my body. Even though Floyd was the reason I was there, I realized right then that I hadn't prepared myself at all for how he might look.

"It's okay, he doesn't have a mark on him," she stated, like she knew all the fearful thoughts that were running through my head. Mainly that Floyd may have horrible, physical injuries.

The sound of my heartbeat in my ears deafened me as Ruth led me toward his room. Once she stopped at the door with an opaque window, I briefly noted that Floyd's room was located opposite the nurses' station. Initially, I drew comfort from this.

At least staff are close by if Floyd needs help. Then this thought was quickly drowned out by a more sinister one of him being situated right there because he might be the person most in need of their attention.

As Ruth opened the door, two distinctive sounds immediately dominated the air. The regular sound of the ventilator intermittently bellowing life into Floyd's body. And the beeping sounds that registered his heartbeat, pulse and oxygen levels from another monitor.

Panic rose to my throat as I fleetingly took in all the sights and sounds in the room. I fought back my fears and tried to focus on Floyd in the bed. His usual shock of messy dark hair was as unruly as normal on one side and completely missing on the other.

Taking a tentative step closer, I saw his face was partially obscured by a coil of corrugated plastic tubing attached to an airway tube. His beard had been partially shaved to attach copious amounts of micropore tape, that held his breathing tube in place on his cheek.

Once the gravity of Floyd's condition sank in, I sucked in a sharp breath as my gaze traced down his arm and noted the IV lines feeding into a three-way IV on his hand. As I took a wider view of him, I realized there was another line feeding directly into his neck.

My heart splintered into tiny pieces as I stared, overwhelmed, toward my best mate in horror. "Fuck," I dragged out in a whisper, too stunned by the sight of him to hold back my feelings.

Apart from the height and build of the man lying in the bed, my best friend was barely recognizable, lying weak and helpless.

"Sit," I heard a gentle voice say. I turned and saw the same nurse as before, prompting me to take a seat. I stared vacantly toward her as I felt light-headed again.

Normally, I was a guy who thought on my feet, often acting on the fly, and mostly getting away with my actions. But in this situation, I was so out of my depth, I had nothing.

"Sit down, Greg." Ruth's instruction was the voice that registered with me. Slowly I turned to face her and did as she'd ordered. I saw even less of Floyd in my sitting position due to his bed being raised to a level that made it easy for the staff to work on him.

"What happens now? We just sit here until he's ready to wake up?" I whispered, mostly to myself.

"The scan results from this morning will tell the doctors the extent of Floyd's brain activity," his nurse explained, thinking I was addressing her.

"Brain activity?" I asked, knowing deep down what that meant, but unwilling to accept that Floyd might have been past the point of no return to health.

"Take all the time you need, Big Man, but you're going nowhere, you hear me?" I warned aloud because I couldn't bear it if he didn't live. I stole a glance toward Ruth and the expressionless look on her face warned me that Floyd's situation was dire.

"The doctor will be up to speak to Ruth soon. He's been in surgery all morning. He'll review all the test results again before he comes back," the nurse offered again as she came round the bed to my side and injected something into the drip in his hand.

The nurse had just finished doing this when the door opened, and Eliza entered the room. "I just saw Floyd's doctor go into his office," she muttered, addressing Ruth. The impression I got was like if she didn't look at me, I wasn't there. My chest tightened again at the look of dread that passed between them.

Considering, I should try to be strong for both women, I finally found the strength to interact with my friend again.

"Hey, mate," I said, focusing on Floyd, and slipping my hand under his heavy, limp one. "Look at you, acting all laid back as usual, with three beautiful women tending to you. Obviously, I know you only have eyes for Ruth," I teased, as the pad of my thumb grazed over his warm, rough knuckles.

I glanced up at Ruth and was rewarded with a small, grateful smile. I took it as her appreciation for creating a tiny window of normality in what otherwise appeared to be an uncertain situation.

"We've sat here for almost thirty hours now," she explained quietly. "I've never prayed so hard in my life for a miracle. I'd take any sign right now that he was going to make it."

Eliza began to cry, and my heart squeezed tight, for Ruth, for Eliza ... for myself. Getting up from the chair, I slowly moved over to Eliza and placed my hands on her shoulders. I half-expected her to flinch but she didn't. Instead, her sad eyes met my gaze, and I wished in that moment I could have said everything would be okay.

As I looked down at her, I dropped my forehead to hers. Eliza drew a sharp breath at our skin-to-skin connection. And her reaction hit me square in the gut. The way her angry eyes immediately flared at my intimate move knotted my stomach.

The thought that Eliza used to be the most important person in my life and that we had been reduced to a little more than acquaintances ... a relative of a friend, made acid burn in my stomach. The girl had been my everything and those eyes that had once burned with passion now regarded me with hate.

"I'm sorry you're going through this," I admitted sincerely. Ruth caught my attention over Eliza's shoulder, her eyes brimming with tears.

"Whatever the news is, I'm going to support you all," I stated, like my presence would somehow fix everything.

Forgetting myself, I reached up to Eliza's head and cradled it in my palms. "I might not be your favorite guy in the world right now, Lizzie, but despite your barbed words, I know that deep down you don't really hate me. Whatever this takes with Floyd, I'm going to be there for you," I muttered.

Eliza closed her eyes, like she wanted to shut me out—either that or she didn't want me to read her true feelings in her eyes. As tears trickled down her face, I leaned forward and met the salty droplets with my lips. Then, as I couldn't find any more words to comfort her, I pressed a kiss to her lips. It was only as Eliza's breath hitched that I realized what I'd done.

The gentleness of the moment was abruptly severed, as her eyes flew wide open, and she quickly shoved me away. "We don't need you to be here for us."

"I do," Ruth muttered. "And the girls will need Greg as well," she said of her daughters. Eliza glared darkly toward her sister-in-law. "You need to forget to be angry for now. How do you think Floyd would feel if he thought you two were at each another's throats?" Ruth challenged Eliza.

"Let Lizzie say what she feels," I said. "I understand she's hurting. There's only love in my heart where Lizzie is concerned," I muttered. "I don't blame her for feeling how she does. It can't have been easy seeing me out there, living a different life to the one we had here." I turned to face my ex-girlfriend. "It was your choice to break up with me and stay here in Ireland. The opportunity I got was a once-in-a-lifetime thing. When I accepted the offer, I never saw that chance as mine alone. In my mind, I'd envisioned a future for us."

"It doesn't matter now, I'm over you," Eliza countered, sounding childlike.

"Then, don't harp on about what neither of us can change. Floyd is our focus right now," I snapped more sternly and gestured toward her brother.

I prayed that he couldn't hear us right then. We had argued in hushed tones while the nurse had been charting Floyd's vitals. If she heard us, she didn't look up.

Usually, I wasn't someone that cared what other people thought about me. But in that situation, I felt ashamed that Floyd was literally fighting for his life while two people he loved squabbled.

The moment the doctor walked in, I momentarily lost confidence in his ability to make Floyd well. For some reason, I'd been expecting a distinguished-looking, elderly person. So, I was surprised when a guy not much older than me strutted forward with authority and tried to shake my hand.

"Hi, we haven't met. Griff O'Hare," he greeted flatly. "I'm Floyd's neurologist. Ruth said you were family." For a moment I eyed him with suspicion. My heart pounded, because I found it hard to believe that someone so young held such prized responsibility for all that was precious to us in his hands.

I then flashed a look toward Eliza and expected her to object to the doctor's statement about me being family, but thankfully she didn't contradict him.

Mr. O'Hare is the leading surgical neurologist in Ireland," Ruth quickly informed me.

Ruth's comment made me instantly thankful for his genius, and I looked at him with renewed respect.

"I've just reviewed Floyd's scans and they look far more promising than we thought. There's plenty of brain activity, but I must warn you that we won't know what this means until he regains consciousness.

"However, from the results I have seen, I'm cautiously optimistic he should do this ... but I can't be one hundred percent on that. What he needs now is rest and—"

"When will you know?" I asked anxiously, cutting the doctor off.

"Ah, that's a loaded question for which I have no definitive answer. It could be days or even weeks before we see any significant changes. We need to have patience.

"My advice would be to keep talking to him. At some point as the swelling subsides, Floyd may begin to respond. Play his favorite music on low, nothing too jarring or excitable to listen to," he mumbled, glancing toward me again. "But I'd advise you all to make sure to get some rest yourselves. If Floyd does regain consciousness, he's going to need your support."

"When he regains consciousness," I corrected. "You don't know Floyd. This guy is an ox," I insisted, unwilling to accept he might not.

Dr. O'Hare raised a brow as if to indicate that it wasn't the first time he'd heard such a bold statement, but he didn't respond. "If you'll excuse me, I have other patients to evaluate. I'll check back in later. Meanwhile, Lindsay will page me if there are any notable changes."

CHAPTER 17

GREG

"Sounds like we'll need to be patient," I mumbled, feeling sick about the distressing wait ahead.

"Yeah, which is something else you're known to lack," Eliza quipped.

"For Christ's sake, stop digging at him," Ruth snapped loudly. The nurse stopped what she was doing and stared pointedly toward everyone.

"Right, maybe I'll go grab a shower at my ma's and put some clean clothes on. I don't want to antagonize anyone further," I stated. The tension in the air from Eliza was stifling. "Can I bring anything back? A change of clothing, food, something to drink?"

"Like whiskey you mean?" Eliza challenged. From what was reported on social media, you can't function without that.

"Enough," Ruth barked as she glared angrily at Eliza.

"Guys, can you take your conversation outside?" I glanced toward Lindsay. Her furrowed brow and pursed lips informed us it wasn't a request.

"It's okay, I'm going," I said, holding my hands up. "Text me what you need, and I'll sort it out," I told Ruth.

I stepped out the lift on the ground floor and saw Raff sitting patiently reading something on his cell phone. I'd all but forgotten about him while I was in the Intensive Care Unit.

"Any news?" he said, standing quickly and shoving his cell phone into his jacket pocket.

I nodded. "Floyd's brain injury is a wee bit better than they originally thought. The doc isn't sure how much damage there is, but he gave us some hope."

"Fuck, what does that mean?" Raff asked as he stepped closer and patted my shoulder. I shrugged, feeling helpless. "Come on, let's get you a shower and some sleep."

"I don't think I can sleep," I confessed. It felt wrong leaving him again when I'd only just arrived, but Eliza's animosity toward me had made the atmosphere in the room feel stale. Floyd needed all the help he could get, and negative vibes from Eliza wouldn't do that.

"Well, you're no good to anyone tired," Raff countered.

"True. Maybe I'll lie down anyway … see if I can doze off. You need to sleep as well. I have a feeling we're in for a few long days," I mumbled sadly.

My heart squeezed when a vision of Floyd lying in bed like that flashed through my mind again. No matter what the outcome for him, I believed that first sight of him would be burned into my brain for life.

Raff had managed to park quite close to the building where the ICU entrance was after dropping me off, so we were fortunate not to run into any fans or people who recognized me. Thankfully, the journey to my ma's house took less time than I thought.

A beaming smile awaited me as my ma flung open the door. Wrapping her arms around me, she gave me one of her extra special hugs. It was the soothing hug I hadn't known I'd needed, until she did it.

"Hi, Son, you must be exhausted," she mumbled, eyeing me with concern. "I've made your bed up and your friend here can have Tim's old room."

"Thanks, Mrs. Booker," Raff replied, sounding tired. I saw him cast a wary eye around the fourteen by ten foot living room that was overfilled with furniture, and guessed he was taking in how small the place was.

"You met Raff already, right?" I asked her, ignoring his scrutiny as I gestured toward him with my thumb.

"I did, but I'm embarrassed to say, I didn't know who of your guards was who. We met so many people that night and the names became a blur as everyone was being introduced. To be honest, I was so enthralled by you, playing on that big stage in Dublin, I couldn't take it all in."

"That's okay, Mrs. Booker, I'm not that memorable anyway," Raff joked to ease my ma's embarrassment.

"I'd say you're the most memorable because you keep my boy safe … and you're the best looking in my opinion," she added as she chuckled. "Everything happened so fast at the end of the concert. And I was also trying to keep Greg's grannie in check …" she trailed off, throwing her eyes to her hairline.

Both Raff and I laughed, because my grannie had channelled her inner rock chick that night, and had proved herself to be a dirty old bugger by flirting with all the men.

"Well, thank you, I'll take that as a compliment," Raff replied modestly. "Feel free to forget my name since you think I'm the best looking of all of us."

"Right, if you're done flirting with my ma," I muttered playfully. "I need a shower and bed," I said, interrupting their small talk since I suddenly felt bone tired. "We'll know more about Floyd in the coming days. I'm going to try and grab a couple of hours rest. Can you ring Ruth's ma and ask her to have some things ready for Ruth and Eliza, that I'll take them back to the hospital."

"And Eliza? You saw her?" she asked warily.

"Not getting into that with you right now, Ma. But Lizzie's at the hospital with Ruth, and they're about the same size. Tell her ma I'll grab their stuff on the way back," I said mounting the stairs. "Come on Raff, I'll show you where you're crashing." The moment I said the word crashing, I winced. Crashing was a phrase I usually used for getting my head down. Now, I understood the ominous meaning of it.

Opening, Tim's bedroom door, I became aware that the single bed, what Raff would call a twin, was nowhere near wide, nor long enough for his tall frame. "What can I say? Irish people aren't known for their height," I joked.

Raff twisted his lips like he wasn't impressed with the tiny bed, and I figured, he'd guessed that a queen wouldn't have fit in the small room. "You know what? I'm so fucking tired, I could sleep on a hedge full of ivy," he muttered.

"You can have my room. It's got a double bed. I'll sleep in here," I decided, not to be polite or ashamed of my roots, just accepting he was much bigger in height and build than me.

"Nah, it's fine. If I can't get on with it, I'll take the floor. My back's killing me from sitting on my ass all night and most of the day anyway."

After insisting, he eventually took my room. The last of my energy had been drained by his opposition so I passed on the shower, stripped out of my clothes, climbed into my brother's old bed and passed out.

"Greg, Ruth's on the phone," my ma mumbled, shaking me awake as I lay squinting up at her. I glanced to my left where I'd been dreaming Eliza had been tucked up against my side and felt instantly disappointed no one was there. My heart sank when I remembered how antagonized Eliza had been by my presence.

Pain shot through my eyes from lack of sleep, and I noticed how the rain lashed against the windowpane outside. I was instantly distracted by the sound of it until my ma's stern voice snapped me back into focus.

Focusing on her holding the house phone out for me, I snatched it from her hand, and I held it up to my ear. "Ruth? What's up?"

"I'm sorry about Eliza earlier," she began.

"Don't even mention that. Concentrate on what's important."

"Thanks, Greg," she quietly mumbled. "I was asking your ma if she would relieve mine at my house, with the kids. She's going to bring a change of clothes for Eliza and me. The reason I asked to talk to you, was to warn you that Eliza has started to date Owen Murphy."

A fiery rage flowed through my veins at the mention of that name for two reasons. Jealousy being the first, and that of all people Eliza could date, Owen Murphy was the last person I'd have wanted her to be with. The guy was my personal nemesis when I was in high school.

Murphy had been waiting for his chance with Eliza since he was fourteen years old. According to Floyd, these days Owen was a car showroom manager, who drove around in flashy cars—even if they weren't his.

Eliza used to piss me off by saying Owen was her smooth, Henry Cavill to my bad boy, Colin Farrell. In some ways this was true. I always appeared to be in trouble back then while Owen had always had his shit together.

Years later, when I was still scraping a living busking in the town center, or playing in local bars, he had graduated with a degree in business studies from Dublin University.

"Right, thanks," I mumbled. My toneless reply to Ruth hid the violent rage that had taken over my body at the mention of his name. The thought of him touching Eliza in the ways I used to touch her, brought bile to the back of my throat. "That fucker," I muttered as I slowly dragged myself upright and handed my ma back the phone.

I sought fresh jeans out of my luggage. "What ... who?" she asked, her face etched with worry.

"Ruth was warning me that Eliza had moved on."

"Well, you did hurt her badly," my ma reminded me, as she noticed I was naked and turned away from me while I got dressed. "It was bound to happen at some point, Greg. Eliza is a beautiful girl. She deserves to have someone."

"Jesus, Ma, what that girl deserves is a good spanking for the way she behaved after I'd won my spot in the band."

"That's your take. Hers would be different, I'm sure."

"I'm not going to argue with you. Anyway, I can't imagine she'll last long with a limp dick, stick-up-his-ass wimp like Owen Murphy. He wouldn't begin to know how to satisfy my Lizzie in bed."

"Is that right, Greg Booker? Do you think a woman's world revolves around what a man can do with his penis? I'm sure if orgasms made babies, there'd be far less babies in the world ... since ninety percent of men can't even get a woman off."

"Ma!" I said, straightening upright and staring pointedly at her in shock.

"Well, it's true. I read it once in a woman's magazine ... *Marie Claire* or some such publication like that ... it was in the doctor's surgery waiting room ... the magazine ... not the woman. Fortunately, your dad was—"

"No, Ma! I don't want to hear it," I muttered as I pulled my jeans over my arse and did up the zipper.

"Then, start thinking with your brain not that ugly, little dangly thing between your legs."

"If I've told him that once ..." Raff interjected playfully to my ma from my bedroom door, grinning. In our small, family house he would have had to be deaf not to hear the whole conversation. "Maybe he'll listen to you because he sure as hell doesn't listen to me."

"Yeah? Whose side are you on?" I challenged, some of my discomfort subsiding when I saw Raff bite back a grin.

My ma laughed at us and trotted down the stairs. I swept past Raff, ignoring his poke at me. I leaned over the banister to call after her. "And for your information my dick might have been a small dangly thing the last time you saw it, but it's a respectable, fat, eight now," I called back.

"Oh, you inherited everything else that was good about your father, so I don't doubt it," she called back, unperturbed by my comment.

"Dear God, shut her up," I mumbled to myself. "That's way too much information, ma. You've crossed a line," I chastised before turning back to look at Raff.

"Fat eight, eh? Something tells me you measured it ... I know your type," Raff goaded, grinning when my head whipped round to face him.

"For your information, Lizzie did," I informed him, finding a moment of humor in my otherwise fucked-up day.

Raff chuckled and shook his head. "Not an image I want to carry around in my head for the rest of the day. Tell me something else quick, before it gets imbedded in my brain."

"Fuck off, Raff," I muttered, shoving him playfully.

"I would but there's nowhere to go in here. These Irish homes are snug," he complained.

"Yeah, I know the brag ... everything's bigger and better in

America," I muttered sarcastically. "Get the fuck off my landing and get ready to leave. We're heading back to the hospital." I pulled out my cell phone and texted Ruth.

Me: Text me Lizzie's cell number?

Ruth: Are you sure about this?

Me: I am. I think we need to at least try to make peace.

Ruth: 399 441 GREG

My jaw dropped when I saw her new number, and I wondered what that could mean.

Me: Are you serious?

Ruth: Lol, Floyd bought her the cell phone for Christmas.

Me: Does she know the numbers spell that?

Ruth: I don't think she's ever given it a thought.

I chuckled as I shook my head, saved the number, and instantly added it to my contacts as 'My Lizzie', even though she was no longer mine.

Me: Thanks darlin'. I'm on my way back to the hospital.

Five minutes later, I read my text conversation with Ruth again in the car again after we'd said goodbye to my ma and we'd set off for the hospital again.

"What are you looking so smug about?" Raff asked, eyeing me carefully before looking back at the road.

I chuckled. "You're not going to believe this. Floyd's not going to die," I said determinedly. "That guy's too much of a genius to go out this way."

"Huh?" Raff asked, eyeing me again, almost a moment too long.

"Watch the road, mate," I muttered. Raff's head snapped back, looking straight ahead.

"So, your buddy is going to be okay?"

I sighed, my chest tightening again. "He's not yet, but he will be," I said, channeling positive energy. "But get this ... he bought Eliza a new phone for Christmas last year and the last four digits spell Greg. The guy's a fucking genius I tell you."

CHAPTER 18

ELIZA

My nerves were fried by the time Greg left the hospital. No matter how prepared I thought I was for our long-awaited reunion, my behavior went to shit the moment I clapped eyes on him.

The moment those lift doors opened and I saw him standing there, I must have had an enormous adrenaline dump because my whole body shook, and I became so lightheaded that I almost passed out. My heart stuttered in my chest the second our eyes met and he held my gaze with those stunning green eyes of his.

I'd been mentally preparing myself for his visit since the moment Ruth told me he was on his way. But the emotional impact of having him in the same space, looking tired but still so sexily appealing, made every preparation I'd done dissolve.

It was then that I realized nothing could have prepared me for the entangled emotions that hit me all at once. But it was my rage that won out as it bubbled up to my chest from my gut and spewed out of my mouth with such venom.

For years I'd imagined how that initial first minute might have played out. Never once did I picture me losing my cool in such an undignified way. However, I never thought for one minute that seeing Greg again would happen in such grim circumstances as my brother being gravely ill.

After he'd gone, I had wanted the clock to rewind and to have a do-over so that I could deal with his presence with more grace. But, his visit to Floyd had been way too brief on one hand and far too long on the other, for me to find my equilibrium and conduct myself in a slightly more eloquent manner.

"Dare I ask how you feel about seeing Greg again?" My steady gaze cut from watching my brother's monitors to my sister-in-law's worried expression. "I mean, I saw how you reacted. I'm guessing you tried to prepare yourself ... but you obviously weren't."

My lips twisted into a wry smirk to convey without words how much I regretted the snide remarks I'd made. "I've had years of anticipation as to how that moment might have played out, and it didn't go remotely like I imagined. I would have been dressed to the nines and he'd have begged to have me back, sorry at what he'd left behind."

"Oh, Eliza, you need to talk to him ... I mean, really talk."

"Ha! Do you really think I'd stand a chance now? Look at me," I mumbled, waving a hand up and down myself. "I must have given him quite the fright with my tear-stained, mascara-streaked face, dressed in this tacky dress and heels."

Ruth chuckled. "No doubt. But it was me that flung myself at him the moment he walked out of the elevator."

"Yeah, when you saw him, it was as if an emotional dam broke inside or something."

"Having Greg here makes me feel closer to Floyd somehow. Does that make sense? When I first began to go out with your brother, they were always together ... we all were always together," she corrected to include me.

"I know what you mean," I admitted, feeling a weight on my chest. "I miss how close we all were."

I especially missed the quiet times Greg and I had together. Nothing made us happier than lying quietly in the dark, my head on Greg's bare chest, him sifting his fingers through my hair.

The sound of Greg's steady heartbeat had been committed to my memory long ago. Sometimes when I was alone in bed at night, if I tried hard enough, I could still conjure it up in my mind.

I shook the thought away and shrugged. "Life felt so simple then," I remarked.

"Until Greg grew grand ideas and headed to fame and fortune, you mean? Don't you ever wish you'd been brave enough to follow your heart?" Ruth probed.

"You know Greg as well as I do. It would never have worked out for us in America. He was hurtling toward the land of opportunity. He's always been an impulsive, carefree, risk-taker. I'm not," I reminded her.

"Sounds to me like you couldn't trust him," Ruth stated bluntly.

I shrugged. "Maybe I didn't, he was always ... unpredictable. I had a feeling my heart wouldn't be safe since his wish to be idolized had been granted."

"That isn't fair. Being famous was never Greg's ambition. He's always been about his music. What you're really saying is you lacked the confidence to believe you could go the distance with him. Let me ask you this. Did he ever give you reason to doubt him?"

"He walked away, didn't he?" I countered immediately.

"You keep harping back to that. Maybe that's how you saw it, but the rest of us didn't. If I may speak frankly, I think you took the shine off his good luck. Floyd and I have talked about this a few times.

"That night when he came into the bar, ecstatic that he'd been chosen for the band, the whole bar erupted in celebration at his good fortune. Everyone congratulated him, we felt it was the recognition that had been a long time coming for him. So, how do you think he felt once you turned on your heels and ran out of the bar, crying?"

"Well, while you were all hooting and hollering at him for winning that spot, all I heard was the beginning of the end of us," I remarked flatly.

"No, Eliza. You decided then and there it would be the end of you in his life," Ruth argued. "Greg was devastated from the moment you refused to go with him. But I'm glad he didn't let his heart rule his head and chased his dream."

"Really? And if that had been Floyd running headlong into a world of excess where he could order up women like drinks in a bar? You'd have been happy to tag along with that?"

"If that had been Floyd's dream, then yes. I would follow your brother to the ends of the earth," she remarked with a note of finality.

"Easy for you to say. You weren't walking in my shoes. You saw how many girls hit on Greg because of his personality. Don't you remember what a huge flirt he was back in the day."

"That was banter, Eliza. Greg's a musician, and what you saw was part of his performance. The moment the music stopped he only ever had eyes for you."

"That's not how it felt on my end. I was the one that had to take the jibes from girls who thought I wasn't good enough for him."

"Perhaps you were too immature to handle a relationship with someone who has such a big personality such as Greg has." Ruth's words stung because it was something I had thought to myself more than once.

Although I never argued with Greg about how he behaved during performances, the by-product of his great gigs was that I felt belittled by how he joked with women in my presence, or how cutting their remarks were toward me.

It was largely due to that flirty banter that I became insecure. A concept that had only begun to dawn on me about a month after he'd left. But by then I had blocked him from contacting me.

During my darker moments, I had almost reached out to him, but then my pride had gotten in the way, and I wouldn't allow myself to admit that I might have been wrong.

That stubborn, iron will of mine almost broke until the day the internet suggested he was over me. Images of Greg, drunk, with a beautiful girl on his lap, beaming happily, had goaded me from my screen …cementing the end of any remote chance that he might come back to me.

"Anyway, that's all in the past. I'm over him. Owen Murphy's my future," I stated, trying to sound convincing.

"From the way you reacted the moment Greg stepped out of that lift, I'd say that's the biggest lie you've ever uttered, Eliza McDade. Did you agree to go out with Owen to hurt Greg?"

"Ruth, I'm tired of saying this. What Greg and I had, it's long gone. Besides, for the first time in a long time, I'm getting good vibes from a man. Owen's great company and he's attentive toward me. Please, let me be happy for once."

"Alright, if you say so. And if that really is the case, you'll cut Greg some slack once he comes back. Perhaps you could apologize for all the snarky remarks you made toward him while you're at it."

An alarm went off on Floyd's monitor and our attention instantly snapped to the flatline where his oxygen saturations were on the screen.

Panic crushed my chest, making it hard to draw breath until Lindsay held a hand up and shook her head. "Don't worry, I'm just changing fingers with his pulse oximeter," she said, reattaching it to his middle one. Once in place, the beeps began to register steadily again.

"I figured that was Floyd agreeing with me," Ruth said, during a rare moment of humor in our otherwise dark day.

As the door to Floyd's room opened, the air shifted and I knew Greg had arrived without the need to look up.

Even though his presence was less unexpected, my heart still fluttered nervously in my chest. Ignoring me, he strolled over to Ruth and handed her a small bag. As they engaged in conversation, I took the opportunity to study Greg closer than I had that morning.

No matter how much I told myself I was him, nothing prepared me to experience that same raw, depth of hurt I'd felt, as the day we'd said goodbye.

Greg looked good … far too good for my liking, because my body lit up like fireworks on the fourth of July and I couldn't tear my eyes away from him. He appeared strong, fit and much healthier than I remembered him. Then I supposed living in the sunshine state had contributed to the gorgeous, bronze glow to his skin. As Ruth and he spoke, Greg flashed her a small, toothy grin, showing his straight, white teeth. My hungry eyes were drawn to his full, sexy lips that had at one time kissed every inch of my body.

A pang of desire shot through me from my head to my toes. The effect of it almost knocked me on my ass. In that moment, Greg looked up as if he had felt me staring at him, and I quickly looked away.

In that brief connection, a thrill coursed through me. I let time pass until I thought it was safe to steal another look and when I did, I realized he was still looking at me. I immediately became self-conscious as he scrutinized me.

I lowered my gaze until he resumed his conversation with Ruth, and I was sure he was no longer focused on me. Then I stole a glance, which gave me the chance to take a closer look at him. Greg was no longer the boyish man who had left me behind and was now a mature, polished version of himself and even hotter than I'd once thought him to be.

An uncomfortable ache in my chest made me realize my heart was beating fast, making me suddenly thirsty, in need of a drink.

"Just going to get some water from the cooler outside," I mumbled. Once outside the door, I gasped as I gulped in air and fought back tears of longing again for the man I had lost.

Seconds later, Ruth came out behind me. "I'm going to change and freshen up. You should go back there." She prompted me and tipped her chin toward the room.

"I can't—not yet," I replied. The warm air in Floyd's room had already made the atmosphere oppressive before Greg had arrived. And since the moment he had arrived I'd found it harder to breathe.

"Oh, God, help me," I muttered to myself in prayer once Ruth was out of sight. I drew in a few steady breaths to loosen the tightness in my chest, but each breath came faster than the last.

"You, okay?" I froze at the sound of Greg's soft, low tone before a delayed shockwave coursed through my body. The tension within me at his sudden presence in the corridor unnerved me. As I took a deep breath, I spun around to face him, and promptly lost my balance.

Greg's strong arms wrapped around, and he immediately drew my body against his chest. "Are you alright?"

Strong memories of how I felt in his arms came flooding back that temporarily drained my anger. At the same time a wall of desperate longing flowed through me that I was too tired to fight.

Tears flowed freely as I clung to the back of his T-shirt. In that moment, Greg was everything I had needed, even if I hadn't wanted it to feel that way. Being held by him as I poured my heart out, was a comfort like no other I'd felt in a long time.

"That's it, let it all out, Lizzie. I know this is scary, baby. But, if anyone can survive the impact of a logging truck accident, it's Floyd." Greg murmured quietly into my ear, rubbing my back, as both of us were briefly united in our concern for my brother.

Feeling him all around me again, his smell, his touch, and the warmth from his hard body, brought a swell of emotion to my throat. Swallowing became painful as sobs made it difficult to catch a breath.

I had dreamed of Greg holding me like this a thousand times or more, but not like this.

A streak of guilt tore through me because Greg believed he was comforting me about my brother, even though my tears had little to do with Floyd right then. They were shed mourning for the love I'd lost.

As I pulled away from Greg, I felt his fingers trace down my back, waist, and inner arms, as if he were reluctant to let me go.

"I'm sor-sorry about earlier," I mumbled as my breath hitched through breathless sobs.

Cupping my face gently in his hands, Greg's eyes filled with empathy, as they connected with mine. His right thumb gently stroked my cheek as he held my gaze. "Don't apologize, Lizzie. You never need to apologize to me for anything. I get it, baby. You must be worried out of your mind."

Deep down I was aware that Floyd had little to do with my reaction, but I accepted his excuse for my anger. "Yeah … I am," I agreed.

As if he realized what he was doing, Greg dropped his hands and stepped back. The moment he stopped touching me, left a pain in my chest. My body swayed toward Greg like it was unwilling to accept the break.

Greg reached out and caught me by my upper arm. "Are you okay?" he asked, his worried eyes ticking over my face in concern. I nodded, even though my heart ached. "Ruth's ma put some clean clothes for you, in the bag I gave to Ruth," he said, casting a glance down my body, and gesturing toward my attire. "Were you on a night out when you got the call?" he probed.

Glancing down at the sexy, figure hugging, red dress I'd worn to impress Owen, it almost killed me to confess where I was going.

"A date?" he inquired gruffly.

"Yeah," I admitted quietly, nodding.

"Anyone I'd know?" he inquired deadpan.

The dark look in his narrowed eyes and the way his jaw moved back and forth like it used to when he was mad put me on guard. I didn't like where the conversation was going so, I shook my head. "I don't think that's any of your business."

"It isn't. I was making conversation. It's been a long time since I could lay claim to you, Lizzie," he said flatly as he dropped his hand from my arm and held both hands up in surrender.

The matter-of-fact way he said this crushed me. Schooling my expression for nonchalance, I shrugged. "That's true."

He had a wistful look in his eyes, but his face was expressionless so I had no idea what his thoughts were.

He let out a tired sigh and stuffed his hands in his pockets. "Alright. Well, if you're sure you're okay, I'm going to head back in and sit with Floyd for a while." He hitched his thumb over his shoulder, then turned toward the door.

Frustration almost got the better of me because I believed there was so much more we could have said ... should have said, but the moment had gone.

As I heard the door click closed softly behind him, I wondered if there would ever come a time when I'd find the closure with him that I needed.

I reminded myself that he hadn't come for me. Floyd was the reason for his visit. He was the person that mattered to Greg. I stuck my hands on my hips, huffed out a breath and shook my head, while distress, frustration and regret warred angrily for the upper hand in my thoughts.

So that was it—My long-awaited confrontation with the man I once thought I would marry. Five minutes of stilted conversation whereby nothing felt final nor resolved in my heart.

Nothing had gone how I'd imagined seeing Greg again would be. All my years of internal arguments I'd played out in my mind were nothing like what had gone down. *Fuck you, Greg Booker.*

CHAPTER 19

GREG

For a few short minutes peace reigned in my heart as I held Eliza in my arms. The all-to-brief intimate embrace we shared was a mixture of elation and torture ... a combination of our own heaven and hell.

The second Eliza clung to me for comfort was all consuming. It was as if the world had fallen away from beneath our feet and nothing else mattered but us. Having her warm body close to mine filled my head full of instant memories of happier times. I couldn't get past how familiar and right she felt in my arms, yet she was filled with grief about her brother.

Distressing or not, I would have given anything to relive those precious few minutes with Eliza pressed against me, her soft hair against my cheek and the familiar scent of her signature Nivea moisturizing cream she'd always used, clinging to her skin.

The moment I held her face between my hands and looked into her red-rimmed eyes, I wanted her. It made me realize that since I'd left her my life had been poorer for her absence. But no matter how desperately I'd wanted to tell her that, I couldn't, not now that she was somebody else's girl.

Besides, I hadn't travelled from the US to antagonize her. And dredging up all those feelings we'd weathered between us would only have brought more pain for us both.

As I re-entered Floyd's room, I acknowledged his nurse and wandered over to his bed again. Before I sat down, I cast another glance over my shoulder.

My heart clenched the moment I saw Eliza's silhouette through the opaque glass door. And vowed to at least try to make things better between us.

As I sat down, I scanned all Floyd's monitoring equipment again while I figured out what to say. Then, paying attention to my friend, I slid my palm under his, closed my fingers around his hand, shut my eyes and prayed.

Even if I were a literary genius, it would still be impossible to describe the scope of emotions while I begged God not to take Floyd from us. Once I opened my eyes, I caught the nurse staring directly at me.

For a moment I wondered if she saw me as the ordinary man that I am, humbled and worried by the unknown fate of his sick friend. I'd hoped so, because Greg Booker the rock star had no business being in Floyd's room.

"Hey, mate, I'm back. Have you missed me?" I joked to my unconscious friend. My normal question to Floyd in that tension-filled situation earned me a small smile from a new nurse.

I had never been one to be stumped for something to say but there was only one thought swirling around in my head. "Don't you dare die, Floyd McDade. Too many people love you," I warned, my tone breaking with those words. The insistent bellows of the ventilator mocked me while I sat there in silence after that.

Time appeared to stand still in the long minutes that followed. Eventually, I dragged my worried eyes away from Floyd and glanced over my shoulder at the door again. My heart ached once I realized Eliza still hadn't moved.

Suspecting she was brooding when I saw her head bent, made me wonder if she was thinking about me ... or us. Much like where my thoughts had been over the previous twenty-four hours or so.

If that was true, I guessed that she would likely keep her distance from me until Ruth came back. Eliza wasn't hard to read, she'd always worn her heart on her sleeve and her stubborn nature like a coat of armor.

I'd always been able to read her. And from my recent interactions with her, I figured Eliza was the same willful girl that had broken up with me. Also, from the angry outbursts she'd had since I'd been at the hospital, they'd given me reason to believe that she felt she couldn't trust me.

Could I blame her? For the first time since about a year after I left, I felt guilty about the reckless reputation I'd earned.

Maybe I should have tried harder with Eliza ... instead of making a show of myself and letting her see what she was missing. She was right about one thing. I was an asshole, as far as getting even went. For the time I had been with Screaming Shadows, the paparazzi lapped up stories of the hedonistic lifestyle I lived, just to forget her.

No wonder Eliza didn't trust me or hadn't been brave enough to expand her reach on the world. Her friends couldn't understand her reasoning when she wouldn't come with me. Most of them would have jumped at the chance to swap their paycheck-to-paycheck lifestyle for an easier life.

Growing up where money was hard to come by, I'd seen firsthand how tough it was for my mother to keep us fed and in clothes that had fit. So, I believed, if I couldn't provide a better life than what Eliza already had, then there was no way I could have committed to her.

The way I saw it, becoming a band member of Screaming Shadows was the answer to everything. Not only in fulfilling my musical dreams, but help to provide Eliza and I with financial security.

When Eliza refused to come to Miami with me and cut all communication, it devastated me. And it took a while for me to come to terms with being in a new country, with a new life. Wallowing in misery at what I'd left behind had begun to affect my concentration. And as I couldn't afford to make mistakes, I decided I had to figure out who I was without Eliza.

The only way I could do this was to throw myself into my new life and embrace opportunity. Consequently, that included a bevy of beautiful women on tap. But those women were mostly looking for no-strings sex, and I'd been happy to indulge in that lifestyle for years now.

However, seeing Eliza upset brought a sense of shame to what I'd been doing. What had happened between us had always weighed on my heart no matter how much time had passed. And the ache in my heart as she shed salty tears on my chest came as a timely reminder that I would never be over her.

As Dr. O'Hare entered the room, his movements pulled me out of my reverie. My eyes narrowed as I followed him from the door to the day nurse. As they spoke in hushed tones, I studied his serious facial expressions while they spoke, in the hope of seeing any positive reaction to their quiet exchange.

Lifting Floyd's chart, he came around Floyd's bed to where I sat and checked out the ventilator. "Is Ruth here?" he asked, twisting his hips to make eye contact with me.

"She's freshening up. She should be back in a few minutes," I informed him. Eliza pushed open the door and came into the room. "Do you want me to get Ruth?" she asked as if she sensed the doctor had news to disclose.

"Yes," both the doctor and I said together. We briefly shared eye contact before I looked back to Eliza.

"What's happening?" she probed, addressing the doctor, sounding anxious.

"Perhaps you could let Ruth know I'm here?" the doctor suggested, giving nothing away.

"Right," she muttered, taking his hint we'd get nothing until his wife came back.

Eliza darted out the room, and seconds later, both women came back. Ruth was anxiously wringing her hands as she followed Eliza inside.

"I'm happy with Floyd's progress," the doctor blurted out quickly, and I guessed he'd read the same fear in Ruth's eyes as I had. Ruth's shoulders immediately sagged in relief.

"The MRI's show no significant injuries to his chest that may have caused the respiratory arrest so it must have been something else. However, if he continues to remain stable, we'll plan to test his ability to breath on his own."

"When?" I asked almost too eagerly.

"Perhaps tomorrow. We're keeping him sedated right now until the swelling subsides. We'll be scanning again to see what progress has been made, but the longer he's on the ventilator the more dependant he'll become."

"Right, and what happens if he doesn't breathe on his own," Eliza asked.

"Then he'll be ventilated again. There's a whole process we go through to ensure that he's not starved of oxygen, but we'd ask for space to carry out this procedure."

"I'm going nowhere—no matter what," Ruth muttered determinedly.

IT WAS four more days before Floyd was successfully taken off the ventilator and he began breathing unaided. However, despite having his sedation dialled down, he had only opened his eyes briefly one time as he drifted in and out of consciousness.

"I thought he would have been more alert by now," I mumbled to Ruth as we both stared at her husband. Floyd's lack of consciousness made me nervous, and I'd begun to feel quite desperate to see more progress.

"Greg, there's a guy downstairs who says you're expecting him," a male nurse, that had been sitting at the nursing station when I had arrived, informed me.

"I need to go. I'm leaving tonight to fly stateside. My band is playing at SunFest in Palm Beach, and I don't want to go."

"There you go again, proving we're not as important as playing music in a stupid band," Eliza chimed in, echoing the same sentiment she'd made all those years ago as I was leaving to join the band.

"That must be the most unfair thing you've ever said to me," I snapped. "Fulfilling an obligation isn't a selfish act. Twenty thousand people have made travel arrangements, will be taking time off work and have already spent their money to see us. The band is contracted to perform.

"You think I wouldn't say fuck it, I'm staying right here, if I wasn't needed? I'm one of five people in a band, Lizzie. My job has nothing to do with my feelings about Floyd, Ruth … or you for that matter. I'm coming straight back to Dublin as soon as is practical, after the gig."

I wondered if there would be some kick-back from Donnie about my plans. However, my other bandmates had called most of the shots over the band's timetable. Personally, I'd always gone with the flow, and I'd never complained.

Nowadays, I felt I had earned my place, and my needs were just as important as the rest of the guys, no matter what Donnie was lining up for us.

"Right, well you know where we'll be," she muttered, nodding her head toward Floyd lying semi-recumbent and unresponsive in his bed.

"I'll only be gone two or three days at the most. We're only performing for one night. Arriving back will depend on how quickly I can get a flight," I mumbled softly.

"Who cares? Go. Do what you want ... just like you've always done."

I scoffed. "And you haven't? I get you're still pissed that I left. You could have come with me. Or do you prefer to forget it was your choice to stay here and fester in bitterness because you couldn't control me?"

"I never wanted to control you ... nor am I bitter."

I snickered. "Right," I ground out, sarcasm dripping from the word as an adrenaline dump exploded and flowed through my veins.

The determined challenge that bored from her eyes to mine made me want to punch something. "Then grow the fuck up and quit ragging on me. I'm getting bored of your abandoned puppy routine. Like I said, I have no choice. Despite what you think of me, I do fucking care—more than you know."

From the way Eliza's eyes widened in shock I could tell I'd intimidated her with my forceful reply. Instant regret extinguished any frustration I felt. Not once while we'd been together had I ever spoken to her like that before.

The second Eliza recovered, she huffed out a breath and pointed toward the lift.

"I believe you know the way out," she barked, dismissing me.

CHAPTER 20

ELIZA

"Fuck, I tore him a new one, again," I muttered to myself once the lift doors closed, and Greg had left. "Why couldn't I keep my big fat mouth shut?" I growled and stamped my feet in a fit of temper.

It had been a while since I'd let my feelings about Greg get the better of me. I thought I'd gotten past wallowing in sentiments of what might have been between us. Yet the second Greg shared the same space as me, all the misery of that time overwhelmed me again.

Regret of what I'd just done brought me to my knees. Kneeling there, dismayed by my lack of control, I stared at the lift's shiny metal doors.

Thankfully the nurses' station was empty and only Greg had heard the venomous words I'd spat … words that still echoed inside my head and made my heart heavy.

What he'd said was true. I had made a choice that I'd regretted. But that remorse had come late in the day … too late by then to undo the damage between us.

Ruth stepped out of Floyd's room, wrapped her cardigan around her and hugged it tightly.

"I know I said this wasn't the place for venting your feelings, but I need to get something off my chest. Eliza McDade, I'm so ashamed of you." Ruth stopped her dressing down of me, the moment she realized I was crying. "Why are you crying?"

Shame filled every fiber of my being because, Ruth needn't have bothered wasting her breath on me, because I already knew how badly I'd treated Greg since he'd come back. I'd behaved horrifically toward him after he'd travelled halfway around the world to be with my brother.

"What if that's the last time I see him? If something were to happen to—" I blurted out.

"Don't you dare consider anything else going wrong. The worst has already happened to us all, and the only way now, is up," Ruth snapped, cutting my sentence off. I hoped she had enough faith for us both because it was something I lacked right then.

As I was smarting from her admonishment, the lift doors opened, and Greg unexpectedly stepped out. My heart skipped a beat as he stalked toward me. "Could we have a minute, Ruth?" The sharp request was more a demand than a question.

Ruth looked from Greg toward me and shrugged. "Keep it down," she ordered, pointing toward his door, like we'd needed to be reminded of respect for Floyd.

Once Ruth went inside, Greg yanked me off the floor, stood me on my feet and pulled me roughly against his chest. "I absolutely refuse to fly across the fucking Atlantic after an argument with you again."

Even though my body initially remained stiff as he held me in his arms, I couldn't resist closing my eyes and breathing him into my lungs.

A wave of emotion instantly rose from within me because,

although he smelled somewhat like how I remembered, there were distinctive differences about him as well.

Anger gave way to relief, the longer I stood there in his arms. All my pent-up tension that had been present within me since he'd come back, slowly dissipated. Then, no matter how many years of pendulous emotions had controled my heart, I remembered how protected I'd always felt whenever Greg held me that way.

"Tell me you're going to let this feud go, Lizzie. I can't bear to think a decision made so long ago is still tearing you up," he demanded gruffly.

For a long minute I didn't reply, choosing instead to focus on the rumble of his voice as it vibrated from his chest to my cheek. I closed my eyes, suddenly swamped with memories of all the little things I had loved about Greg.

Without pulling out of his grasp, I glanced up. Still a little unsure, I bit my lip, then gave him a small nod.

"I think that was a yes," he murmured softly, as he assessed me through narrowed eyes.

"You're right. We're both very different people now," I admitted. Despair flooded through me at my words because they drew a line under what we had been.

Is that what I'm most angry about? That he no longer looks like the pale-skinned, Irish boy I fell in love with? That he now looks every inch the sexy, rich, international rock star? That I no longer measured up for his affections? If the internet was anything to go by, Greg wouldn't see me the way he used to anymore. Why would he, now that he was used to dating Oscar winners who spent more time preening themselves to perfection, than I spent at work every day?

Releasing me, Greg took a step back. "No more, Liz, you hear me? It breaks my heart to see you so upset."

"You're right," I said, sounding defeated. "I think my reaction was a combination of shock from me being stressed about Floyd and seeing you after all this time ... here in the hospital of all places," I added, trying to find a valid excuse for my explosive reaction. "Now that it looks like Floyd's chances are better, I can see that I probably took my stress out on you."

"Come on, Lizzie, we both know that wasn't about Floyd," he insisted, calling me out.

"I'm done," I stated.

Greg's gorgeous eyes scrutinized me like he knew I was talking bullshit. "We could sit down and talk when I come back at the very least," he offered.

"There's no need for that. I'm dating again now," I blurted because the more time I spent with Greg the more I felt myself caving to the feelings I'd locked away.

He chuckled. "You told me … Owen Murphy," he muttered flatly. If I'd expected him to be furious, I was disappointed that he didn't appear to be. When I agreed to a date with Owen it wasn't to punish anyone. "Hope he gives you everything you deserve."

My initial thought about that was that there was no other man who could ever replace what I had with Greg.

Taking my hand, he turned it over and placed a soft, lingering kiss to the center of my palm. I gulped in air as my throat constricted as he did this. Then he lifted his eyes to look at me with his lips and breath still on my skin.

The explosive heat in his eyes filled my heart with longing. Then, before I was ready, he broke the kiss and stood tall. Slowly he closed my fingers around my palm, trapping his kiss in my fist.

"Alright then," he said in a sad tone. "Take care of yourself, Lizzie. No doubt we'll see each other once I get back."

The lump that had grown in my throat burned with unshed tears because Greg's gesture with his kiss was the same goodbye kiss he'd given me the day he left me for good.

I swallowed down a wave of emotion that threatened to break me as Greg stepped back. He continued to hold my gaze, as if he was committing the moment to his memory again. Then he turned, strode back to the lift, and pressed the call button again. The doors immediately opened, like it had been waiting there for him all along.

"Alright, Greg?" a huge guy with an American accent asked. It was then that it hit me. The last time Greg had left as an ordinary man. But now, the world knew his name, and he was so famous that he needed someone to protect him.

CHAPTER 21

GREG

As the elevator doors closed, I crouched down to the floor and slapped my hands on my head. Inhaling deeply, I blew out a long breath while I tried to relieve the crushing pain in my chest. "Damn that fucking girl," I mumbled in frustration to myself.

"Trouble in paradise," Raff asked, sounding sarcastic.

I'd done plenty of complaining about Eliza's pissy moods to Raff every time I'd gotten drunk and nostalgic.

Snickering as I stood tall, I shook my head in defeat. "That woman can bring out the best and the absolute worst in me. I've never met anyone else like her ... she's a real, stubborn fuck."

"If she was your girlfriend, I figure she would have needed to be. Your ass is so wayward, I imagine you'd need someone to tell you no and to mean it. However, I can imagine how explosive the angry sex would be if you ever made up with her," Raff mused deadpan.

I chuckled and stuffed my hands in my pockets. "Yup, been there and done that many times, so you're not wrong on that score. But do you know what gets me? Even though she's been acting all furious and aloof, I've had a raging boner whenever she's been around."

"TMI, dude … but it sounds like being dominated," he stated, laughing. "If that's the case, I want a ringside seat the next time the two of you clash. I could use some tips on how to handle you."

"Me? I'm not hard to handle," I mumbled. I let out a small chuckle at my lie despite the uneasy feeling I had about leaving Eliza behind again.

I considered Raff's comment about him needing tips to manage me as we walked to the car. Most of his duties involved me these days. He had worked with Korry and Deakon as well, but since they had gotten steady partners, that dynamic had changed. Bodhi was always with Jude, and Mikey had taken over Levi and Deakon's security since they lived near one another. So, as Korry and Bernadette almost never left home unless it was band stuff, Raff was practically always with me.

"You got a girl?" I asked, feeling selfish that I'd never asked him before.

"Someone I see from time-to-time," he muttered, sounding evasive.

"Fuck buddy?" I probed, narrowing my eyes to watch his reaction more closely.

"Not really … it's not like that," he said flatly. He shrugged off that comment with another. "This job makes it hard to have a long-term thing."

We fell quiet as I digested his last remark until we reached our rental car.

"Greg," a female voice shouted. One of three girls that had just climbed out of a car near ours, waved over at me.

"Get in," Raff quickly demanded.

I did as he asked, and he started the engine. As he began to drive us out of the parking space as the girls began to run alongside. "Stop for a minute before one of them ends up under our wheels," I ordered.

Raff did as I asked and the girls caught up to us, panting breathlessly. "Don't open the door, and only a few inches on the window," Raff demanded. "We don't want them grabbing you."

"Hi, ladies, how's it going?" I asked with a warm smile.

"Good. We didn't know Screaming Shadows was back in Ireland," a small blonde gushed excitedly.

"Ah, we're not. Only me," I said, frowning like I was upset by that fact. "I just came home to visit my ma."

"What are you doing at the hospital?" a tall brunette with them wondered, her eyes narrowed as she studied me closer.

"Dropping a family friend of my ma's off to visit with someone," I replied in a white lie. The last thing I needed was them hounding Ruth and Eliza about their connection to me.

"Where are you going?" the nosey brunette asked.

"Never mind where, can we come," the last and curviest of the three asked. All three girls started cackling like she'd said the funniest thing ever.

"I'm afraid not, girls. We're on our way to the airport. The band is headlining at SunFest in West Palm Beach this weekend."

"Where's West Palm Beach?" the blonde probed.

"Florida," the brunette told her, looking stunned that she didn't know this.

"Aw, I wish we could go to America," the curvy girl uttered.

"I'll tell you what. Ring the London office for the record label. Ask for Bernadette and tell her you met Greg Booker at St. James's Hospital, and he asked you to tell her this and that next time we play in Dublin you three will be our guests."

"Oh. My. God. Seriously?" they chimed in together.

"Nah, I'm joking," I teased. "I watched the smiles fall from their faces and chuckled. "Of course, I'm serious."

Fortunately, my cell phone began to ring, and when I saw

Korry's name, I cut them off. "All right, we need to get going. Thanks for the chat, girls."

Taking his cue from me, Raff slowly rolled the car forward until he was clear of them, then put his foot on the gas as I answered Korry's call.

"'Sup?" I asked.

"Checking what time you land later, and if there is any update on your buddy," Korry mumbled.

"Why, are you sending a welcoming committee?" I joked.

"Sorta," he said flatly. "How's your buddy?"

"Regarding Floyd, I'm far more optimistic than I was when I got here," I admitted. "He's breathing on his own, but not fully conscious yet. I'm coming straight back to Ireland once the SunFest gig is over."

"Cool, you do what you need to do. Stand your ground with Donnie and any of the others, should they start making demands," he advised. "It's about time you were taken seriously. The other reason I'm calling is to make sure you'll be here for dinner. We thought it might do you good to have some support after all the stress you've been under."

"Take off is 11:00 a.m. so, I guess we'll be there by 4:00, depending if the flight leaves on time, and allowing for traffic," Raff said, filling Korry in on the details.

"Okay. Bernadette is arranging a band dinner at the penthouse for us this evening. It'll give us a chance to catch up and sneak in a practice of the set for tomorrow. It's been a while since it's been just us guys."

It felt good to know that it wasn't exactly a couples' group social evening that had been arranged. Raff pulled into the private plane entrance of Dublin airport and showed them our passes. "Right, we're at the airport now. See you when we land."

Cutting the call, I stuffed my phone in my pocket, and by the time I'd done this, Raff had rounded the front of the car and opened the passenger door. "Thanks, mate, let's hope there's no turbulence so that I can catch up on some sleep."

CHAPTER 22

GREG

I entered the penthouse in Miami with mixed feelings that evening. There was a sense of relief at being around people who understood the pressure of our obligations but at the same time, I felt guilty that I'd had to leave Floyd.

"How are you holding up, buddy?" Deakon asked, hugging me the moment I walked through the door.

"Better now he's off the vent," I said. "Although I'm far from happy with needing to be in two places at once."

"I can't imagine what you're going through. Floyd's a great guy." Deakon had met him in Ireland and joined in with our conversations sometimes when I'd FaceTimed Floyd. "Do you want to freshen up or are you ready to eat? It's still early here, but it's got to be around 9:00 p.m. in Ireland by now."

I nodded. "I think I could eat," I said, suddenly finding my appetite. Heading over to the kitchen counter where the food was all laid out, I filled a plate and sat at the dining table beside everyone else.

"Sorry about your buddy," Levi muttered. "We've been worried for you."

Jude nodded. "Deakon's been keeping us up to date on how he's doing." The genuine concern in Jude's tone meant everything to me.

"Thanks, it's been an anxious time for sure. Is Donnie coming to the meeting?"

"He texted to say he was half an hour out, so he'll be here any minute," Levi replied.

"Good, I want a word with him."

"You look shattered. Do you need something to help you relax? A smoke, some whiskey?" Levi offered.

"Quit smoking," I mumbled. "But I could murder a whiskey."

"Coming up. Dude, we're relieved to have you back. Donnie was worried that you might sit the festival out."

"I know you all think I'm a flake, but I'd never bail on a gig."

"That's what Deakon and Korry told Donnie," Levi muttered. Levi glanced toward Jude and a sheepish look of guilt passed between them. I knew instinctively they weren't convinced I'd be back.

"I'm not that guy," I reiterated, my tone slightly pissed that Jude and Levi had thought less of me. "I broke up with my girlfriend to be in the band."

"Sorry, Greg. Just with the circumstances back home ... we weren't sure that we'd still be your priority."

I nodded because I got where they were coming from. "You know, I'll admit there were times when I felt as if I couldn't walk away from that hospital. But now that Floyd's stable, off the ventilator and slowly coming around, I feel more confident about him. I weighed up the risk and figured if its only for a day or two, I had to focus on the band. That's why I need to talk to Donnie. If PR intends to line up more promotion, you guys can do those without me, right?"

"Absolutely, there's nothing else planned for a month now that the album's out. The numbers are looking fantastic by the way.

Social media is doing its work and we're all past due for a break," Levi muttered.

"Although, we just need to make Donnie think it's his idea," Jude chipped in. We all laughed as the service elevator door opened at the far end of the penthouse and our manager trotted in, wearing a bright green Hawaiian shirt and a pair of white, stay-pressed, suit trousers.

Deakon began to hum the tune to that old TV series *Hawaii Five O*, making us all snicker.

"Ah there you are, thank fuck you made it," Donnie gushed, oblivious that the tune was in reference to his attire, as he slapped me on the back.

"Yeah, I'm here," I said flatly. "Then I'm out for a bit. I'm heading straight back to Ireland after the gig. And if you want the best of me, you'll keep whatever thoughts to the contrary to yourself."

"So much for making Donnie think us taking a break would be his idea," Deakon mumbled, amused.

"It just so happens I was thinking the exact same thing," he said, casting a sneaky glance in my direction. "You boys have earned a break," he announced, taking credit for our time off, even though I'd given him no choice. "Meanwhile, tomorrow morning, 9:00 a.m. sharp, I expect all of you to polish that set list. You're headlining on the Ford Stage after XrAid, so I imagine you'll want to get there early to spend some time with the band."

"Crakt Soundzz aren't playing this year?" This surprised me as it was a home gig for them as well. Alfie Black's record label usually organized for his and his wife's bands to play at the same festivals.

"They're flying back from Reno, tomorrow morning. They are performing there tonight," Donnie offered.

"Right," Donnie agreed, but they'll be around after the festival tomorrow night. Cody has invited all of us to a party at his place after the gig. It's home stomping grounds for us all. Apart from that, I love hanging out with him."

"I'm not drinking. I'll come along for a while, but I don't want to drink. If you don't mind, Bernadette, would you arrange a flight back to the UK the day after tomorrow … in the morning. A commercial flight will do fine."

"No can do. The flights across the pond leave early evening to arrive the following day. Your best chance of a daytime flight would be to hire another charter."

"Get him charter, Bernadette. It'll be on the band's dime. Raff will be going with you in any case," Donnie insisted, sounding more upbeat than I'd ever heard him.

I stole a glance at Raff, and I could see he looked put out. He'd been with me for over a week already. Not to mention that he hadn't had time off since we'd been in California before that.

"Does your girl have a passport?" I asked Raff. "If not, I think if you really think I need someone, then one of the others should come. Raff is entitled to a life of his own as well. He's been carting my arse around for a while now."

"It's fine. I'll be happy to come back with you. I don't think the girl could come with me. Oh, and we're staying at a hotel or you're renting a house this time. That bed of yours isn't long enough. I don't think any of them are at your mom's."

I chuckled. "Of course, we can go somewhere else. My ma won't be offended. She likes having the place to herself."

Raff grinned. "All right then, that's settled."

A SOFT KNOCK at my penthouse bedroom door woke me the following morning. I'd been sleeping so deeply I only realized my cell phone was ringing as Raff opened the door. I reached for my cell and when I saw it was Ruth, a jolt of electricity shocked my heart.

Dread filled my heart as I sat up and answered.

"Hey, Greg, I heard I missed you," Floyd rasped in a hoarse tone down the line.

My heart did a somersault, as tears instantly sprang to my eyes. An emotional swell made my throat constrict, as I ran a hand over my head and I struggled to talk.

"Fuck me, it's so good to hear your voice," I eventually choked out. Relief flowed through my body that he was awake.

"Likewise. You should have hung around," he mumbled playfully.

I paused the conversation while I gathered my composure.

"You still there?" he asked in a tired, raspy tone.

"Damn, you waited for me to leave to wake up on purpose, didn't you?" I joked as my voice broke. The wave of emotion I'd tried to swallow down overwhelmed me and I cried.

"That too," he replied, ignoring my sobs of relief. "I heard Eliza bitching at you, and well … you know me. I didn't want to get in the middle of that," he suggested playfully.

"Jesus Christ, did you?" I asked as a pang of shame squeezed my chest.

"Yeah, but that was on her," he croaked. "I'm so tired, mate. I'm going to pass you back to Ruth. I only called because she nagged me that you'd only believe this was true if you heard me for yourself."

"Your wife's a smart woman. She knows me well," I praised. "I'll be back in Ireland, in a couple of days."

"It's me, Greg," Ruth said, having taken the phone back. "Don't worry, I'll let him know. We can't believe he's recovering so well. The doctors think he's had a miraculous escape. Dr. O'Hare reckons he might be discharged on bedrest at home in a few days."

"I told you he was tough," I gushed as I climbed out of bed. "Listen, I've slept in for band practice and I need to run. I'll call you when I'm on the way back."

We quickly said our goodbyes and I hung up.

"Good news I take it?"

"Floyd's awake. Man, he sounds so fucking good considering where we were last week."

"We're still going back?" Raff asked with a raised brow.

"Absolutely, he's not out of the woods yet. But he's well enough that I can afford to take my mind off him and focus on the band now."

CHAPTER 23

GREG

*I*n my world, nothing compares to a beat pulsing beneath my feet. And nothing brings more peace to a bassist, than those vibrations resonating in their chest and the sound of that steady thrum those chunky wire strings make under their fingertips.

Although I wasn't looking forward to playing a gig, it turned out to be exactly what I needed. I hadn't realized how tightly wound I was from all the traveling, Floyd's accident and seeing Eliza again, until I got on stage to do my job. Concentrating on the set forced me to temporarily forget everything for those couple of hours.

"Isn't the lineup here at SunFest the best yet? How are you guys doing tonight? Have you had a good day?" Levi asked.

A roar of appreciation went up from the crowd as Levi gave us the nod, and Jude and I counted the rest of the guys into the song that even the baby boomers in the crowd couldn't fail to recognize.

The moment Deakon struck the first chord on his guitar the audience cheered in recognition. Then, a few numbers later, our real fans amongst the audience almost lost their shit as Levi belted out the words of the song that had made Screaming Shadows famous, long before my time.

Levi was buzzed, high from playing live again. Life was good in his world, and his high energy performance reflected this.

As other bands in the festival lineup finished their sets, the crowd in front of our stage grew denser as people migrated to us. Daylight had given way to a clear night sky, and watching the fans singing in the crowd brought its own brand of magic to the gig.

By the time Levi finished the last song in our set and attached his mic back on the stand, the fans looked as exhausted as we were. "Thank you, SunFest. You guys have been on fire," he screamed, raising another resounding cheer from everyone. "All right, let's dial things down a little since it's been a long day for y'all. I want to sing one last song that I heard on the radio yesterday for the first time in ages. He then put in a heart-felt performance cover of Keane's old hit "Everybody's Changing".

That was the thing about Levi, his true genius was showcased best when he took songs other bands had made famous and put his own spin on them.

For the duration of that song the audience was silent, completely enthralled by his talent. Not forgetting Korry's incredible keyboard arrangement, which in my view was better than the original version of the song.

By 10:00 p.m. the outdoor temperature was still a humid ninety-two degrees. Levi and Jude caved, and both lost their T-shirts, causing a frenzy of screams from most of the females and quite a few of the males as well.

Levi was rewarded by a collective ear-piercing shriek of delight as fans scrambled to catch the sweat-soaked T-shirt he'd been wearing that he tossed into the crowd.

As usual, Levi, Jude and Deakon were the showmen of the band, and like with most other bands, the bass and keyboard players tended to be mostly overlooked.

Korry and I might not have been as popular with our fans as our other bandmates, but were an essential part of what made Screaming Shadows great.

What people didn't realize was that the bass guitar, like the drums, was the heart of any band. We kept the pace and timing on point and usually covered up mistakes. But if Jude or I put a beat out of time there was a possibility of throwing the rest of the guys off.

As I stood on the stage keeping time, my heart felt fuller than it had in days because I'd heard Floyd's voice. Raising my eyes to the night sky, I silently thanked the stars for letting my friend live.

Floyd's accident was the third major trial I'd had in my life. The first being the death of my father, and the second, Eliza's lack of faith in me.

After seeing Ruth and Eliza distressed at the hospital, it gave me much to consider because the people I loved mattered.

As the encore finished and the crowds began to disperse, I found Flynn Docherty waiting for me in the wings. Flinging an arm around my shoulder, he drew me in for a manhug. "I hope you don't mind me gatecrashing your gig. Your security guy Ralph let me in."

"Raff," I corrected.

"Right," he muttered as he flashed me a sheepish smile. "He was telling me about Floyd. Have you heard how's he doing?" he asked, his tone turning anxious.

Flynn had also met Floyd when Tim was helping Flynn with his genealogy research in Ireland. During that time he'd gotten to know Floyd and my brother quite well.

"He's awake at least. I won't be happy until I get back to see him for myself."

"Me and the band, we were staying at Kane Exeter's place over in Jupiter for the week. We're off to Cody's party tonight, but we're flying to the UK tomorrow. I was hoping we'd just hang out with everyone, but as Raff told us you were heading back to Ireland, I figured I'd offer you a ride. I can ask my pilot to arrange a pitstop in Dublin and drop you off. I caught your PA ... Korry's wife ..."

"Bernadette," I prompted.

He nodded. "Bernadette ... and explained the situation."

"Seriously? That would be awesome. Wait, do you have space for two of us? I'll be taking my security guy."

"Of course, I'm sure Kayden and Lexi will enjoy having you on board."

"Oh," I muttered and cleared my throat. "Lexi ..." I rubbed the back of my neck, smirked and let out a tired sigh. I wasn't sure if Flynn knew of my previous involvement with her.

Flynn leaned in and whispered. "You tapped that?"

I winced, nodding. "First time I met you all."

"Fuck," he muttered, and ran a hand through his hair. "You're not alone. I think Lexi is an occupational hazard for musicians." He huffed out a breath and grinned.

"You as well?" I asked, surprised he would cheat on Valerie.

"Jesus, no. Not that she didn't set her sights on me in the beginning. Of course, Valerie handled her like a champ." We both laughed because Flynn's wife was also his manager, and a force to be reckoned with. "Alright, my advice is to pretend that you don't remember her," Flynn said, with a glint of mischief in his tone.

"Won't that piss her off? Although she might be grateful ... isn't she going steady with some guy right now?"

"*Was going* steady," Flynn chuckled. "Her guys never last long. To be honest, I think she wears them out. Don't worry."

"I don't want to cause any trouble if she hits on me on the plane."

"Leave that to me. I'll give Craig and Simone a heads up to pin her in her seat and keep her occupied. You'll be sitting with me and Valerie, so she won't have an opportunity to get you alone."

Craig, Flynn's guitarist, was Flynn's best friend. He trusted them to handle Lexi, but I wasn't sure I could.

I learned my lesson about having sex with women in bands after her. Lexi stalked me for weeks, and paid crew members to pass me messages. The woman even sent me pictures of her pussy via my social media inboxes.

"Are you sure you want me on your plane with her?"

"Leave Lexi to us. She won't be a problem," he said again, chuckling and shaking his head. "Okay now that the transport issue is settled, are you're coming to Cody's party?"

"I was going to show my face, but I'm drained, dude."

"Fair enough. Be at West Palm Beach Airport at 5:30 a.m. with your guy. I know it's an early start, but Valerie sent the kids on ahead and she wants to be in London to see the kids for dinner."

"Right, I'm grateful for the ride. See you in the morning."

CHAPTER 24

GREG

I tossed and turned for most of the night in anticipation of the flight ahead. Eventually I got up and showered at 4:30 a.m. and was ready to go by the time Raff came to wake me.

Mikey drove us both to the airport and was uncharacteristically cheerful as he mumbled along to Meghan Trainor's "Dear Future Husband".

Raff cast an incredulous look in my direction with a raised eyebrow, and I smirked knowingly in return. Hearing Mikey singing a bubble gum pop song was too good of an opportunity to miss. So, even though it was only 5:00 a.m. in the morning, Raff whipped out his phone, videoed him and posted it in our WhatsApp group.

Once we'd arrived at the airport, we were ushered through the private jet owners' security check point and onward to Flynn's plane. I felt we'd barely been seated before we were in the air.

"Sorry to hear about Floyd," Valerie said. Her tone sounded heartfelt as her huge, gorgeous green eyes filled with concern as we took off.

I nodded, figuring Flynn had discussed Floyd with her.

"Thanks. I'm just glad he's alive. We can work on the rest." I scanned the others onboard and acknowledged Craig, their guitarist and his girlfriend Simone, with a nod. Lexi immediately leaned forward with an outstretched arm and scratched her long nails on my forearm.

"No one told me we'd have the pleasure of your company for this trip," she said, sounding seductive.

"Greg has a family emergency back in Ireland. He's not in the mood to be sociable today," Flynn warned her, cutting her off.

"We're happy to help you get home quickly," Valerie said, winking.

Lexi slumped back against her seat, pouted and stared out the window.

As the flight attendant served us a continental breakfast of coffee, croissants, and orange juice, Flynn turned his attention to me.

"Does going to Ireland mean seeing Floyd's sister?" he asked carefully. Unfortunately, at one time, I'd poured my heart out about Eliza, after having a few drinks, to anyone who would listen. Flynn happened to be one of those people.

"Flynn told me what happened between you," Valerie admitted.

I shrugged, an ache forming in my heart again raking over my past. "She wasn't as mature and worldly as other girls of her age. Plus, she wouldn't leave her ma. At that time, she didn't know anything other than the local community where we lived," I explained defensively.

"Age doesn't come into it. I wasn't quite sixteen when I fell in love with Flynn," Valerie stated, flashing him a sideward glance.

"You and Lizzie are two very different people. She's lived in a small community all her life. Where I come from there are plenty of risk-takers. However, there are also people whose circumstances make them scared of change. I guess Lizzie was brought up to believe good things only happened to other people."

"We thought that too for a while," Flynn countered.

"It's hard to understand how someone like Eliza thinks," I explained. "Life hasn't been easy for her … nor for most of the hard-working people where I come from."

"Before Flynn and I got together our lives weren't exactly smooth sailing either," Valerie insisted.

I nodded because Flynn had told me their harrowing stories. But they were exceptional people. Not everyone in this life is as resilient and inspiring as them.

"True, and I admire the fight in you both. But you both have very different personalities and mindsets to Lizzie. As children, my mate and his sister lived with domestic violence. They were so used to living in fear and being neglected that they thought their life was normal.

"They often went to bed hungry. Floyd told my ma that when the rent money was due, they weren't fed for days at a time," I argued. "After that my ma fed Floyd and Eliza at least three times a week."

"Gosh, that poor?" Valerie commiserated.

"Their father worked so they shouldn't have been in that position. But he was controlling, verbally and emotionally abusive toward all of them, and a heavy drinker. Floyd tried to stand up to him to protect his ma and sister more than once, but every time he did, his da gave him a hell of a beating."

"Anyone would think Eliza would have wanted to get as far away from that life as possible."

"Shortly after Lizzie left school and got a job in a clothing factory, their da was found dead, behind a pub. Eliza's wage went into the house to keep a roof over their heads. Their father's death was recorded as suspicious, but the garda never put much effort into finding out who did it."

"How awful," Valerie muttered. "Some people can't catch a break in life."

"To be honest, I think Floyd and Eliza saw their da's death as their lucky break because I never once saw any of that family mourn it."

"I get that ... they probably felt relieved ..." Valerie trailed off with an angry look in her eyes. I could see by the empathy in her eyes that Floyd and Eliza's story had made an impact on her.

Revisiting the memory of what the McDades went through, made my heart clench tight. There were even times when our home became their sanctuary.

After hearing my account of something I'd witnessed myself, my ma invited their mother, Carol, to come hang out at our place whenever she needed to. Ma's tea and sympathy went a long way during that time, and I'm glad to say Carol and her remained close friends to this day.

"Looking back, apart from Floyd, I was probably the only positive thing in Lizzie's life. And it shames me to say that at one time I had promised I'd never leave her.

"So, from her perspective I made a false promise by auditioning for Screaming Shadows. I never thought for one minute the guys would pick me. I just thought it would be a cool experience to play with a world-class band."

"So, your big break must have felt like a double-edged sword when she refused to go with you," Flynn suggested.

I nodded. "The way she still sees it, I turned my back on her, so it's no wonder she's still pissed."

It was only once I had aired my thoughts aloud, I considered Lizzie's perspective again. Trauma had followed her since childhood, and once her father had died, life was suddenly calm.

"But look at the life she could have had with you," Flynn mumbled.

"Lizzie feared change and became afraid of upsetting the small peaceful sanctuary her family home became. I should have recognized that she felt secure for the first time in her life and tried harder. Instead of that, I broke my promise to her by choosing the band over her."

Right then I needed to know if I could convince her to talk to me. "The plane has Wi-fi, right?" I asked, pulling out my cell phone.

"Yeah, RedA connection," Valerie stated. "She then gave me a password that encrypted my SMS.

Me: It was a relief to hear Floyd's voice. See you tomorrow.
My Lizzie: Who is this?

I chuckled because I'd forgotten she wouldn't have the new number the record company issued me with.

Me: Not your favorite person.
My Lizzie: Greg? angry emoji. **How did you get this number?**

I laughed.

Me: Does that really matter? I have it and I've committed it to memory now. I should be back in Ireland later today.

My Lizzie: And what exactly am I supposed to do with that information?

Me: I'm not sure. Maybe you'd like to grab a late dinner at my hotel ... we could have that talk?

My Lizzie: What talk? We have nothing to say to one another, and I doubt Owen would be happy about that.

Me: Owen wouldn't be happy about you having an innocent dinner with me?

My Lizzie: From what I've observed of you since you left, there's no innocence left in you.

Me: Come on, we should at least try to be friends. I'm going to be around and us arguing isn't going to help Floyd's recovery.

My Lizzie: I have all the friends I need, thank you.

Fuck. My chest tightened in frustration at her stubborn reply.

Me: How many of them would buy you dinner?
My Lizzie: Is that supposed to impress me, Mr. Moneybags? I

remember a time when you used to fish down the sides of your ma's couch to find money for a bag of chips.

This was typical of Eliza. The girl could cause an argument in an empty room. My gut twisted further in frustration until I couldn't ignore my discomfort.

Me: ***My bank account has nothing to do with this. I'd be grateful if we could talk this out ... for Floyd's sake, if nothing else.***

It took Eliza a few minutes before she responded this time.

My Lizzie: ***Text me the address and time. I'm not making any promises. I'll make my mind up then.***

"Fuck, she can be so difficult," I muttered before glancing up at Flynn.

"Well, it looked like there was a back-and-forth exchange at least, so that's something," Valerie said, sounding encouraging, like the glass half full woman she was. Flynn pulled Valerie's head toward him and pressed a kiss to her forehead.

"I'll take it. It's better than nothing," I muttered.

"Anything's better than nothing," Flynn agreed. "Right. I'm going to catch some sleep. I suggest you sit back, relax, and do the same. Sounds like you're going to need your wits about you with that girl once you see her," Flynn muttered as he reclined his seat, folded his arms, and closed his eyes.

I nodded. "Thanks, guys. I appreciate you letting me talk it all out," I said, of my history with Eliza. I grabbed the blanket on the seat next to me, reclined the luxury seat and closed my eyes.

CHAPTER 25

GREG

It was raining again as we touched down in Dublin. Just like it had been when I'd left three days before.

Once we'd landed, I'd called Ruth who asked that I leave my visit with Floyd until tomorrow, citing the reason that the doctors had been doing cognitive tests on him, and he was wiped out.

After learning this, I asked Bernadette to move my meeting with Eliza up and arrange a private dining room for 8:30 p.m. Despite Eliza's barbed tone in her texts, I was confident she would come.

It was almost 7:00 p.m. by the time we arrived at The Croke Park Hotel in Dublin. Bernadette had checked us in there for the night due to the secure property she'd found for us not being free until the following day.

There were chaotic scenes in the small reception area of the hotel as two Gaelic football teams were also checking in. Raff frowned, concerned at the crush, and shielded me with his body.

In the lounge a massive TV showed a video of Daughtry singing "Battleships" as we waited for our turn at the desk, and I figured with all the interaction going on between the players no one would pay attention to me.

"Fuck me, if it isn't Greg Booker," a massive, thickset guy in his mid-twenties mumbled in a Northern Irish accent.

With cropped black curly hair, I supposed him to be a good six inches bigger than me, and only slightly smaller than Raff. He looked as if he'd been in a fist fight. There was a plaster over his broken nose, a freshly missing tooth, and his right eye was swollen closed. "I'm a fan," he said, slapping a huge hand over his chest. "Got every Screaming Shadows album. The latest is dope, man," he said excitedly, talking a mile a minute. "I saw you guys when you played here in Dublin a while back. I was stoked when you got picked as their new bass guitarist."

I beamed, instantly relaxing to know I was among one friend at least in the mass of enormous guys. "Thanks, man, that means a lot."

"Oye, Shamus, you want breakfast in the morning?" someone called out. His eyes instantly shifted from me to the desk, where the voice had come from.

"What kind of stupid question is that?" he retorted. "Do they do an all you can eat buffet breakfast? If not, I'll need two full Irish." His gaze turned back to me. "So, what are you doing here in Dublin?"

"Seeing my ma," I said quickly. "My security guy is too tall for the beds at her place," I mumbled, making him smile.

"I get that, I always have trouble with beds," he sympathized, glancing at Raff for the first time.

"We're set, Shamus, move it," the voice at the front urged.

"Well, that's me. Nice to meet you, Greg. Tell your manager not to leave it too long before you play here again."

I grinned. "Got it," I said, watching him move through the crowd. Raff followed him and disappeared for a few seconds before reappearing by my side.

He caught me by my elbow. "Got the keys, come on before the rest of them spot you."

For security purposes, Bernadette had reserved two comfortable family suites with adjoining doors. After Raff found someone to deliver the bags to our rooms, we headed up to them.

"Don't go anywhere," Raff warned, once we were inside mine. "I'm going to check out the private dining room."

I nodded. "I'm going to take a shower."

"Bernadette booked the private dining room for 8:30 p.m. I'll be back at 8:20 p.m. Don't open the door to anyone," Raff muttered as he left, like I was a child.

After freshening up, I texted Eliza again.

Me: I'm at the Croke. Tell me you're coming to dinner, and I'll send a taxi for you.

My Lizzie: Owen said you want to flash your cash.

Fuck. Owen fucking Murphy. Sounds like he feels threatened.

I took a deep breath reminding myself to keep calm. Nothing would get settled between us if I lost my cool with her about that guy.

Me: The only reason I'm not staying at my ma's is because the beds aren't big enough for my security guy. Tell Owen he has nothing to worry about. Our dinner is to try to find an amicable relationship. We should be on talking terms. Ruth and Floyd don't need the stress of us being at each other's throats.

Had I said those words aloud they would have stuck in my throat. But now, I'd take being friends over not talking to her at all.

It was a long, painful five minutes before Eliza responded.

My Lizzie: Right. I'm leaving now. I'll get the bus.

"That fucking woman," I yelled, and threw my cell phone at the wall. Fortunately, it hit the padded headboard and landed on the bed in one piece.

"What? What's happened?" Raff asked, rushing through the adjoining door, wearing only his boxer briefs.

"Lizzie, she's a pain in my arse," I grumbled. "She's getting a fucking bus here."

"Dude, I thought something drastic had happened," he muttered, irritated.

"It fucking did. I offered her a taxi and she turned me down. I can see how tonight's going to go already."

"Greg, if Eliza's as volatile as you say she is, you'll get nowhere with her if you lose your cool."

"True. She might have chosen not to come at all, so I should see this as a win."

"That's the spirit," he said, hanging onto the handle of the door. "Take a deep breath. At least you're finally getting the chance to sit down and talk to her."

"Yeah, like we should have done years ago."

"Right. Am I safe to go and finish getting dressed or will there be more drama before that?"

"Fuck you, mate," I replied, smiling as he closed the door again.

My Lizzie: *I'm outside.*

"What? She won't even come inside?" I muttered. My heckles were instantly raised, frustrated again by her obstinate behavior. No one could agitate me like she could. Taking a deep breath, I let it go and texted back, guessing it would be the first of many of my temper-control techniques I'd need to take before the dinner was over.

Me: *My guy is coming to get you.*

Raff insisted that I wait in the dining room while he brought Lizzie to meet me. As the lounge beside the entrance was full of drunken rugby players, I had no choice but to accept his demand.

For a full five minutes I sat there anticipating the moment she'd walk into the room. Then as time passed, I grew concerned that she'd bailed at the last minute.

I had begun to convince myself that the latter was a real possibility when Raff held the door open, and Lizzie came into view. My heart skipped a beat as I took in how gorgeous she looked, dressed in an olive-green, figure-hugging dress. The color made the copper in her hair more vibrant set against it.

Eliza scanned the décor of the private room before she allowed her eyes to settle on me.

"Is the restaurant not open tonight?" she asked, looking confused.

"This is a private dining room. It'll only be you and me here," I explained, standing up as she walked hesitantly toward me.

"Is this supposed to impress me?" she muttered, eyeing me with suspicion as she shrugged off the small cream jacket she wore. The movement made her ample tits jiggle, and although I did my best not to become distracted by them, I could hardly miss those double D's.

"No, it's to give you both some privacy ... and to keep my guy safe," Raff countered sternly before I could speak.

"Right," she said in a far less haughty tone, after being put in her place by someone else.

"Come, grab a seat." My heart raced because she was near to me. I placed my hand naturally on her upper arm and led her to the booth I'd been sitting at. My body hummed the second her warmth seeped through her sleeve into my palm. "Still drinking spiced rum and coke?" I asked. Eliza's eyes grew wide, like she couldn't believe I'd remembered this.

She nodded. "Yes. I'll take a double if you're offering," she replied as she placed her jacket on the booth seat beside her.

I nodded toward Raff and watched him wander to the server who stood at the end of the dining room, before I turned my attention to Eliza.

"Thank you for coming, Lizzie. You look beautiful, as always," I said honestly as I took in her long auburn hair and lightly freckled features. The freckles she constantly complained about. Eliza hated her fair complexion and the color of her hair. Yet to me, they were the perfect combination for her.

I used to think she glowed beside all the other girls and how that light sprinkle of freckles across her nose and cheeks gave her a sun-kissed look, even in winter.

A smile lifted my lips as my gaze dropped to her ruby lips and I recalled how the world felt as if it had stopped spinning whenever we used to kiss.

"So, are you just going to sit there, smiling and staring at me?" she asked in a sharp tone, bringing me out of my reverie.

"No," I replied, snapping back to the present. I cleared my dry throat. "Excuse my indulgence at taking you in. It's been a long time since I've seen you."

"And whose fault is that?" she bit back.

Ignoring her caustic comment, I continued to stare at her. "Lizzie, I've never forgotten what I left behind," I confessed, cutting to the center of our hurt. "I thought I had won the lottery when you agreed to go out with me. You were gorgeous then, beautiful when I left to go to the US, but the stunning transformation in you since then is blowing me away," I replied.

"That silver tongue of yours won't work on me, Greg Booker. So, you can quit with the compliments. I'm not yours anymore. I'm with someone else now." Eliza's body stiffened in her seat, but she was a fool if she thought I hadn't noticed her study me every bit as closely, as I had her. A warm glow burned within me when I recognized passion in her eyes.

"Did I say you were?" I accepted she wanted to hurt me. I'd even prepared myself for this by thinking of all the hurtful things she might say. "Do you need to be mine before I can express an opinion?" I challenged. We fell silent as Eliza's eyes burned with determination as she held my gaze. The pause in our conversation made the air thicken between us, as each of us got lost to our own thoughts.

Once the stretched silence became too much, she broke the connection. But as she shifted uncomfortably in her seat, her gaze dropped to my mouth, and suddenly I felt thirsty. As I licked my lips, I heard Eliza let out a soft sigh.

I swallowed roughly and took a deep breath. "Look, Lizzie, can we start again? I'm going to be here for a whole month. I'd like to spend as much time with Floyd as possible and that means running into you. Wouldn't it be better if we could leave the past behind us and start over as friends?"

"How can we be friends? Am I supposed to just forget what we had in the past?"

"No, I'd never want you to forget the great times we had. I wouldn't swap what we had together for anything."

"You already did," she snapped in an instant.

"You know what I mean. You were my first love, Lizzie. You hold a special place in my heart. You're someone I'd never forget. But you've moved on, right?" I suggested, quoting the bullshit excuse she'd used to warn me off.

The guarded look in her eyes immediately softened, and I believed my candid admission had hit home. The effect was brief but recognizable before her emotions were masked again. A small smile toyed at the sides of my mouth. Despite the angry front she showed me, Eliza hadn't forgotten how special we were at one time either.

"Don't. I know what you're doing," she scolded.

"Oh, yeah? And what is that?" I asked nonchalantly.

"Making me miss what we had."

"Is that what I'm doing? Is it working?" I probed, sounding serious as I raised a brow.

"Did you ask me here to fuck up my life again or to torture me about how great we were together?"

"Neither. My only intention with what I said was to acknowledge what we once had. Lizzie, that chapter of our lives was over a long time ago. And I just feel it's time we came to terms with the choices that we made. My only regret is that I hurt you, but I've made peace with my decision. You have told me you're with someone else," I shrugged, pausing to give her time to respond but she didn't.

Hurt flashed in her eyes as she grabbed the edge of the table to brace herself. Nervously, she tucked her long hair behind her ear and began to fidget with a small gold hoop earring. "I am," she stated too quickly.

Liar. Her reaction showed me she wasn't into Owen Murphy in the least. I'd wanted to call her out on that statement because it might have been a while, but Lizzie was as transparent as tissue paper when it came to telling lies.

"I asked you to come and have dinner with me for a few reasons. The first was to apologize for hurting you. Somewhere deep inside of you, I think you know that wasn't my intention. Our lives could have been so different today if you had shown faith and come with me."

"Like you said, that's all in the past," she muttered, shutting down my line of conversation.

As she shuffled to the edge of the booth, my instincts told me she was making to leave. "Have you eaten?" I asked quickly, placing a hand over hers and waving the server over with menus.

Eliza's gaze dropped to our hands and she appeared fascinated by them for a few seconds before she met my gaze. She slipped her hand from beneath mine and huffed out a breath. "What are we doing here? What are you hoping to gain from this, Greg? Do you think you can buy me dinner then take me upstairs to your bed for old time's sake?"

"Is that what you think? Who the fuck mentioned anything

about sex?" I question angrily. As the server stood awkwardly with the menus clutched to his chest, Eliza opened her mouth to say something else and clamped it shut. "I've been traveling all day, and I haven't eaten. I'm hungry," I explained flatly as I acknowledged the server by looking up at him. "Do you still like that Italian dish your ma used to make?"

"Spaghetti carbonara? How do you remember something like that when you've taken hundreds of women out?" she challenged, bluntly. I hadn't but as this was her perception, I went with it. "You never forget the important things in life, Lizzie," I stated, ignoring her remark.

Eliza wasted no time in challenging my promiscuous behavior. "Is that right? Funny how what I liked to eat was important, but you could move on quick enough," she countered. "All those girls in such a short time, Greg," she persisted when she wouldn't allow her previous comment to drop.

The server made to walk away until I held my finger up for him to wait. "Yes, I admit to that," I said, holding my hands up in surrender. "All those women because I couldn't get over you, Lizzie. They meant nothing, none of them. But you'd made it perfectly clear that if I set foot on that plane, we were over."

I wasn't going to tell her I went through nearly two months of hell, waiting for her to take that stubborn stick out of her arse and reach out to me.

"Your silence made it obvious to me, we were over. The way I saw it, there was no going back since you'd already carried out your threat, so I had to try to get on with my life.

"It's unfortunate my life was made public by the power of social media. But believe me when I tell you, I never slept with any of those girls to flaunt my new life in your face. You have no clue what it felt like to be on the other side of the world and knowing you were willing to let me go."

"You must have known how heartbroken it would have made

me to see that," she argued.

"To be honest, I never gave it a thought. I was a broken man. Do you think I read all that shit they post about me? By the way, you don't have the monopoly on being heartbroken. Imagine me on the other side of the world, experiencing all the amazing things that were happening to me daily, and the void that I constantly carried because I didn't have you to share it with. You have no clue how fucking lost I was."

"I wasn't lost. I've been here the whole time. You were the one that ruined us."

I sighed exasperated with her because I wasn't the most patient of people at times, and this was one of them.

"Fuck. We're not doing the same cyclic conversation again, it's boring. We've had years to wallow in regrets since all that went down. You've told me that you're with someone else now, so I don't see the problem.

"As hard as that is to know I lost you, I accept that you've found love again. I can't be bitter that you're happy because I chose a different path. I want you to be happy.

"Leaving didn't mean I didn't love you enough to stay, Lizzie, but I will never understand why you preferred to stay here than to take the ride with me. All that said, I've taken responsibility for the consequences of that."

"I'm thankful that I didn't go with you," she argued. "I wouldn't have survived the humiliation of your whorish behavior."

Those barbed words stung and filled me with shame. "I never fell in love with anyone else. From what you said, you can't say the same."

"That's none of your business," she growled angrily.

"No, it isn't. So why have you made it your mission to poke your nose into mine?" I countered.

"See, I knew this was a waste of time coming," she disclosed, reaching for her jacket.

"It is if we're going to constantly rehash the past. We've been here almost half an hour and our breakup has been the sole topic of conversation. I was hoping we'd find some peace between us tonight. Surely you don't want to only remember that one event about us. We used to love hanging out together, Lizzie. Wouldn't it be better all-round if we could be friends."

She stared at me for a long minute, like she was considering my suggestion. However, it wasn't long before she was silently checking me out and I saw the war with lust and desire within her gorgeous hazel eyes.

"Why are you smiling?" she asked. I hadn't realized I was until she pointed this out.

"I'm happy to see you," I replied, shrugging. I could hardly tell her the truth, that she was full of bullshit … that she still wanted me.

My comment unexpectedly disarmed her, and she gave me a small smile in return. Relief flowed through my body because to me, it was a smile of hope. I reached over the table and stroked two fingers across the back of her hand. Her gaze immediately fell to what I had done before she glanced back at me.

"Let go of all that bitterness, darlin'. We can't be angry forever. I make a great friend … ask your brother."

She gave me a wry smile. "You really believe we can be friends?" she suddenly asked in a complete change of tact.

I nodded. "I've missed you in my life, and if we can't be together, why shouldn't we be friends?"

"Alright, I'll try," she said in a soft tone. "Right, you can start by feeding me. Where's this spaghetti carbonara, you promised me?"

I glanced up at the server and he shifted uncomfortably from foot to foot. "You heard the lady, spaghetti carbonara and I'll take a rare fillet steak, please."

Relief washed over the server as he jotted our order on the pad. "And you can bring us a couple more drinks, thanks."

CHAPTER 26

GREG

*D*inner with Eliza went better than I'd expected. There was nothing like good food and wine to mellow the conversation. After her double spiced rum and coke and a few glasses of wine, Eliza soon forgot I was the enemy and began to loosen up.

Once I had managed to keep the conversation in neutral territory, she also became less self-aware.

I was surprised when she began reminiscing without prompting about some of the crazy things we had done in our past together.

"Do you remember that night when we climbed onto the cinema roof? We sat there watching the world go by for most of it."

"God, yeah. The weather was fantastic all summer long that year as I remember … we had very little rain. As I remember it ended hilariously too."

Eliza's big round eyes glittered with humor as her whole face lit up at the fun memory. "Oh! That's right, I ripped my jeans on a jagged piece of tin roof and got stuck." She giggled. "When you couldn't get me free, you called the fire brigade to get me down," she recalled, wagging her finger at me.

My heart squeezed to hear the sweet sound of Eliza's laughter … a sound that had been all too rare. As she threw her head back laughing, she exposed the long column of her neck. I fixated on the fact that I'd kissed every inch of her neck many times in the past and recalled how soft her skin felt when I'd done that.

"You left me up there alone and hid while they used their rescue platform to take me down, Greg Booker. To this day my ma thinks I was sleepwalking when the garda took me home."

"What a stroke of genius you had, pretending you had no idea what was going on," I commended.

"Who knew my ma was so gullible?" As she laughed, Eliza looked more like the girl I once knew.

"What's your favorite memory?" I probed, observing her carefully.

A delicious blush crept up her face as she shrugged. "I'm not sure," she remarked.

I believed she was lying because every time we had ever spoken about a particular event that we'd shared, her face had always turned crimson, just like it had right now.

"Want me to tell you mine?" I suggested, ready to call her out.

Eliza cringed as she twisted her lips, like she knew what was coming.

"We had many amazing nights, but I think it must be the night we missed the bus home. Standing there in the dark in that bus shelter … with all those cars whizzing by, while I ate you out," I muttered in a low tone so Raff couldn't hear me.

"I remember every single second of that encounter. Right from the first hitch of your breath as I slid my hand up your skirt and slipped my finger along your hot, wet seam. The sound of that thud your head made as it fell back against the Perspex window the moment you gave yourself up to me."

She shook her head, her eyes heavy with lust at the memory, and shrugged. "Why would you go and bring that up?"

"Maybe because it was what sprang into your mind, but you couldn't bring yourself to say it," I replied, leaning back against the seat. I lifted my wine glass, eyed her carefully over the rim of it, took a swig of my Chianti, and placed it back on the table.

"You're so cocksure of yourself, aren't you," she stated. It wasn't a question.

"I am. Did me talking like that make you wet? You used to love when I talked dirty to you."

She squirmed in her seat. "Don't..."

"Why? You asked me a question and I answered you. The thrill from that night had little do with us being in public. It was how easily you gave yourself to me no matter where we were. The way you were standing there, trusting me to do what I wanted.

"Even now, if I shut my eyes, I can still see you vividly in my mind from that night. Your head tipped back, the moon casting light over the ecstasy on your face. I can still feel the impression of your leg hitched over my shoulder whenever I remember that. My jeans were soaked ... my face was too, come to think about it." I chuckled.

Eliza shook her head, her cheeks stained a pretty shade of red, as she clamped her eyes shut. She squirmed again and I imagined she was reliving the moment but was too embarrassed to face me while she did that.

"I was nuts for you, Lizzie. Can you remember how I could never keep my hands off you? So, you can imagine that night has been committed to my memory forever.

"There were a few times I almost came in my jeans just from your soft, breathy moans and the sounds of my tongue, lapping up your sweet nectar ..." I groaned. "Hands down, it has been the most unexpectedly erotic, sexual encounter I've had in my life."

Eliza looked flushed, as lust and desire shone in her eyes before she quickly closed them. But she was too late because I already seen her reaction to my recount of that event.

Suddenly her eyes snapped open. "Jesus, there you go, trying to reel me in. I have no idea why I didn't stop you from saying all that. But I'm going to mark it down to temporary insanity," she muttered, sounding tipsy. As she stood up, she tottered around to get her balance. "Anyway, I better be going," she mumbled, sounding reluctant.

I stood before she'd had a chance to lift her jacket. I swiped it off her seat and held it out for her to slip her arms into it.

"Right, thanks for coming," I said, instantly snapping back to the amicable version of myself.

For a second Eliza froze, then cast a glance over her shoulder toward me. There was a wistful look in her eyes, and I sensed she had expected me to plead with her to stay. It might have been some time since I'd been around her, but if I had learned one thing about her, it was when not to try to coax her.

"I'm taking you home," I insisted. My gaze drifted to Raff and at my nod, he left to organize our transport.

"I'll get the bus," she argued defiantly. *Like hell you will.* I scoffed and she cast me a dark glare.

Sticking my hands in my pockets, I arched my back and glanced up at the ceiling. Standing tall again, I shrugged like I couldn't care less. "Good, I'll wait in the bus shelter with you."

I chuckled when her body went rigid, her cheeks pinked up and her big eyes flared with lust.

"You'll what?" she asked, instantly flustered from my bus shelter reference again as she tried to put her hand in her jacket pocket several times but missed it. As I bit back a grin, her eyes met mine and softened.

"Jesus, Greg Booker, I should knock you the fuck out," she mumbled quietly.

I nodded. "You could. I've always thought you were a knock-out," I mumbled, chuckling again.

"Tonight, hasn't been as painful as I thought it might be," she admitted.

"Friends?" I suggested, even though there was doubt in my mind that we could ever stay platonic.

"I'm not sure ... I'll try," she admitted but I could hear in the placid tone of her voice I was winning her over.

"That's okay, I'm here for a month, darlin'. Take your time," I replied sarcastically.

My cell phone buzzed on the table, and I picked it up.

Raff: I'm in the parking spot out front. Let me know when you're in the elevator and I'll catch you on the way out.

"About that lift? Bus shelter or a safe ride in a car with someone chaperoning us?"

"Car," she muttered. It wasn't exactly a surrender, but I took that as a win.

AFTER ELIZA GAVE Raff the address to punch into the GPS, she slid into the back seat. As I climbed in after her, my shoulder brushed against hers as I sat back in the seat. I left it leaning against hers and was surprised when she didn't make space between us.

"You're going to stay at The Croke for the month?" she asked, her face only inches from mine. My hungry eyes dropped to her lips.

"No, moving to a house tomorrow," I muttered quietly, then I held my breath for a moment while an almost overwhelming urge to kiss her hit me.

Tearing my eyes away from her mouth, I searched Eliza's eyes, and for a moment my heart almost beat out of my chest once I believed she wanted that. As our gaze grew intense, the sexual chemistry between us was almost palpable.

As if the buzz became too much for her, Eliza turned her head and looked out of the car window.

"A house?" she muttered, picking up the thread of our conversation.

"Yeah, somewhere with less eyes on me all the time. Nothing fancy, just a place with more security," I explained.

She nodded and fell silent. As the silence stretched between Eliza and I, my eyes met Raff's the rear-view mirror, and he winked. He fucking winked at me, while I was trying to have a serious conversation. I bit back a grin.

Sitting close to Eliza felt like home. I was enjoying the quiet, peaceful moment between us, so I leaned back in the seat, tipped my head back and closed my eyes. A few seconds later I felt her body shift a little, like she was turning into me. Then I heard her inhale deeply, like she was breathing me in. At that moment, my heart begged me to make a move and take her into my arms, but I was determined to stay in control.

Moving positions, I straightened up in my seat and looked down at our laps. Eliza had been so distracted when she'd gotten into the car, she hadn't put her seat belt on. So, thinking of her safety, I automatically leaned across her body and reached for her belt.

For a moment our eyes locked and I swallowed roughly while her soft breaths wafted over my face. It would have been so easy to close the space between us and kiss her, like I'd wanted to. But she wasn't mine anymore. Sitting back, I pulled the belt with me, around her, and buckled her up.

"I'll get that. I'm not helpless you know," she said, her hand closing over mine as I clipped it in place.

"But it's more fun if I do it," I whispered seductively, fucking with her despite my resolve not to touch her. A shiver ran through her before she met my gaze again. "Don't do that ... stop flirting with me," she ordered in a tone far huskier than it had been all evening.

"Why? Because you can feel yourself getting drawn to me? Are you forgetting Owen already?" I goaded.

"No, I'm not," she snapped. A small smile curved her lips.

"Liar," I teased, smiling. "I could make you forget ... make you forget your own name. Do you remember when I used to do that?"

"I knew this was a bad idea. Why do I put myself in these positions?" she mumbled, like she was aggravated by me.

"You can put yourself in any position you want with me, baby," I replied, smiling. "But I'd like to remind you how it feels when I take you from behind."

"Stop it," she snapped, more sternly this time.

"What? I'm only prompting your memories. I can't see how that is offensive."

"You're being an arsehole."

"No more than you are," I countered quickly. "Women can be arseholes too, you know."

She chuckled. "Grrr, stop being ... you."

"Why? Because you love me?" I asked, playfully nudging her again with my elbow.

"You can quit all that playful, mischievous shit because I don't," she said a little too quickly, then turned her attention to the view outside again.

"Liar. Admit it," I teased with yet another nudge in the ribs to goad her.

"I'm with Owen."

I scoffed. "Yeah, you said. How long is that going to last? Does he turn you on with words? Can he make you wet by staring at you? Does he make you feel how I did?"

"That's my business."

"Does he find you so irresistible that he loses control with you, like I used to? More to the point, would you let him eat you out in a bus shelter?"

"Greg!" she squealed, instantly red faced, stunned by my outburst. With pursed lips she drew daggers toward the back of Raff's head.

"Lizzie, he's a rock star's security guy. Raff's as good as a blind-mute when he's on the job. He doesn't hear a thing. Nor would he ever repeat anything we said either."

I'd forgotten how funny it was seeing Eliza in a meltdown of embarrassment. Her nostrils flared as her teeth bit her bottom lip, and her face was almost purple with rage.

"This is why I didn't want to come," she disclosed.

"Sorry, why? Because I remind you of the best orgasms of your life?"

"No, because you're a grade A arsehole."

"Likewise," I shot back. Eliza folded her arms and huffed loudly.

"See! Can't even deny it," I insisted.

Raff chuckled and tried to cover it up with a cough.

"He's listening to every word," she muttered, horrified as she pointed to the back of his head.

"Then he's being entertained, right?" I said, unfazed.

Eliza shook her head and looked like she might combust in her seat, which gave me a rare attack of guilt.

"Put the radio on," I ordered Raff to combat the suddenly stale silence in the car. Raff did as I asked, and I cringed when I recognized James Bay singing "Let It Go"—a song about a couple who were once happy, breaking up.

Eliza pinched her closed eyes with the thumb and forefinger of her right hand, as if the song affected her, and stilled. Her left hand was on her lap next to me, so I lifted it and held it in mine.

At one time, holding hands was a natural act for us. However, with that song playing, I felt our connection right down to my bones. Then a wave of belonging washed over me, one like I had only experienced when we were together.

Eliza sat motionless, letting me hold her hand until the song had ended before she dropped her hand from her eyes and sat quietly, still with her other hand in mine.

"Are you going to see Floyd tomorrow?" I asked, giving her hand a gentle squeeze.

"Yes, of course I am. They're doing some more cognitive tests and deciding when he can go home."

"Is he mobile?"

"Not yet. They've been doing physio with him lying in bed. I believe they are going to try to get him to stand tomorrow." Eliza continued to stare straight ahead, instead of looking at me as she said it. My intuition told me that she figured she would need to let go of my hand if she gave me eye contact.

If I was right on that, then she wasn't ready to let me go. And the possibility that she liked her hand in mine, made my heart full.

"Ruth's worried that he won't manage the stairs at home for a while."

I held her hand tighter and made her look at me. "That's why I'm here. I want to see what he needs. Whatever it takes, Lizzie. If his accommodation is the only reason they're keeping him in the hospital, then I'll rent somewhere until he can manage."

"Are you serious? Just like that?" she asked, her tone rising an octave from one question to the next.

"Of course. Ma won't let me buy her another house … she loves her neighbors, so the money I paid for her ex-social housing place wasn't much. I would have offered to buy Floyd and Ruth a place years ago, but he's a proud man. I'd never dream of suggesting anything that made our friendship unequal."

"But wouldn't you be doing just that if you got somewhere now?"

"These aren't normal circumstances he's facing. He has a

perfectly nice house, but it doesn't suit his recovery right now. I have all that money sitting in the bank, doing nothing. It's about time I did something worthwhile with it. In fact, I should buy a big enough place for all the family to move into, until Floyd's well enough to go home."

Eliza stared at me for a long time, then shrugged. "Why would you buy a house in Ireland when you live in Miami?"

"Why not? Ireland's my home. I need a base here at some point. The band is based in Florida, but I live all over the world when we're on the road promoting or recording. Mostly in rental properties... or at the band's penthouse in Miami.

"The rest of the guys in the band have bought places now that they are in solid relationships. They're way ahead of me in terms of their finances. But I don't spend like they do either. I've got a tidy sum of money in the bank. I know you think I'm reckless, but I've never been reckless with money. Apart from keeping my ma comfortable, and donations to Tim's chapel, I've barely touched what I've made."

She looked contemplatively toward me. "Thanks for the offering to do this. I'd normally tell you to shove your money up your arse—but this is my brother. I want to see him get out of the hospital as quickly as Ruth does." Eliza turned her head and looked out of the window, like she had nothing else to say on the matter.

"Don't mention it," I said sarcastically, responding to her backhanded acceptance of my generous offer.

CHAPTER 27

ELIZA

Why does Greg Booker need to be everything I love in a man? What is this hold he has on my heart that makes me not able to be happy without him?

It had only taken one meal with Greg to realize I'd die if I never shared another with him. A few minutes in his company was enough to temporarily stall how angry I felt inside. In truth, it was because I still mourned what we'd lost, that and the fact I had never been able to stop loving him.

During dinner, Greg was as enthralling as I remembered, and I was pleased to find parts of Greg that fame hadn't changed. Luckily, he had retained much of that same quick wit and cocky flirtatious banter that had drawn me to him as a teen.

Less fortunate for me, was that Greg had also retained his ability to push my buttons at will, bluntly calling me out or by making crude remarks to embarrass me.

Then, apart from his familiar traits, there was that new, worldly man, who used his experience with women to captivate me. His ability to disarm me—by soothing my troubled heart with his all-encompassing, magnetic stare—created a sense of intimacy between us during our dinner.

However, I was pleased that during his time in the band, Screaming Shadows hadn't redefined who he was as a private person. Underneath the designer clothes, flashy cars and expensive dinners, Greg's caring core had essentially remained the same.

As he sat casually talking about the places he'd been, places I knew little or nothing about, I recognized that we were both different people now.

We had managed an evening with each other without me exploding in a spiral of hurt again. More than that, there were times during dinner where memories of how incredible he'd once made me feel led me to fantasize about him.

Each new topic he spoke about made me feel we had less and less in common now because my life had remained small and relatively uneventful.

As the night wore on, I realized I'd barely had a steady breath all evening due to the connection we shared. So, I'd had to keep reminding myself that this was the man who had chosen another life —one that didn't include me—even if I had been responsible for that.

Greg's rise to fame had changed him in ways that had done nothing to curb my attraction toward him but at the same time, the void between his world and mine convinced me there would be no going back.

Apart from the many complications due to my fucked-up emotions about Greg and life in general, we'd agreed to try to be friends. He was right about one thing, being friends meant we wouldn't need to avoid each other. At least that would be a relief for Floyd—if not for me.

Being friends sounded simpler in theory than I imagined the

practical side of that title would be. Mostly due to the shockwaves that ran through me from each lightest touch of his hand, or even from just being near him.

As we sat side by side in the car on the way to my house, there was an air of expectation between us that I couldn't define. Perhaps it was the thought that he might try to kiss me ... and maybe I believed if he tried, I would be too weak to resist him. *Worse than that, how would I feel if he didn't try?*

We're totally different people with different outlooks on life. Greg hasn't allowed the grief he face during his formative years to define him. He isn't a damaged soul like the rest of us after a traumatic event. And he always appears to be thankful just for being alive.

"You've gone quiet. What are you thinking about?" Greg asked, breaking into my thoughts.

I realized my mind had wandered after Greg had stunned me with his offer to buy a house for my brother to live in.

"Garth Flannigan, you remember my neighbor with the Doberman Pinscher dog?"

"Yeah, nice guy. What about him?"

"He was my boss at the factory. He sent me to college ... saw something in me no one else did."

Greg flashed me his sexy smile and my heart clenched tight at the sight of it. "I'm not surprised by that. I always knew you were smart, Lizzie."

It was true. Every time we had our report cards from school, my grades were excellent. Not that my parents cared. Dad would lecture me that he didn't see the need for studying hard at school, because he thought it would make me discontented to work in the factory.

"You really didn't talk to Floyd about me, did you?" I asked, eyeing him carefully in the darkness of the car.

"No, but not because I didn't care," he added quickly. "No

matter what you thought or think of me now, losing you was excruciatingly painful. Talking to Floyd about you wouldn't have changed what happened. I don't know—perhaps I chose not to talk about you in case he said something that might have made me come back. Anyway, whatever the reason, Floyd's your brother. It wouldn't have been fair to put him in the middle of us."

I sat quietly as I mulled over his comment about the breakup being painful until he changed the subject.

"Can I tell you some more about my life with the band?" he tentatively asked.

"No point in asking if you like being with them. I've seen by the way you flash that wide grin whenever you're on stage, you do."

"Then let me tell you a little about the guys when we're not on stage," he pleaded, placing his hand on mine before curling his into a fist around it, and giving it a squeeze.

I nodded. "Okay."

"They're a great bunch of guys, all down to earth, and protective of one another. When I first joined Screaming Shadows, I thought they might regret the choice they had made. Now, I think that they think I'm quirky, but they've accepted me. I don't think I could play with anyone else after being with them."

"In the pictures you're with Deakon or Korry more, are they closest to you?"

"I would say I'm closest to Deakon, but him and Korry are the two guys that I've spent most of my time with. Deakon is cocky, self-confident and hilarious. We have similar personalities, I think. He has my back. Korry's a good guy. He's a thinker, laid back, but he's no pushover. He's the quietest … and he's brave. The kind of guy who fights for what he believes in."

"What you did was brave," I countered.

"Brave? Me … what did I do?"

"Flew across the world to chase your dream."

Greg stopped talking to process what I'd said. We'd had so

many fights about him going, and I'd wasted so much of his time arguing when he should have been excited.

Leaning toward me, Greg held my chin between his thumb and forefinger, then pinned me in a serious gaze. For a few seconds he said nothing, then he sighed. "I wish you'd been brave, Lizzie," he replied quietly.

I sat back, breaking his contact with me. "See, this is why this being friends won't be easy. Everything always leads back to us."

"We'll get past it," he said confidently.

"Will we?" I replied, sounding skeptical. If I still felt the same after all these years, I doubted that.

"Trust me," he muttered calmly, squeezing my hand he was still holding.

"If only I could," I replied honestly. Anytime someone said those words to me, my brain instantly blocked that request.

The damage from my past ran far deeper than anyone could have imagined. I'd never been able to trust anyone one hundred percent. Not even my brother … or my mother.

CHAPTER 28

GREG

*A*s we turned into the area where Eliza still lived with her ma, my eyes scanned ahead to her house. The lone figure of a man sat on the doorstep, and I intuitively knew it was Owen. My gut twisted as I shifted in my seat and let go of Eliza's hand.

After Raff parked, I climbed out of the car. When I offered Eliza my hand to help her out, she ignored it and stepped out herself.

Owen pushed past me, laying claim to Eliza by sliding an arm around her waist. He briefly pulled her against his chest before pushing her away to check her over.

"Are you okay?" he asked, moving his hands to her shoulders to gain her attention.

"I'm fine … it was only dinner," she said curtly. The way that she said it was like she was confirming that nothing else had gone on between us.

"Right," he muttered, giving me a side eye. I hadn't seen Owen in years, spoken to him in even more years than that. Yet I heard the relief in that one word. "Thanks for bringing her home," he mumbled to me, before addressing Eliza again. "You should have gotten a taxi. I would have paid for it."

Eliza eyed him with suspicion as she stepped back to create some personal space. Owen's possessive statement told me how threatened he felt by my presence. I also suspected that he thought the only threat to him and Eliza, could be my money.

As there had been several references about my money from him, via Eliza, it highlighted how little insight Owen had as to how Eliza ticked. If money had been her driving force, she would have come to Miami with me, where she would already have had it all.

"Thanks for dinner ... and for bringing me home," she said quietly, almost shyly for once.

"It was my pleasure, Lizzie. It's been great to catch up a little. I'll see you at the hospital tomorrow," I said. Moving past Owen, I habitually slid my hand into Eliza's silky hair and kissed her cheek. I let my lips linger there for a beat and heard her breathe me in. Breaking contact, I stepped away from her. "Do you want a ride to the hospital in the morning?"

"I'm taking her," Owen piped up.

I gave him a small smile but didn't respond to his comment. Whether that was to fuck with him, or to let him know I saw how threatened he was—I wasn't sure. I secretly hoped it was the latter because from the way Eliza had checked me out earlier, Owen Murphy had plenty to worry about.

"Alright, I'll see you tomorrow, Lizzie."

"Eliza," Owen corrected. His jaw worked back and forth in irritation because I'd called her by my nickname for her.

"Night, Greg," she replied with a hint of a smile on her lips.

"Don't do anything I wouldn't do, Owen," I said as my parting shot before I climbed back into the car. Raff closed the door as I muttered to myself, "Not that you'd know where to start with a woman like my Lizzie. Owen couldn't begin to imagine half the stuff I could do with that girl."

As Raff slid back into the driver's seat, I opened the window a few inches.

"I bet he asked you to get back with him," I heard Owen say.

Eliza shook her head before she glanced in my direction. I turned and looked straight ahead, like I wasn't paying attention, because I wanted to hear her reply.

"Relax, that wasn't even mentioned. When he's hanging with the likes of Lori Sinclair, what would Greg Booker want with me these days?"

"Then what *did* he want with you?" Owen asked, emphasizing his question, sounding perplexed.

"Before the meal, I'll admit the conversation was a bit strained between us. But when all's said and done, he only wants to be friends ... for the sake of my brother. Now, Owen, tell me—how was I supposed to say no to that?"

As Raff pulled away, Eliza looked toward the car again, and cringed when she realized my window was open, letting me know that I wasn't supposed to hear their conversation. Her reply took the shine off my night because until she'd made that comment, I figured we'd made some headway.

"You ready to go?" Raff asked when he knocked on my bathroom door. I stood staring into the mirror while I considered Eliza's comment from the night before again.

"Yeah, just got to brush my teeth," I replied. Applying toothpaste to the brush, I brushed vigorously while thoughts of that smug look on Owen's face bugged the fuck out of me.

Eliza's last words that caused the tightness in my chest. I had never been one to dwell on much, except when it came to her.

However, that comment she made warned me that although

there were spades of sexual chemistry arcing between us, I believed Eliza was still set in her mind about me.

Sitting with her last night confirmed how much I still loved her. That depth of feeling about her had never gone away. It was an emotion I had been fighting during the early days of the breakup, which became a permanent feeling I'd learned to live with and accepted it had become part of my DNA. However, enough time had passed that I had learned to mask those feelings in public. As for Eliza, she appeared as if she didn't need me to breathe anymore, not like she used to.

Seeing her and Owen together made me wonder how she could be willing to trade our raw passion for what Owen Murphy could offer. One look between them was enough for me to recognize there wasn't the spark in her eyes she had whenever she looked at me.

Then again, perhaps I was wrong about that, reading into them what I wanted to see. For the first time ever, I considered that maybe Eliza just hadn't loved me as deeply as my feelings ran for her.

Ten minutes later, Raff had me sit in the car while he checked us out of the hotel. Katy Perry mocked me on the radio with her apt number "Thinking of You".

During the short journey to the hospital, I sent a text to Bernadette. I asked her to contact estate agents in Dublin who could find me some houses to view. My only requirements were that there should be a downstairs bathroom a few reception rooms that we could use to turn into bedrooms and there should good security and immediate possession.

It was a tall order, one I wondered if it could be fulfilled so that Floyd could convalesce in comfort, with his family all around him. However, seeing how quickly Deakon and Levi had managed to purchase properties, I figured that cash buyers with great legal teams could close a deal in days.

As I was about to go into the lift at the hospital without being seen, Levi's name flashed on my cell phone screen.

Fuck, what now? I asked myself, stopping to take the call. I had been bursting to see Floyd, but I believed if Levi was calling, then it had to be something important.

"Just checking in. Do you need anything?" he asked.

"I am about to go into a lift to visit with Floyd."

"Can I send anything?"

"Nah, I'm good. Thanks for asking. I spoke to Bernadette via text about maybe buying a house to help Floyd out for a bit. Everything goes a bit slower here when it comes to buying property though. It's not like the states where you can get it all wrapped up on a dime."

"How desperate are you? Can't you rent?"

"Not sure. It'll depend on any equipment Floyd needs. His wife's worried he won't make the stairs to the bedroom in their own house."

"Right. The only thing I can think of is that you go to auction. If you wire the money and pay the fees you can get the keys almost straight away."

"I hadn't thought of that. Thanks, Levi. I'm taking the month by the way."

"I know. I just didn't want you to think because you were gone nobody cared."

I smiled. "I'm so used to that feeling ..." I admitted.

"Listen, I get it ... I know it was hard for you in the beginning. Coming into a band where everyone has been living in each other's pockets for years couldn't have been easy. Don't think we don't value you, buddy. You might be a little out there in terms of impulses, like getting married and diving off balconies. But you're most definitely one of us."

My heart squeezed because Levi was usually the person that cut me off at the knees for my behavior. "That's good to hear," I admitted. "Alright, I need to shoot. I'm standing in a foyer of a hospital. Any second someone might recognize me, and then I'll need to be sociable."

Levi laughed. "I hear you. Don't forget to look after yourself as well as your buddy. Oh, and a word of warning for you. Beth told me that Deakon, Sadie and her, have been talking about going to Ireland for a bit of R&R. I thought you might like to know."

"I'd love them to come and see me," I said. "Cheers, Levi. I'll be in touch."

"Well, that sounded like a heartwarming phone call," Raff said, chuckling.

"Right?" I said lifting a brow in surprise. "He's the last person I would have expected to check up on me. Do you think they're drawing straws back home, and the one with the shortest must check up on me?" I asked, laughing.

"No, not where Deakon and Korry are concerned. I think they're the real deal … not that Levi and Jude aren't of course. Levi, Jude and Bodhi are just closer because of their long history as kids."

I nodded. "What about you? Who are you closest to?"

"Probably the same as you … you, Korry … Deakon … sometimes with Mikey. Bodhi, not so much. He prefers to pair with Mikey when it's a two-man security requirement. The rest of the time he's joined at the hip to Jude."

"So, you feel out on a limb?" I asked, considering his confession about his colleagues.

"Not at all. I don't mind being sent to do extra trips. It lets me get to know you on a personal level. And it beats hanging around the penthouse all day when everyone else is at home," he remarked, as the lift arrived and we stepped inside.

"Well, I'm glad it's you that's here. I find your style of security less invasive than the others. I regard you more as a friend than my security protection. Plus, you're easygoing, not intense like Bodhi is."

"Thanks, I try. It can't be easy having a sitter all the time."

The lift doors opened on the ICU floor, and I placed my hands on his chest. "It's a pain in my arse, but necessary once shit gets real. Some of our fans are nuts," I admitted. "Anyway, I'm happy you're here with me. Now, go, see Dublin for a while. Have lunch in one of the pubs. I recommend the Roast Beef dinners. I swear to God, I'll text you when I need you to come back."

"Thanks, that is if you're sure."

"I am. Nothing is going to happen in here. Floyd is more likely to get mobbed than I am."

Raff chuckled as the lift doors closed, leaving him inside. As I turned around Eliza was waiting outside the lift door.

"About last night ..." she began as she walked toward me.

"It's fine," I replied, holding a palm out in front of her to stop her from coming closer. "You gave him your honest thoughts. I appreciate that. You can tell Owen I'm not a threat. I have no wish to rehash all the shit that we went through again," I said sternly.

Eliza stepped directly in front of me and placed her hands on my chest. Gripping her wrists, I moved her gently to the side and stepped past her. "Like you said, friends for Floyd's sake. Other than that, what you do with your life is up to you. I won't be interfering."

My heart cracked the moment I voiced those words because nothing could be further from the truth. However, Eliza's tone had been laced with bitterness when she'd made that comment, and it appeared that Owen was the guy she wanted. So, despite how I felt, I figured for her sake, I'd try to be okay with that.

Eliza's eyes flared in shock, her hazel eyes transforming from bright to dull as the impact of my words hit home. The pleading look that had been in them to start with was now a glare because

I'd shut her down. Seeing this gave me a small measure of hope that she was torn.

Without looking back, I inhaled a cleansing breath as I pushed open the door to Floyd's room. Relief eased that tight feeling within me the second I saw Floyd, sitting up in bed. He looked alert and smiling as he sat bare chested, even if he needed a good barber's service.

"Is that a new look you're sporting?" I asked, seeing half his hair and beard all gone on one side.

"Tell me about it. Ruth tried to trim my beard on the other side, but I don't trust her enough with a razor. Damn, it's great to see you," he murmured weakly. "Now you're either back because I'm getting better or I'm dying … nope definitely improving," he decided.

"Yeah? How do you figure that?" I asked, chuckling.

"Because if I was seriously ill, they wouldn't let your clumsy arse near me."

I grinned as I leaned forward to hug him. As he lifted an arm and slung it around me a wave of emotion closed my throat, almost choking me. Hugging him extra-long, I whispered, "What the fuck did you do, mate? Don't you ever do that to me again."

"How else am I supposed to get you to visit Ireland?" Floyd countered, in good humor.

"Nice to know the part of your brain that processes sarcasm is still intact," I joked. My face fell as I stared more intently toward him. "Fuck, mate, I thought you were mincemeat from the way my brother broke the news to me, over the phone."

"To be frank, when I first tried to wake up, so did I," he muttered flatly. "I had this light aversion and what felt like the biggest hangover of my life. Then there were dizzy spells, and I couldn't remember what day it was."

"So far there's been no recollection of the accident at all?" Floyd shook his head. "What's the last thing you remember?"

"Singing to Bruno Mars "The Lazy Song"," he muttered, chuckling.

"Well, you didn't need to take that part about lying in bed so literally," I joked.

"Agreed," he replied, smiling. "God, it's great to have you here. You make me feel better already. If anything had happened to me Ruth would—"

"Have been taken care of," I interjected. That thought felt too huge a burden to discuss. "So ... what's the plan? Everything moving okay—nothing broken?"

"Mostly a lot of stiffness and numbness in my legs, a crush injury around my pelvis where the seatbelt was. It's some muscle weakness, but no permanent paralysis my doc thinks. Dick still works so that's the main thing," he remarked, wagging his eyebrows.

"I'm sure Ruth's delighted to know your junk is in order."

"She is. It was her that noticed I had a boner before I was fully awake."

"Little nymph," I teased.

"My little nymph," he corrected. I grinned. "So, you finally faced Eliza. How did that feel?"

"Like I was being dragged naked through broken glass and fed a crate of sardines through a funnel, while someone scraped their nails down a chalkboard," I remarked.

"Better than you expected then," he shot back, laughing.

"She's with Murphy now," I mumbled, not willing to mention Owen's name if I could help it.

"Ruth said she's serious about giving him a go," Floyd said, nodding as the smile fell from his face.

"It's for the best," I blurted, then considered how acidic those words had felt on my tongue.

"Is it. Fuck, she's a silly girl in my opinion," Floyd muttered, shaking his head.

"At least she's moving on."

Floyd's eyes widened in panic. "Hey, what if Owen Murphy becomes my brother-in-law?"

I shuddered. "If that's what she wants, then my opinion won't matter. Anyway, enough about Lizzie. When are they going to let you home?"

"They're not sure. I won't manage stairs for a while. My legs feel weak, and the sensation is as if there are lead weights around my ankles. They're not sure to what extent the nerves at the bottom of my back are damaged. They're hoping physiotherapy will help. I'm worried that I won't be able to drive."

"Worst comes to worst, you can get hand controls, so let's not dwell on that. You're a determined guy, I know you'll work hard with the physio regime. Lizzie said Ruth was worried about the stairs as well."

"Yeah ... but I'm alive."

"You are and we're all thankful for that. Now listen, I want you to hear me out, because I think I might have a solution. Don't take this the wrong way because I get that you're a proud man. So..." Floyd was already frowning, and I hadn't disclosed my plan yet. "I'm going to buy property here in Ireland, and I want you to convalesce in it. I'm looking for one with suitable access for your family on one floor."

"No, Greg. We've got savings. If we need to move out for a while, I'll rent somewhere."

"Yeah, well if you feel you need to do that, you can rent it from me," I stated. "It'll be a win-win. I'll have someone who'll take care of my property, and you'll have somewhere that meets the requirements for any equipment you need."

"I can't let you buy a fucking house for what might only be a few months," Floyd argued again.

"It'll be an investment. The money's just sitting in the bank, earning a shitty interest rate. It's about time I invested in bricks and mortar anyway. I could potentially double my money in ten years or so."

"Greg … I can't."

"Please, Floyd, think of your family. It'll cause the least amount of upheaval for the kids and Ruth. It's not all about you. I can furnish it so everything will stay as it is in your own place. And it'll be less upheaval once you are ready to move back."

"What did I do to deserve you as a friend?"

"No doubt, it would have been something beyond naughty," I replied. We both laughed and I could see Floyd begin to come around to my idea.

From that point on, it took us a while to hash out some minor details of my plan, but eventually Floyd agreed. Plus we both suspected, it would likely be the only way he'd get out of hospital quicker.

I had only been by Floyd's bedside for about an hour when I noticed he'd grown tired. "I'm going to leave for now, and let you doze for a bit. Is Ruth coming in later?" I asked.

He nodded, smiling gratefully. "Yeah, she's bringing the girls in with her."

"Right, well, I'll take the rest of the day. See what I can find out about houses, auctions and shit like that. I'll drop by again tomorrow. If there's anything at all I can do, give me a ring."

"Thanks, Greg. Wait, how did you get to be so responsible, checking up on me … buying houses and such? Where did my flaky, impulsive little buddy go?"

"Oh, he's still here," I said as I leaned in and gave him another hug. "I've just been reeling him in, until I knew you were on the road to recovery," I muttered. Floyd's eyes blinked closed as he smiled. "Nap, mate. I'll see you tomorrow."

"Greg," Floyd called out as I reached the door.

"Yeah?"

"You're one in a million. I love you, mate."

"Fuck! Now I know you're dying?" I teased, grinning. Opening the door, I stepped outside and as the door clicked closed tears sprang to my eyes.

"What's wrong? Is my brother, okay?" Eliza asked, jumping out of the chair she'd been sitting on. It dawned on me that she'd sat there for the whole of my visit.

I nodded. "Yeah, he's on the mend … I know this because he was giving me shit. It's just hard to see him like that when he's always been the one that's had my back."

Relief washed over her face as she clutched her chest. "You're leaving already?" she asked, sounding disappointed.

"He's wiped out. I'm leaving to let him nap. I'll be back tomorrow. Meanwhile, I'm going to see what I can do about that house."

"Floyd agreed?" she asked, her huge eyes rounded in surprise.

"Yeah, he knows it's necessary if he wants to get out of here. He told me a bit more about his injuries and I'm going to check out if I can get a care package together for whatever it takes to help him."

"Thanks, I told Ruth … w-we appreciate what you want to do for them," she said quietly.

I nodded, pleased I'd made them happy. Next, I pulled out my cell phone and asked the nurse at the desk if it was okay to send texts.

"Texts are fine," she replied.

I texted for Raff to come back, and as I put my cell away, I realized Eliza was still standing, hugging herself. "Aren't you going back in?" I asked.

"Not if he's sleeping," she mumbled. "I'll be leaving soon. I'm only waiting for Ruth and the girls to come. We don't like leaving him alone."

"Right. Good plan. You can put me on the rotation to sit with him as well," I informed her and sat down to wait for Raff.

"Thought you were leaving?" she asked, frowning.

"I am. Just waiting for Raff, my security guy, to come."

UNTIL GREG

"I see," she said quietly. "I forgot about that."

"About that?" I probed.

"You, being a rock star, and stuff." she chuckled, looking a little embarrassed.

The lift doors opened, and Ruth stepped out with her girls.

"Uncle Greg, you're really a person," her oldest daughter Aria called out. I laughed because I'd only ever spoken to her on Skype or Zoom. She ran over and excitedly hugged my leg. Bending, I picked her up and was rewarded with another tight hug. Ruth smiled as she carried their other, dribbling, eleven-month-old daughter Myra.

My cell buzzed with a message. "That's what I call timing. My ride's here darlin'," I told Ruth. "Eliza brought you up to speed on the house?"

Ruth nodded. "I can't believe you'd do all of that for us."

"I'd do anything for all of you. It's nothing. Go ... see your man. I'll call you if I have any news. Otherwise, I'll catch up tomorrow."

I wandered over to the lift while Eliza and Ruth had a short exchange, then Eliza came and stood beside me.

"You're leaving now?"

She nodded. "Want a lift home?" She shook her head. "What, you're mute now?" I teased.

"No ... look Greg, about yesterday ..." The lift opened and Raff stood inside, so she stopped talking. I gestured for Eliza to go in and I stepped in after her.

"Your timing is everything. I was on my way back to you," Raff mumbled. "Bernadette's sent you details of a property she thinks might be suitable that's in an auction this afternoon. It starts in an hour and a half. The details are in your email."

I glanced at Eliza who was watching us both with interest. "Do you want to come with us? Another opinion is always good. You might see something I don't."

"Me? Sure, but what would I know about buying houses?"

"About the same as me," I replied, shrugging. "You ever bought a house?" I asked Raff.

"Nope, I inherited my grandma's."

"Lucky bastard," I joked. "Okay, so we're three rookies. This should be fun."

"You really want me to come after what I said yesterday?"

"What did you say that was so offensive? You could hardly say no," I remarked, remembering what she'd said. "That sounded like it felt you were obligated to come because of Floyd. It was an honest answer, and I know where I stand."

"That's not how I felt … not really … I just …"

"Look, I'm not about to get in the middle of you and Murphy," I snapped, unwilling to hide my frustration about the whole situation—about loving her, at the thought of leaving her behind with someone like him. Yet … I couldn't admit that to her. "You already told me that your love life is none of my concern. Now, let's just concentrate on finding your brother's family somewhere to live. Nothing else matters apart from that."

"Don't you have someone to bid for you by phone?"

"And miss the excitement of buying my first house? Nope. I'll take responsibility for that."

Raff sighed. "Alright, but if I say we need to leave … we're leaving."

CHAPTER 29

ELIZA

I couldn't believe when Greg wanted to include me in trying to purchase a house. Especially after my slap down in front of Owen.

Since then, I'd been unwilling to process my remark because I'd wanted to take it back. It wasn't as if I'd been with Owen a long time and owed him my loyalty or anything, so I had no idea why I'd tried to appease him.

Before Greg suggested dinner, I thought we'd never be in the same book again, never mind on the same page with our points of view. It had only taken a few hours in his company before my mind had begun to shift.

So why did I make it sound as if it had been a chore, when all-in-all dinner with Greg had unexpectedly been the most exciting event in my life in years?

"Sounds good, doesn't it?" Greg asked, breaking into my thoughts. I'd been distracted and I hadn't been paying attention to what he'd said. He gestured to the auction listing and once I had read it, I stared in disbelief at the imposing, seven bedroom, six bath, country house in Baily, Howth.

Situated right on the coast in the northeast of Dublin, it was the poshest house I'd ever seen, and a world away from Tallaght, the housing estate we all grew up in.

My heart pounded when I saw the starting bid price of 5.3million euros. "This isn't just a house, it's a EuroMillions lottery winning house," I mumbled incredulously. I stared at the pristine whitewashed stately pile, featuring a huge pool and a whole basement with games rooms. There's even a separate apartment.

"Forget about the price tag, it has an indoor swimming pool, a sauna, beauty room with a massage table, a gym, and the best bit is it has three bedrooms all on the ground floor. One even has a huge ensuite bath and wet room. It has everything Floyd needs. If we can get it for a decent price, I bet I'd double my money in ten years or so."

The 'we' in his explanation wasn't lost on me. If only …

"You seriously have the money to buy something this expensive?"

Greg nodded and felt oddly embarrassed to admit to having so much money. "I wouldn't be here otherwise." Greg's eyes narrowed and he looked seriously toward me. "I'm not bidding on this to impress anyone, Lizzie. It's got decent security, and a deep-water dock at the back. I could get a boat if I want one … I've always wanted a boat. Most importantly, I'd be anonymous if I lived there."

"But you don't. You live in Miami," I shot back. A pang of hurt at my acid remark tightened my chest. Disappointment flashed in Greg's dull eyes at my outburst, and it made me check myself. I sighed. "Look, it's way too much of a house. Think of the heating bills, the maintenance…"

"Like I said, I'd find a way to help it pay for itself," he countered. "Weddings and small conferences are two events that would love this place for a start. You'd be surprised at what guys with big bucks would pay."

"Can you hear yourself. You want privacy, then you're renting it out? What did you do with Greg Booker?" I asked, staring pointedly toward him. "The old Greg would never have imagined himself attached to a place like this one on the sheet," I said, flicking the pamphlet.

"It's an investment, Lizzie."

"It's a money pit," I argued, talking sense.

As it happened, Greg stopped bidding on the big house at 6.2 million and it eventually went for 7.1 million.

"I'm glad you were priced out of that house. It would have been a millstone round your neck. And I like this house much better," I said, staring down at the picture of the substantial two-story, brick built modern house he ended up buying.

The six bed, four-bathroom family house with a swimming pool, tennis court with a great secluded driveway had a far more palatable price tag of 2.95 million euros instead. Although him buying a house in the millions still freaked me out.

Grinning, Greg looked pleased with his purchase as he laid down the auction paddle in front of the auctioneer. Next, he produced a black credit card and his identification, then called his legal and financial advisers to arrange the details for the purchase with the auctioneer's office.

"I wasn't priced out of the white one, darlin'. I just didn't think it was worth that kind of money. It's worth six million at the most." He frowned. "See the problem with being famous is that everyone thinks you should pay more. Or people want to one-up me like those two dickheads that were bidding against me. They forgot about the investment because they were so hellbent on outbidding me.

"Once I dropped out, that guy in the black coat's ego made him determined to outbid the other one. They've obviously got more money than sense. I can imagine the guy that won boasting to anyone who'll listen that Greg Booker wanted to own his house." I nodded, understanding how that could happen.

"Anyway, you're right. I was looking at the other one like a business venture. This one is a family home. It has everything Floyd needs—and room for Aria to play safely outside ... and it's secluded."

"It's more than Floyd needs," I muttered cautiously.

"You know, I think we should all move in with him when he first comes home. We could help for a bit. Ruth is going to be run ragged looking after the two girls and Floyd. It can't be easy ... all that stress of two little kids, and that crazy puppy of theirs running around." His gorgeous green eyes searched my face expectantly as he waited for my reply.

In theory it sounded like everything I'd ever dreamed of ... sharing a house with Greg. And nothing that was good for my resistance toward him as well.

"You don't need to be there. I'll help when I can. My company has been great giving me this week off, but I need to go back. I'll go there after work to help with dinner, then clean up while Ruth puts the kids to bed."

"I'll hire a housekeeper to do all of that. But I still feel that you should move in. You could help with the kids in the morning and go to work from there. This house is nearer to the factory for a start. Plus, it would save all the back and forth to your ma's place at the end of the day. Even if Raff drove you, it would be twenty-five minutes each way."

As Greg's eyes searched my face, I felt my resolve melt away and I found myself thinking it might be great.

"Come on, Lizzie, you know it makes sense," he coaxed. I felt any resentment toward him from our past crumble because, he had done an amazing thing by removing a potentially stressful situation for Floyd, Ruth, the girls, even my ma and me.

Could we stay under the same roof without things becoming messy?

All I knew was ... for a reason I had yet to determine, I wanted to try.

"Alright, I'll stay."

The smile that lit up Greg's face made my heart clench tightly. For a long moment our eyes locked. In that instant, I had to do something to break the spell that had begun to develop between us, so I averted my gaze to the pamphlet and began to babble.

"This bedroom on the ground floor has an ensuite bathroom. Do you think the dining room and office on either side of that could be Aria and Myra's rooms for now?"

"Anything that makes life easier for everyone, Lizzie," Greg agreed quietly.

"THE KITCHEN HAS a table and ten chairs so the dining room likely wouldn't get used anyway," Greg excitedly told Floyd as he relayed the suggestion I'd made about the girls' bedrooms.

"Man ... this is too much," Floyd mumbled as he sat in his hospital bed. My brother bit his lip and the way his eyes kept darting between us told me how uncomfortable he was by Greg's financial layout on his behalf.

"Nonsense. It's the least I can do," Greg said modestly as he shirked Floyd's discomfort off. "Now, the house has a drawing room and sitting room, so I figured maybe turn one of those into a playroom for the kids. There's a huge basement with a self-contained apartment down there. What would you say if Lizzie, Raff and I moved in for a while?"

Watching Greg divert the conversation, reminded me of how

diplomatic he used to be as a boy when he invited my brother and I back to his ma's for tea, whenever he'd sensed there was likely nothing to eat at home.

My heart pounded in my chest as I silently willed Floyd to agree.

Floyd glanced warily toward Ruth. Once she nodded, my brother grinned widely at Greg's suggestion. "God, I'd love that. We'd get to spend time together like we used to."

"That's what I hoped you would say. And don't worry, Raff and I will fend for ourselves," he told Ruth. "I make a mean sandwich these days."

As my brother, Ruth and Greg joked, I couldn't wait for the house move to happen. My heart fluttered excitedly at the thought of seeing Greg every day for a few weeks.

Then, once again I warned myself that this arrangement was a *very* temporary situation. Greg's priorities were the band and my brother, nothing to do with me. The moment Floyd was well, or his band needed him, Greg Booker would disappear from my life … just like he did before.

"I … I need to get going," I said as I smiled at my brother.

"Alright, sister," Floyd said, smiling. "Thanks for being here. Enjoy yourself tonight."

My heart stalled because I had a date with Owen, and I suddenly felt guilty about that. Greg didn't speak but I felt him watching me as I made for the door.

"Lizzie," Greg called out as I opened the door.

I turned to look at him and my heart flipped over when he flashed me his perfect smile. A thrill ran through my body at how something so simple could light me up inside. He stood and made his way over to me, wrapped his arms tightly in a hug, with his face close to my neck. "Thanks for coming with me today, you made buying my first house special."

I nodded and pulled out of his embrace, swallowing roughly as I did this. "Glad I was able to help."

As I headed toward the lift, I heard Floyd's door close softly. The lift doors opened and closed with me inside. I felt thankful that Greg couldn't see me cry. It had once been my biggest dream that Greg and I would buy a house together. Something that he'd made happen today. Just not how I had imagined it would be.

CHAPTER 30

GREG

"That was a cunning move," Raff muttered as he drove me back to the rental house after I'd explained the plan for us all to move in together.

"I want what's best for Floyd," I protested.

"And for you. Dude, she's snarkier than Sadie ... and she's seeing someone else," Raff mumbled, turning to eye me carefully. "Must I remind you about the ultimatum she gave you?"

"I know ... but she's grown up a lot since then. The old Eliza would never have agreed to dinner ... or the auction today. You didn't know her back then she was as stubborn as fuck. At that time, if she held a grudge, it was for life."

My cell rang. "This will be Deakon, Levi said he might call," I mumbled, as I shifted my weight and pulled my phone out of my pocket.

Lori's name flashed on the scene and my heart sank. "Fuck."

"What?" Raff asked, his head spinning in my direction.

"It's Lori Sinclair," I said my lips twisting in thought. For a moment I felt reluctant to answer.

"I thought you really liked her?" he probed.

"I do," I insisted.

While we were talking, Lori's call cut off. Seconds later my voicemail alert went off.

Raff nodded briefly at my cell phone in my lap. "Now she thinks you're avoiding her."

"Am I? You've seen how full on it's been since I saw her. I spent one night with her ... it's not as if I'm in a full-blown relationship with her yet."

"The way I see it, your focus is in one camp—here. You're making time for dinner with Eliza. Buying houses for Floyd. Arranging for all of us to move in together ... what the fuck is it with that?"

I flashed him a dark scowl. "What do you mean?"

"You and me moving in with your buddy, I get that ... but insisting your ex-girlfriend—"

"Floyd's sister," I reminded him.

"Yeah, keep telling yourself that's the only reason," he mused flatly, as he stared straight ahead at the road.

"I'm not avoiding Lori," I said changing the subject back to his original comment. "I'll call her when I get indoors," I insisted.

"So, you're definitely calling her?"

"I said so, didn't I?" I argued. From my point of view, I hadn't been putting it off. The truth was I was kidding myself. I hadn't given Lori a thought since I'd had dinner with Eliza.

My gut told me Lori would be easy to be with ... might even hero-worship me. That wasn't what I wanted from a partner at all. Eliza wasn't easy to be with, but if I couldn't have her, I didn't want anyone else.

"You know what? I am going to call Lori, she deserves my time, but I've decided I won't go and see her—not when I feel how I do about Eliza."

"She's with some other guy ... and she won't leave Ireland, you said so yourself," Raff mumbled.

"Maybe not, but I'm established enough with the band, that when I'm not working I can be here."

"Just like that?"

"No ... it would be fucking hard, but ... I don't want to live without her in my life anymore."

"Right, there's only one small problem with that," he muttered.

"Yeah, I know ... she's stubborn."

"And there's the guy," he said again.

"I see the way she looks at me. She doesn't want him she wants me."

"You think?"

"Oh, I know so ... and you know something else?"

"What?

"I won't take her back until I think she's ready. She knows I still love her, but I'll be playing down wanting her back."

"You sound pretty confident about that."

"I am. Watch this space, Eliza McDade for all her stubborn ways will be mine one day."

HAVING GROWN up in Dublin I knew my city well, so when Raff took a turn off the main road that I wasn't expecting I paid attention.

"This isn't the way to the rental house. You should have stayed on the main road."

"We're not going home."

"We're not?"

"Do you know The Merry Ploughboy Gastro Pub?" Raff queried.

"Floyd raves about it all the time," I said, nodding. "Not eaten there before though, why?"

"I booked us a table tonight for dinner. It's a small place that you won't get mobbed. And there's live music ... folk music. So, I figured since I'm here for a while, I should get the full Irish experience. It's either that pub or a chain place like Nando's takeout or something."

"The pub sounds good. I could do with revisiting my roots and getting sloshed."

Raff gave me a dark look as he shook his head. "Sloshed? If you get drunk, you'll do something stupid."

"Me? Embarrass myself in my hometown? Never," I said, crossing my heart playfully with my fingers.

Raff slowed down and eyed me skeptically before he focused back on the road. "Alright, we'll go. But ... if you get pissed and start a fight or something, I want a bonus."

"Deal," I replied, grinning.

Raff's cell rang as he was driving, and I saw it was Deakon. Raff glanced at the caller ID and huffed. "For fuck's sake, can't anyone leave us alone?" he muttered before he answered on loudspeaker.

"Raff, dude, how's our Irish wild card holding up?"

I put my fingers to my lips and Raff smiled knowingly.

"Pissed drunk, flat off his face. You have no idea what I'm putting up with here. I have no clue what I'm going to do with him."

"Aw, fuck. When I spoke to him, he'd sounded like he had it together. We were coming to Dublin to surprise him tonight as well," Deakon said, sounding bummed.

"We?" Raff asked.

"Yeah, Sadie, Beth and Me. We figured he could do with a night out. Sounds like we're too late since he's hit the sauce already."

"The drink I can handle. It's how he dropped his pants and pissed in the street that's too much."

"Jesus, in daylight?" A snort escaped my nose and Raff's hand instantly clamped over my mouth, silencing me.

"Yeah, he got a fine from the Irish police," he said. As Raff silently laughed, he hunched briefly over the wheel.

"Oh, God. Did anyone film it?"

"Dude, it was more like who didn't film it."

"Fuck, Donnie's going to go nuts. Where is he now?" Deakon asked, concerned.

"He's passed out in the back of this rental car, I'm driving."

"Fuck me. Is the place you're staying secure ... I mean there won't be people around when you get him out, will there?" Deakon asked, chuckling.

"Yeah, that's private. If I'm going to be dealing with this shit all the time, I want a raise."

"Dude, his best buddy almost died. We need to cut him some slack on this one," Deakon argued in my defense.

I started laughing aloud and Raff did the same. "Deakon, I love you, dude. You're a true friend," I called out.

"Are you fucking serious? Raff ... your ass is fired," he bellowed down the line.

Raff grinned. "Are you sure about that because me and your buddy are just about to hit an Irish pub. Do you trust that I won't be needed to cart his ass home anyway?"

"Fuck you," Deakon replied, laughing in defeat. "As for you, Greg Booker, you owe me big time. To think I was trying to do something nice for you—"

"I appreciate it," I said, cutting him off. "Can't wait to see you. When do you get here?" I asked, changing the subject.

"We're about an hour away."

Raff nodded even though Deakon couldn't see him. "Okay, we'll be at the pub in ten minutes. I'll text you the address and the driver can drop you all off there. I can put your luggage in the back of the car."

"Sounds great, see you soon," I chimed in.

Deakon cut the call and we both cracked up laughing. "I think that's the most fun I've had with him sober," Raff mumbled, chuckling. "Sounds like our night is suddenly about to get a wee bit livelier."

CHAPTER 31

GREG

Raff's face fell once we entered the pub. "What the fuck? I asked for a quiet spot." The tables were all pushed together and lined in up rows from the stage to the end of the bar, facing the small stage.

I laughed. "Don't stress, if we sit right on that last row at the front, or the very back, once the entertainment starts no one will pay attention to us."

"Evening, guys, table for two?" the host asked us.

"I already booked in the name of Montgomery," Raff muttered. "But since then, we have three more people coming. Can you fit five of us in?"

Raff frowned as the host scratched his head and began using a pen to count to himself. As he did this, he pointed toward each of the tables and muttered names aloud to himself. He looked puzzled as he glanced back at us.

"Dude, apart from us there are only two other people in here," Raff prompted, confused by all the host's calculations.

"It's banquet night. All those seats are reserved, but I think I can squeeze in another table at the front. Can you sit at the bar and give me five minutes to shuffle stuff round a wee bit?"

Raff shrugged again. "Suuure," he said, not sounding convinced at all.

I ordered two pints of cold Guiness. "I shouldn't be drinking," Raff muttered. "I'm working remember?"

"Ah you won't need to do much. I'm among my own here. No one will give a fuck who I am. They'll be more interested in the other performers tonight."

"You think?" he asked, curling his lip, unsure.

"I know so. The Merry Ploughboys are legendary in Irish folk music circles. You're in for a treat. Can't wait to see what Deakon makes of it."

"Table's ready, lads," the landlord stated.

Moving us from the bar, the landlord placed us exactly where I'd wanted to be, next to the stage. We were starving but as it was a banquet and everyone ate together, we had to wait for the place to fill up.

Fortunately, that didn't take too long and by the time we were on our second drink the pub had begun to fill up. As we were in the last row and I was facing in toward Raff, I was correct in my assumption that no one noticed me at all.

The server was setting down our third drinks when Raff got a text.

"Deakon and the others are almost here. You should be alright here until I get back. Don't talk to anyone," he warned.

Anticipation got the better of me and I turned to look at the entrance. My heart lightened the moment I saw Beth, Levi's sister wander into the bar by herself.

As she scanned the room to look for me, I shot up an arm. Beth's face lit up in recognition the moment our eyes connected. She flashed me a warm smile as she slipped off her jacket and wandered toward me, down the opposite side of table.

Plonking heavily onto the chair next to where Raff had been sitting, she grinned. "Surprise," she shrieked theatrically, making jazz hands in the air, and drawing attention to herself.

"You can surprise me anytime, sweetheart," a young lad in a group of eight said. They were seated at a table on the row next to us.

Beth laughed. "That's it, dream big," she replied. The lad's friends roared with laughter at Beth's cocky come back.

She glanced toward the door and mine naturally followed. Deakon and Sadie strode in behind Raff, and he was immediately spotted by the same group of guys.

"What the fuck?" one of lads called out. "Deakon Brody ... is that you?"

"To be sure," Deakon replied with a fake Irish accent, as he gave them a theatrical bow. They all laughed. "What the hell are you doing here?" demanded a bald lad, sitting in the middle of their table.

"Visiting the best bassist on the planet," he replied, as he stretched up onto his tiptoes to search for me.

The scraping sound of wood on wood as I pushed back my chair and stood, drew everyone's attention toward me. "Could he mean me," I said, waving playfully. A roar of appreciation came from the eight lads, and they began drumming their fists on the table and stamping their feet in support of me.

"Oye, there's people here to enjoy themselves," the landlord warned them. He swiped a dish towel catapult style at one of their heads, and then slung it over his shoulder. "Don't make me regret dropping that ban you all had already for your rowdy behaviors."

"Sorry, my fault," I said, raising a hand. "Their bill for the night is on me," I said, circling my finger around at their table, as I smiled at the landlord.

"What, this lot? They drink like fish," he replied.

"Then I'm in good company," I remarked. "And might I remind

you why Irishmen drink like fish? It's because it's always pissing with rain and Ireland's surrounded by water."

Everyone laughed and I saw the landlord relax. "Alright, have your fun. But when the music starts and the food comes out, I'll remind you to behave yourselves."

"Fuck me, the shenanigans have started already," Raff muttered to himself as he reached our table and sat down next to Beth.

"Take that stick out of your ass and relax," Deakon advised Raff. "We won't be needing a bodyguard tonight unless that lot start a fight. I doubt it though, since they have a new buddy that's paying their bill," Deakon said, nodding toward me.

"Listen to you," Sadie mumbled. "If you hadn't pointed him out, Greg might have gone unnoticed." Deakon scoffed and pulled a face. Sadie frowned. "What?"

"Greg might have gone unnoticed at that moment, but this *is* Greg we're talking about. I'm betting that there won't be a soul in this bar that doesn't feel his presence before the night ends."

"No, they won't, because Greg's going to behave himself, right Greg?" Raff muttered, eyeing me darkly.

I even felt the hint of mischief in my smile as I nodded but, I wasn't a liar, so I couldn't confirm I'd heeded his warning in words.

"Damn that food was incredible," Sadie praised as she placed her fork on her plate. She leaned back in her chair, rubbing her stomach.

"How can you eat three desserts and still look like that?" Beth remarked.

"You put a fair bit away yourself, Miss Bethany. I don't know how you maintain that magnificent figure of yours either," Raff remarked, complimenting Beth.

Beth's cheeks pinked up and she looked at her lap. Her reaction was unusually shy for her.

"Hey, everybody. I think we should start the night off with a jig. So, would you please put your hands together for our champion Irish dancers."

We all applauded and cheered as three girls and one guy stepped onto the stage and began dancing a jig. Beth turned to Raff, and they chuckled. The music started quite slowly and as it increased in pace, so did their feet.

"Oh, my, God, it's a wonder they don't get confused and fall over. I've never seen anyone's legs move so quickly and independently of their still body," Sadie mused.

"Fuck me, that fiddler is incredible. What's that tune called?" Deakon muttered, his eyes fixated on the dancers.

"Ah, that jig is called "I Buried My Wife and I Danced On Her Grave," I replied straight-faced.

"You're shitting me, right?" Deakon replied, laughing over the drink he'd been about to put to his mouth.

I shook my head laughing with him. "Nope, that's the God's honest truth."

"And I thought The Hill Billies had hilarious titles for their tunes," he muttered to himself.

For another fifteen minutes we watched the dance troupe execute their performance with precision. Then when it finished, there was another ten-minute break.

Sadie had ordered us shots, so we downed a fair few of those, then I switched to my favorite Irish whiskey.

"I thought you were easing up on the drinking?" Deakon queried.

"Not here. I'm with good company, and Raff will cover my ass if I get out of hand." As I explained this to Deakon, The Merry

Ploughboys took to the stage. Then, from the moment that the folk group began their set, the atmosphere in the pub switched from polite, dinner conversation to their full-on, interactive musical gig.

The acoustics in the bar were incredible, and the wooden floor, a perfect addition to the vibe as the collective foot stomping and tapping sent vibrations up through my chair.

As I stole a gaze around at the patrons, there wasn't one of them that was untouched by the music. Seeing the audience engrossed as they clapped and tapped their feet, reminded me what the power of music could do to unite people.

Watching all their happy faces made my heart feel lighter than it had in days and the vibration of their beat was another kind of music to my soul.

I half-expected a what-the-fuck face from Deakon when I cast a glance at him but was surprised that he was also lost in the music, even if heavy metal was his thing.

As the gig neared the end, their bass player Eoghan Heneghan, spotted me at the front. Wandering over to the mic, he said, "For those of you who haven't spotted him yet, Greg Booker from Screaming Shadows is in the house tonight."

The middle table of guys, smashed out of their heads drunk, all cheered heartily at the mention of my name. Eoghan shushed them by waving his hands for them to pipe down.

"Now you know what real music sounds like," Eoghan jibed playfully to me.

"I can play a jig or two," I replied with a smug grin.

Eoghan scoffed. "He says he can play a jig folks," he announced to the audience, like he was challenging me. I stood, turned and bowed at everyone, which brought a roar of appreciation that I was playing along.

"Permission to come on stage?" I asked politely. I cast a glance at Raff who was slowly shaking his head. I flashed him a demonic grin and laughed.

"Aye, come on up," Eoghan's brother Liam, their guitarist and accordion player agreed.

By that time, I was drunk, probably past my best for the challenge I had in mind. But being among my fellow countrymen I knew they'd forgive me the odd mistake.

Eoghan moved to take his bass guitar strap over his head. I waved it away because I didn't want it. He looked puzzled as I strode over to Dermot Daly and held my hand out for his fiddle.

Dermot frowned and shook his head. "You're not fucking up my baby," he mumbled warily.

"Trust me, I can play. My da taught me," I said quietly. Dermot eyed me carefully, unsure if I was lying or not. "Seriously dude. I can. Tell you what. If I break it, you can pick any fiddle you want, and I'll replace it." Although Dermot still looked unsure, he reluctantly handed his precious instrument over to me.

Taking my turn in front of the mic, I grinned. "Right then boys, what are we playing?" I asked but before any of them could reply, I said, "I know. Irish Washerwoman."

The guys in the band laughed as I wandered over to take the spot where Dermot had been standing. "Alright, we're starting at three-quarter, ninety-five bpm and moving to one-twenty bpm on the second round," I said, regarding the speed we'd play the piece at. "Alright, on my tap of three," I ordered, counting them by stomping my heel.

The moment I began playing the fiddle, the bar erupted in cheers. Then, as the tempo shifted to the faster pace, Deakon's jaw dropped, stunned at my skill, with a look of wonder on his face.

I grinned, and he shook his head, clearly blown away that I had this little gem of talent hidden up my sleeve.

Then he quickly fumbled in his pocket for his phone and began to video the band. Beth and Sadie caught my eye as they had gotten out of their chairs, and were performing a cute, little jig together.

A commotion in front of me drew my gaze away from them to two of the lads at the middle table who were creating havoc by trying to dance on the table. I stopped playing and wandered over to the mic.

"Get your arses off that table and sit the fuck down. You're distracting me. I'm trying to concentrate on not making an arse of myself."

Everyone laughed as they climbed down with their heads hung low. They were about to sit back in their seats, but the landlord threw them out.

I shrugged because that was fair … they'd been warned. After they'd been carted off, and their protests had died in the air, I nodded at Eoghan, marked time with my feet, and we all picked up the tune from where we left off.

Once the performance ended, the bar patrons erupted in a rowdy round of applause. Garth Campbell, another member of the band slapped my back.

"Well, that'll teach me not to challenge the likes of Greg Booker in a hurry," Eoghan muttered into the mic. "It was a fucking pleasure to play on this stage with one of Ireland's great men," he said, patting my shoulder.

I turned and gestured to The Merry Ploughboys as a collective while I handed Dermot back his fiddle. "These guys are exceptional musicians who do it for the love of music. I can honestly say it was an honor to share a stage with them all tonight."

I jumped off the stage, took my seat, and Deakon bumped me on my shoulder as I lifted my whiskey. "What the fuck was that? How do I not know you can play the violin?"

"Fiddle," I corrected. "The fiddle was my first instrument," I explained with a shrug. "My da wouldn't let me play anything else until I could play Irish Washerwoman on the fiddle."

"I wish I could have met your dad and shook him by the hand, because what I just saw was a whole other side of you that I never knew existed."

"There's a lot you don't know about me. What's the saying? People only know what you want them to see."

"Well, buddy, I'll be watching you more closely from now on," he remarked as he held up his glass to toast me.

CHAPTER 32

ELIZA

Owen had a flat tire on his car, and this made us late in arriving at The Merry Ploughboys for their banquet night. By the time we got there the staff had already given up our places to somebody else.

Owen pleaded with one of the servers and slipped them a twenty euro note, which earned us being squeezed in at a small table right at the back.

From the moment Owen had picked me up, I'm ashamed to say my thoughts had been preoccupied with Greg. Now that we'd pushed past the hurt in our hearts, my conversations with him had been flowing better.

A thrill shot through me when I remembered the way he'd looked at me earlier in the day. In fact, since he'd been back, there had been times when I had lost my train of thought by being so lost in his intense gaze. Sometimes it had mesmerized me so completely that I couldn't break our connection.

It had been years since I'd felt my heart flutter excitedly in my chest. Yet a simple smile from Greg had done that to me. The casual way he dropped my nickname when he wanted to appear sincere had made me feel special, like he viewed me as one of a kind.

No one else has ever called me Lizzie, not before him or since. And if they did, I would never have answered to it.

Unbeknownst to Owen, he'd been talking to himself for most of the night before the entertainment showed up. And apart from a couple of digs at Greg showing off, by buying Floyd somewhere to convalesce, I'd missed almost every word he said.

When I'd agreed to a date with Owen, I never expected to cross paths with Greg that evening. Yet there was Greg, the rock star, larger than life, bowing and playing up to the audience.

My heart had stopped for a beat the moment his name was mentioned. And I barely a drew breath from the shock of it before Greg was up on the stage with The Merry Ploughboys, with a fiddle in his hands.

"Fuck. Is he following you?" Owen grumbled, looking more than a little annoyed.

"Hardly, since he was here first," I snapped back.

"Did you mention we were coming here?" Owen probed, studying me with narrowed eyes.

"Jesus, what is this? No, I didn't mention it, and I didn't know he was coming here. Haven't you heard of a fucking coincidence." I threw my hands up, "Who knows, maybe it's fate." I almost laughed at the dark glare he cast me at that remark. "Now, will you leave me in peace to enjoy my night or do you have any more questions to interrogate me with?"

The tension in Owen's back made him rigid in his seat. "What the fuck is he doing? Can you believe we've come here for a relaxing night out and this joker is stealing the show? He's always been willing to make an arse of himself, if it gets him attention," he grumbled.

"That's not fair, Owen. Eoghan pointed him out. It's not like he was trying to disrupt their set."

"Oh, you've changed your tune," Owen said, sounding sarcastic. "Last week he was still the scumbag that dumped you to seek his fortune. And now here you are, defending him."

"This malicious jibing needs to stop. I'm here with you, aren't I? So, you can quit with the petty jealousy." Owen's eyes narrowed suspiciously. "Well?" I prompted flatly, needing him to stop with the nasty comments.

"Aye, you're here with me, but he's the spectacle. Look at him acting like an eejit and making a show of himself," Owen grumbled.

"Don't make me regret coming here with you tonight."

"You can't blame a guy for being suspicious. I mean, this place was your suggestion."

This was only our second date, our first being disrupted by Floyd's accident, yet Owen and I were arguing about my ex-boyfriend already. Greg coming back hadn't helped matters though. Not when he appeared to be constantly in my face, stirring up feelings of longing within me from the past while I was doing my best to get over him.

Seeing Greg again had made me feel torn about dating Owen because my mind had been consumed with thoughts of Greg since the day he came back. Thoughts that drowned out any fledgling ones I might otherwise have had about Owen.

That made me consider whether I really wanted a third date with Owen? Or, if I was using him as an excuse to keep my distance from Greg.

While we were arguing, the band struck up a jig, and I realized Greg had gotten up on stage. I couldn't prevent the smile on my face when Greg began to play the fiddle.

In my opinion, he had a natural flair for the instrument as he tapped his feet, and played effortlessly, without a nervous streak in his body.

Then again, Greg could get a tune out of anything. I'd even

heard him play two spoons, and some paper and a comb like a kazoo. A wave of nostalgia hit me square in the gut at the familiar tune they played. And I remembered the first time, he'd played "Irish Washerwoman" for me on his da's old fiddle as I sat in his ma's living room.

Watching him engage the audience as they sat enthralled felt different to how it had made me feel years ago. Instead of being eaten by jealousy, my association to him gave me an instant sense of pride.

As part of Screaming Shadows, Greg wasn't the most obvious member of the band on stage. However, I'd bet money none of them could pick up any instrument they hadn't played in years, like the fiddle, and play with skill in another genre of music, like The Merry Ploughboys played.

Ruth was right. Greg didn't play music for fame, fortune or the women that musicians attracted. He played because it made him happy, and because music was in his blood.

CHAPTER 33

GREG

Raff ordered us a cab because he'd had as much to drink as me. Then, as there were people still mulling around, waiting for Deakon and me to go outside, the bartender invited us to stay inside until the taxicab arrived. So, we sat at a table near the restrooms at the back while Sadie and Beth went to pee.

Deakon and Raff were deep in conversation, and during a reflective moment for me, my mind drifted to Eliza. My heart raced at the thought of getting time to know her better again by living with Floyd. Yet, as caution gnawed at my heart, I wasn't sure if that was a good thing or not.

Buying the house and suggesting we all stayed there was either a stroke of genius on my part … or insanity. Not that having us all there had initially been a plan in my mind when I'd bought the house.

"Sorry, I forgot my bag." For a second, I couldn't make sense of Eliza being there, in the pub.

"Lizzie?" I muttered quietly, confused. I stood up too quickly and lost my balance. Eliza immediately reached out, grabbed, and steadied me.

"Are you really here?" I half-joked, as my hands automatically slid to her hips. My fingertips sank into her flesh beneath the thin dress pants she wore. Our eyes connected and I guessed by her narrowed ones she had assessed that I'd had too much to drink.

"Hey, Lizzie. This is a nice surprise," I whispered close to her ear.

I felt her tremble as a shiver ran through her body, which made me smile. I watched her eyes widen then she stared a moment too long before her back stiffened, like she suddenly remembered what was happening. "I-I forgot my bag. I left it under the chair," she mumbled, still staring, but she didn't move to retrieve it.

"You were here?" I asked softly, as I leaned closer to her ear again. A more distinctive tremor ran through her body as she pulled back and held my gaze. This time the primitive electricity arcing made us both reluctant to break our connection.

"Alright, buddy?" Deakon asked in a slurry voice, as he came alongside me and nudged my shoulder. Still close enough to Eliza to breath her in, I cast a small, sideward glance toward Deakon as Sadie held him up.

Knowing Eliza thought I was drunker than I was, I decided to use this to my advantage. With a ghost of a smile on my lips, I said, "Deak, Sadie ... this is ... my Lizzie ... the fucking love of my life," I confessed honestly. As I slid my hands from her hips to her head, Eliza's breath hitched in response. Cradling her face between them, I stared intently into her gorgeous hazel eyes, and pressed my forehead to hers.

The way her breath hitched again, instantly deepened the already sizzling connection between us and I felt her body soften to my touch. "You're so ... fucking beautiful," I whispered desperately as the air around us thickened even more.

At that point I fiercely contemplated kissing her, but I knew if I did, my action had the potential to open old wounds. Wounds we had that were only healed at surface level. So instead, I allowed time to stand still as we took each other in, oblivious to anyone else, until she swallowed roughly while her curious eyes searched mine.

"What are you doing, Greg? Don't you dare kiss me," she murmured back, her lips barely moving.

"You know me, Lizzie. You know better than to challenge me like this. I'd say you want me to kiss you. The old Greg would have pounced on you for setting such a dare. But ..." I paused and let my eyes tick back and forth as they soaked in the lust I saw in hers. "I'm not that guy anymore. If you want that to happen, you'll need to be the one that makes the first move."

"Eliza?" Owen's stern voice questioned, interrupting me. Startled by his tone, Eliza stiffened again, like she suddenly remembered who she was with, and what she'd come back for.

"You're drunk," she muttered and abruptly pushed me away. Ducking beneath the chair I'd been sitting on, she stood up straight again with her bag. Flustered, she placed the strap of her bag over her shoulder, then toyed with it.

"Keep your hands to yourself, Booker. If you touch her again, I'll lay you out," Owen threatened in a menacing tone.

I chuckled because I thought he was funny. But Raff had heard enough.

Stepping in front of me, Raff closed the space between Owen and me, placed his hands on his hips and cleared his throat. Owen tilted his head back, stared up at him. I swear I saw him gulp. Towering at least six inches above Owen, Raff flashed him a sinister smile. "Yeah? You and whose army?" he asked in a low, intimidating tone. "If you lay him out, that would mean you'd have gone through me. Got that in you, big boy?"

Deakon and Sadie started laughing as Beth came back from the rest room. "What's funny?" she asked, frowning.

"This," Deakon muttered, nodding toward Raff and Owen. "Nothing like a good scrap to finish a night on the town,"

Deakon remarked, nodding toward the standoff between the two men.

"He knows better," Owen bravely remarked to Raff about me. Owen twisted his body and poked his head past Raff to make eye contact with me. "Eliza isn't interested in you. You had your shot and look how that turned out. I should thank you for fucking that up because Eliza belongs to me now."

"Stop talking about me like I'm a piece of meat. No one owns me," Eliza chided sternly, sounding pissed.

"Uh huh," I goaded, nodding toward her in acknowledgement of what she'd said. "Whatever ... she might be with you for now, but she's only marking time," I suggested, goading him.

"Greg Booker," Eliza ground out in a warning. My eyes darted toward her, and her mouth was set in a line which informed me how frustrated she was with me. That condescending look almost killed me.

"Right," I muttered, knowing for once when to stop. Besides, I was in no fit state to challenge Owen Murphy. I'd likely embarrass both Eliza and me if I had let the standoff continue.

"Come on, baby, let's get out of here," Owen demanded. As Owen slid an arm around Eliza's waist, I growled. Raff slapped a hand on my shoulder to stop me from moving in on him.

Leading her out of the bar, Owen looked back over his shoulder. "In the future, I'll thank you to leave Eliza the fuck alone," he ordered.

"Or?" I challenged on impulse because I wasn't going to let a jumped-up little shit like Murphy order me around.

When he smirked, shook his head and turned away, I made to go after him. Raff caught me by my arm and stopped me dead.

"Dude ... that's a bad idea. I believe you could take him, but probably not tonight. And not for Eliza's sake. Think with that drunken head of yours not the one in your pants. You're pissed drunk and beating up her boyfriend isn't going to improve your relations with Floyd's sister now, is it?"

My jaw ached until Beth reminded me of something Eliza said. "Sounds to me like that girl wants to be claimed. If she was into that guy, she would never have made her 'no one owns me' statement."

I wandered over to Beth, grabbed her head and pressed a quick kiss to her lips.

"My thoughts exactly, sweetheart. If I know my Lizzie like I think I do, Owen Murphy's shot with her will be over soon."

CHAPTER 34

ELIZA

"What the hell were you doing, letting Booker go head-to-head with you like that?" Owen barked as we reached his car. He opened his door and climbed in, leaving me standing in the street. I climbed in beside him and noted the tension inside between us immediately.

"I asked you a question," he probed, turning to look at me. His knuckles were blanched white as his hands gripped the steering wheel.

I was still reeling from what had just happened in the bar and had yet to process it. A visual, of the soul-searching gaze in Greg's beautiful green eyes flashed through my mind. So, I closed my eyes and took a deep breath, as I relieved the moment.

"I'm waiting, Eliza," Owen prompted, breaking into the tender thought.

I opened my eyes and stared blankly at his face, then realized I felt nothing for him. I knew then and there that continuing to date him was pointless. I shrugged. "Honestly? I don't know why that happened."

"What the fuck do you mean, you don't know?"

I shrugged again. "I ... I can't explain it. He almost fell over and I caught him. Then before I could consider what was happening, his forehead was pressed to mine."

"I didn't see you doing much to push him away," Owen challenged as he started the car and began to drive us home.

I shrugged. "True. I'll admit to that. I don't expect you to understand the connection we once had—"

"You're right, I don't," he snapped, cutting me off. He banged his palm angrily on the steering wheel. "I never knew what you saw in him. That guy was the class joke. Now, you're either with him or with me," he barked again. For a second my heart stilled, then in a moment of clarity I digested his words. Although his ultimatum was on a much smaller scale than the one I'd given Greg, it was an ultimatum, nevertheless.

In that instant, I understood that I had to do what was right for me. Just like Greg had done when he'd gone to join the band.

"You know what? I don't think this is going to work," I said, wagging a finger between us. "Even though I'm not with Greg, my history with him makes it impossible for you not to compete with my past. What happened tonight was pure coincidence, even if I can't begin to unpick what you just saw in the bar between us."

"Ha! And there it is. Us. You said us because you still think of the two of you as an us. I never stood a chance with you ... not now that he's back in the picture."

"You don't stand a chance because instead of proving you're a man that is worthy of my time, you chose to bitch about my past with my ex. Greg Booker will always be in my life, in one way or another. Floyd and Greg are like brothers. Greg's had years to come home for me and he didn't. He's here for Floyd. But you have so many bad feelings about Greg that he would always come between us."

We both fell silent as the hostile atmosphere in the car became oppressive. Once we arrived at my place, he just stared straight ahead and made no attempt to talk to me.

"Thanks for bringing me home," I said, opening the door and stepping out. I'd barely closed the car door again before he zoomed off down the street, then turned so fast at the junction that his tires squealed.

Inhaling deeply, I stared up at the night sky. Then I growled and stamped my feet right there in the street. "Men. They're more fucking trouble than they're worth," I muttered as I stomped up the pathway to my family home and let myself in.

"Eliza," my ma called out from the living room.

"Coming." Taking off my jacket, I hung it up in the hallway and headed to see what she wanted. A soft smile spread on her lips as I pushed open the living room door.

"Did you have a good time, sweetheart?"

"No, I bloody well didn't. Between Greg Booker and Owen Murphy, I'm sworn off men," I replied.

"I thought you said Owen was nice," she queried, looking puzzled.

"I did, but that was before Greg Booker showed his ugly face back in Ireland."

My ma chuckled. "I don't think any woman could find Greg ugly. That's the hurt in you talking, Eliza."

I growled. "That dick was in the same bar as Owen and me tonight, and as usual he took pride of place."

Ma sat up straighter. "Sit. Tell me what happened," she prompted, gesturing toward the seat next to her.

Huffing out a breath I sat heavily on the couch and poured my heart out. When I'd finished, she frowned.

"I hate to tell you this, but you've still got it bad for Greg."

"No, I haven't," I barked, insistent that it was Owen's jealousy that had made me call time on us.

"And lying to yourself is only going to create a new world of hurt," she added in contradiction to my protest.

"I mean what the hell did he think he was doing, telling his bandmate I was the love of his life? I'm sure he only did that to fuck with my head. And another thing. You know he bought a house and he's moving Floyd in there tomorrow?" My ma nodded. "Well, the latest is that I'm to move in as well—to help Ruth with the girls in the mornings, before work."

My ma nodded. "I think that's fair. She's going to have a lot on her plate, so that makes sense. I only wish I was fitter, then I'd move in there to help too."

Our ma suffers from Rheumatoid Arthritis which has slowly reduced her mobility. Nowadays she used a walker or a cane to get around the house. She had been newly diagnosed right before Greg joined Screaming Shadows, and although Greg hadn't known about my ma's condition, this was one of the main reasons why I'd refused to go and live thousands of miles away.

"Yeah, but Greg is moving in with his bodyguard as well. That's going to be hard for us both. I mean, I'm barely speaking to the man. The last thing I need is to catch feelings for him again, and for him to leave like he did the last time."

"Eliza, be honest with yourself. You can't catch anything because your heart is already riddled with feelings for Greg Booker."

"You haven't seen him since he's been back, Ma," I whined. "It would help if he'd gotten uglier, but he hasn't. And the adoring look he gave me earlier—how the hell am I going to cope with shit like that?"

My ma eyed me skeptically and shook her head. "Do you know

how many woman would give their right arm for a man like Greg to look at them, the way I've seen him look at you?"

"That was years ago, Ma. Long before he had all these glamorous women falling over themselves for him."

"It's been years, Eliza. If glamor was what turned Greg's head, he would have been taken by now. Have you ever heard of him being with a long-term girlfriend since you?"

"No ... but—"

"No buts—go to bed, think on that, then get some sleep. You're going to have your work cut out, working at the factory and sorting out Aria and Myra."

"I know she needs help, but what about you?" I asked, concerned.

"How many times have I told you, I'm fine. Your life was affected enough by your da without me being a burden to you. I won't have you fretting about me. I have my usual carer four times a day, and Martha's only next door. You know how fabulous she is," she reminded me about our neighbor and ma's close friend. "Martha pops in to watch TV with me most nights. I'm perfectly happy."

"Right, but I'll be coming back and forth to the house, to make sure you're okay."

"Don't worry about me. Besides, I think it'll be good for you to spend time with Ruth and your brother."

Ma was right about that. It had been a long time since I'd spent quality time with Ruth and Floyd. So, after my discussion with my independent mother, I swore to try to look at my temporary house move as positive—even if I was worried about how I would cope around Greg.

CHAPTER 35

GREG

"Is there any chance Raff could pick up Eliza's suitcase from my ma's?" Floyd asked as I supported him with his walker, while we headed for the indoor pool.

My heart fluttered excitedly at the mention of Eliza's name, despite my determination to play it cool with her. I was still disappointed with myself that I'd been caught off guard by her presence the night before.

"No problem," I replied.

Floyd had been discharged home from the hospital to my house earlier that day. Fortunately, I had done a deal to buy the contents of the house as well. So, after a brief tour of it to acclimate him to his new surroundings, he had lunch and a nap.

My mate was the kind of guy who had never let the grass grow under his feet, so he'd arranged for his physiotherapist to call, to get started on his rehabilitation.

Floyd sat on a chair by the pool while the private physiotherapist I'd hired, helped him out of his jeans. This pause gave me time to text Raff to organize a cab to collect Eliza's luggage.

"Want me to stay?" I asked Floyd, giving him the choice. He was a proud man and the last thing I wanted to let him think was that he was dependent on any of us.

He shook his head. "Nah, I'm fine. Go relax for a while."

"We should be about an hour," the physio told me, helping Floyd to stand. I watched with bated breath as Floyd sat at the edge of the pool and eased himself into the water with his strong arms. The instant his body was submerged, he kicked back and swam on his back.

I breathed a sigh of relief when I saw he could get himself out of trouble if necessary. "Okay, I'll be back then and I'll bring fresh clothes for you to change into for dinner."

Raff: Can't get a cab, it's rush hour. Heading to the address to pick it up myself. DON'T GO ANYWHERE WITHOUT ME!

The doorbell rang as I was walking back along the hallway. Ruth came out of the living room, and waited until I was out of view before she opened it.

"Geez, you're soaked. You should have rung Floyd or me. I'd have come to get you," Ruth muttered. As she appeared to know who it was, I stepped into view.

Eliza stood looking adorably drenched to the skin, in a tight, black, pencil skirt and heels. Her cotton blouse had turned see-through as it clung to her chest, revealing a white lacy bra. I'd never seen her look sexier.

I became fascinated by how her pale, wet skin glistened as rivulets of rainwater dropped from her updo auburn hair, then streamed down her cheeks, past her neck and disappeared into her cleavage.

"Dear God, woman, did you swim here dressed like that?" I asked playfully, snapping out of my mesmerized state.

Eliza smirked, but just shook her head, obviously too tired to argue back after her day at work. I walked over to the cloakroom in the hallway, grabbed a towel, and handed it to her.

"Come on. I'll show you to your room," I offered. Without

waiting for her to argue I headed for the stairs, leaving her no choice but to follow me.

The room I had given her was the first at the top of the stairs opposite mine. First because I wanted her near me, and secondly because, if Floyd needed help other than Ruth, Eliza and I would be nearest. Raff was in one of the other two bedrooms at the far end of the hallway to the back of the house, separated by a family bathroom on one side and a large linen closet on the other.

"This is lovely," she remarked as I led her into the mainly cornflower blue room, accented with creams and light shades of gold.

"Good, I'm glad you approve," I said, pleased she liked it.

Lifting her hands to her head, Eliza untied her hair, bent over and shook her long, wet locks out. Standing straight, she casually towel-dried her hair, oblivious as to how sexy she looked as she did that.

She continued to look a hot, sexy mess as she kicked off her wet heels and padded in her stocking feet over to the window. "Did my suitcase arrive?"

"It should be here any minute. Raff has gone to your ma's to collect it himself. Wait here …" I said, leaving her room and cutting across to mine. Grabbing a clean, white T-shirt and a pair of boxer briefs I'd never worn from my suitcase, I took them back to her. "Here, you can change into these until he gets here," I said, holding them out.

"I'm not wearing your clothes," she muttered flatly, frowning darkly.

"It's either these or you sit naked until they arrive. Floyd only gave me the message ten minutes ago, so your luggage might be a while."

"You're seriously asking me to wear your briefs?"

"If you're worried you might catch something, I've never worn them," I explained, hurt by her reaction. "All I am offering is a kind gesture, Eliza. Wear them or don't. I don't care," I lied, leaving them on the bed. "I'll leave you to get settled. Raff will bring your suitcase once it arrives."

Leaving her standing in her wet clothes from the rain, I left her room and began to go downstairs.

"Fuck you, Greg, playing the martyr like I'm some damsel in distress."

I briefly stopped when I heard her speak, but after hearing her pissy comment, I chuckled. Her behavior was Eliza all over, stubborn as fuck. However, as obstinate as she was, I wouldn't have wanted her any other way.

"Dinner's at 7:00 p.m. Ruth wants to eat without the kids. When you're done cussing me out, and you've found your sociable side, you're welcome to join us," I called back from the stairs.

The groan she let out, told me she was mortified I had heard her. Smiling, satisfied I had gotten the last word in, I continued down the stairs.

CHAPTER 36

ELIZA

*E*ntering the ensuite bathroom, I caught sight of myself in the mirror. My eyes almost bulged out of my head at the sight of my soaked blouse and I slapped my hands over my breasts.

"Fuck. You can be such a smart-ass sometimes. I can almost see my nipples through this stupid shirt," I mumbled to myself. "And—you're going to get locked up at this rate. Since Greg Booker's been back, you've done nothing but talk to yourself," I grumbled aloud, wagging a finger at my reflection in the mirror.

Stripping out of my wet clothing, I turned on the shower and stepped into the hot water. It instantly calmed me down, then it wasn't long before I felt the animosity within me slowly wash away.

Refreshed and warmed up from the power shower, I decided that perhaps I'd been hasty in how I'd responded to Greg's offer of clothing.

Still naked, I tiptoed back into the bedroom to retrieve the T-shirt from the bed, where Greg had left it.

I was six tiptoe paces into the room before I realized I wasn't there alone. Shocked, I let out such a blood-curdling scream that

Greg appeared in my bedroom in seconds. Meanwhile, his bodyguard stood frozen, mid-stride with my suitcase still in his hand.

Instead of darting back into the bathroom like any normal person would, my mind went blank so I instantly dropped to the floor, and curled up in a ball.

"What the fuck?" I heard Greg ask his bodyguard as I lay mortified with my eyes closed. The air around me shifted, then I felt a warm towel being draped over me.

"How the fuck was I to know she was in there?" Raff mumbled, sounding amused. "You never said she was here when I passed you downstairs in the hallway."

"You could have fucking knocked," Greg barked.

"I did. She didn't reply."

"Right, out," Greg demanded.

I heard the door close then I felt the air shift again and Greg's presence next to me. Laying a hand on my back, he mumbled, "Come on, he's gone you can get up now."

"No, I'm naked," I muttered back, sounding defeated.

"I know, I saw," he said, chuckling. "The way I see it, you have two choices. You can stay there rolled up like a fetus under a towel, or you can stand up, wrap the towel around you and get clothes out of your suitcase, since my T-shirt wasn't good enough for you."

"You need to leave. I'm naked," I muttered again.

He chuckled again. "We've established that. I even saw that for myself. Gorgeous body by the way."

"I don't want you to see my body," I mumbled in a whiny tone.

"Baby, I've kissed and licked every delectable fucking inch of your delicious body. What's the point in being shy now?"

"It's different. We're not together," I snapped.

"Oh, I didn't know that was a thing," he remarked. "You never used to be shy about me seeing you naked."

"Can you just not be an asshole by continuing to fucking argue with me, and leave please?"

He sighed. "Alright, have it your way," he agreed. "But I just want to say, in wet clothes or no clothes, you look amazing today."

By 6:50 p.m. I was starving, having only had a slice of toast to eat that morning. Usually, I had dinner at 5.30 p.m. with my ma, so although I would have preferred to skip going downstairs and facing everyone, I had little choice but to do it.

Wearing a pair of black yoga pants, a tank top and a fleece over the top of this, I was modestly dressed as I wandered into the dining room. Raff and Greg were already seated with my brother at the table. And from the loud conversation they'd clearly been drinking whiskey.

"Ah, there she is. Have you recovered from your embarrassment?" Greg asked, instantly going where I'd rather have forgotten. Raff snickered and from the condemning look he gave me, I felt sure that he didn't like me.

"I have. Did you all see enough or would you like a repeat performance of me digging my way to Australia?" I replied, brazening my embarrassment out with a bout of good humor. All three men laughed as I shrugged off my mortification and took a seat beside Floyd.

"Good day at work?" Floyd asked, placing a hand on my back.

"So-so, but it never stopped raining all day. I'm starving because I forgot my umbrella so I couldn't nip out for a sandwich."

Ruth poked her head around the door. "Eliza, would you mind carrying some food to the table?"

I immediately felt dreadful because Ruth had cooked dinner and put two little ones to bed while I'd sat in my room acting childishly from the moment I'd arrived through the front door.

"Sure," I replied, feeling guilty.

Grabbing dishes of mashed potato and green beans I placed them at the center of the table while Ruth brought through chicken, Brussel sprouts and peas. She went back to the oven and took out ribs and some soda bread, while I topped up drinks, and opened a bottle of wine.

"So, Greg was saying you shouldn't give up your day job because you've got no chance as a professional streaker," Ruth remarked with a straight face, as she dropped a dollop of mashed potato on her plate.

"All right, you've had your fun. Cut it the fuck out now or you'll give me indigestion. Anyone would think you'd never seen a naked woman before."

"We did ... a couple of hours ago," Raff informed me, laughing.

"I thought bodyguards were seen and not heard?" I challenged, glaring determinedly toward him.

"I learned from your ex that if I did that, he'd take the piss. I need eyes in the back of my head with this one, or I never know what he'll do next."

"Sounds about right," I conceded. "Greg has a talent for getting himself into trouble, from what I remember."

"Yeah, his wife wasn't too happy when she woke up and found they were married."

My heart stopped with the shockwave that shot through my body and my fork fell out of my hand. Disappointment didn't nearly cover the devastation I felt with Raff's words. "You ... your wife?" My voice was an octave higher than usual as I fought a wave of panic that threatened to overwhelm me.

"You didn't hear the news this side of the pond?" Raff asked, sounding amused again.

Greg didn't break stride in loading his dinner plate but glanced up at me and shrugged, like it was nothing. "It happened."

I fought to remain in my seat because I wanted to run away right then. "Happened? You're married?"

"Was ... I was married ... although I'm not sure if I should say I was married or it was a non-marriage?" he muttered, considering that out loud. "Annie and I got an annulment."

"Annie?" I was conscious that I was repeating most of the keywords he said, but I couldn't stop myself from doing it. "You had a wife called Annie?"

"I did," he mumbled as he cut a piece of chicken and put it in his mouth.

"You didn't know?" Raff asked, glancing toward Floyd. The moment he did this, I believed Floyd and Ruth had heard about this.

"It was a mistake," Greg muttered slowly.

"A mistake?"

"Yeah, we were drunk, and we'd taken some recreational stuff ... it was a bet ... I ... it wasn't my proudest moment."

I scoffed. "And you're mocking me for being embarrassed at being naked in my own room?" I asked sarcastically.

Greg put his fork and knife down, placed his elbows on the table, clasped his hands and rested his chin on them.

"Annie's friend bet Annie she wouldn't ask for a kiss. Well, she did, and I kissed her. That should have been the end of the story." He shrugged. "But as usual ... when in Vegas ... things went too far, and we all got drunk. Then the same woman bet us $10k we wouldn't get married. You know me ... a bet ... a dare ..." Greg shrugged again, opened his hands, and waved them in the air before picking his cutlery up again. "Hence the hasty marriage and annulment. But to clarify my status to you, I'm not currently married. And as far as the Catholic church is concerned, I never was."

"Wow. That stunt confirms everything I thought about you. No risk is a bad risk ... until it is," I argued.

"Did I say that?" he snapped. "It was a stupid mistake, but it ended okay."

"Weren't you supposed to stop him getting into fixes?" I asked Raff.

"I usually do. But I was as sick as a dog that night."

"That was convenient," I remarked, still reeling from the news that Greg could do something so stupid. Or be so drunk that he had no idea what he was doing.

"I'm sure it was the weed. I don't do weed anymore," Greg explained.

"Fuck me, Eliza, give him a break. He's a rock star. Of course, he's going to do stuff that shocks the rest of us," my brother said, defending Greg.

"Floyd McDade, don't you dare defend him. This guy could run off the edge of a cliff and you'd blindly follow him."

"Leave Floyd out of it," Ruth said, coming to Floyd's defense.

"I think I liked her better when she was naked on the floor with nothing much to say for herself," Raff commented.

Raff's off the cuff remark caught me in a weak moment, so in frustration, I grabbed a handful of mashed potato off my plate and slung it straight at his face.

Everyone stilled, stunned into silence because I'd lost control like that. My brain went into meltdown as I sat shocked by what I had done.

Calmly, Raff lifted his napkin and wiped the potato from his expressionless face. "You know what?" he said quietly. "You two are a match made in Heaven." My heart pumped fast as he pushed his chair out and stood up. For a second, I thought he was leaving the table, until he wandered over beside me.

Paralyzed by fear as to what he might do, I couldn't move. After a few beats Raff leaned between Floyd and me on my right and picked up the bowl of Brussel sprouts. "You serve from the left, yes?" he asked as he moved to the other side of me and dumped the green vegetables into my lap.

"That was your one free pass, Eliza. You need to think before you act. Next time you throw something at me, I'll spank your ass —Greg or no Greg."

Raff returned to his seat like nothing had happened and lifted his knife and fork. My eyes darted toward Greg who sat still and didn't react. I felt relieved that he hadn't reacted.

"These ribs are amazing, Ruth, what kind of sauce is this," Greg asked quietly.

Ruth answered him while everyone else resumed eating like nothing had happened, until Greg glanced up at me and flashed me a warm smile. "Would you mind passing me a few more sprouts, darlin'?"

Realizing my chest was tight and my heart was pounding from fright, I huffed out a breath. "I'm really sorry I did that," I mumbled to Raff. "I've had such a rough day," I mumbled again, as I began picking the sprouts off my legs.

"Apology accepted. Now perhaps you can put that temper of yours on hold until we finish our dinner," Raff replied, sounding authoritative.

Embarrassed, I glanced back down at my lap with tears in my eyes, surprised Greg was allowing him to talk to me that way. Then I continued to pick the spouts one by one and place them back in the bowl.

"I'm sorry too, Lizzie," Greg said, sounding genuinely apologetic.

"For?" I asked sarcastically, still staring at my lap.

"Taking the piss ... for getting married while in a drunken stupor ... for ... being me, I guess."

"Never apologize for being you, Greg. I've never met a more honest person. I count myself lucky that I know the man behind what we read in the papers. It would seem only a few people get to know who you are beyond your public reputation," Floyd remarked.

My brother's words were sobering because everything Floyd had said was true.

With my feelings more in control, I looked up. "Floyd's right. I'll accept your apology for the first two things. But you should never apologize for who you are. I know I get frustrated sometimes but no one wants you to change that crazy side of your personality. It was why I fell in love with you in the first place."

Greg's gorgeous green eyes softened as he looked across the table at me. But the moment I felt his gaze grow intense, I went back to cleaning my lap.

"Well, since the vibe in the room has turned amicable again, I think it might be safe to offer everyone another glass of wine," Ruth stated flatly.

CHAPTER 37

GREG

"A word," I said calmly to Raff after dinner. Everyone left the kitchen and went into the living room, when I pulled him aside.

"I know I'm your boss but we're friends, right?" He nodded, his eyes narrowing to study my mood. "I think we can both agree that what Lizzie did at the dinner table wasn't cool. So, don't think I thought that.

"The point I want to make is that she knows she embarrassed herself. She didn't have the words to argue with you. Now, let's face it, you're a huge man—an intimidating man to most. Would you agree?" He shrugged. "If you ever threaten any woman in my company again, no matter the circumstances, you're gone."

"You saw what she did," he protested in disbelief, looking shocked. "I'm your bodyguard, not hers. I don't need to take shit from people like that."

"People like that?" I remarked. "She's a woman. And I've admitted that I'm unhappy with what she did. But if that's all it takes to make you so pissed that you'd threaten a woman, then maybe you're in the wrong job. I'm the first to admit us guys all behave badly, and you, Bodhi and Mikey put up with a lot of shit. However, Lizzie is an ordinary girl, not some badly behaved groupie that can shrug comments off.

"That girl suffered the most horrific domestic violence at the hands of her father for years before he died. So, when you make physical threats toward her, the effect of your words doesn't bounce off like it might in the circles we move in."

"Fuck, I wasn't thinking like that."

"I know, and that's why I've waited until now to talk to you. The last thing I would have done is to make a scene at the table. That would only have exacerbated the situation."

"I apologized. Do you want me to talk to her about it?" Raff said, genuinely concerned.

His reaction confirmed what I'd always thought about Raff. He was a good guy, a great guy, which was why I was warning him and not booting his arse out the door.

"I'll speak with her. I imagine she was already freaking out about needing to be here at the house. Then there was the incident up there in her room. But I agree, she needs to manage herself better. Meanwhile, please just be mindful of the words you choose around her."

"Fuck, I get it. And I really am sorry ... not for the sprouts, she deserved those ... but the spanking part," he clarified.

I smirked. "The sprouts were funny ... mashed potato even better," I replied.

He gave me a wry smile. "Thanks, Greg. Do you want me to step back? Ask Mikey or Bodhi to come over?"

"Fuck, no, I just need you to be more mindful, that's all."

"I will. Eliza ... kid gloves from now on," he muttered.

It was only 8:30 p.m. by the time Floyd was worn out and retired for the night. Ruth went with him, glad to have her man back in her bed beside her.

Deakon called, asking us to go out. So, I swore to Raff I would be staying in and he went off to look after my bandmate. As I passed the living room, Eliza was watching TV. I knocked gently on the door to catch her attention.

"Would you mind some company?" I asked softly, praying she'd say yes.

She glanced toward the TV where she had been watching a program about an off-grid, cabin community, and then back toward me. "No, this is nearly finished though."

"That's fine, I've seen this already," I informed her. Instead of choosing a seat away from her I sat next to her on the couch. Eliza stiffened but didn't look at me, keeping her focus on the TV. We sat quietly until the credits rolled before I spoke. "About earlier," I began.

"Totally my fault. I embarrassed myself," she said, making a cutting motion with her hand like she was drawing a line under the incident.

"Which time? When you flashed yourself or when you hit my 6'5" bodyguard with mashed potatoes?" I asked playfully to lighten the mood.

She smirked. "Fuck ... your bodyguard saw me," she mumbled mortified again.

"Baby, don't sweat it. Sure, he got an eyeful of a beautiful woman, as I did," I said, nudging her shoulder with mine. "You can relax, it was probably the highlight of his week. I doubt he'll be bleaching his eyes anytime soon." She chuckled. "But there is something I wanted to clear up with you. Raff was out of order threatening to spank you like that."

Eliza shrugged. "I knew exactly what you and Floyd were both doing when neither of you reacted to that. It helped that you didn't defend me. You and my brother know any escalation to Raff's initial comment would only have made my anxieties escalate more."

I nodded, reached out and held her hand. "I want you to know I've spoken to Raff, and he's sorry."

"He shouldn't be. I started it."

"No, technically he did with his crass remark. I'm not going to defend what he did. However, I will say that he's dug me out of more holes than anyone else ever has. Raff's the guy you want in your corner if you are ever in trouble. He's normally calm and level-headed. Everything he does is measured. I mean look how carefully he poured those sprouts in your lap."

Eliza laughed. "He must wonder what you ever saw in me," she mumbled.

"See in you, Lizzie," I corrected. "You're the most beautiful woman I've ever met ... a loving woman, with a difficult past. And I hurt you. I know this, but I can't change the past.

"However, I'm here, trying to make amends. Even if that means we can only be friends—I'll take it. I have never hidden how I feel about you, but my schedule overseas is as hectic as ever."

"I know," she said quietly in resignation.

"I'll admit that I could have come home more often. But in the beginning, it was easier not to see you. That was supposed to give you space since you blocked me everywhere. Not being with you ... seeing you, it almost killed me. Then, as time passed and you didn't reach out well ... all those other women became a way of dealing with how much hurt I had inside."

She stared at the TV again for a minute before she turned back to me. "I don't know if I can do this," she confessed.

I frowned. "Do what?"

"Be here ... live with you like this, knowing you'll be leaving again."

"So, you still love me?"

She nodded her gaze softening with pain. "I think I'll always love you ... even if it's from a distance."

My heart raced with the window of opportunity she'd handed me. "Then come with me."

Eliza stared pointedly and sighed. "Don't."

I nodded even though I hated the thought of another frustrated rejection. "Owen?"

Eliza scoffed. "What about him?"

"Do you love him?"

"You know ... I don't even think I like him," she replied with a raised brow.

I chuckled. "Good—he's a knob."

She nodded in agreement, smiling. "That's a good word for him."

"You know, in the past, people have asked me, why you?" I admitted.

Eliza winced. "I know they see me as difficult, hard to handle, not easy to love ..." she trailed off, one shoulder lifting in a half shrug as she toyed nervously with the remote in her hand.

"Lizzie, you've got that wrong. Loving you comes so easy to me. It's the easiest thing I've ever done in my life. Living without you—has been the hardest."

Tears sprang to her hazel eyes, and she looked down at her lap. "Too much has happened since we were together ... but I think it would help if we tried to be friends."

My heart sunk because I'd felt our conversation had been going so well that for a brief time, I believed I was making headway with her.

"Okay since I spend nine months of the year in the US and you still refuse to come with me, I guess friends is what we will be." The ache I felt in my heart grew exponentially once I admitted that fact to myself. Then, I began to regret asking Eliza to stay at the house.

"You can go back to your ma's if this is too uncomfortable for you," I said, giving her an out.

"No, you're right. Ruth and Floyd need all the support we can give them, I'll be happy to stay now that we've cleared the air."

"Can we hug it out?" I asked, holding my arms out because I didn't know what else to say.

For a moment she stared longingly into my eyes before she replied, "Okay."

Once Eliza made the first move, I enveloped her in my arms. This time, there wasn't the same initial tension in her warm body as I'd felt the previous times. And the feel of her small frame as it melded into mine had never felt so right.

The moment her soft cheek rested against my hard chest, I instinctively slid one hand up, and protectively cradled her head against it.

A sign she was crying only registered with me when my T-shirt began to feel wet. I leaned back to look at her. "Lizzie, are you okay?"

"Yeah ... just emotional."

I swallowed back a lump in my throat at her response, kissed the top of her head and moved my hand from her head to rub her back. "You must be tired. Come on, let's turn this off and you can get into bed."

Nodding, she pulled away. My heart felt heavier the moment we lost touch. Stifling a sigh, I grabbed the remote, turned off the TV and followed her out to the hallway. Side by side we climbed the stairs until we reached the landing.

"What time do you need to leave for work in the morning?"

"There's a bus at 7:45 a.m.," she replied.

"What time do you start?"

"8:15 a.m."

"Then I'll take you. We'll be ready to leave here at 8:00."

"Really? Thanks, Greg," she replied, sounding grateful.

"What for?"

"Being you ... beneath that sexy rock star thing you've got going on, you're still Greg Booker. It seems you are still the same fabulous, caring guy you always were."

"I'll take that," I said, smiling. Leaning forward I cradled her head in my hands, pressed a kiss to her forehead and breathed in her scent again. "Night, Lizzie. Let me know if you need anything."

As she turned to go to her room, I felt her reluctance to leave me. Watching her door close tore me up. Everything in me wanted to go with her because nothing would have pleased me more than if I held her all night in my arms like I used to.

With a heavy heart, I climbed into bed and stared up at the ceiling. The bed was comfortable, but the amount of tossing and turning I did, anyone would think it was a cold, hard, concrete slab. I should have been tired after the day I'd had, receiving Floyd and his family to the house. But my mind just wouldn't shut off.

Knowing Eliza lay sleeping less than twenty feet away across the hall didn't help either. So near ... the nearest we'd been to each other in years—yet she might as well have been a thousand miles away.

And so, the cyclic questions began in my mind as they'd done thousands of times. What could I do to help her let go of her past? How could I show her she could trust me? Then, I searched for solutions for how I could be with her, and still live across the pond for most of the year?

Other couples did it, but I supposed it only worked, if there was trust. Considering my behavior since I'd joined the band, with all the well-documented one-night stands I'd had, I guessed she never figured she would now.

At some point I must have drifted off to sleep but woke to the sound of whimpering in the distance. It was a sound I knew well—Eliza softly crying in her sleep.

Throwing the duvet back, I pulled on some briefs, padded across the hallway, and opened her bedroom door. Her crying sounded way louder once I'd opened the door.

"Lizzie?" I murmured softly as I stepped closer to the bed. Her head thrashed back and forth in distress during her nightmare. I knew not to touch her, so I tried to gently rouse her by talking to her again. "Lizzie, baby, wake up," I muttered with a little more force behind my tone.

"Huh," she mumbled as she sat bolt upright in the bed and clutched her duvet to her chest.

"It's okay, it's me. You were having a nightmare, baby."

Eliza flopped back against her pillows and covered her face with her hands. "God ... sorry," she croaked.

"It was a bad one, huh?" I asked, validating her fears.

"Even though my da's dead, I still hate him."

"I know," I said, tucking my foot under my arse as I sat on the bed beside her.

"Well, that's all the sleep I'll be getting tonight," she confessed.

I remembered that about her. She couldn't fall back to sleep unless I stayed with her.

"Do you want me to stay?" I asked warily, like it might open a can of worms for both of us.

"No," she muttered quickly.

"You sure?" I probed.

"I do ... but it might be too hard for me ... for us," she confessed.

"I'll take my chances," I said, lifting the duvet and getting into the bed beside her. "Come here," I ordered, lifting her arm, and sliding my arm under her neck. Reluctantly, she turned over and rested her head on my chest.

For a few seconds she lay awkward against the side of my body, then I heard her swallow roughly before she sighed, and I felt her relax into me. Inhaling deeply, I breathed out a contented sigh as I wrapped my arms around her and tucked her closer to my side. "Better?"

"Yes and no," she muttered.

I chuckled. "Same," I confessed as I lifted my head and kissed the top of hers. "I know this feels messy, but we'll deal with that later. Don't overthink this. Just take the comfort I'm offering and get some sleep."

CHAPTER 38

ELIZA

My alarm buzzed annoyingly on the nightstand as I rolled over in bed and turned it off. Then it dawned on me that I was alone in the bed.

Did I dream that Greg was here last night? The nightmare felt real enough.

Turning over, I grabbed my pillow and inhaled its scent. It smelled like Greg.

I headed to the shower, then got ready for work.

Floyd was still in bed when I went downstairs and found Ruth in the kitchen. Both girls were at the table, Myra in her highchair.

"Hello, Auntie Eliza," Aria squealed as she jumped down from her chair and wrapped her hands around my skirt in a hug.

"Aria. Don't get cornflakes on Auntie Eliza's work clothes," Ruth admonished.

I bent to meet my niece eye-to-eye. "If you did, that hug would have made it worth it," I said, winking.

Baby Myra pointed at me with her chubby finger, blew a series of raspberries and focused back on the bowl of fruit that sat on her tray.

"Exactly," I mumbled as I slid onto a seat, grateful for the cup of coffee Ruth had placed in front of me. "Alright, who am I getting dressed today?" I asked glancing from one girl to the other.

"Me!" Aria exclaimed, jumping down from her chair again and bouncing on her toes.

"And me," Greg's sexy, low tone murmured softly from behind me. Goosebumps riddled my body as I turned to look up at him, shirtless, bare-footed, his jeans hanging low on his hips.

"No, Greg-Greg, Auntie Eliza is getting me ready for school," Aria admonished. "Mammy can do you," she replied.

"I think your da would have something to say if your ma did me," Greg replied, loading my niece's reply with innuendo she had no idea about it.

Ruth laughed. "Hm, you could be right."

Greg's cell phone rang, distracting him from the conversation. He frowned as he fished it out of his pocket and saw who was calling. "I need to take this," he muttered as he wandered back out in the hallway.

"Hey, Jesus, I'm sorry I didn't get back to you yet," I heard him say softly. Don't ask me why, but there was something in the way he answered that made me believe it was a call from a woman.

I glanced at the time and calculated back five hours from Miami time.

"Wonder whose calling him at this time in the morning? It's only 2:30 a.m. in the US," I mused aloud.

"Rock stars never keep office hours, Eliza. Greg has been known to call Floyd at all hours of the day and night. He doesn't pay attention to time zones," Ruth informed me as she buttered some toast, cut it into small slices and placed it on Myra's tray.

"I've got a feeling it was a woman," I said flatly.

"What if it is?" Ruth replied, obviously tired of me after the way I'd behaved the night before.

Amy Winehouse mocked me on the radio singing "You Know

I'm No Good" as my heart stung while stared back at my sister-in-law.

I shrugged. "I'm just sayin'."

"Are you coming?" Aria interrupted us, tugging at my skirt hem.

"Sure. Take me to your room and we'll have you ready for school in no time."

By 7:50 a.m., Floyd was up and in the pool with the physiotherapist, while Ruth buckled both kids in their car seats and headed off to her house to pick up some more of their belongings before she dropped Aria at school.

I was shrugging myself into my suit jacket when Greg reappeared downstairs, dressed and ready to take me to work. Picking up a car key from the hall table, he smiled. "Ready?" he asked. My heart leapt from the appraising look he took of me, and I nodded.

Greg surprised me by opening the car door for me before getting into the car himself and began to drive.

"How did you sleep?" he asked as he concentrated on the road ahead.

"It's a comfortable bed," I informed him, still apprehensive of what happened in my bed before.

"Yeah, mine is too. I must check out the make of the mattress. I could do with a new one in the band's penthouse at home."

"Why have you worn the one you have out?" I asked, then cussed myself for my too quick, snarky inference.

"Are you asking if I fuck women in my bed there, Lizzie? If so, the answer is no. We never shit where we eat. No one takes females other than partners back to our communal space," he replied bluntly.

Just the inference of him fucking women at all made my chest tighten and my heart ache.

"I'm sorry ... that just came out. What you do is none of my business."

Greg stole a glance at me before turning back to the road. "You know, it doesn't need to be like this, Lizzie. Just say the word and I'll take you with me," he told me sincerely.

His offer made my heart flip over because it was so unexpected. I fell silent, wishing it were that easy. But I knew better than anyone, love, faithfulness and trust didn't necessarily go together. My ma trusted my da when she married him and look at the life she had—the life she has now that her best years are behind her. Being left alone with a mobility condition isn't how she envisaged her life turning out.

As we rounded the corner to the factory that I managed, I tried to lighten the mood. The last thing I needed was to spend the day all broody about my last words to Greg before he'd dropped me off.

"I must say, you're full of surprises. You're such a careful driver," I praised, changing the subject. "When did you pass your test?"

"Test?" he smirked. "I haven't taken a test."

"You're joyriding?" his disclosure sent a bolt of electricity through me with shock.

"Jesus, Eliza, don't be so dramatic. I've been watching Raff, Bodhi and Mikey driving for years. It's not that hard. The trickiest part is knowing what the street signs and lines on the road mean.

"You drove me to work without a driver's license? Are you crazy?"

"I got you here in one piece, didn't I?" he challenged.

"Fuck, Greg. You could have gotten us both killed," I admonished.

"But I didn't," he said deadpan. "Do you want picked up tonight?" he asked like our safety didn't matter.

Leaning over, I swiped the key from his car. "I'm getting the bus home ... and so are you. I'm not letting you drive this machine. It's a deathtrap without someone qualified at the wheel."

"Give me the key, Lizzie," he said tiredly, holding his hand out.

"No. You could die," I shrieked.

"Promise, I won't," he replied deadpan, looking innocently toward me.

Quickly, I opened the door and got out. "No. Call Raff to come get you. I'll give him the key." With my heart pounding in shock, I left him sitting in the car, and pulled my cell phone out as I made my way into the factory.

"Ruth, is that you?" I asked when she answered.

"You know it is, I'm on speed dial on your phone," she replied sarcastically.

"Get Raff up and tell him to get his ass over to my factory. Greg's outside in the car."

"Is he being mobbed?" she asked, sounding alarmed.

I sighed. "No. The point is that he drove me to work, and he doesn't have a fucking driver's license."

"What?" she yelled.

"You heard me," I snapped. "The guy had a cheek to ask if I wanted him to pick me up after work. I've taken the key off him, and he won't be getting it back. So, get Raff's ass in an Uber to get down here and rescue him.

"And you all wonder why I wouldn't go to the US with him? I must admit, my resistance was waning since he's been back, but this has reminded me, Greg Booker is a law unto himself. Give Raff my number and get him to call me when he gets here."

CHAPTER 39

GREG

The tight, thin line on Raff's lips warned me that I was in trouble the second he stepped onto the pavement from an Uber.

"What happened to the promise you made to me?"

"That was a promise for the US. You never said anything about what I couldn't do here," I argued, not knowing whether that was the truth. "Anyway, all I was doing was driving Lizzie to work. I thought I'd only be out of the house for half an hour."

"She's got the keys to this," he said, circling his finger in the air inside the car. "Want to tell me why?"

I chuckled. "I was stupid, but I couldn't help fucking with her."

"After everything you told me about being wary of her mindset, and you go and do that? Come on, tell me …" he muttered, making a winding motion with his index finger for me to get on with it.

"Okay. She asked me when I passed my test … and I asked, what test?"

Raff caught on straight away, bit back a smile and barely managed a frown. "So, you let her think you had no driving license?"

I nodded then chewed the inside of my cheek so as not to laugh.

"Well," he said holding his hands up to gesture that I was sitting stranded because of my joke. "Like I said, she knows how to handle you. You know, I've got a mind to catch an Uber back to the house and let your ragged ass sit here until she finishes work today. Actually, if you weren't famous and I'd lose my job for doing that, it's exactly what I would do."

I nudged his ribs with my elbow. "Come on, you know it's as funny as fuck. You should have seen her face." I chuckled.

"And you told me not to scare her. She's probably traumatized about riding in cars as well now," he muttered deadpan.

"Nah, I know the line. Maybe I just get a kick out of seeing the flames in her eyes, the moment she gets riled up."

"You're playing with fire. That woman must be an incredible lay because I don't know how else to reason your undying love for her. Eliza has the shortest fuse of any woman … or man, that I've ever come across."

"You don't know her like I do, is all."

He sighed. "At least promise me not to piss her off while she's cutting vegetables with a sharp knife, carrying rope, or anything that could do you permanent damage."

"So, are you going to go get the keys?" I asked, laughing, and ignoring his comment. I nodded at the steering wheel.

"Only if you tell me you'll come clean to her and apologize."

"I will, promise," I replied, crossing my heart with my finger.

"Yeah, your promises are like farts in the wind, Greg," he muttered as he opened the passenger door, climbed out and closed it again. A group of young women passed him. And I watched as every one of them glanced back over their shoulder toward him as he stood on the pavement, figuring out how to get in.

Their reaction to Raff showed me what a great looking man he was. Then I considered that he really did have the shit end of this deal in our relationship. I got the fame, the money and the glory, while he got the aggravation. I vowed to myself then and there I'd find something to reward him with.

I WAS in the pool with Floyd when Eliza made it home from work. After helping Floyd get dried and dressed for dinner, I headed back to the kitchen where I'd ordered take out for everyone for dinner. Ruth had already bathed the girls for bed since they'd also been in the pool. She went to settle them down minutes before Raff arrived, having brought Beth, Sadie and Deakon over.

"Nice house," Deakon beamed as he stepped inside and glanced up the staircase.

Ruth came rushing back downstairs, patting her hair, and smiling with her eyes fixed on Deakon.

"Oh, this is Floyd's wife, Ruth. Close your ears, Sadie, she has a crush on our boy, Deakon."

"I. Do. Not," Ruth admonished way to fast.

"She does," Raff and Beth said in a chorus. Sadie laughed, which made Ruth sigh in relief. "Ruth McDade, meet my bandmate, Deakon Brody."

Deakon stepped forward and kissed both cheeks, leaving Ruth looking flustered and holding her bright red cheek.

"Who is that pawing my woman?" Floyd bellowed as he came from the kitchen, using his walker. The physiotherapist insisted he use it after an hour of exercise in the pool.

"Where's the basket for that shopping cart?" Deakon joked about his walking aid.

Floyd laughed. "Get your ugly ass over here and give me a manhug."

Deakon strode toward him but stopped short of my friend. "You gave us all a fright, big man."

"Gave myself an even bigger one," Floyd joked back.

Deakon fell, serious. "All joking aside, what's the verdict?"

"Getting stronger every day. Still some numbness, but the physio reckons I'll be as good as new in three to four months."

Deakon glanced toward me, and I was surprised to see relief in his eyes. "Six and we're going dancing. No jive moves mind you," he joked, winking.

"Right, are we all going to stand here in the hallway, or would you prefer a seat at the kitchen table while we finish the introductions. The takeout food should be here any minute." Ruth gestured toward the kitchen, then everyone followed Floyd.

Leaving them to get seated, I ran up the stairs and knocked on Eliza's door. "Deakon, Sadie and Beth are here," I informed her, before stopping short to take her in. Dressed in a short teal-colored, figure-hugging dress, Eliza looked sensational.

"Right," she muttered quietly, as she grabbed a hairbrush and ran the brush through her hair.

"You look incredible, baby." Eliza ignored my compliment and kept brushing her hair. "I owe you an apology for this morning," I said softly.

"For taking me joyriding?"

I smirked. "It was a joy, taking you to work. But I have a confession to make. We weren't really joyriding. I do have a license. I passed it in the USA about six months after I left here."

"And you let me think …" Her lips flattened in a line of frustration as she looked pointedly toward me.

Before she could tear me down, I stepped toward her, pulled her in for a hug, and held her tight against me. "I agree it was a sick joke. I was about to tell you the truth when you grabbed the keys and left me with a 'fuck you'. But I need to be honest with you. It was either make you mad and get out of the car or I was going to kiss you."

"Don't kiss me," she quickly muttered.

"Not even if I feel that need down to my bones, every time I see you?"

She shook her head. "Maybe I should go back and stay at my ma's?"

"I'd be sad if you did that. But I'd understand. Is that what you want to do?"

Eliza looked thoughtful before lifting her hands in a helpless gesture. "To be perfectly frank, since you've been here, I have no idea what I want," she said honestly.

"Are we going to talk about what happened last night? Or do we pretend that it never happened?" I asked bluntly.

"Last night?" she asked nonchalantly. If it hadn't been for the fast pulse in her jugular vein, I'd have believed she had no idea what I meant.

"The nightmare," I prompted.

"You held me until I fell asleep."

"How often do you still get them?"

She shrugged. "They happened about every other month ... but more since you've come back."

"So, I'm responsible for that sick fuck of a father you had, torturing you in your sleep?"

"No ... I think seeing you has stirred up my feelings ... that's all."

The doorbell rang and I guessed the food had arrived.

"That'll be the food. Can we discuss this later once everyone has gone?"

"Sure, although I don't think there's much more to say than what I've already said."

"Come on," I said, instinctively reaching out and grabbing her hand. Instead of fighting me on my gesture she held it tighter and let me lead her to the door. "You really do look stunning tonight," I mumbled softly, close to her ear.

Her cheeks turned pink at my compliment. "I hate to say it, Greg, but so do you."

"Maybe we should just stay here and fuck all the anger out," I said, stopping to stare into her gorgeous eyes.

"If we did that, we'd likely die of exhaustion in the process," she replied, placing her free hand on my chest, and pushing me back.

I grinned. "See … no one else gets you," I remarked, lifting our hands and pressing a kiss to her knuckles.

"Greg." Her eyes flashed a dark warning to me.

"I was just testing how sharp your knuckles were … in the event you throw a punch."

Eliza let out a genuine laugh which was music to my ears. "Come on, feed me, I'm starving hungry," tugging at my hand for once.

"Me too," I replied, although what I left unsaid was I was most hungry for her.

CHAPTER 40

GREG

It had been a long time since I'd seen Eliza laugh freely, but Deakon, Sadie and Beth's stories, regarding the other guys in the band, had her in hysterics. Especially when Deakon told the story about the guy Joe, that I had replaced, baking a cake, and the time when Korry got Bernadette stoned.

Ruth and Floyd had gone to bed, exhausted but happy around 9:00 p.m., while my friends and I continued to reminisce. Eventually, Raff took the others back to their rental house while Eliza and I tidied up.

"You looked as if you had fun tonight," I remarked as we walked upstairs together.

"I did. They're lovely people, and Deakon thinks a lot of you."

"He's a good guy … he's funny as fuck, and bold. It's only since he got with Sadie that we've really gelled as friends. Levi and Jude are like brothers. I suppose they don't have much time for the rest of us now that they have families to share their time with as well."

"You're the last single guy in the band now … that must bring you a lot of female attention."

I nodded. "I'm not going to lie and say it doesn't. But that shit has gotten old. Seeing the others settled down makes me wonder what I'm missing."

"There's no one that ..." she trailed off, hinting at the question do I have someone else.

"I dunno ... there might have been ..." I admitted, regarding Lori. Even as I said it, I knew Lori was a non-starter now that I'd seen Eliza again.

"I see," she muttered, looking destroyed.

"You asked so ..." My heart clenched when I read the devastation in her eyes.

"No, honesty is important," she muttered bravely. "Right, I'd better get to bed," she said, hitching her thumb over her shoulder. "Good night, Greg. Thanks for tonight ... the food ... and the company," she mumbled as she walked into her room and quietly closed the door.

My heart burned as I stared after her, feeling helpless as to how to fix us. I raised my hands and clasped them behind my head as a lump formed in my throat with that thought. Then I dropped to my knees on the soft carpet, still facing her door. "Fuck."

"You, okay?" Raff mumbled as he came up the stairs and found me still kneeling there.

"Yeah," I replied, glancing up at him.

"Another argument with sunshine in there?" he asked, nudging a thumb in the direction of her door.

I shook my head as I climbed to my feet. "Nah, I need to stop torturing myself about her. She won't budge, and for as long as she has my heart, we'll be doing this forever."

Leaving Raff standing there, I headed into my room, stripped out of my clothes and climbed into bed.

I WOKE startled and disoriented by the same pained cries in the night as I had heard the night before. Once I'd gathered my bearings, I edged my way out of bed and headed across the hall to Eliza's room.

"Lizzie," I muttered, this time moving to her bed and sitting on the edge of it.

"Mm," she mumbled, sounding disoriented. "Was I doing it again? I'm sorry," she said, sounding broken.

"Move over," I ordered as I lifted the duvet and climbed beneath it. Unlike the night before there was no tension as she rolled on her side, lifted her head and placed it on my chest.

"Thanks," she whispered, immediately accepting me with her. She nestled her head on my chest to get comfortable and it felt so natural because she'd done that a thousand times before. Then she slid her hand over my stomach, pausing to graze her fingertips slowly over each divot in my abs. My cock pulsed and I realized I had no underwear on.

"Fuck ... sorry," I mumbled, still half asleep.

"What for?"

"I forgot to put boxer briefs on."

Eliza stiffened a little but didn't reply. She then laid perfectly still until her body relaxed as her breaths deepened and evened out.

Right then I felt the happiest I'd felt in years. It was all I wanted in life—to make music and to be happy. Having Eliza in my arms, holding her, protecting her—showing her what love was—it was what I felt born to do. That was right before my reasoning kicked in again and I remembered I was also born to make music.

Eliza might have fallen back to sleep and slept like a baby in my arms, but it was at least an hour more of thinking before I eventually joined her.

I WOKE from the deepest sleep I'd had in years with Eliza still in my arms. It was 3:30 a.m. The dim glow from the featured lights in the front garden gave off enough light that the room wasn't in complete darkness. Eliza had barely moved all night, except for one of her hands that was currently nestled between my thighs, painfully close to my balls.

Silently cursing my morning wood, I lay quietly and conjured up images of fish guts and any other gross thing that usually turned my stomach, as I willed my cock to go flaccid.

Eliza stirred, I closed my eyes because I wasn't ready to leave her or for any regret I might read on her face. However, I was even less ready for her wandering hand that swept over the soft hairs on my thigh.

The moment that I heard her inhale my scent, my tender heart picked up its pace. The sound of it brought blood rushing through my ears. Then, as if Eliza felt my heartbeat race, she lifted her head off my chest to look at my face. The second I felt as if she was staring at me, I opened my eyes. Immediately the air in the room grew thicker from the instant sexual chemistry there was between us.

Even though I wanted to take her then and there, I lay motionless, wary of what that might mean, but more importantly to gauge Eliza's next move.

Tentatively, she swept her hand up my side, glanced at the tattoo under my left pec then appeared to study it more closely. A small smile curved my lips as she read what it said. As she began to trace the intricate design she found there, I sucked in a breath and held it until she gazed at me in awe.

"Even after everything, you put my name over your heart?" she asked softly, sounding incredulous. I glanced down at the small golden, Irish harp tattooed on my body, with six strings that subtly spelt the name Lizzie."

"Yeah, I didn't know anyone else with six letters to their name?" I teased, playfully. "Floyd only has five."

She smiled then bit her bottom lip for a few seconds. "When did you do this?"

"The day I passed my driving test," I told her with a cocky grin. Eliza rose off me and took a playful swipe at my chest.

Reacting faster than her, I grabbed her wrist, rolled her onto her back and fixed both hands above her head. Then, before I'd stopped to consider what I was doing, the tip of my wet cock brushed over her thighs as I settled my body between her open legs.

The stunned look in Eliza's wide, lust-filled eyes made me realize what I'd done. "Well, fuck. This isn't awkward," I mumbled sarcastically, as I stared down at her serious, searching eyes.

"Not awkward at all," she murmured back humorlessly. She swallowed roughly as desire burned in her gaze. I recognized that look in a heartbeat—she wanted me.

"Fuck, you have no idea how easy it would be to slip your thong out of the way, and slide deep inside you," I openly confessed as I dropped my forehead to hers. "You have no idea how … desperate I've been … to kiss—touch—taste … to fucking consume you." A wave of emotion rendered me speechless while a lump that had formed in my throat reminded me what a bad idea that would be.

For a few seconds we stayed in that position, our souls connected and suspended in time. It felt like we'd entered an emotional no-man's land. It was one surrounded by our mutual desire, passion and endless infatuation toward each other. We had always been aware of the chemical lust there was between us. But in that moment, I was mindful that it had been tainted by years of heartache and pain.

"Please, Lizzie … tell me to leave," I ordered because right then, with her beneath me like I'd dreamed of for years, I hadn't the strength to make that decision myself.

"I can't," she admitted, her voice shaky in response.

"Then you need to know that I'll be leaving here again," I warned.

For a long moment I thought she'd find the strength to push me away. Then she bit her bottom lip, still staring me down, and whispered, "I know." Tears pooled in her eyes. They glistened as she shook her head. "I don't care, make love to me."

"Fuck," I breathed hoarsely in response as both relief and concern for us squeezed at my chest. My hungry eyes searched her face, convinced I had heard her wrongly. And for a long minute, I stared back at her in disbelief. "You need to do better than that, Lizzie. Prove to me this is what you really want."

"Let go of my hand," Eliza ordered, struggling to free her right hand from my grip. Once I did as she asked, she traced her free hand down to my hips. Her sensual touch felt featherlight as it trailed down my V line and eventually gripped my hard length in her fist. As her small hand surrounded my cock, I let out a long hiss.

"Fuck, baby," I breathed as my eyes rolled back in my head while I savored her initial touch. When I opened them again, I saw lust mixed with a desperate, intense look as she held my gaze. Then she began to pump my cock in firm but slow motions.

"Is this convincing enough?" she asked quietly through ragged, excitable breaths.

I stared into her blown, excited pupils. "We're crossing a line," I warned in a husky tone. "I don't want to hurt you … I don't want us to fight about this afterward or what happened to us in the past anymore," I mumbled.

"I need this," she whispered, ignoring my protests. "I'll die if you leave me like this." Any resolve I held within me dissolved the moment she said this. Letting go of the arm I still held above her head, I rose to my knees and sat back on my calves, taking the duvet with me.

"Don't say I didn't warn you that this was a bad idea," I muttered as I lifted her pajama tank top over her head and watched her tits spring free.

"Holy shit, baby," I muttered as I bent forward and immediately sucked hard on one of her perfect, pebbled nipples. I palmed them both in my hands to reacquaint myself with them.

"Oh, Greg," she breathed out as her back bowed sexily off the mattress. The sound of my name on her lips sounded more tender than at any other time since I'd been back.

That made me smile as I moved my mouth from one nipple to the other to pay her girls equal attention. Sitting back on my calves again, I flicked them both hard and gave them both a small playful pat.

"Christ," she muttered as she increased the speed of what she was doing, and my cock grew much firmer.

"Fuck, wait," I said, gripping her hand and releasing her hold on me, because it was my Lizzie doing that and it felt too good, and if she didn't stop right then, she would make me come.

I'd waited years for that moment, I never thought it would happen again, so I willed myself to hold back, to make the most of it.

"I need you inside me," she muttered impatiently, reaching for my cock again.

"And you'll get me ... all in good time, Lizzie," I promised seriously.

Eliza growled, grabbed my hips and tried to pull me down onto her. I stopped her by restraining her wrists firmly on either side of my body.

"Stop. Believe me, baby. If we're doing this, I won't let it be a ten-minute fuck. I need to take my time with you."

Once I was sure she was back in control, I released her wrists and reached for the sides of her thong. Slowly, I tugged on the thin material and began to take it off. Eliza lifted her arse to let me pull it free from under her.

The moment I'd stripped her bare, I ran my hands lightly over her silky skin, from her feet, up over her shins, thighs, hips and belly, until I eventually stopped to worship a breast in each hand.

"Your tits are even more magnificent than I remember," I praised, thrumming both of her nipples with my thumbs, making her smile. Bending, I took her mouth in a soft, tender kiss and let our feelings slowly grow between us.

Once our desires turned desperate again, our raw need set fire to the smoldering embers of love that had lay dormant with in us for years.

Years of frustration unleashed the animal within us, making us lose control in an unbridled connection of passion so enormous that neither of us knew what to do with it.

Frantically, we took everything the other could give as we bit, licked, and sucked upon sensitive, intimate flesh as we marked our claim to each another.

Once I couldn't hold back it only took a couple of heartbeats for me to nail her in a sixty-nine position, with her arse in the air, her cunt in my mouth, and my thick cock in my Lizzie's throat. Then for however long we were in that position nothing in my life had ever felt better.

"Fuuck... I... I'm going to come," Eliza mumbled around my cock as her body began to twitch and jerk. Quickly, I wrapped my arms tightly around her hips and lapped at her clit faster. A few seconds later I was in paradise when she screamed out my name and came all over my face.

"Oh. My. God," she muttered breathlessly as she shot forward, collapsing face down, over the length of me. Laughing, I slapped her arse, and rolled her to the side of me.

"Shit, got any condoms?" I asked, as I sat up.

"I've had the birth control jab. Are you clean?" she asked.

"Haven't been with anyone since I got tested ... are you?" I asked, rolling her onto her back so I could see her face.

Eliza looked affronted and smacked my pec hard. "You've got a cheek," she muttered.

"And you've been with Owen Murphy," I ground out. That thought almost killed me. "According to Floyd, Murphy's been sharing himself around since his divorce," I told her.

"I never slept with Owen ... and we're not together now anyway," she muttered, sounding embarrassed she'd had to say this to me.

My heart instantly lightened to hear her confirm all this and I was relieved to know that Eliza hadn't let him inside her.

"You really feel safe about not using anything?" I pressed. Before, when we'd been together, it had been a long time before she'd let me go bareback.

She nodded. "If we're only going to do this once, then I don't want anything between us."

Her realistically harsh comment felt like a jolt to my heart. It clenched at the mention of those words because I already felt addicted to her again. I'd equate fucking with Lizzie to that one hit of the purest cocaine I'd ever tried, and immediately swore myself off it because I could see how easily I could have gotten addicted.

Lifting her knees, Lizzie parted them in front of me in a completely unabashed way, which was far removed from the fetal position she had assumed on the floor only a day before. As she had made an exhibition of her position in front of me, I took the time to admire the display.

"Sweet, baby Jesus, look at you," I mumbled, sliding my middle finger gently over her glistening, deep pink flesh. "So fucking pretty," I muttered, lifting my finger and sucking it, unable to resist another taste. The word 'mine' was on the tip of my tongue like I used to say whenever I saw her like this.

Lowering it again, I traced it through her slick juices and slid it into her entrance. Eliza gasped as her hips bucked up for greater contact.

"Does that feel good, baby? You're as tight as I remember." I slid my finger out, replaced it with two, then three, all the while slowly fucking and stretching her gently in readiness for taking me inside her.

"I need you …," Eliza whined impatiently, as she reached out to grab my hips.

"That's what I was waiting to hear," I remarked, playfully as I grabbed hold of my cock and began to stroke myself in front of her.

"You really don't know how sexy you look doing that," Eliza remarked.

I looked from my cock to her eyes full of arousal and grinned. "Would you rather I kept doing this, than …"

"Fuck no. Please, Greg—"

Eliza's words died on her lips, as I placed my cock at her entrance and slowly stretched my way in. "That's the word I needed. And now that you've begged me …" I advised. I stopped talking and bit my lip in concentration because she felt so fucking good that I almost came.

"Ohhh, fuck that's …" She winced and shut her eyes tight.

"Breathe, Lizzie," I mumbled, cradling her head in my hands with my focus instantly off myself, and on Eliza. "You know it'll feel good once it's all the way in."

She opened her eyes wide. "You mean you're not already?" she joked.

Dropping my head, I kissed and bit her neck in the places I knew always made her extra wet while I slowly pumped my hips back and forth until I eventually bottomed out.

"Fuck ... it's been a minute since I did this," she said, looking more relaxed once she'd gotten used to my girth.

I smiled and pulsed my cock inside her, drew my cock almost out of her and slid all the way back in. I repeated this a few times until I felt Eliza's hips rise to meet mine, it was the green light to move faster.

"God, I've never forgotten how good this feels with you," I muttered into her neck. Eliza shivered with my mouth on her sensitive spot. She hitched her leg over my hip to let me sink just a little bit deeper.

"Fuck me harder," she suddenly demanded. "Don't hold back, Greg, I'm going to come any minute," she disclosed as she sunk her long nails into my back and scored them into my flesh.

I'd never seen Eliza more beautiful than with her eyes rolled to the back of her head as she screamed behind my hand, as her pussy milked my orgasm from me.

We both finished in an orgasmic meltdown of blinding heat just a few minutes later. I guessed sex had been a while for both of us. It had been a few weeks for me at least.

Listening to Eliza panting as she caught her breath had to rank as one of the most incredible sounds ever because even with vanilla sex, I'd managed to leave her breathless.

"Wow," she breathed as she flung an arm over her eyes and continued to heave deep breaths. "I'd forgotten how fantastic we are when we're together like this."

"Liar," I teased. "If you're anything like me, you've been getting yourself off to memories of times like the one we've just had, for years."

Eliza took her arm from her eyes and stared pointedly toward me. "Alright, I'm not going to lie," she mumbled, chuckling.

CHAPTER 41

ELIZA

"Shit," I muttered as I stared at my washed-out complexion and puffy eyelids in the bathroom mirror. Was I angry with myself? No—not mad—fucking furious that I'd let my weakness for Greg get the better of me.

Was it worth it? Having sex again with Greg? Of course it fucking was ... and it wasn't. One night was all it had taken to make me feel as bad as I had the night Greg prepared to leave me. *You're a fucking eejit, Eliza McDade.*

In that initial post-orgasmic glow, I had basked in the security of his strong limbs all around me as I drifted off to sleep, too tired to even think. That was my main problem with Greg, he had the ability to make me forget to think ... or at least to see sense at the worst possible times.

What did I expect to happen this morning? That I'd wake up and Greg would tell me he couldn't live without me? That the sex was so incredible he was going to stay after all, when he'd already made it clear he wouldn't.

If I was honest, somewhere along the line, while we were being intimate, I might have given that thought an outside chance.

That was before I had the best night's sleep in years and woke up in bed upset and alone this morning. I'd fallen asleep almost immediately after Greg had cleaned me up, which left me wondering if he had only waited until I was asleep, then he'd snuck back out to his own bed.

During the time we'd spent together, I'd figured there was the same deep connection between us. However, since Greg made a point of letting me wake up alone, he'd left me feeling used.

It was my own fault, considering it was me who had begged for him to fuck me. What man would turn that down. Even so, Greg was the one with all the words of caution. Yet, I had ignored every one of his warnings, in my desperation for that one last chance of intimacy with him.

By the time I had showered all traces of Greg's scent from my body and dressed for work, I could no longer put off showing my face downstairs. Reluctantly, I grabbed my bag and jacket and went down to find Ruth to help with the girls.

"Morning," my sister-in-law said, busy as usual making breakfast. Floyd smiled at me as he sat at the table with their children.

"This is a surprise seeing you up so early," I mumbled and kissed his cheek as I made my way around the table. I poured myself a coffee and took a deep breath. "Is Greg not up yet?" I asked, knowing he'd been getting in the pool early with Floyd for physio.

"Yeah, he's gone out already. Said something about a meeting at some hotel," Floyd muttered.

"Hotel meeting? What would that be?" I asked intrigued.

"I said the same when he told us," Ruth chimed in. "I mean, this is his home, he could have held his meeting here." She stopped what she was doing and took a closer look at me. "Have you been crying?"

Fuck. Trust her to notice. "No, I'm using new makeup wipes and I got shampoo in my eyes this morning," I lied, quickly averting my gaze and staring into my coffee. "It's early for a rock star meeting, right?" I asked, distracting everyone from staring at me by asking another question.

"I think someone flew in to see him. You know what these famous people are like. They arrive and leave at all hours of the day and night," Floyd muttered. "Aria, go get your uniform on," he said, digressing from the conversation to instruct his daughter.

"I'll help, come on," I said to my niece as I followed her out of the room. It took almost half an hour to finally have Aria ready for school as she made constant interruptions to her routine, by wanting to share pictures she'd drawn the day before. After that, she demonstrated her reading to me by reading a thirty-page book with pictures.

"Aria, come now ... you too, Eliza. Unless you want to be late for work. We'll drop you off. Floyd has a hospital appointment this morning," Ruth ordered.

It turned out my whole day was a series of distractions, mostly with me being preoccupied with Greg and the thought of facing him again. But there were machine breakdowns and logistical problems with our supply chain at work I'd had to deal with.

At least the issues at work reduced the amount of times I had checked my cell phone for texts and found there hadn't been any.

Near to clocking out time, I began second-guessing how Greg would react to seeing me and doubts crept in that he might choose to avoid me. I decided to go and check on my ma and told her I'd bring something over for dinner.

The moment I walked through the door, she knew something was wrong. Placing takeout fish and chips on plates, I placed hers on her tray in front of her and sat on the couch with mine.

"Right, come on. Out with it," she ordered flatly.

"Out with it?" I asked, doing my best to sound confused.

"What's happened … and before you lie to me, Eliza McDade, remember, I'm your mother. I have a built-in bullshit detector as far as you and your brother are concerned."

I shrugged. "It's hard being around Greg all the time."

"Even harder being without him," she countered, playing devil's advocate. "I still don't get you, Eliza. That man would have been good to you."

"Please stop … it's too late now for all that," I muttered, stabbing three chips onto my fork and stuffing them into my mouth. If I needed evidence for that, I only had to remind myself that I had woken alone that morning.

"It's never too late if you love him."

"He's not the man that left, Ma. He does what he wants—when he wants—how he wants to do things now."

"What the hell is that supposed to mean? And I might remind you that you're not the girl he left behind either," she suggested.

"Aren't I? Everyone knows how awkward and difficult I am. I've never met a person that hasn't been frustrated by my mood swings and suspicious nature."

"So, what you're saying is that your da has won."

I stared in shock because she hadn't mentioned my da in years. "My da?"

"This is exactly how your da wanted you to be. Scared to live, mistrusting everyone, afraid to let yourself be happy. He wanted you to think you were less of a person than everyone else, like he did with me. That's how he controlled all of us. Floyd got it. At least he tried to stand up to him."

"It was different for Floyd, he …"

"Bullshit. Floyd took beatings for standing up to him. He had the determination not to let your da crush his spirit. Wake the hell up before it's too late. Life's messy, Eliza, but you've still got to grab it by the balls."

"First Floyd, then Ruth, now you?" I whined. "It's easy to form opinions when you're not the one taking risks."

"Don't you dare talk to me about risks. I risked my life every day living with your da for the sake of you and your brother."

"Yeah, and I didn't see you grabbing life by the balls and leaving him," I mumbled as my heart raced in frustration about that fact. "How do you think Floyd and I felt seeing him beat you? My da treated you like shit and you allowed that to happen." The stunned look on my ma's face told me I'd gone too far. "Oh, God, what am I saying? I'm so sorry—"

"No, you are spot on," she replied, after stoically cutting off my apology. "I didn't try to get out of that situation. Why? Because he told me if I ever left him, he'd find me and kill all of us. Crazy right? But you know him, he was a clever, devious, manipulative man who never made idle threats. We had nowhere to go that I believed he couldn't find us. So, I stayed because I couldn't see any other way."

"God, I never knew that. Why haven't you told us this?"

"And burden you like that? I wasn't much of a mother to you and your brother growing up, but at least I spared you from knowing that." We fell silent while my ma ate more of her food. My appetite had gone as I glanced down at mine. "Anyway, enough about that deadbeat man in the ground."

"I'm so sorry you went through all of that." I stared silently at her for a few minutes before picking up our conversation again. "What happened with Greg had nothing to do with my da," I said gently.

"I beg to differ. You used your da as an example and didn't go with Greg because you were scared that he'd let you down."

My mind instantly flew to earlier in the day and I nodded. "He did let me down ... and he'd continue to do that, if I let him."

"So, you think he'd be unfaithful? Whore around and humiliate you if you were with him?" I shrugged because I felt ashamed to admit to that, and I wasn't sure if I had mentioned that before.

"I read those articles on the internet as well, Eliza. If you really think he would have taken you all the way to the US only to turn on you that way, then I don't think we're remembering the same person. The Greg Booker I knew back then had no room in his life for another woman, because he only had eyes for you."

"Everyone says that, so why am I so hesitant to believe them?"

"Because you live in survival mode. When have you ever taken a risk?"

"Greg took enough risk for the both of us."

"Ah, so there it is. Greg's ability to do that scares you to death. And I'll bet money that something happened yesterday, hence your hasty visit to me right now." There was no use protesting about that because my ma would only have seen through me. "The fact you're not arguing back to me speaks volumes, Eliza. If you want my advice, you'll get your arse over to that man's house and clear up whatever brought you here."

"And what would you have me say and do?" I challenged.

"You could start by shaking off that stupid resentment you harbor about the past because he did the right thing. Or would you rather your da's cruel behavior ruin Greg's life as well? Look at how your da affected you. If Greg had stayed and put up with your crippling fears, your da would have controlled him too—through you. Let me ask you this. If Greg Booker was to ask you to go with him now ... give you a second chance to be with him, would you take it?"

"Ma..."

"Oh, and before you say it, don't you dare use my condition as another excuse. Floyd and Ruth are here ... and I have Martha, and the carers. It's time you lived life the way I imagined it for you the first time I held you in my arms."

Tears welled in my eyes as my heart pounded inside my chest, because every harsh word my ma had said to me was true. I'd been afraid to go with Greg because I thought it would go wrong. All I had done was make myself unhappy living without him anyway.

"Carol, it's only me," Martha called out from the hallway, letting herself into my ma's house with the hidden key.

Quickly, I roughly swiped at my tears, stood and lifted my tray with my barely touched food.

"Right, I better be getting back to Floyd's. Ruth will be waiting to bathe Myra." Leaning over my ma, I pressed a kiss to her cheek.

"Mind what I said, Eliza. Breathe, and if that man shows any hint of making up with you, I suggest you swallow your pride and hear him out."

CHAPTER 42

GREG

Soft knocking and Raff's voice pulled me from a deep sleep. It took me a couple of seconds to realize where I was. Eliza lay next to me, her back facing my front but we weren't touching. Gently, I slid out of bed and crept out into the hallway.

Shooing him into my room, I followed him and closed the door. "What time is it?"

"6:20 a.m.," he said, standing dressed in his suit, ready to do his duty. He sniffed. "Jesus, Greg. You don't need to tell me what happened last night."

I smirked. "I think I fucked up."

"From the smell on you, I'd say you most definitely fucked something... or someone."

"Don't," I warned sheepishly.

He stuffed his hands in his trouser pockets. "Looks like you've made yourself a new clusterfuck to keep you busy," he pointed out.

"Fuck, when don't I?" I scoffed and scratched my head.

"Okay, you're late. You've got less than twenty minutes before we leave."

"Right, let me grab a shower. Grab some jeans and a shirt and put them on the bed for me. I'll be out in a minute."

"So ... dare I ask?" Raff wondered as the car we rented rolled quietly out of my driveway.

I shrugged. "Lizzie had a nightmare," I explained.

He chuckled. "Was that nightmare you fucking her or ..."

"Don't be crass. I heard her crying and went in to comfort her."

"By fucking her?" Raff asked, quickly glancing at me again.

I shook my head. "Quit ragging on me. It had also happened the previous night ... her crying due to a nightmare, I mean. I had gone in to comfort her.

"She doesn't sleep afterward unless someone is there, so ... Anyway, it happened again last night, louder this time. I heard, got out of bed and got in beside her. The only difference being that the first night I had stopped to think and pulled on some boxer briefs. I wasn't thinking last night and I—"

"Climbed in naked," Raff finished.

"I swear to God that I tried not to take advantage of her. I even warned her I'd be leaving again. In fact, after last night, I know I'm fucking up right now and I shouldn't be doing this today. But for obvious reasons this is something that needs to be done in person."

Raff scoffed. "How gallant of you."

"It isn't like that ... But last night ... We couldn't have resisted what happened."

"So why are we going here this morning?"

"I never asked her to come ... told her not to come. Hell, I even told her about Lizzie. But she's come all the way from Greece."

"Dude. It was one fucking night. What did you do that made you so special?"

"I guess I gave her false hope ... although at the time, I was serious when I said I'd see her again. Then after seeing Lizzie ..." I shrugged.

"Lori ... she's keen to come all this way, I'll give her that—or confident she can change your mind."

"She won't. Not since I saw Lizzie again ... and especially after last night."

"What does that mean for you? Eliza is a gorgeous looking girl, but dude, that temper ... that ..."

"No one is asking you to get her. I do."

"You're obviously a sadist," Raff said dryly, as he pulled up at The Shelbourne hotel. I glanced at the clock, which read 7:00 a.m.

"Stay with the car. Give me ten minutes. I'll go up with him," I said, looking toward Bruce, Lori Sinclair's bodyguard, who was standing by the entrance. "If I'm not out by then, come and get me. I'll text you the room number."

Once out of the car, I strode through the foyer close to Bruce with my head down, thankful when there appeared to be no one else around.

I was texting Raff the number when Bruce opened the hotel room door with his keycard. Lori immediately rushed forward and hugged me before I entered, as if she'd been standing there waiting to pounce.

Peeling her arms from around my neck I held her by her wrists and walked her back into the room. The moment Bruce closed the door, I let her go and stepped to the side.

"I asked you not to come here, Lori," I said quietly, sticking my hands into my pockets to ensure I wouldn't inadvertently touch her again. The last thing I wanted was for her to get mixed signals, no matter how innocent any contact might be.

"Yeah, I know. But I thought if we could just talk, that we'd—"

"No, I'm sorry. I didn't mean to lead you on. I like you ... I think you're a beautiful girl, but my feelings for ..." I sighed. "I'm in love with somebody else and I shouldn't even be here this morning."

"You told me that it didn't work out."

I considered this and nodded. "It didn't then … but I have new reason to hope we might find a way forward."

"Greg … I-I really like you." I heard the plea in her tone as she slowly sat down.

There was no doubt most men would figure I was mad to pass up a chance with her. Lori was bright, beautiful, sweet and straightforward. But in my heart, she would never compare to Eliza. Guilt washed over me again that I'd left Eliza in bed to be there, to let Lori down.

"Listen, you're going to find someone amazing. A man who'll treat you like the princess you are. But that guy isn't me. I've already met my princess … and her name is Lizzie."

"Stay … just spend the day with me," she mumbled seductively, ignoring what I'd just told her.

"No, I'm sorry, I can't do that. Firstly, it would be wrong since I already told you where I'm at. And secondly, that would be disrespectful to Lizzie."

"But you're not with her," she challenged.

"In my heart and mind, I am. I was with her last night," I confessed. "Look, I don't want to hurt you, I told you that on the phone yesterday. Yet here you are—all the way from Greece. Did you think I might have a different answer for you once I saw you in person? Seeing you anxious and eager like this makes me think that night we spent together should never have happened because I'm afraid you have feelings I can't return."

I pulled out my cell phone.

Me: I'm done come to the entrance.

Seconds later Raff replied.

Raff: On my way.

"Alright, Lori, that's my cue to leave," I said, gesturing toward my cell phone. "Take care of yourself, princess. There's a great guy out there for you ... you just haven't met him yet."

As I opened the hotel room door, I heard a sob break free from her throat. My heart sank, but I ignored it, and closed the door behind me. "Right, mate, can you take me back to the entrance."

"Well, I take it that didn't go down too well," Raff muttered as I slipped into the passenger seat and told him to drive.

Taking a deep breath, I sighed. "Some people won't take no for an answer."

"How did you leave it?"

"I tried to be a nice guy, but I figure I probably sounded pretty unfeeling."

"Then you drew a line in the sand for her," he stated firmly. "Can't do more than that. So, where are we going now?"

"To my da's graveside," I mumbled. It had been years since I'd been to see it, and being famous, I had to do private stuff at times when there was the least chance that someone would see me.

"Sounds like he was a great guy," Raff said after listening to me for what felt like an age, as we sat on the damp bench directly across from my father's headstone.

I'd been reminiscing about my childhood with him and all the great skills my father had taught me. "So, you owe your musical talent to him?" Raff suggested.

"I do. Since the day he died, I tried not to look back on his loss with any lasting regrets. He was an armchair philosopher, my da, and he preached that we should always look forward."

"He taught you well because apart from Eliza you always live in the now."

I stood up, stole another glance at my da's polished marble headstone and sighed. "Anyway," I shrugged in my reluctance to leave, "we need to be getting back." Sliding my cell phone from my jacket pocket I checked the time. My stomach bottomed out because it was already 8:25 a.m. "Shit, I was hoping I'd make it back before Lizzie left for work."

"That's what I meant about making a clusterfuck decision earlier."

I pulled out my cell phone to text Eliza but there was a text from my cell phone provider telling me they were doing essential work in the area, and they would text when the signal came back.

I growled and shoved my cell phone back in my pocket, thankful at least that I'd gotten that text in to Raff at the hotel before it went down.

"No signal," I said, gesturing with my cell phone. Raff and I were on the same network so there was no use in asking to use his. "Take us to the rental house. We'll spend the day with Deakon and the others."

"What about Floyd?"

"Aria is at school. Myra is spending the day with Ruth's ma and the physiotherapist isn't due until 4:00 p.m. because Floyd had an early hospital appointment today. If he's been seen on time, they'll be back home soon. We'll give them some space because it's about time Floyd and Ruth had some alone time together."

"Dude, you're really a good person behind all those antics you pull," he mumbled.

"Except that I left Eliza this morning," I reminded him. "What the fuck was I thinking?"

"Ah, see, now you're getting into my head, Greg. If I'd had a dollar for every time I'd had that exact same thought about you, I'd be a rich man by now."

"Fuck you, Raff Montgomery. With the amount of free accommodation, food, worldwide travel and expenses you get, I bet you've barely ever touched your paycheck."

Raff grinned. "Ah, dude, I think you might have a point there."

***

"THERE HE IS." Levi beamed with his perfect smile through the huge screen at the rental house. Beth had linked her laptop to the TV screen, and the rest of the band were all FaceTiming on the house internet when we arrived.

"Are you all missing me?" I asked, smiling.

"No," Jude mumbled in his low, brooding tone, after he poked his head into view. Everyone laughed.

"What the hell time is it there? It's not even 9:00 a.m. here yet."

"Ah, that's just it, we're not in the US, we're here," Levi mumbled as he turned his screen around, and we saw the Eiffel Tower.

"You're in Paris?" I asked surprised.

"Yeah … a sixsome vacation before we hit Dublin for Levi's bachelor party."

"Sixsome?" Levi swung his screen in the other direction. Korry and Bernadette, Esther and Trinnie waved back.

Levi looked sheepish for a moment, licked his lips and pulled a serious expression. "Surprise. Donnie got us a private gig. A Parisian socialite's 21st birthday bash."

"No," I said flatly.

"Yes," he and Jude muttered, nodding.

"It's two and a half million bucks, for three hours work," Levi disclosed. "Private plane, all expenses paid, and it's right here in the center of Paris. And before you say no again, Jude needs this as a favor."

My eyes flew wide. "You do? Why?"

"Temporary cashflow problem. We've seen a property near Deakon and Levi's place. Esther wants to live in the keys. My accountant says we're about half a mil short to buy it, without selling our condo in West Palm Beach. The change in lifestyle for the kids would be fabulous."

"I'm loaning him the money to make the deal, but the stubborn bastard is now talking about liquidating assets to pay me back. The accountant doesn't want him to do that so ... gig in Paris."

"It's not a good time for me," I muttered, playing coy but knowing I'd do it anyway.

"I know, but it's one night. You could fly over the morning of the gig and fly back the morning after. You'll only be gone slightly more than a day."

"Sounds like I don't have a choice," I muttered still pretending to be bummed.

"See, that's the spirit," Deakon exclaimed with a cheesy grin as he slapped my back.

"Dude, I owe you," Jude muttered humbly.

"Mate, you owe me nothing. Of course, I'll do it. If it was any of the others, I'd have told them to kiss my arse. But you were the one who shouted the loudest for me to join the band."

"So now that business is out of the way, Bernadette will send everyone schedules," Levi interjected before I could change my mind.

"When is this gig?"

"Friday night."

"I'm more interested in hearing about this bachelor party," Deakon probed.

"We figured the day after the gig we'd all fly into Dublin to party. The date for the wedding is the following Saturday."

"I won't be there," I stated deadpan. "I'm supposed to be taking a month out, remember?"

"Dude, it's not work. We'll get Floyd and his family over there. A holiday will do them good. They can stay at our place since we'll be on our honeymoon in the Maldives and Gabby will be at her dad's."

"I'm not sure if he's …"

"I've already spoken to Ruth and Floyd this morning. He's cleared it with the neurosurgeon to fly, and they're excited to come," Deakon mumbled.

"Sounds like a lot of plotting has gone on behind my back."

"Not plotting, just making sure you'll be there," Levi explained.

"I'm surprised you think I'm an essential," I shot back.

"Dude, you're a brother … oh that gives me an idea. Do you think Tim would conduct the proceedings. I mean, we found a pastor but somehow having your brother sounds much cooler."

"Seriously?" I chuckled.

"Sure."

"I think he mentioned once he can usually only marry people in church. Are you even Catholic?"

Levi nodded. "We both are … and if that's what it takes …"

"I'll ask him," I said, laughing. "I can't wait to see his face when I run this one past him."

We spoke for a few minutes more, then Levi concluded the call.

"Anyone got mobile signal?" I asked after checking my cell phone again. Everyone looked at their cell phones and shook their head.

"Nope, still down. There's a message from the service provider saying they are doing essential work," Beth said, confirming what I already knew.

K.L. SHANDWICK

"Right, we're going back to bed," Deakon mumbled as he stood and hauled Sadie to her feet.

"You're quiet," Raff remarked to Sadie as she leaned on Deakon.

"Time change, partying—" she began.

"Noisy fucking," Beth interjected. "These two sounded like a couple of foxes in heat last night. Meanwhile," she gestured to herself. "They're doing nothing for my dry spell over here."

"Anytime you need help with that," Raff mumbled behind his hand, close to her ear.

"Yeah?" she asked playfully, her brow cocked suggestively. "You never know your luck. I might just take you up on that," she muttered, wagging a finger at him.

"Now it really is time to go back to bed if Raff's flirting with Levi's sister. I want to be the deaf mute in the room if that's going down. Otherwise, I'll be stuck in a hole if he questions me because I'm a bad liar," Deakon joked. We all laughed as Deakon led Sadie back to their room.

Once they'd gone, Raff went to the bathroom leaving Beth and I alone. "You could do worse than Raff you know," I suggested.

"I know … a lot worse." She pulled out the neck of her T-shirt and mumbled into it, "Had worse, too."

I laughed. "From the way he was watching you the other night, I think he might have a wee thing for you."

"From the knot in his pants, I'd say it was more than a wee thing," she replied.

"Damn, you are hard up," I said, chuckling.

"Like I said, the offer's there," Raff interjected, having heard the last part of our conversation.

"Sounds like you're hard up as well," I muttered, eyeing Raff with a sideward glance.

"Well, we can't all crawl out of bed reeking of sex when we have jobs to do," he replied.

"Oh?" Beth queried. "Is that a recent reference or a historical one?" she asked.

"My lips are sealed ... NDAs and all that," Raff replied, making a zipped motion across his lips.

Beth laughed. "Not the woman in the bar ... the one with the angry boyfriend?"

"Not her boyfriend," I muttered.

"Oh, so it was her? Eliza is it? I thought you weren't going to go there again?"

"It-it's complicated."

"So, it was her. Floyd's sister? The love of your life?" she mumbled, using air quotes to repeat what I'd said at The Merry Ploughboys.

"Like I said—complicated. But I'm going to try to put it right."

"By doing what you did this morning ... that kind of right?"

"Fuck. That's not fair, Raff," I replied, glaring. What I'd done had left a bad taste in my mouth, but I believed Eliza would see what I did in the same light as my bodyguard.

AFTER MULLING over the situation with Eliza and Lori all afternoon, I took out my cell phone to check to see if we finally had phone signal again. Once I saw we did, I pulled Eliza's number up.

Me: So sorry about this morning. I didn't get time to explain that there was something I had to take care of this morning. Can I take you to dinner tonight?

Ten minutes later she sent a text back.

My Lizzie: Already ate with my ma.

Fuck.

Me: Are you still there? We'll come and pick you up.

My Lizzie: *Already on the bus.*

There was no need for me to try to decipher the content of those texts. Eliza was pissed with me. I couldn't blame her because I'd crept out of her bed before she'd woken up and at least had a conversation with her.

CHAPTER 43

ELIZA

As I walked into the driveway, I saw Ruth taking the girls out of her car. I noticed Raff's rental car was there as well, so I knew Greg was home.

"Good day?" I asked, knowing she had spent it without the kids.

"Yeah, it was lovely to spend time with Floyd on my own. You have no clue how good it felt to say all the things I had never told him before. There were so many things that had come to mind as he lay unconscious in the hospital that I felt I needed to say."

"I can't imagine," I said, placing a hand on her forearm to empathize with her. She smiled, tearing up a little before she distracted herself by passing Myra over to me. Aria had already run ahead into the house and left the door open.

"What about you? How was your day."

"Work was fine … the rest—not so good," I replied, eyeing the door to the house with dread, reluctant to go inside. All day I had felt ashamed because I woke up and Greg had left me without a word.

"Oh, maybe you can tell me over dinner."

"For reasons that will become apparent at some point, I can't do that. Anyway, I'm not hungry ... that was part of the not good. I took fish and chips over for Ma."

"Uh, oh. Something tells me there was a conversation about Greg. With him being here and knowing your ma is one of his biggest fans, I'm guessing she had plenty to say."

I nodded and gave her a wry smile. "Yeah, and she tore me a new one ... actually the way she spoke to me, you and I should be covered in shit, because it was a doozie as well."

She laughed, then her face grew serious again. "Have you and Greg had a chance to talk properly ... I mean without you getting angry and tearing him down?"

"Is that what I do? No. Don't answer that, I know that's been part of our problem since he's been home." I sighed. "My ma thinks my da has won if I don't try to make up with Greg."

"And what do you think?" Ruth asked as we wandered into the house. We passed Myra back and forth between us as we took off our coats.

"She's right ... I'd never looked at it that way. There was some historical stuff from when my da was alive that she disclosed to me today. It made me think again about my life and ..."

"You're going to talk to Greg about this?" she asked, sounding hopeful.

"I'm not sure. I mean, I feel sick at the thought of him leaving this time. Would I be making the same mistake again if I just let him go? Can I possibly get past the hang-ups I have, and at least try to trust him?"

"Floyd trusts him ... I do too, otherwise we wouldn't be here," she said, holding her arms out and gesturing around the house. "You know your brother. He can be as stubborn as you are when it comes to taking care of his family. Could you imagine Floyd accepting this kind of help from anyone a month ago?" I shook my head. "He's put his faith in Greg. I don't think Floyd could ever do that with anyone else."

I nodded, accepting what she said was true. However, the one thing I'd had on my mind all day was still bugging me.

Was I considering something that was now beyond my reach? Was last night for old time's sake, or might what we did be a steppingstone to a second chance together?

"I'm just going to nip upstairs and change," I informed Ruth, gesturing at my formal suit.

"All right, honey. If I start running a bath for Myra, would you listen while Aria reads. Her homework reading book and report log are in her schoolbag."

"Sure. Tell her to get it out and I'll be down in five minutes," I said as I headed upstairs.

The moment I opened the door, the scent of what we'd done the night before hit me in the face. Greg's scent hung in the air around me, and the crumpled bed sheets were a sad reminder of how I'd felt when I woke and found him gone.

Shaking off the hurt that had begun to form in my heart, I quickly stripped and remade the bed, freshened up, then changed into jeans and a T-shirt.

Taking my hair out, I ran a brush through my long locks and left them down. Then, somehow it felt like the walk of shame as I headed downstairs to face Greg again.

Voices I recognized as Greg and Raff's carried through the hallway as I walked reluctantly toward the kitchen with my heart pounding. The moment I entered the room the talking immediately stopped. Greg stood, his concerned eyes on me. "Hey, Lizzie. How was your day?" he asked, smiling like nothing was amiss.

I wasn't sure if he was brushing off what happened between us, or whether he was playing it cool because there were other people around.

"It was work," I said flatly, shrugging. "Aria, bring your reading book, honey," I called out as I wandered toward the kitchen door again, and called to her down the hallway.

Floyd came out of the bathroom and walked toward me with a walking stick. "See my new trick?" he asked, grinning.

"Wow. What happened to the walker?" I said, my heart instantly lighter for seeing my brother walk with minimal aid.

"Physio said I'd worked so hard these past couple of days, that I was ready to ditch it unless I go out of the house. So, I feel like a hiker with this baby now."

I laughed. "Maybe when your beard grows back, we'll get you a rucksack and you can join one of the local walking groups," I joked.

"Here I am," Aria said, hopping down the hallway with her books under her arm. "Miss said I only need to read five pages tonight," she informed me, instantly negotiating the minimum allowed because she disliked reading books without pictures.

Leading her into the living room, I sat on the chair, and she climbed up on my knee. Following her pointy finger, she began to read a story about someone going to buy fish and chips in a shop—which I found to be a ridiculous coincidence, since I had just done that. Aria read the words in a mechanical fashion and as soon as five pages were done, she slammed the book closed, hopped down and ran out of the room.

"Well, that was riveting reading material. I can see why you don't want to do that," I said to myself. How were kids supposed to be inspired when they were given a book about boring everyday life.

"What's boring about fish and chips?" Greg asked as he came into the room, wandered over to me and sat on the arm of my chair.

"Were you eavesdropping on us?" I asked as my heart hammered in my chest in anticipation of the conversation to come, about us hooking up.

Greg looked reflective as he curled a finger around my hair and gave it a small tug. "I'm really sorry about this morning." I glanced up at him and our eyes locked in a connection that gave us another pause in our conversation. He looked thoughtful as he gathered more of my hair up together and slowly wrapped it around his fist. "I'm fucking useless," he mumbled.

I frowned and shook my head because I still wasn't sure where his conversation was going. I immediately felt I needed to save face and protect myself. "It's fine ... I didn't expect anything. It was one night."

"Lizzie, don't. It isn't fucking fine, and I really didn't brush you off. Don't you know me? I'd never use you like that. I was already going out early this morning. I had something ... fuck—" His cell phone buzzed in his pocket, and he ignored it.

"Stop, Greg," I said, putting a hand up. "We're good. Let's face it, fucking was probably something that needed to happen. Now that we did, we can at least be adult about it."

"Adult about it?" he repeated incredulously with wide eyes. "Would you just breathe for a minute? You have every reason to be royally pissed with me, so don't pretend that you're not."

I stopped mid-breath and sighed. Who was I kidding? I had never been able to hide my feelings. Greg had a torn look in his eyes, and I felt his apology was heartfelt.

"Can we have a reset?" he asked softly. "What do you say we get out of here for a while and talk ... just the two of us?" he asked with a pleading look in his eyes.

Taking the advice of Ruth and my ma, I nodded because I believed the moment where we ironed everything out was now or never. "What about Brutis, your pit bull?" I asked, regarding Raff.

"If we find somewhere quiet, he can stay in the car," he informed me.

I nodded and once I had agreed we should talk, I underwent a mental shift. I was tired of fighting my feelings—tired of feeling angry. Tired of being without him. "Okay. Let me get a coat and shoes," I mumbled, standing.

Reaching out, Greg caught my wrist. He had a look of relief in his gorgeous green eyes. "Thanks, baby. I'll grab a jacket and let the others know we're heading out for a while."

Raff drove us to a small, village pub about ten minutes into the countryside. Leaving Greg and I in the car, he went inside, came out less than a minute later and gave us the thumbs up. Greg immediately got out of the car and led me out after him.

"You won't have any problems in there," Raff muttered, smirking as he got back in the car.

Greg held the door open, and I stepped inside, instantly understanding Raff's relaxed attitude. The barman looked to be in his sixties and there were two men around the same age as him playing darts on the other side of the room.

After ordering us drinks, Greg guided me to the furthest of the four tables in the small bar, near to a fireplace.

Placing my drink in front of me, he sat down, flashed me a nervous smile and huffed out a breath. "Right," he remarked firmly. "I've been watching the clock all day waiting to speak to you about last night. I had hoped to be back before you left this morning, but …" he shrugged because we both knew he wasn't.

My heart pounded because in that moment I felt my life hung in the balance. Since I'd come home, Greg had been saying all the right things, but without saying much at all.

"If you're going to ask if I regret what happened—my answer is no," I confessed. "Did I feel foolish and humiliated when I woke up and found you gone this morning?" I shrugged. "If you were in my shoes how would that have made you feel."

The pain in Greg's eyes told me he really did understand how demeaning his actions were. But then I remembered Greg was no ordinary man and his schedule couldn't change to match my expectations.

"Okay, I'm just going to put this out there. I don't regret a single second of last night. I wish I could wind back the clock and be there when you woke as well. Last night was so unexpected that …" he paused and fidgeted with his whiskey tumbler, "… half of me is still processing that it actually happened."

My head was nodding before I realized I was doing that because I felt the same. "So, now what? Do you want me to go back to my ma's?"

"Fuck, no. That's the last thing I want. But since you were the one that egged me on to cross a line last night, maybe you can tell me what you do want to happen."

"You say that like I can have anything," she mumbled.

"Well, that would depend on you taking my circumstances into consideration."

"You mean living in Miami?"

"I do, since that appeared to be the main sticking point last time."

"Tell me, Greg. Why do you love me? Why me?"

He scoffed. "Seriously?"

"Yes, I'm serious. I see the way people look at how we are together. I can tell they're silently asking themselves, why her? They don't get how you could possibly put up with someone who is a constant pain in your arse."

"As if I give a fuck what other people think? Who cares, do you? No one else needs to get you. I do. If you believe there's someone out there for everyone, then—*My. One. Is. You.* You're my person, that one beautiful human being that my heart is in sync with. My one mind, body and soul connection that makes everyone else pale to insignificance.

"You branded my soul the day I met you, Lizzie. And I'm yours, whether we are together or not. The difference between you and me is that in my world, I don't need to own you to love you. We've both said that you're not mine, but that's bullshit." He slapped a hand across his heart. "As long as this ticks, I'll believe that you belong with me."

"If that's how you think, you wouldn't have wanted anyone else."

"I don't. For you, our relationship comes down to trust, and for whatever reason you feel that I'm not a safe bet. I need to accept something in my make-up makes you feel that way.

"However, the way I see it, unless you can find the courage to take that leap of faith, you'll never know if you can. You need to understand there's no way of proving trust until after the fact. Trust is a retrospective concept. It can only be evidenced by looking back. No one can confirm its truth until later."

"Greg, what about all those women?"

"Those women you keep throwing back in my face, you mean? Even though I've never stopped loving you, I thought we were done for good. I didn't take a vow of celibacy like my brother, Lizzie. A man has needs. Those women were hookups that wanted me. Women I obliged in exchange for releases—temporary company that I vented my frustrations, mostly about us, on. None of them have ever held a piece of my heart, because I have always been in love with you."

"You told me there might be one ..."

"No. I know I did, but I was lying to myself," I replied, shutting that conversation down. "Like you, I thought I might try ... the way you did with Owen, but I know since seeing you again, it would never have gone anywhere with her."

"So ..." I said. "Where does that leave us?"

"That depends entirely on you, Lizzie. I've made it clear what I'd love to happen. But I understand what it is that I'm asking," he muttered.

"Ask me," I suddenly blurted out.

Greg reached over and placed his hand over mine as his eyes searched my face. "Come with me, Lizzie. Come with me to the US, and I swear I'll do everything I can to make you happy."

"My ma ..." I replied so choked up that I had no words for what

I needed to ask, deciding it was time for answers to our dilemma, instead of trying to create more barriers.

"Floyd and Ruth have been discussing your ma going to live with them for quite some time. He's told me in the past the only reason your ma won't go is because you still live with her," he mumbled, lifting his drink and swigging it down.

"He's never discussed that with me," I stated flatly. "That must have been a while ago. I've no doubt they might have thought they could cope before, but since Floyd's accident—I can't walk away and leave Ruth to deal with Floyd, the girls and my ma," I replied, my brow raised as if to ask if he was thinking straight.

"Floyd's getting better every day, and we can employ a housekeeper for them, if Floyd would accept it. Would you at least let me talk to all three of them about it. No pressure, Lizzie. Just a quiet chat to see if there's a solution that would make you happier to come with me."

Knowing our ma was comfortable and had people on hand would resolve some of my worries at least. But my fears about trust wouldn't just disappear by hiring someone to deal with them.

I considered what Greg said about trust being proven in hindsight, and I guessed the chances of that would come down to my own self-esteem and faith in our relationship.

"Yes. You can talk to them. I'm tired of remembering how we were ... and of being a memory to you. Of us being nothing but memories. Life's what you make of it, right? But I swear if you hurt me, Greg Booker, I'll never forgive you again."

"Feel this," he told me, grabbing my hand and placing it over his heart. "My heart is racing. The fact that you're willing to try has made me the happiest man on earth." His hands framed my face and he stared intensely at me. Then with the scent of whiskey on his breath he pulled me in, pressed a soft kiss to my lips, leaned back to see me and smiled. "You won't regret this, Lizzie."

Whether it was that I had matured since Greg had left, the

discussion I'd had with my ma, or I simply valued myself more, I wasn't sure. I didn't feel as resistant to change as I had been until Greg had come back.

For the first time in my life, I felt willing to take a risk, and prayed that Greg was being truthful, that I was the only woman he wanted in his life, and his promise to make me happy.

Greg checked the time on his cell phone. "Come on, if we get back now, Floyd and Ruth might still be up," he muttered, impulsively jumping to his feet, and tugging me by my hand.

Leading me out of the pub, he waved to Raff who immediately drew the car up beside us. As we climbed in, Lady Gaga was playing "Always Remember Us This Way" and the lyrics of the song weren't lost on me.

Neither Greg nor I had forgotten how we used to be, and it was those memories that had kept our love alive, despite the passing of time.

CHAPTER 44

GREG

I felt like I was walking on air as Lizzie and I left the pub, confident a solution to her coming to the US was in sight. As we climbed into the back of Raff's rental car, I pulled Eliza toward me and pressed a soft kiss to her lips.

"Short trip," Raff remarked because we hadn't even been in the pub an hour before we'd left.

"It achieved what we wanted," I remarked. "Can you put your foot on the accelerator, I want to talk to Floyd before he goes to bed."

Raff did as I asked while Lizzie and I sat quietly, gripping each other's hand.

I breathed a sigh of relief when I saw the glow from the TV through the living room window as Raff pulled into the driveway. The moment he stopped the car, I climbed out, leading Eliza with me.

"Hey, where's the fire?" Raff muttered as he climbed out afterward, then went to close the back passenger car door I'd left open.

Ignoring him, we headed for the sitting room, where we found Ruth lying on the sofa and Floyd in a reclining chair.

"Can we talk?" I asked, being economical with my words.

Ruth sat up and reached for the lamp on the end table near the sofa. "Sure," she agreed as Floyd turned the sound down on the TV.

I held up our joined hands. "We've been to the pub," I stated, grinning.

"And you're so drunk you've forgotten that you're sworn enemies," Floyd muttered sarcastically. "You've been gone less than an hour. Even happy hour couldn't get you both so drunk you've forgotten how my sister hates your guts."

"Ah, but that's just it. She doesn't." I turned to Eliza and squeezed her hand. "Tell them," I coaxed.

"I don't."

"And what's brought about this miraculous change of heart. Did you get a brain injury as well?" Floyd asked, his tone lighter now.

"Shut up," Eliza mumbled, her face reddening to a cute color of pink.

"It's about time you woke up, Eliza. If this guy here ever wronged you, he knows we'd no longer be friends."

"I do," I agreed. Floyd loved me like a brother, but he was as protective of his women as my bandmate Levi.

"So, what did you want to talk to us about?" Ruth asked.

"Lizzie's coming around to the idea of giving the US a try ... but she's worried about all of you ... especially your ma."

"Don't sweat it, Eliza. We've been waiting for you to get a life so that we could ask Carol to come and live with us. The girls don't see enough of her right now, and I know it would make life easier for everyone. Between the amount of time Floyd and I take visiting her, I'd rather she lived with us."

"Would you consider continuing to live here?" I asked.

"Here? We have a house Greg," Floyd stated.

"I know you do and it's a very nice house. But think about it. Once you're fighting fit again, you could all move upstairs. Then your ma could have the room you are currently in and one of the girls' rooms as a living room. She'd have space from the girls, and you'd have space from her when you want some alone time."

"There's even room for Martha to come and stay without the girls losing their playroom," Eliza remarked.

"What would I do with our house?"

"Rent it out."

"If we did that then I'd insist on paying you a proper rent to live here."

"No, I'd want you to put that money into savings plans for the girls."

"What if I can't go back to foresting?" Floyd asked, sounding like he was considering this.

"You could always try lecturing. That guy from Dublin University is always asking you to consider teaching the post graduate forestry courses. With your land management skills and the master's program degree you have through your work, you're well qualified."

Floyd looked thoughtful. "I'll admit that it's something I've been thinking a lot about since the accident … first when I wondered if my legs would ever be as strong as they were again. Then since I've been home bits and pieces of the accident have been coming back …"

"See, I was thinking, there's a little land at the side of the house. I could put one of those ready-built, German kit-houses on there. A housekeeper could live there to keep house for you all. That way she won't be live-in, but it would give Ruth some support around the place."

"No to the housekeeper," Floyd insisted. "If we're going to live in this posh house, we're doing it on our own."

"That's settled then. I'll expect the first rent check to be deposited in the girls' bank account the month after your house has been rented out."

"Did I agree to something there?" Floyd asked, confused.

Ruth smiled and nodded. "Yeah … and I can't wait to tell your ma she's coming to live with us."

"And I can't wait to tell her we've finally offloaded that snarky bugger over there … and even better, she'll be thousands of miles away," Floyd joked.

"I haven't said I'm going yet," Eliza remarked.

"Oh, you're going, even if I've got to drag your sorry arse to that plane myself," Floyd informed her, chuckling.

"God, am I really going to America?" she mumbled aloud.

"Yeah, you are … but you need to put in your notice at work first," I replied, smiling.

"That's not going to be easy. I've been working there since I was at school."

"Then it's high time you had a change," Ruth coaxed. "I've always said you give too much to your job. Like I have always said, it'll still be there when you're not."

"Okay," I said, taking a breath and letting everything sink in. "Got to strike while the iron is hot, baby. Tomorrow you're putting a week's notice in."

"A week? It says in my contract I need to give a month."

"And you want to stay here after I'm gone to do that?" I asked. "What's the worst they can do? It's not like you're going to need a reference, is it? Not when you're going to be with me."

"I'll need to do something," she insisted, frowning.

"Oh, you will. Let's just get you over there. Then there will be plenty of time to figure out what you want to do."

CHAPTER 45

ELIZA

Waking up to Greg gently snoring in my ear was the greatest thing that had happened to me in a long time. As he lay on his side facing me, I studied his beautiful features for ages while I listened to him breathing.

It was hard to believe that he had done so much, was so famous that some people would do anything just to be near him. And yet, I was the lucky one that got to see him so vulnerable and relaxed while he slept. The snoring stopped and he stirred beside me.

Next his strong hand swept from my back to my arse, and he left it there. "I hear you thinking," he mumbled, although he had yet to open his eyes.

"How the hell can you do that?" I asked.

"What? Feel you looking at me?" he questioned.

"Yeah, it's freaky."

Greg gave my arse a firm squeeze. "I can feel your sweet breath on my face, it's even and light so that makes me think you're awake. And if you're awake and you're facing me, then the chances are you're taking me in. It's what I do to you, whenever the opportunity arises so ..." he trailed off after confessing he did the same to me.

"I love you so much it hurts," I confessed. An incredible feeling of calm washed over me for being able to say those words without holding back.

"Ditto. There were days when I didn't think I'd make it ... loving you and not being with you," he quietly mumbled.

"Let's not hurt each other anymore," I suggested.

"I never meant to hurt—" I pressed my fingertips to his lips to stop him from repeating the same sentence that usually led us into a spiral of hurt.

Instead of protesting, Greg rolled to his back, pulling me on top of him.

"You're right, let's not waste time raking over stuff that can only depress us, and try to erase some of those memories." Then he made slow, tender love to me. "Jesus, it's 8:20 a.m. I'm going to be late for work," I cried. I jumped out of bed and ran into the bathroom.

"My name isn't Jesus," Greg joked as he stepped into the doorway of the bathroom and leaned on the door frame.

"Ha! Funny. I'm going to be late for work," I stated, quickly showering my body.

"I'll tell Raff you're late because we were fucking and to meet you in the car park."

"No, you bloody well won't!" I shrieked with wide eyes as I stepped out and wrapped a warm towel, from the heated rack, around me.

Greg laughed. "I'll tell him you slept in and to meet you at the car. Just concentrate on getting ready."

In less than five minutes I was running down the stairs with a bare-chested Greg, hot on my heels.

"Can you get the day off Friday?" he asked.

"What? No. It's not enough notice and I need to do the wages Friday."

"I need to be in Paris on Friday for the gig."

"I don't own a passport."

"Fuck."

Greg looked bummed when he realized there wouldn't be time to get me a passport for Paris. Then and there he took his cell phone out and told me he was messaging Bernadette to get forms sent. He then advised me to get photographs and the necessary documentation from my ma's, so that we could have the application notarized by someone when the time came to apply.

Once the text exchange was completed, he pressed a small kiss to my lips, as his cell phone buzzed again. He took it out and glanced at the screen.

Suddenly, his eyes flared wide and a dark look came over his face as he read the message. His eyes flicked up to meet mine. "Go, you'll be late," he mumbled.

As Raff turned the car around to leave, I saw Greg pull up a social media platform. "You've got to be fucking joking?" I heard him shout as he strode toward the house while we drove away.

"What's wrong?" I asked Raff.

He glanced at me in his rear-view mirror. "What do you mean?"

"Weren't you watching? Greg's angry about something."

"Nope," Raff replied, nonplussed. "And if I had a dollar for every time one of the band guys was pissed off, I would already be retired."

Temporarily calmed by Raff's remark, I sat back in my seat. My heart sank once I checked the time on my cell phone and saw it was 8:35 a.m. But I no longer cared how late I was because the dark look on Greg's face as he read that screen was the only thing that concerned me.

"You haven't had much to say for yourself this morning," Raff said, breaking into my thoughts as we drew up to the curb next to my work.

"I'm a bit preoccupied about Greg," I confessed. "When you go back can you ask him to text me, to let me know he's alright?"

"Greg? Nothing much fazes that guy. Whatever you saw, I'm betting it's been forgotten by now."

"You think?" I asked. I considered Raff's comment and figured he was probably right. Nothing held Greg down for long. However, as the knot in my gut was still there, I prompted. "Probably, but for my piece of mind would you ask?"

"Jesus, I don't get you two at all. One minute you look at him as if you could kill him, and the next you're fretting over a text he received."

As I climbed out onto the street beside him, I frowned. "Please, Raff, for me?"

He sighed. "Sure. I'll make sure he texts you … happy now?"

I smiled and patted his chest. "There … see, I knew there was a kind gene hidden somewhere inside that fancy suit."

"Don't push it," he mumbled, smiling.

"Or what? You'll 'sprout' me?" I asked sarcastically, reminding him of the action he had done as I walked away.

"Fuck, you know … maybe you and Greg do deserve each other," he said, laughing.

CHAPTER 46

GREG

"This has never been more important," I barked down the line to our PR guys in Miami.

"It's only 4:00 a.m.," the PR rep replied.

"Don't give me a time check, I don't fucking care what time it is. I want this piece of fiction retracted, and an apology issued, or I am suing," I responded furiously.

"Be reasonable, Greg. It's spin, you know how this goes. It'll be old news in a few days. The same shit happens all the time in this game."

"My life isn't a fucking game. The perspective of this story couldn't be further from the truth," I countered. I stared at the bullet point timeline of Lori Sinclair landing in Dublin, checking into her hotel and me turning up a half hour later. "And where's the fucking bullet point of me leaving less than ten minutes afterward in this article?"

"If that was the case, it wouldn't be newsworthy now, would it?" the PR rep replied. "What do you want us to do?"

"I want you to print that I went there to blow Lori Sinclair off. Her visit wasn't welcome. Hell, I even told her not to come."

Raff appeared at my bedroom door, his hands hanging from the top door frame. "What the fuck's going on?"

I threw my iPad across the bed toward him. Leaving the door frame, he came in and picked it up. "Ah, fuck," he cussed. "I told you not—"

"Shut the fuck up, Raff. I don't have time for I told you so. What the fuck am I going to do? Just when I was getting somewhere with Eliza. I can't afford to fuck this up."

Raff blew out a breath. "Best thing you can do is come clean with Eliza. I thought that's what you were doing yesterday when you took her to the pub.

"To be honest, Lori didn't cross my mind during our conversation. It was a fucking non-event as far as I was concerned."

"Well, it isn't now."

"No shit…"

"Greg are you still there?" the PR rep asked, making me realize he was still on the line.

"Get Lori Sinclair's people on the line to discredit the story. Tell them she has to say it was a business meeting or something. Maybe a discussion about being in a Screaming Shadows music video. I don't know, make something the fuck up. If she dares to tell them anything else to save face, say that I'll go to the press and tell them she stalked me.

"Remind them that there's CCTV in that hotel that can back me up. It'll show the time I entered her room and the time I left. I couldn't have been in there more than what … six or seven minutes since the rest of the time was going to and coming back from it."

I hung up and threw my phone on the bed. "Fuck me. Lizzie will never trust me now."

"Has she ever?" Raff asked. "Look, I was there. I can back you up."

"She'd say you're paid to back me up," I replied, scowling toward him.

"Text her. Tell her you want to meet her for lunch," Raff suggested. "You need to tell her about this shit before she reads it for herself."

My heart pounded as my gut filled with dread, and I had the start of a headache coming on. "Fuck, I only pray she believes me."

Me: What time is lunch?
My Lizzie: 12:30 p.m. Why?
Me: Meet me for lunch. I'll bring it with me.
My Lizzie: What's the occasion?

Fuck. I stalled because I had no idea how to answer that. Then I figured the best thing that I could do for her would be to be honest.

Me: I want to talk to you about something. Got to go, I'm in the pool with Floyd this morning for some conditioning training.

———

BY THE TIME Raff and I reached Eliza's factory, the anticipation of the conversation I had to face made me feel sick. "Dude. Don't try to sugar coat this. Quick and to the point … like ripping a Band-Aid off. There is no palatable way to make this sound any better."

We'd stopped in a multi-story car park while Raff ran to a baker's shop and bought filled bread rolls, sodas and cakes.

"She'll likely choke me with these," I mumbled as I stared at the brown paper bags full of food that sat next to me on the seat. Raff chuckled. "Not fucking funny mate, I'm serious."

"Now when I think about it, crusty rolls … they could be painful. Maybe I should have bought something softer, like mashed potato," he said. I smiled despite the agonizing pain I felt in my gut. "Here she comes," he informed me.

Raff walked around and opened the door for Eliza.

"So, what's this all about?" Eliza asked, her curious big hazel eyes studying me, warily.

"Raff's just going to find somewhere quiet to park, then we can have a chat," I said. "Meanwhile, I got you a ham and cheese roll, they used to be your favorite."

Eliza smiled. "Still are. I can't believe you remember so much about me," she said, opening the bag, taking out her bread roll and taking a huge bite out of it.

I swallowed hard. "Like I said, I remember everything about you."

Raff stopped the car and got out. "Back in ten," he mumbled.

"Okay, what's so important," she mumbled around a full mouthful of food.

"There's an article that's circulating on the internet ... I think these influencers call them blind items. It's circulating stories about celebrities, and people either prove them or debunk them. This one about me has made it in print, in some rag in LA." I turned to face her as much as I could in my seat. "So, you know I went out yesterday morning before you woke up?"

She frowned. "Yeah? An article?" Eliza looked anxious and I hadn't even explained myself.

"A couple of days ago I had a phone call from Lori Sinclair."

"I fucking knew you were talking to a woman. That happened the other morning, right?"

My heart squeezed because I could see her already getting distressed. "Yes, that's right." She stuffed her roll back in the bag and slammed it down on the seat. "You left me to meet her?" For a second, she looked like she was having trouble swallowing then she gasped out a breath. "You left my fucking bed to go and meet another woman?" she yelled at me, her face red, as she grasped at the door handle but couldn't get out.

For once I was thankful to Raff, who always put the child lock on every car to stop me from disappearing on him.

I put a hand on her forearm to stop her, and to gain her attention again. "Please, Lizzie. I need you to hear me out."

"What the fuck is there to say. You had sex with me, knowing you were going to meet another woman that morning."

"It wasn't like that. Fuck. Please …" I muttered as I ran my hands through my hair in distress. "You have every right to be furious with me. But you could never be as pissed as I am with myself. But please, I beg you, at least let me explain."

"I doubt anything you have to say would make what you did any better."

"I know, but … fuck, Lizzie, I'm here, fighting for us."

Eliza had drawn a breath, no doubt to unleash another tirade in my direction but my comment somehow hit home. Stopping midbreath, she let her body sag and stared me down.

"Right, you have two minutes, then I'm leaving," she barked as she stretched her neck to look ahead, to see where Raff had gone.

"You know I accompanied Lori Sinclair to the Oscars a while ago, right?" She nodded, but the hurt look in her eyes slayed me. "Well, we got along okay. She was a nice girl,"

"This is the girl who you thought could be someone …" she trailed off leaving the rest of that sentence unsaid.

I nodded and shook my head immediately after. "I was kidding myself. The moment I saw you again, it confirmed to me that I couldn't settle for anyone else."

"So, you left my bed and went to meet her anyway? That makes no sense to me if this is you trying to defend yourself."

"I agree. Look, let me get this out or you'll only get frustrated about it and leave before you understand what happened."

"Right, I'm listening."

"When we were in LA I said I would go and see her in Greece, where she's filming. Then, I got busy with the band and didn't call her back. We texted back and forth a few times, but nothing intimate. She's rung me twice since I've been here. Once the night we were on our way to The Merry Ploughboys, and then the other morning. I swear I blew her off and told her not to come here."

"If that's the case, what were you doing in her hotel with her?"

"Telling her to go home, that I wasn't interested, that you were the love of my life."

"And I'm supposed to believe that?"

"You can do what you want with it, Lizzie. But it's the truth. I know how much trouble you have with that." I let my comment sink in before I continued. "I had already decided to meet her in person to tell her to her face before I slept with you. Fuck, even Raff told me I was creating a clusterfuck by telling her in person. Did I listen? Do I ever?" I asked, frustrated. "But I swear, I was in that room with that girl less than ten minutes, because the only purpose I was there for, was to tell her I was in love with you."

"I don't know if I believe you," she mumbled quietly.

"Then we're done before we've started because shit like this is going to crop up from time-to-time, and I don't want to be constantly challenged. When all's said and done, I thought I was doing the right thing by telling her in person. I figured by doing that the calls would stop and she'd realize I was no longer interested."

"No longer interested?"

"Fuck. Don't twist what I'm saying or pull a comment out of context. I already told you the moment I saw you again, I believed it was you or no one."

"I'm going to go back to work now. Can you find your babysitter and ask him to let me out of this fucking car?"

"That's it? You don't want to discuss this anymore?"

"Unlike you, I have a job to do today. I need to be back for the afternoon shift change."

"Are we going to talk more about this?"

"I'm not sure. I'm going to go back to my ma's tonight."

"Why? Fuck, Lizzie. I'm here fighting for you. Don't you want to fight for me?"

"Is that what you want me to do? Right now, I haven't even seen the story you're talking about, and I already feel humiliated. So, like I said, I'm going to my ma's house tonight. I want some breathing space. Once I've digested everything you've said, I'll decide what to do from there."

Raff wandered into view, and she knocked on the window to get his attention. Once she had it, she pointed to the door handle.

Raff unlocked the door, and Eliza climbed out. "Don't worry about driving me, I can find my way back."

CHAPTER 47

ELIZA

Tears streamed down my face as I made my way back to the factory office. For the first time in my life, I'd felt truly happy. That feeling had lasted for less than a day before Greg's shady past had caught up with me.

Am I supposed to believe he thinks I'm better than Lori Sinclair? The woman was everything I wasn't and was a much better fit for the lifestyle Greg now had.

Suddenly a truck horn blew, and a screech of tires scared me back to the present. "Christ, woman, are you trying to get yourself killed?" an angry construction worker barked at me from out of his window. He then realized I was crying. "Wait here," he told his workmate. He hit his hazard lights and jumped down. "Are you okay?"

"Yeah, I'm sorry. Boyfriend trouble," I replied truthfully.

"Show me where he lives and I'll crush his nuts for you," he muttered, frowning.

I smiled despite the news I'd received. "The way I'm feeling, I'd rather do that myself."

He laughed. "That's the spirit darlin'. Don't let the bastard grind you down. And if you ask me, he's a fool. I mean, bejesus, look at you."

"I see you failed to hit me with your truck, so you're hitting on me instead?" I joked.

He held up his wedding ring finger. "Got a fabulous woman already ... not that you aren't, you understand."

I chuckled. "I think we should leave this conversation where it is, because I don't think I can handle two rejections in one day," I teased again.

"Can I give you a ride?"

I laughed because of the innuendo implied, considering the previous remarks. "No, fortunately I work at that factory over there."

"Right. Now mind what I said. Don't go throwing yourself under a truck on account of any dickhead."

"I won't," I said, crossing my heart with a finger as I watched him climb back in his cab. As he opened the truck door, the sound of a Screaming Shadows song spilled out. "Oh, I love this song," the driver informed his workmate before he took off his handbrake and drove away.

"WHAT NOW?" my ma asked seconds after I arrived at her house with a pan pizza for tea.

"I still live here," I reminded her. "I'm coming to stay here tonight ... to keep you company."

"Liar. Tell me what happened?" she muttered, waving for the pizza box to be taken over to her.

I grabbed two plates, dished a couple of pieces each onto them and laid the box on the side.

"Right, start at the beginning," she demanded.

I felt like I was sixteen again, admitting to my ma that I'd slept with Greg. Fortunately, she didn't pull any faces that showed she had an opinion about my decision in one way or another. Then for half an hour I explained everything that had happened since I'd been sleeping overnight at his house. Lastly, I told her about Lori, which I was most embarrassed about.

"Do you think he's telling me the truth?" I asked my ma.

"Does it matter what I think? I'm not going to be around for the rest of your life, Eliza. It's going to be up to you to judge when someone's being honest with you. What did your gut say when Greg told you what happened?"

"My gut said he was sorry that he'd been there ... other than that ..."

"Let's look at the positives in this scenario. First, the same night as this happened, he offered you a second chance to go to America with him." I nodded. "Then he was talking about me moving in with Floyd and Ruth ... he wouldn't have suggested that, if he wasn't planning to spend his future with you."

"Yeah," I admitted.

"Then today when the shit hit the fan about that woman, he did offer a plausible excuse ... you said yourself, that you had heard him take a phone call, and thought it might be from a woman."

"That's true," I mumbled, feeling more hopeful.

"Greg also confronted what he did by speaking with you face-to-face, because he wanted you to hear his truth ... much like he did with that Lori girl. In my opinion he was trying to show respect and taking responsibility for his part in hurting both of you. Not that he didn't cock up though," she added.

"You make it sound so easy to accept what he says."

"How else can you be with someone if you don't put your faith in them. Greg is not anything like your da, Eliza. I mean he's an honest man, what else can he do? From what you said, he told you he was there less than ten minutes. I seriously doubt Greg would blow his future with you for a quickie in a random hotel. He might be impulsive but he's not stupid."

"I don't think I can do this ... be strong, shirk things off that sting the way this has today."

"Then don't, tell him you aren't interested."

"I am interested," I argued, shocked at her apathetic reply.

"Then you need to get past all this aggravation and put your relationship with him first. To do that you need to accept Greg's version over some crappy, blind article pushed out for money."

I sighed because what she said made sense. "I'm going to think hard and sleep on it. That's not a bad thing ... to take breathing space and be sure of everything?" I asked, needing reassurance.

"Normally, I'd say what are you waiting for. But I know you need to be sure. Once you are there's no backtracking this time, Eliza. Greg's waited this long, but that doesn't mean he'll wait forever."

CHAPTER 48

GREG

"Dude, are you up?"

"Yeah. You just caught me. I'm heading with Floyd to the pool for another physio session."

"Right. Tell him we were asking after him."

"Will do. So, what's up?"

"I just got off the phone with Bernadette. We're heading over to Paris early. We're getting together before the gig tomorrow night. Mikey's meeting us at Charles de Gaulle airport at 4:30 p.m. Apparently, we've been added as members of some private club. Is your Eliza coming with us? If so, Bernadette said you need to contact her with Eliza's details."

"No, only me," I informed him sadly. "Lizzie doesn't have a passport."

"Fuck. What a bummer. Still, we'll all be back in Dublin on Saturday afternoon for Levi's bachelor party," he commiserated. "She'll be able to join us then."

"Right," I said, sounding flat and wondering how likely that might be.

"Is everything alright with Floyd?"

I figured took my one-word answer to mean I was preoccupied. "He's good," I replied. "Look I should get going. I'm still lying in bed," I informed him.

"Alright, I'll let you get off. Just make sure you and Raff are at the airport no later than 1:30 p.m."

"You look rough," Floyd muttered that morning as I slid into the seat at the kitchen table next to him, with a cup of coffee in hand. It was a rare moment of just him and me. Ruth had gone to her ma's with the girls, and Raff was still in bed.

Leaning on the table, I pressed the heels of my hands into my eyes. "Your sister's going to be the death of me."

"What has she done now? Wait you know we're breaking our rule not to let her come between us?" Floyd asked.

"Yeah, but I need to talk," I admitted. "I fucked up."

He gave me a small, sympathetic smile. "Right, let me have it."

"You don't want to hear it, mate."

"If I didn't, I wouldn't have asked," he countered deadpan.

I explained what had happened with Eliza's nightmare, what happened after, in no graphic terms, and then how I went to speak with Lori.

"You're a dick, but I'd say this is a classic Greg Booker move. Not your finest, although I don't believe you'd ever fuck Eliza over."

I pulled my hands away and gave him direct eye contact. "See, I knew you'd get me. All that I wanted was to do things the right way."

"I agree that the caring sentiment was there. But as usual, you didn't see how that might look to Eliza … to anyone really, mate."

"I was going to tell her, but I was so swept up with how she'd agreed to come back to the US with me, that I didn't give the thing with Lori a thought."

"See, this is the kind of shit you do because you're a good guy. You could have blown Lori off in a text instead of going there."

"I'm not that guy," I argued.

"I know," Floyd said, nodding. "The thing is, the more you protest about something like this, the greater people will feel that there's no smoke without—"

"Exactly," I said, cutting him off. I knew he'd get it. "But if I don't publicly deny this, Lizzie will think there is truth to the story."

"How did your conversation with her end?"

"I told her I was there fighting for us because the article was a lie. She said she felt humiliated and left."

"She texted Ruth that she was staying at our ma's last night. I thought it was strange since the two of you were finally back together," Floyd admitted.

I sighed, exhausted from the stress I had caused for myself. "Look, Levi spoke to you about the gig in Paris, yes?"

Floyd nodded. "I was surprised to get the call. Bernadette must have given him my number."

"I need to head over there today. There's a charter at 1:30, but I hate leaving things like this."

"Don't. Go to your gig. Make music and forget about the drama here for a while. It'll give Eliza the chance to miss you. Then when she sees your life's going on as normal without her, she'll figure it out one way or another. There's no better advice I can offer."

"As usual, you're right. I've got no choice but to go there anyway, so I might as well try to enjoy it."

At that moment my brother rang. I sighed and answered.

"Hey, Tim. I'm sorry I haven't been in touch with you since I've been back again, but it's kind of full on here. I'm leaving for Paris in a few hours, but I wanted to run something past you."

"Wow. That's a lot of information, an apology, an itinerary, and you're begging a favor all in one hit," he said, chuckling.

I laughed. "I'm sorry but you know how life gets," I insisted.

"I do. Two weddings, a funeral, and four baptisms since Friday," he replied, telling me what he'd been doing as well.

I smiled. "There's definitely a set of wings being made in your honor, bro," I joked.

I almost felt the eye roll I imagined him doing. "So what's this favor?"

"Levi asked if you could perform the wedding ceremony for him and Trinnie."

He gasped. "Marry them? Isn't his woman divorced?"

"Yeah," I frowned.

"Is her husband still alive?"

"Yes."

"Then no, it's against the rules."

"Ah. Well, I'm not going to get into that debate. I'll just tell him you said no," I replied decisively.

"I'd still like an invite to the wedding though," he went on.

I chuckled. "They're all coming over to Dublin this weekend. Want to hang out with us on Saturday night?"

"Sounds grand. Nothing says I can't take a dram or two. Message me with the time and the place."

"Will do … come in plain clothes, and you're not to try to do any converting," I teased.

"Or you could all dress up as priests," he muttered deadpan. I laughed. "See you on Saturday, remember … text me the details," Tim mumbled and cut off the call.

WHEN WE LANDED at Charles de Gaulle airport in Paris, it was the first time I felt as if something was missing since that first time I had landed in Miami. I knew that 'something' was the woman I'd had within my reach until I'd fucked up.

I was surprised when I saw two cars on the tarmac, until Mikey informed us he was picking up Levi and Trinnie on the way back from a visit to some purse store, where Trinnie had booked a visit to buy an exclusive bag.

"I think Levi should bring you on stage for a song tomorrow night," I told Beth, who sat between me and Raff in the car.

Beth laughed. "I think if you're being paid a vast sum of money, the last thing the birthday girl will want is a brother and sister indulging in a spot of karaoke."

"Never, it would be a bonus. You're an incredible singer," Raff muttered, slapping a hand on her knee.

"Jesus, would you two get a room?" I asked, chuckling.

"Why? Sounds to me like you're jealous," Raff countered. "Me and Beth go way back. Don't we, sweetheart," he joked.

A flush crept over Beth's face but stood her ground. "Knock it off, Raff, or you'll start the rumor mill going. You see the spotlight these guys are under. I'd hate that kind of focus upon me," she admonished. "Talking about rumors, I saw that blind item thing from that influencer on TikTok."

"It's bullshit," I mumbled. "Can we not talk about it. It's a mess, and I've got a job to do."

"Got it," she mumbled.

"So, you're all going clubbing tonight," Raff stated as he read his texted itinerary from Bodhi on his phone while the car took us to our hotel. Raff using his cell phone reminded me I still had to switch mine over from flight mode. The moment I did this, my heart pounded once I saw there was a text from Eliza.

My Lizzie: Can we meet away from the house to talk later?
Me: I'm in Paris.

I stared at my cell phone screen waiting for her to respond until we arrived at an exclusive private hotel in Saint-Germain-des-Prés and had transferred to our suites for our two-night stay.

After Raff left me and headed into his adjoining suite, I kicked off my shoes, and laid on the bed. I hadn't slept much at all the night before, yet the turmoil inside me made the thoughts in my head feel relentless. Clasping my hands behind my head, I stared up at the ceiling and wondered if my life would always be like this with Lizzie.

Am I kidding myself that Eliza swapping the mundane, routines in life for the unpredictability of mine could make her forget the bad times?

Somehow in the recesses of my mind, I'd hoped it would. I'd missed her so much—missed how she made my world brighter whenever she smiled.

Eventually, I dozed off until Raff knocked at my door. "Dude, are you going to freshen up and change?"

"What time is it?" I asked, staring at the shaft of light coming from our adjoining doors.

"Almost 8:30 p.m."

I struggled up onto my elbows in bed and stared at him, still a bit disoriented. "What time is dinner?"

"9:00," he replied.

"All right, I'll be ready. Give me fifteen minutes."

A text message alert sounded on my phone.

My Lizzie: Are you coming back?

I huffed out a breath and ran a hand down my face in frustration.

Me: Why would you think I'm not?

My Lizzie: I should have stayed and talked things through with you.

Me: That would have been better than running away to your ma's.

When it became clear that she was mulling my comment over, I went to shower and get ready for dinner.

"Do you know how hard it is to get a membership for this place?" Korry mused, looking impressed for once as we headed to the hotel's private members' club directly after dinner.

"This is why we should never turn down these one-off gigs. I don't care how entitled this girl is that wanted a private show, if it gets Jude his house."

"A membership to a place like this is only one of the perks that comes with the job. Donnie did an amazing deal to get us such an exclusive package," Levi informed us as we were escorted by a guy in an expensive suit to the nightclub portion of the premises.

Inside the nightclub there were some discrete domed alcoves with walls of neon artwork, in typical Parisian style. Our party was led to a reserved one near to the dance floor, where there were four bottles of Armand de Brignac 2013 champagne already chilled, waiting on the table.

Within minutes our heads bopped automatically to the perfect bassline beat in the room. The DJ's sick skills on the deck were incredible, as he took ballads we all recognized and dropped or cut the song at the hook or riff with perfect timing—the guy was a music genius.

My unresolved issue with Eliza had left me more anxious than I had let on, and I hit the bottle hard. First the champagne, then some shots Sadie and Beth insisted we drink, then I went on to whiskey.

"So, you're getting married in a little over a week?" I asked Trinnie, to make conversation while Levi danced with his sister.

Trinnie's eyes widened like she was shocked at the thought, then drew in a sharp breath and let it out steadily again. "Yes."

"You're perfect for each other," I told her, giving my honest opinion.

"I think so too. I wasn't in any hurry to marry again but…" she glanced toward the dance floor. Following her gaze, I saw Levi in a deep conversation with his half-sister, Beth.

"He's besotted with you," I mumbled, nodding.

"I know … aren't I lucky?" she replied, grinning, clearly pleased with herself.

"Indeed," I agreed, laughing.

"What about you? Deakon was telling Levi you met up with your ex-girlfriend or something. Floyd's sister, right?"

"Eliza … Lizzie to me," I replied. My heart sank at the sound of her name on my lips since we'd left things the way we had.

"And?"

"And it's still complicated, mostly because of me this time."

"Stick with it if you feel it's worth it. Jump if it feels toxic," Trinnie advised. I stared pointedly at her because I took that as sound advice, since she'd been divorced once already.

"Gotcha," I muttered, and threw another whiskey down my throat.

"I mean it, Greg. Value yourself … and if you need to talk, I'm a good listener."

I smiled because Trinnie had kept Levi grounded, and apart from our band families, Floyd's family and my own, I didn't meet many level-headed people in the music business.

"Thanks, Trinnie," I replied. "Look at us bonding. You'll be asking me to be a bridesmaid next," I joked to lighten the mood.

We were both laughing when Levi took his seat back beside her. "Beth wants a dance," he mumbled, nodding toward her dancing by herself on the dance floor.

"Right. Duty calls. Can't be neglecting the boss's sister," I mumbled. I stood and pulled the legs of my trousers down before I headed over to Beth.

In less than five minutes with Beth, I was laughing out loud. I cracked up as Beth leaned in and shimmed her tits at me, twerked her ass in my direction, and generally made a drunken arse of herself. I liked the free spirit that alcohol set free in her.

"What? Just because you can't bust the moves like I can," she challenged when I flared my eyes at another of her antics.

"No? Get a load of this then?" I replied and proceeded to make a real tit of myself by trying to breakdance.

Beth, not one to be beaten tried to join me, obviously forgetting the short dress and thong she had on. Fortunately Raff stepped forward, covered her up with his jacket and dragged us both to our feet.

"You're both done for the night," he scolded, as Beth and I bent double in fits of laughter.

"And when Joe got the boot, I was supposed to be the wild one of the band," Deakon mumbled, pretending he was pissed that the spotlight was on me, instead of him.

"Would you rather I partied like Korry?" I challenged, nodding toward him locked in a slow dance with Bernadette, despite the mash-up rap medley that Beth and I had been boogying down to.

"That guy is whipped," Deakon said, sounding like he thought there was no hope for his bandmate.

"And so are you," Sadie mumbled, grabbing Deakon's junk, and challenging him with a determined look that made us laugh again.

"As am I … he's as whipped as I am," he mumbled, amused before he grabbed Sadie by the scruff of her neck and stuck his tongue down her throat.

"Hey, remember where you are," Levi muttered, nodding at the people around us.

"You think I give a fuck where I kiss my woman? It's not as if we're ever likely to come back here," Deakon reasoned. "I was just teaching Sadie a lesson," he joked.

"Yeah?" Sadie muttered, shooting one of her legendary death glares at him. "We'll see how good that lesson you taught me is, once you're tossing yourself off in the bathroom later." True to form, Sadie wasn't giving Deakon any wiggle room.

"Right, we're heading to bed," Jude said. He stood and slid an arm around Esther's waist.

"Aww, that's a shame. I mean, you've hardly been the life and soul of the party tonight … considering we're here for your benefit," Deakon muttered, calling him out for not joining in the fun.

"I'm tired. Wait until you have kids," Esther mumbled. She looked washed out, which was rare for her.

"We were up at 5.30 a.m. this morning with Honey. Then Esther was spewing rings around herself with morning sickness," Jude countered.

"That'll teach you to manage your contraception better, dude," Deakon mumbled.

"You know, I think I'm going to head up as well," I said, interrupting their conversation. "I didn't sleep last night. But don't let us lightweights spoil your night. Feel free to keep partying."

"I'm headed to bed as well. I've had too much to drink, too quickly tonight. I don't want to be hungover tomorrow," Beth mumbled, holding her head.

"I'm staying," Levi muttered, raising a hand to Deakon.

"Thank God." Deakon slapped his hand on his chest as if he was in shock. "For a minute there, I thought the rock n' roll lifestyle was dead."

"You might want to remind Korry he's a rock star. Him and Bernadette look like they're at a grade nine formal with all that shuffling in circles," Levi mumbled deadpan, nodding in Korry's direction.

We hadn't seen Bodhi all evening, yet as if by magic, the

moment Jude stood up to leave, he appeared by Jude's side to escort him back to his room.

It occurred to me that Mikey hadn't had much to say for himself either. But according to Deakon, Mikey was pissed that he'd had to come because he'd had plans with his girlfriend. I'd had plans too, and I hated how I'd left things with Eliza.

"The set will be ready by 11:00 a.m. Bodhi just got a text from the crew," Raff muttered to me, after Bodhi had spoken into Raff's ear.

"Can you order breakfast in bed for me in the morning, I'm too wasted to do it myself. It's been a while since I've drank this heavy. Is there a sauna in this place where I can sweat the drink out?"

"Yup, on the breakfast. As for the sauna, I'll check that out and text you," Raff muttered, then escorted me to my room with Beth in tow.

I nodded. "Good job, now go, take Beth to her room then go to bed."

"You got it." Raff smiled. He'd almost closed my door before he pushed it open again. "And Greg, don't you fucking dare go walk about. I mean it."

CHAPTER 49

ELIZA

What an idiot I've been if everything my ma said was true. I had every intention to message him once I arrived at the factory to tell him that too, but as soon as I got to work all hell had broken loose. Then, as it was one problem after another, I never got to it until I was on the bus on the way back to his house.

The moment I read that Greg had already left for Paris, my stomach sank. I wanted to tell him I had regretted my decision to stay away the night before. I hadn't done it to punish anyone, least of all Greg. I also hated that I'd needed some extra time to conclude that I believed him. However, with the years apart and the changes in him, I felt justified in taking my time, given all I had read about him.

As I sat staring at his few words my chest tightened until I realized I'd held my breath. I then spent the rest of the journey back wondering how to put things right between us.

"You look impressed with yourself," Floyd muttered in a sarcastic tone, the minute I walked through the door after work.

I shrugged. "I'm guessing Greg told you what happened?"

"He did, and it was a dick move, but he's going to make those, Eliza. It's the way he thinks. But I'd bet my house that guy would never cheat on you."

"Ma says the same," I mumbled.

"I think it's time you wake the fuck up, sis. Greg isn't a normal man anymore. Drama will be part of the deal if you do get back together. You need to decide whether you're tough enough to have a relationship with a public figure. If not, then cut the ties right now, and put the guy out of his misery."

"It isn't as easy as that. What the hell do I have that an Oscar winning actress doesn't?"

"At this minute in time? Greg. You have Greg, Eliza. He came clean and told you what he'd done. For Christ's sake, he went there to tell her to stop contacting him. Would you rather believe an article written by some stranger on the other side of the world than the guy you love, facing you to explain it?" I didn't reply so Floyd continued. "You'd better be sure of the choice you make with Greg this time, because I don't think he'll try again."

"Ma already gave me 'the talk', and after a sleepless night, I know in my heart I can trust that he's telling me the truth."

"What do you want for that? A Medal? Have you told Greg this?"

"I messaged him wanting to talk but he'd already gone to Paris."

"Then what?"

I narrowed my eyes. "What do you mean?"

"Then, what did you do?" he challenged.

"I asked if he was coming back."

"Best advice I can give you is this. If you want him, you need to go after him. He told me what happened with you and then Lori, and to be frank, he's devastated. Greg usually acts before he thinks and then realizes he screwed up. But the one thing he wouldn't do is intentionally hurt you."

After Floyd's dressing down and Greg's last text message my mind went around in circles. If I had found it hard to sleep in my own bed at my ma's the night before, it was nothing to how my mind fired off scenarios in all directions in the bed I had shared with Greg. Then, I had the lightbulb moment that shocked me to my core.

What if Greg comes back after his couple of days away and tells me he's given up?

Once that thought had gone around in my head on repeat, I grabbed my cell phone and sent him another text.

Me: I'm sorry. I hate that I missed you, before you had to leave.

Shock made my heart pound when those three little message dots instantly start to bounce because, it was past 2:00 a.m. here, 3:00 a.m. in Paris.

Greg: Can't sleep?
Me: No, I was thinking of you.

My cell phone vibrated, the second I sent my response.

Suddenly I felt both anxious and nervous he was calling me because I wasn't sure what he might say.

"I'm sorry, I'm a fuck up," Greg mumbled, slurring.

"No, I am," I muttered quietly. "I should have listened."

"We're a pair, huh?" he stated, sounding resigned.

"In more ways than one," I admitted. "I …"

"I get it. I know how it looked. Fuck, I told her not to come, Lizzie."

"Did you sleep with her?" I blurted out, my heart pounding.

"Fuck, Lizzie, what is this? I told you. I was there less than ten minutes."

"I don't mean when you saw her in Dublin," I explained. "I need to know."

"So that you can torture yourself with my answer?" he asked.

"I'll take that as a yes," I said flatly.

"All right, since you've asked, I'll give it to you straight. Not to hurt you, but to let you know I aim to have no secrets from you. I did—once. The night of the Oscars. But fuck, do I regret that now."

"Do you?"

"I just said so, didn't I? I'm in love with you, Lizzie. Fuck, sometimes I think it would be easier if I wasn't."

"Is that how you feel?"

Greg let out a long sigh. "Of course, it isn't, I'm drunk so my heart is a wee bit anesthetized. But I'm tired, Lizzie. With or without you, this thing between us will never end. That doesn't mean I can take being crushed again. This back and forth is killing me."

"I believe you," I blurted out. "I've realized I'm hurting us both with how I behave. I couldn't bear being without you last night. Those few nights in bed beside you were enough to teach me what I've been missing … and I don't mean the sex. Let me say this, then I'll drop the subject.

"For the first time in my life, I felt ready to try to be everything you want me to be. Learning you left me to go to her devastated me. It was like you respected her feelings more than mine. Then I thought you went because she was a huge star, so more important—"

"No one is more important to me than you, Lizzie," he said, cutting me off. "I swear that I only went to see her to get her to leave me alone."

"I know that now. And I guess if we're going to do this, I need to grow a tougher skin, like Floyd suggested. That's not going to be easy."

"Baby, you'll get all the support you need from the strong women the guys in the band have surrounded themselves with. Sadie's a ball breaker, Beth … well, she's been to hell and back, and she came out the other side. Sadie—I'm sure she'll tell you her story once you get to know her."

"I wish I was there with you, in Paris," I confessed.

"Lizzie, you have no idea how much I wish you were here."

"Would you do me a favor?" I asked quietly.

"Anything for you," he said playfully.

"Would you tell me about your life in Miami?"

"Sure, there's no time like the present. Do you want me to start now while you're lying in bed?"

"I didn't mean now, I meant—"

"It's not as if I have anything better to do. I'm lying here all alone in this huge bed. And I want you to know because once I get back, we'll be making plans."

Greg then described in vivid detail where everyone lived, what happened when they went on tour, how important it would be for me to travel with him.

Just lying there listening to him at the other end of the line made my heart feel full, but the things he told me made it race. Suddenly I was no longer scared about what the future held because I was ready to put my faith in him.

"Jesus, is that the time? It's after 7:00 a.m. I need to help Ruth with the girls," I mumbled as I started to get out of bed.

"Yeah, and I'll grab a couple of hours sleep before I go to our band rehearsal."

"Break a leg," I said, smiling. "I love you, Greg. I can't wait to see you tomorrow," I said as my heart ached that I had to hang up.

"I love you too, baby." I was about to put the phone down when he said my name again. "Lizzie?"

"Yeah," I said, putting my cell phone back to my ear.

"I can't believe we're finally going to do this," he muttered with a vulnerability in his tone I'd never heard from him before.

"You'd better believe—" I mumbled and abruptly stopped because my cell phone battery died.

CHAPTER 50

GREG

As I laid talking to Eliza for hours, I felt able to say things I had only dreamed of sharing with her until tonight ... or rather this morning by the time we finally said goodnight.

Even though I was exhausted when the call abruptly ended, there was a wired feeling inside me, that just wanted the gig we had to do to be over, so that I could get back to her.

I wasn't so stupid to think that since she'd agreed we couldn't live without each other that everything would be smooth sailing from now on. After all, you don't wipe out a lifetime of fears in a heartbeat like that.

There had been certain times when I'd looked at Raff during the past few days and figured he thought Eliza was unhinged, and to an outsider there were times she gave them cause—like the mashed potato incident. But I suspected that Sadie and Deakon got her, because Sadie had trust issues of her own.

It was almost an hour after our call before I finally felt settled enough and I was just dozing off when I heard the faint sound of moaning coming from the direction of Raff's adjoining suite. I smiled, until I remembered the last time I saw him, I'd told him to escort Beth to bed.

Turning over, I buried my head with a pillow to block out the noise because if it was her in there, Raff was either braver or more stupid than I thought he was. Especially since Levi tended to be overprotective about the women in his life.

"Morning," Raff greeted, much more chipper than he had been in weeks, since getting laid.

"It is," I said in a hoarse tone.

"Breakfast is here," he announced before wandering over to my hotel room door and taking the breakfast trolley from the server outside.

Instantly, my mind went back to Eliza and my heart flipped over in my chest when I remembered how happy I'd felt after we'd left our conversation earlier. Reaching over to the nightstand, I grabbed my cell phone and sent her a text message.

Me: Morning gorgeous. I just want to say I love you and I can't wait to see you tomorrow. I hope you have a fabulous day.

"Come on, get your ass out of bed," he ordered as he pulled back the drapes and set the trolley beside the small dining table in the living room part of the suite.

"You're too fucking cheerful this morning, anyone would think you got laid last night," I muttered, pretending I hadn't heard the noise from his room.

"I've got plenty to be cheerful about. It's Paris and it's not pissing down with rain."

"It doesn't rain in Dublin all the time."

"All the time I've been there it has," Raff retorted as I poured myself some coffee. I lifted a sausage from my platter and bit it in half. "I was on the phone half the night with Eliza."

"Oh, and how is Miss Sunshine?"

"Cut that the fuck out," I muttered. "Once you get to know her, you'll love her."

"I can't wait," he mumbled sarcastically.

"Alright, I wasn't going to go there," I said, feeling pissed by his response. "Was that Beth I heard in your room last night?"

"Beth?"

I laughed because he almost choked out her name because I'd caught him off guard.

"Don't give me that shit. Oh, Raff," I mimicked in Beth's breathy, American accent. "How many other American women do you know in this hotel?"

Raff gave me a sheepish grin and shook his head. "Not a fucking word," he mumbled as he rubbed the back of his neck.

"I think you'll find Oh, Raff is two words," I replied, enjoying watching him look uncomfortable for once.

He grabbed a cup from the coffee tray in the room and sat down beside me. Taking my pot of coffee, he poured himself one. "We were waiting until after the wedding to tell everyone, but Beth and I have been an item for quite a while."

"Jesus, you kept that quiet."

He shrugged. "It's a delicate situation … I mean it's in my contract that I can't fraternize with band members or their relatives," he disclosed.

"What? I never knew that. Who wrote up the contracts?"

"Bodhi, with the legal team."

"This isn't a fuck buddy kind of deal, is it?"

"Nah, it's getting serious now. That was one of the reasons I mentioned Kane Exeter's band. When I was approached to join their security team, being with Beth made me hesitate about taking the job. We weren't that serious at that point, but now …

let's just say if it wasn't for the friendship I've developed with you, I'd be gone already."

"Would I be selfish if I said I'm glad you stayed?"

"Nah, I never took the time to get to know you before. Being in Dublin has made me realize you're actually a really good guy."

"Well … that's high praise indeed," I joked, as I lifted some toast and buttered it.

"So, things might change after Beth and I tell them we want to be together."

"It won't. I won't work with anyone else either, not now that I've spent time with you."

Raff smiled. "Thanks, Greg. Look at us having a bromance moment."

We laughed. "Where is Beth now?"

"Gone back to her room. We came to mine because we felt there was less chance of being caught at mine. Bodhi or Mikey always text what's happening, but one of the girls may have called on Beth."

"Don't worry. I've got your back. You might take some shit for overstepping, but you signed that contract before you even knew Levi had any sisters, right?"

Raff nodded. "True," he mumbled as a text message alert came on my cell phone.

My Lizzie: Good morning. I miss you. Why can't it be tomorrow already?

I smiled because she missed me. I missed her too, and like her, I couldn't wait for us to be back together.

Me: All good things come to he/she who waits.

My Lizzie: I feel like I've waited a lifetime already.

"Okay, let me finish my breakfast and put our love lives aside, because I have a two point five million-dollar job to do."

The venue we were playing at was an upmarket nightclub that had been rented out for Josephine Odette Devereaux's twenty-first birthday bash. No expense had been spared for her family and some five hundred guests.

As we'd arrived, a truck was loading some of the many birthday gifts she'd received, under the watchful eye of two security guards.

"Fuck me, did you see the car lot outside? There are hundreds of millions worth in hardware out there. It's like they've taken Maserati, Ferrari, Pagini, Lamborghini, Aston-Martin, Bugatti and Rolls Royce showrooms and transported them here for the night."

"I blame the owners' parents for indulging their kids like that. They've got more money than sense. I mean how else can they afford rides like those at their age?" Deakon mused.

"At any age," Jude countered in agreement.

Earlier in the day we'd all turned up for a quick rehearsal and found out that we were one of three bands, and our set time had been reduced from three hours to two. Apparently, there was a French pop star on before us, and some French band none of us had heard of, headlining.

Personally, none of us could care less where we were scheduled to play because this wasn't about status, it was simply the birthday girl's personal preference.

"I've never seen so many twenty-one-year-olds draped in jewels like that before. Not even at an award ceremony," Korry muttered after we'd spent over an hour in the politest meet and greet that I'd ever encountered.

Then again, it always felt weird talking to people through an interpreter if they didn't speak English.

"At least they're not dressed in ball gowns," Deakon argued as we reached the designated dressing room with our band name in golden letters stuck on the door. "Fuck me, so this is how the other half lives?" he muttered.

We were used to people treating us well, and having privileges others would never see in their lifetimes, but unlike some of the venues we played, the dressing room looked palatial, with four sectional sofas, individual mirrored booths, a large screen TV, and a well-stocked drinks cabinet. It had to rank as the poshest one we'd ever been in.

As we entered, Bodhi and Raff set our bags down, while Mikey went off to check for weak spots in the venue, security wise. Then, Levi turned, placed his hands on his hips and frowned. "Right, females out. Band warm up time," he demanded, probably because Trinnie wasn't there.

Esther, Sadie and Beth did as he asked. However, Bernadette, as our band PA, took out her famous Tupperware box and shook it in front of her.

"Right guys, you know the drill," she mumbled, tapping the side of the plastic tub. We each took out our cell phones and dropped them inside the box. "Lovely. Don't worry, I'll bring them back as soon as you're finished. Have fun and break a leg, everyone," she informed us.

Before she left, Bernadette reached out and grabbed Korry by the hem of his T-shirt. She planted a kiss on his cheek and whispered something into his ear. Korry snickered and shook his head, clearly amused by whatever she'd said.

"That looked like a promise from where I'm sitting," remarked Jude with a chuckle.

"It was. The sex is always explosive after a gig."

"Guys, cut it out. I'm the only one not getting any tonight," I grumbled.

"Oh, please, stop playing the poor me card. Look at Bodhi and Raff. They won't be getting any either," Deakon argued.

Raff was still in the room at that point and cast a glance over toward me. "Yeah, poor Raff, he never gets any," I replied deadpan.

IT NEVER GOT old that no matter how people were dressed where we performed, or that there might be a language barrier, we had fans in all walks of life.

Seeing everyone pulse in unison, in response to the beat, and singing in the language the song was written in, was a point of fascination for me.

Sure, there were songs that I didn't understand the lyrics, but could still appreciate the technical aspects of the music and the melody. But it still made me wonder what fans of our music that didn't understand the lyrics got out of it. Was it a superficial groove that made them like it, or something else.

For me, my favorite songs were usually because I loved the beat first, then the melody. But the songs I had the deepest connections with came from a combination of those, and how clever or profound the lyrics were that accompanied everything else.

Levi certainly gave them their money's worth. When it was disclosed that Josephine played the guitar, her friends suggested she join us on stage. There was a few minutes of gentle persuasion. I saw straight away that she wanted it to do it, but like most precious, spoiled drama queens, she milked the crowd coaxing her to perfection.

Dressed in a purple velvet one-piece jump-suit, the beautiful brunette girl climbed onto the stage. Then she clung tightly to Levi's side.

"So, Josephine," Levi mumbled into his mic.

Josephine's guests went wild, and she pretended to be shy, by burying her face in Levi's chest. Again, her timing was perfect as she waited for the vibe of the crowd to change before she lifted her head and nodded.

"What should we sing?" Levi asked her into the mic.

She leaned toward him with her hand cupped around her mouth.

Levi pulled a face, his nose wrinkled like he didn't like the choice she made but when Josephine pouted, he relented and nodded.

"All right," he said, shrugging. He turned to Deakon. "She wants "Waiting For a Girl Like You" by Foreigner."

Deakon chuckled. "Bet you're glad Trinnie isn't watching, she'd have your twins for singing that with another woman," he said, nodding at Levi's crotch.

Once our guitar tech had given Josephine an acoustic guitar, Deakon found the key and played softly over her acoustic version as she and Levi began to sing.

Josephine's guests went crazy, cheering and singing along in support, to the mellow soft rock ballad, while she grinned up at Levi for indulging her.

Given her status and money, the girl wasn't all show, she had some serious talent and added some tapping into the version which added a positive to their performance.

When the song finished, she bowed and had the grace to hold her cheeks like she was fangirling. "Thank you! Levi Milligan, you made my dream come true. I've wanted to sing with you since I was eleven years old."

Levi chuckled and leaned in to talk in the same mic as her. "And that doesn't make me feel old," he muttered. The members of the audience who could understand English laughed.

Once the guitar tech took the guitar off her, Levi asked for a sharpie. He signed the back of the body, passed it to each of us and we signed it as well. "From Screaming Shadows to you. Happy

Birthday," he said, passing it back to her again as he gave her a kiss on the cheek.

My mind immediately went back to the piles of gifts we saw being stowed in that truck and figured that relatively low-value guitar would become one of the most prized birthday presents she got.

AFTER OUR SET, Mr. Devereaux came to the dressing room to talk to us with his wife. "Thank you so much for coming all the way from the US to make our daughter happy. We appreciate you all taking the time out of your busy lives to make our beautiful daughter's birthday so special."

He sounded gracious in his appreciation. "Please feel free to leave anytime because I'm sure if you tried to join in the festivities out there, you'd only get mobbed," he mused in his perfect English with the slightest hint of a French accent. He thanked us again and left the dressing room.

"Well, that had to be the easiest gig we've ever done," Jude mumbled. "Thanks guys. I really appreciate you doing this for me as well."

"Don't mention it, buddy. I can't wait to have you as a neighbor," Deakon muttered.

"Fuck. Don't make me regret the move. You're not going to pester me every five minutes, are you?" Jude grumbled, making us laugh.

Bernadette knocked on the door. "Um, this is a first," she muttered, waving an envelope, looking more ruffled than usual.

"What's that?" Korry asked, snatching it from her and reading the typed wording on the front. "To the band and crew," he read out loud.

"Well, open it," Deakon prompted, as intrigued as the rest of us.

Korry ripped open the envelope and pulled out a check. "Oh, fuck, it's the paycheck for $2.5 million."

Bernadette shook her head. "No, it isn't. Mr. Devereaux paid your fee before you guys left the US. He said this is a tip for a job well done."

"He double bubbled us?" I asked, confused.

Everyone sat and stared at each other, stunned that someone would do this. It wasn't often we were left speechless by anyone … actually, I think that was a first.

CHAPTER 51

GREG

"Can I have a word?" Bernadette asked, tugging my T-shirt as I was walking back to the dressing room. The worried look in her eyes, and the solemn way she said it, told me that word would be bad news.

As we dropped back behind the others, I was conscious Raff had done the same.

"What am I supposed to have done now?" I asked, instantly ready to defend myself.

"Were you with Lori Sinclair last night?"

My jaw dropped and my eyes flared wide. Her question immediately made me feel anxious and sent my heart racing. "Excuse me? Why the hell would you think that?"

"Raff asked me not to say anything until after the gig," she muttered, glancing at Raff.

"He asked you not to say what?"

"Greg, I called bullshit on that story anyway, so I didn't see any reason to upset you right before the gig. I know exactly where you were because I put your drunken ass to bed last night and woke you up this morning."

"Would someone mind telling me what the fuck you're both talking about?"

Bernadette fired up the tablet she'd been clutching to her chest along with the Tupperware box with all our cell phones inside. The moment a picture of Lori Sinclair popped up, I almost blacked out in frustration.

'How far will Lori Sinclair and Greg Booker go to keep their love affair under wraps?' read the headline.

As my eyes scanned the article, I stopped breathing the moment I reached the quote from Lori. "Don't you guys have anything better to do than track my love life?"

When asked if she was with Greg last night Lori was quick to reply, "No comment." She went on to add, "What Greg and I do in our private lives is none of your business."

"Bitch," I muttered. "How the fuck did she know I was here? And that statement she made is so ambiguous that even I think it suggests she could have been with me. You had no fucking right to tell Bernadette to keep this from me. I can't imagine what Eliza thinks of me now," I ranted at Raff.

"We only saw it ten minutes before you were due to do the gig," Raff argued. "There would have been no time for you to process it before you went on stage. Admit it, you'd have been all over the place with your performance."

I gave him a death glare because even if he was right, I had needed to have that information the moment it was discovered.

"Once you calm down, you'll see what I did was for the best. I made a decision because an hour here or there wouldn't make any difference because that story had already been out there since early afternoon."

"What the fuck is she playing at?" I grumbled, glancing at the image of her smiling for the camera. "Did anyone tell her I was coming here?" I asked Bernadette.

"No. Apart from Donnie, the band, the crew and me, no one else knew about this gig or where you were staying," she replied.

"Get my cell phone out, I need to call Eliza," I said, nodding toward the plastic box in her hands. "Then get me someone from the press to talk to. I want to make a statement." Bernadette opened the box with our phones, and before she could find mine, I grabbed it and hurriedly pulled it out. "Give me ten minutes, I need to make a call." Bernadette glanced at me with concern.

"Go check on the others and give them their phones. I got this," Raff muttered. I glared at him while I waited for my call to connect.

"Look at how you're reacting. Could you have handled this and then gone into that gig, doing your best?" he challenged.

"That would have been my shit to deal with."

"Yeah? And because I know you so well, I figured there was a real chance that the band wouldn't have had a bass player tonight," he replied, calling me out. "You'd have been in a cab on the way to the airport as the rest of the band walked out on that stage."

I blew out a breath as my call to Eliza connected.

"Lizzie, I swear I wasn't with her," I blurted out before she even spoke.

"I know," she said in a calm tone, surprising me. In fact, it was probably the calmest I'd ever heard her. Her even response took the heat out of my temper.

"I have no clue what the fuck what Lori was trying to do, making that statement," I protested.

"Oh, I do. She was warning me off. You told her about us, and she figures that if she makes waves, I'll think the worst of you."

"So, you believe me?"

"Please, Greg. Of course I do. I know you weren't with her last night because you were with me. There's no way we could have had the kind of conversations we had if you'd had her in the room. Even without ever knowing that, I noticed how smug she looked.

That expression is one that warns people that she usually gets her own way."

"Well ... she won't get her way with me," I affirmed.

"I know," she agreed quietly.

"Fuck, you don't understand how relieved I am," I replied as my heart began to relax. "Although, Lizzie, what happens in the future if shit like this happens?"

"I'll need to believe you until I'm proven wrong," she replied, sounding determined. "I should thank her because it's made me realize how easily this can happen. I was convinced that Lori was trying to teach me a lesson or attempting to keep the rumor about us going with her little stunt."

I smiled. "Thanks, baby. You have made my day."

"I'd rather make your night tomorrow," she muttered cockily.

"Oh, you will," I confirmed, smiling wider.

"So where are you now?"

"Just finished the gig. I literally came off stage to that fucking article. You can't imagine how pissed I was when I read it."

"Forget about it ... and her."

"I will now that I've spoken to you. I'm just going back to the dressing room, then we'll be heading back to the hotel. I can't wait for tomorrow to see you again."

"I've missed you."

"Me too, even five minutes apart is too long right now," I admitted.

"Oh, now you're starting to sound clingy," she teased.

"Oh, I'll be clinging alright," I said, glancing up and seeing Raff standing, leaning against the hallway wall. "Right, I better get off before Raff vomits. He's standing here watching this lovefest."

"He still doesn't like me, does he?"

"He doesn't know you. Once he does, he'll love you," I replied, not denying Raff had his reservations about her.

"Night, Greg," she mumbled, sounding tired.

"Night, baby. See you tomorrow."

CHAPTER 52

ELIZA

"Jesus, Eliza would you sit still for five minutes?" Ruth grumbled as I stood up and glanced out at the driveway for the tenth time in as many minutes. Greg had messaged me from the airport that he and the band were on their way to the house.

The doorbell rang and my heart instantly pounded in my chest. "They're here?" I asked, confused because the driveway had been empty when I'd sat down.

I shot out of the chair, my nerves suddenly jangling while an adrenaline buzz filtered throughout my body. Taking a deep breath, I exhaled slowly and attempted a composed walk to the door.

My disappointment must have shown on my face once I opened the door, because the smile on the delivery woman's face that looked back at me fell instantly.

"Oh good, the food's here," Ruth mumbled, ignoring me and opening the door wider. I glanced over the woman's shoulder, and I saw a local boutique restaurant's delivery truck.

"I did tell you the band's PA had arranged for a food drop for when everyone got here, didn't I?" Ruth muttered. By the over-eager tone in her voice, she knew she hadn't shared that with me.

When the delivery woman had gone, Ruth began the task of laying everything out on the table. Once the cakes, pastries, open sandwiches, and hot BBQ food in insulated containers was laid out, we grabbed plates from the cabinet and stacked them at one end with napkins and silverware beside them.

While we were finishing this chore, the front door opened, and a cacophony of conversation spilled into the hallway. It sounded as if everyone was talking at once. Then my heart almost burst out of my chest because that noise registered that Greg had come back.

As I hurried out into the hallway, Aria came bursting out of her room, almost knocked me over, and ran past me. "Uncle Greg, you're back," she screamed excitedly and flung herself at him. Raff stepped back to let her connect with her favorite person.

Greg wrapped his strong arms around her, lifted her up and kissed her cheek. He smiled widely as he glanced up at me. "See that's how you greet someone who's been away," he informed me as he set Aria back on her feet.

"And if I did that, they'd have been scraping you off the drive-way," I said deadpan as I smiled, walking toward him.

"I like her already," the smooth-talking lead singer of his band said, chuckling, as he smiled toward me. "Levi, and you must be Lizzie," he said, placing a hand over his chest, before he leaned forward and kissed my cheek. A mixture of excitement and shock ran through me in another rare fangirl moment.

"Eliza," Greg muttered darkly, correcting his bandmate. Greg moved in on Levi and put his arm around my waist. "No one calls her Lizzie, except for me."

Levi grinned. "Damn, I never thought I'd see the day where Greg Booker puffs his chest out to protect what's his," Levi droned out, amused. "This is my soon-to-be-wife, Trinnie," he said, pulling a beautiful woman slightly in front of him. His eyes softened the instant hers met his, and then she focused her gaze on me.

"Hey, Eliza. Greg tells us you're coming to live in the US. Florida is my home state. And being in real estate, I've discovered some real hidden gem places. I can't wait for you to come over so that I can show you around," she informed in a friendly tone.

I stared for a second, basking in the connection I made with Levi's partner, because like Beth she had a warmth to her that made me instantly like her.

"I can't believe I'm actually going to the US. I'm so nervous. But I'll look forward to your offer, and to getting to know you better," I replied.

"We're a pretty close-knit bunch of people. You'll soon get sick of the sight of all of us," Deakon teased.

"You're not joking," Sadie muttered. "Some days I have to go visit Levi, just to get away from you," she replied to him.

Deakon laughed. "Yeah, then you remember what I'm packing and come running back," he muttered playfully. His comment earned him a punch in the arm from his girl, which made everyone laugh.

"I'm Jude, and this is Esther," Jude Collymore informed me, stepping around Levi, like I wouldn't know who they were. He sounded every inch as broody as the TV interviews I'd watched. He hitched his thumb over his shoulder. "This is my security guy, Bodhi," he muttered, introducing a mean-looking guy with what looked like a permanent scowl on his face.

"Would everyone like to come into the kitchen," Ruth suggested as the hallway was overrun with people. Aria was still dancing around and getting under everyone's feet.

As everyone moved along the hallway, I noticed Korry and the woman I recognized as their PA, from the internet, Bernadette, standing outside.

"Come on, you two," Greg demanded, waving them in.

"Nice place," Korry praised as he and Bernadette stepped inside. "Hey, Eliza, isn't it? We've heard so much about you from Greg. It's great to finally meet you," he added.

"I've been hearing some things about you two as well," I said, smiling as I recalled Greg telling me on the phone how Korry got Bernadette stoned the time they had to share her motor home.

"Yeah, yeah," Bernadette said, waving her embarrassment off, but her cheeks pinked up anyway. "Good to meet you, Eliza. I guess we're going to be seeing a lot of each other."

"That's the plan," Greg interjected. "Come on, I'm starving. I can smell that delicious food you ordered from here." Guiding them into the kitchen, Greg pulled out a seat for me, then one for Bernadette.

Once I sat down, I looked around the table and began to take everything in. Floyd had joined everyone and sat at the head of the table, with Ruth squeezed along beside him.

At that point, I zoned out for a couple of minutes. I sat in silence as everyone spoke around me while I stared at Levi Milligan, lead singer of Screaming Shadows directly in the flesh, in front of me.

Is any of this real? Is this really my life now?

"Right, Lizzie?" Greg asked, pulling me out of my reverie.

"Huh?" I asked, making Greg chuckle.

"You're going out with the girls tonight while us guys take Levi on his bachelor party."

"I'll stay with Ruth, keep her company," I offered once I knew Floyd was going with them.

"My ma's coming to babysit," Ruth informed me.

"Okay," I said tentatively, wondering how I would hold my own in the company of four other rock stars' partners.

While everyone ate, the chat at the table was rowdy and full of fun. Then, after we'd eaten, Greg stood and pulled me out of my seat.

"Right, guys, if you'll excuse us. I haven't seen my Lizzie since before Paris. We need some time before us guys leave for the rental house." Gently, he slid an arm around my waist and led me out of the kitchen, and upstairs to my room.

I'd barely cleared my bedroom door before he spun me around and shoved me back against the nearest wall. Closing the door, he kept his distance but slapped his palms on the wall on either side of my head, like he was scared to touch me. Taking a small step forward he rested his forehead on mine and searched my eyes.

"Baby, no more hurt on either side. I can't bear to be away from you anymore," he admitted.

"I hated it too. The other night devastated me that I couldn't be there with you."

"We need to sort that passport out fast, Lizzie. Levi and Trinnie's wedding is only a week away, and it would kill me if I couldn't take you back with me."

"I got all the forms ready, and I've had them notarized. The passport takes ten days as it's my first-time passport."

"Fuck. I'll speak to Bernadette, see if there is some way the passport office can speed it up."

The more positive my thoughts were about leaving Dublin for a new life with Greg, the greater my excitement grew. Then I was instantly anxious I might not get to leave with him on time.

"Am I getting a kiss or what?" I asked since I was dying for that to happen, because he hadn't kissed me once since he'd been back.

"I'm scared to," he admitted, smiling.

"Scared?" I asked. He lifted his forehead from mine and instead of kissing me on the lips he kissed my neck instead. Goosebumps instantly sprouted all over my body while a thrill ran down to my core. He moved his hands from the wall to my hips, then he pressed his body so hard against mine that my spine flattened against the wall.

"Fuck, you have no idea what I want to do to you, Lizzie."

"Show me," I murmured seductively, goading him on.

"It would take me all night to do you justice. I don't have the time right now," he said, sounding pained by his confession.

"Now you show restraint?" I asked. "Where's the impulsive guy that acts first and thinks later?" I goaded.

"He's still here," he said, pressing his erection against my pubic bone and grinding it in small, delicious circles.

"But I'm thinking with this one," he said, pressing his forehead to mine again. "I'm desperate to do this right for you this time, Lizzie. I can't afford to fuck up again," he whispered seriously.

My heart clenched at the note of anxiety I heard in his explanation. His words immediately resonated with my own sentiments regarding how anxious I was to put things right between us.

"Okay, don't kiss me because I already know that one kiss won't be enough. Go, have fun, but when the night is over, you come back to my bed, you aren't sleeping anywhere else."

"Dude, put your dick away. Mikey's back and we want to get to the rental and freshen up before we hit the town," Deakon called from the bottom of the stairs.

"And that's my cue, baby. Like I said … I need a night, not a few stolen minutes with what I have in mind for you. By the way, I'm not drinking tonight, and you can bet your sweet arse, I'll be in your bed tonight."

Placing his hands on the wall, he pushed himself free of me, stuck his hand down his jeans and adjusted his cock, giving me a sheepish grin.

"You wouldn't believe the protest that's going on down there," he teased. "Have a great night with the girls, Lizzie, you're going to love them."

Opening the door, I smiled when I heard him cuss to himself. "I can't believe I'm leaving us both hard-up like this, to spend a night with a bunch of drunken, hairy-arsed rock stars."

CHAPTER 53

GREG

It was almost 8:00 p.m. when we arrived at 37 Dawson Street. As it was Saturday night, the bar was heaving. They didn't usually take reservations, but once Bernadette explained who we were and what the occasion was, the owner made an exception.

My brother was already waiting outside, having been dropped off by one of his parishioners five minutes before. After some quick introductions and reintroductions we headed inside.

On entering the trendy, eclectic place, our party was led to a mezzanine floor with a huge, wooden table and a great view of the bar downstairs and several Mahatma Gandhi images hung on the wall behind us.

"Let's have some shots to get the party started," Levi informed the pretty server. "Let's go cliché and have tequila. Two bottles. Bring tumblers, a bottle of Jameson's whiskey, a good bourbon, some gin and some vodka as well," he ordered, eyeing each of us individually and mentally assessing what we all drank.

"A glass of chianti for me," Tim mumbled awkwardly. I glanced toward him and took in for the first time what he wore.

Dressed in a mustard-colored, Arran, roll-neck sweater, under a green tweed jacket, a pair of black pants and some brown suede boots, he looked completely out of keeping with the rest of us. While we were dressed for a casual night on the town, my brother looked as if he had been heading for the nearest literary society.

As the server went off to get the drinks, Jude frowned as he assessed his best buddy. "Easy, Levi," he warned. "Remember that promise you made to yourself," he added, reminding him of the bad decisions he'd made while drunk in the past.

Levi's expression darkened. "I do remember," he snapped. "But I'm allowed to get shit-faced tonight. It's my bachelor party."

I didn't miss the concerned look that passed between Jude and Bodhi. In the past, drink had been Levi's demon, which had caused him to make some poor decisions around his fidelity with women. Decisions that had brought unwelcomed public attention about his behavior.

Jude waved a hand for Mikey to lean in and he whispered something to him, covering his mouth with a hand. I didn't need a degree in intelligence to know he was tasking Mikey to shadow Levi's movements closely.

It only took around thirty minutes before the first females ventured upstairs and began asking for pictures. Naturally, we obliged. We downed half a dozen or more of tequila shots each, and a couple of shots of whiskey, therefore, I had mellowed a lot and had a slight buzz going on in my body.

Fortunately, I had Eliza on my mind, so I decided I'd skip the booze from then on and switch to soda water. It had never been in my interest to stay sober during previous nights out, but it gave me a rare opportunity to watch the dynamic of the group that I hadn't noticed before.

Uncharacteristically, Levi hit the whiskey hard, drinking half a bottle, after the shots, in less than half an hour. Knowing he had gone to rehab in the past and drink being part of his problem had obviously made everyone else on edge.

Jude was being measured in his alcohol intake, more so than usual. I suspected that was due to his concern about Levi acting recklessly.

"So, when are the strippers coming?" Levi asked playfully.

"Unless the stripper is called Trinnie, that won't be happening, dude," Jude muttered, looking agitated. "It's bad enough that you're getting pissed out of your head, without having your twins castrated by your girl, a few days before your wedding."

Deakon stood and wandered over to the server, mumbled something to her, and passed her a wad of euros. I stood to go to the restroom and passed him on his way back to the table.

"I've asked her to get the barman to water down the next bottle of whiskey. We're all going to take a shot to finish the one that's still on the table," he advised me.

To an Irishman putting water in the whiskey was sacrilege. But for the sake of Levi's future, I forgave Deakon's action because he'd only made that decision out of necessity.

It had been years since Levi had taken alcohol to excess, and knowing that Trinnie meant everything to him, we as a band gave our support to see him through the night without fucking his future up.

Levi stood and swayed slightly, before he headed toward the restroom as I was coming back. Mikey and Korry immediately stood and went with him.

"Guys, I think we need to change venue and call on the girls. I haven't seen him go off the rails like this in years," Jude mumbled. "If I'm honest, I think it's the final commitment thing."

"Final commitment?" I asked, not sure what he meant.

"You heard the stories about him picking up women, and that he was in an open relationship before Trinnie. It was one of the reasons he headed to rehab. There's a lot of history surrounding his father, he wasn't the best role model for Levi growing up. Anyway, I know you know some of this, but he had a shit time and that fucked with his ability to manage fidelity."

"Right," I said, being able to relate somewhat since I had spread myself around due to not getting the commitment I'd wanted from Eliza.

"Do you want me to talk to him?" Tim asked.

"No. There's no point. The only way around this is distraction. I'm going to message Esther to meet us at another club. I'm confident that once Trinnie's around, he'll get his shit together," Jude informed me.

"Let me text, Eliza. I'll tell Lizzie to meet us at Pygmalion. It's a great nightclub and a bit of a walk from here. That should sober him up a bit before he gets there."

Deakon grabbed the bottle of watered-down whiskey and slid it into his jacket pocket. "If he's drinking anything else, he'll be drinking this." He sighed. "Fuck, I could do with a smoke, want to come with me?" he asked, nodding down toward the exit.

"Go. If you're all outside, it'll be easier to get Levi to leave," Bodhi muttered, then hung back with Jude, Tim and Floyd while Raff accompanied Deakon and I outside.

"Fuck, I haven't seen Levi so hell bent on getting drunk in years," Deakon said as he pulled a bashed joint out of his inside jacket pocket and squeezed it back in shape. "Hey, boys," two young women, with skirts up to their arses and enough cleavage to distract a monk, stated.

"Hi, ladies," Deakon replied, playing up to them.

"Oh, Jesus, it's Greg Booker," one of them said before her jaw dropped in surprise.

"Oh, wow. It's sexy Greggy," the other remarked, wandering closer to me. "Show us your abs," she demanded, winking.

"Not fucking likely, it's freezing," I mumbled, trying to sound playful.

"Show us your tits," Deakon shot back. I knew he meant his remark in response to her demand on me, rather than an actual request. She twirled around quickly and stared him out.

"Deakon fucking Mosely," she mused. "I'll show you mine, if you show me yours."

"Alright, but you first," Deakon remarked, nodding toward her top. We both figured his comment would have given the girl pause for thought and she'd leave, but without hesitation, she lifted her shirt and flashed her black lacy bra. "There," she said and pulled her shirt down again. "Your turn."

"Ah, that wasn't your tits, that was your bra," he countered.

"Fuck, me," she muttered before she lifted her top up again, hooked her fingers under the wires on her bra and her tits sprang free, right there in the street.

"Ah, see ... now, that's what I call flashing," Deakon praised, glancing at me with wide eyes, like he couldn't believe she'd done it.

"Your turn," she coaxed Deakon, nodding toward his junk.

"Alright," he agreed much to my surprise.

For a second, he placed his hands on his belt, glanced toward me and shot me a grin. Then in a flash he moved his hands to his T-shirt and lifted it up his chest. "There you go," he said, then quickly pulled his T-shirt back into place.

What the fuck was that? That's cheating," she mumbled, frowning.

"Cheat—me—never," he replied, scoffing.

"You promised," she mumbled, pouting. I turned to look for her friend, and saw she'd left and was sitting at a table on the other side of the window of the pub with another group of people.

"I did promise," Deakon agreed. "And I delivered. You showed me your tits and I showed you mine."

"I meant your cock," she muttered angrily.

"Ah, you should have been more specific. I'd never have made that deal. I'm not in the habit of exposing my junk in public."

I laughed because she stamped her feet and punched her fists against her hips. "I'm never buying another Screaming Shadows album again," she threatened.

"How many do you own?" I asked to distract her.

"None, but that's not the point," she replied before she stopped and stared at me. "You let him do that to me, and you call yourself Irish?" she said, not making sense.

"Firstly, I never let anyone do anything to you. You made a deal with him, and he delivered. Secondly, I don't know what being Irish has to do with you flashing your tits in public. But if it makes you feel any better, I'll reprimand him for you."

"Go on then," she goaded.

"Don't ask women to see their tits again," I said solemnly.

"Thank you, Greg. At least there's one gentleman among the Screaming Shadows band." Without saying anything else she turned on her heel and walked up to the bouncer at the door, as the others were coming out. Catching sight of my brother, I silently thanked my brother's boss there were no exposed breasts to embarrass him.

"Deakon. Don't ask women to show them your tits. It's bad form," I mumbled quietly.

"She started it," he retorted.

"And if I tell Sadie what you did, how do you think she'd respond to that?" Deakon's eyes widened and he winced. "Got it, boss. I will never ask a woman to show me her tits again."

"NOT SEEN him like this for a long time," Raff muttered, as he fell into step with me and Deakon, and nodded toward Levi.

Levi was staggering between Bodhi and Jude while Korry and Mikey were walking in front of them.

"Is Levi an alcoholic? I know everyone says he wasn't but the way he was throwing back the drink tonight—"

"No, he's not an alcoholic. More like a binge drinker, I suppose," Raff remarked, cutting me off. "But you know him well enough. How often have you seen him drink more than two whiskeys since you've been with the band?"

I nodded. "True." I hadn't. "I hate seeing him like this," I remarked.

"I can tell you now, he's going to hate himself tomorrow," Raff informed me.

"Then it's up to us to make sure that his night ends well," I replied.

My cell phone beeped in my pocket. Checking the screen, I saw it was a message from Eliza.

My Lizzie: We're inside. Brian Last from school was the bouncer on the door. He spoke to his mate, and they've sorted out a private section of seating for us.

Me: Great. We'll be there in about ten minutes.

My only hope was that Levi would treat Trinnie with the same respect that he had for her when he was sober.

CHAPTER 54

GREG

"That's it," Jude told Levi as he chucked his dinner into a gutter, near an alleyway.

"Fuck me, I feel rough," Levi mumbled quietly, holding his head.

"I think you're done drinking alcohol tonight," Bodhi ordered, but somehow made his remark sound like a suggestion.

"Maybe we ought to call it a night altogether," Levi suggested, looking pale.

"No can do, big man. We're going dancing with our women," Deakon informed him, pushing past his comment. It was like Deakon felt Levi had to see through his slip and face Trinnie as a reminder of everything good in his life.

"Well, that's a lame move. A bachelor party is supposed to be men only," he grumbled.

"No, a lame move was you getting pissed out of your mind an hour into your shindig. However, part of the fun of a bachelor party is the groom making an ass of himself."

"Yeah, you achieved that with flying colors, since you've spewed up in a public gutter, and I had to hold you up while you took a piss because you almost pissed on your pants in a restroom," Mikey remarked.

"See, it's barely 11:00 p.m. and you've crammed so much into your special night already," Deakon remarked.

"Amen," Tim muttered in agreement.

Jude smirked because Deakon and Mikey didn't hold back but he didn't defend Levi, which was a first, in my recollection of events where anyone took a pop at Levi.

"No more drinking, Levi," Jude ordered. He pulled a small bottle of water from his jacket pocket and passed it to his friend. "Here, swill your mouth out and sober the fuck up. It's been years since you lacked control like this."

Levi's skin appeared to have a slightly green tinge wnder the street lighting, as he did as Jude instructed. Until that moment, I'd always seen Levi as one of the two strongest alpha males in the group, but the way he did as Jude instructed, showed me who was the true alpha between them. "Right, now we're going to find you some strong coffee before we meet the girls."

We traipsed around for twenty minutes until we found a late-night café. Everyone stayed outside as Mikey went in and bought four cups of black coffee. Levi downed the first then retched. "Fuck, I don't think I can do another."

"Yeah, you can, stop being a pussy and get the next one down," Jude told him. I eyed my brother who had wandered off and was in conversation with two homeless people. I saw him take out his wallet and hand each of them a note. *Tim truly is the best of us.*

I began to shiver standing there in the street because I was a lean guy, and I was only wearing a thin jacket.

Raff eyed me carefully. "I'm calling the transport to come and get us. This is lunacy, hanging around with all of you. All we need is some drunken arseholes to take exception to any of you."

Levi had managed his third coffee by the time the passenger van turned up and we all climbed inside.

"Feeling better?" Deakon probed, slapping a hand over Levi's knee.

He nodded but didn't speak. "At least you're presentable for when Trinnie sees you," Jude muttered. "What the fuck were you thinking, going on a bender like that?"

Levi shrugged. "I just thought I'd let my hair down."

"Well, if you pull a stunt like that again, I'll shave it the fuck off in your sleep," Jude warned.

"The galling part of that is, if you did shave his head, he'd still look better than the rest of us put together," I mumbled to Jude, chuckling.

"Oh, yeah, because he really looked stunning barfing back there, right?" Korry suggested in a sarcastic tone.

"All right, you've all had your fun. So, I lacked pace after not drinking much for so long," Levi argued.

"Lacked pace? You could have won the Dublin Marathon with the speed you put that whiskey away," I told him, speaking out against his behavior for the first time.

"Right, we're drawing a line under what happened. Better get your act together before we face our women," Deakon told Levi.

Luckily, we pulled alongside the club at that moment, so there was a natural distraction of us migrating from the van into the club. There was the usual buzz at the door, with fans calling our names, screaming hysterically, and cameras flashing in our direction. Each of us went into professional mode, then waved and had one or two exchanges with fans, who stood on the curb by the entrance.

"Hey, Greg! How's it going, man?" Brian Last, the rugby team captain from high school, greeted as he held out his massive fist. After I bumped his with mine, he pulled me in for a one-sided hug. "I was surprised to see Eliza tonight with all those American women. Then she told us you guys were all on your way, and it made sense. Don't worry, we've made space inside, so you won't get harassed by the clubbers."

"Thanks, man. Meet the guys, Jude, Deakon, Korry, and Levi," I said pointing to each one. My bandmates shook hands with him, then another doorman swapped places with Brian, and he led us inside.

As he weaved his way through to the seating area where our women sat, I saw Eliza on the dance floor, smiling and dancing with Beth. Trinnie, Esther, Ruth and Sadie sat at the table. Sadie stood the moment she saw Deakon and he moved around Brian to wrap his arms around her.

"Thanks, Brian, can you stay for a drink?" I asked.

He shook his head. "We're not allowed to drink while we're on duty."

I thanked Brian again, then headed straight for the dance floor. "Mind if I dance with my woman?" I asked Beth, but didn't take my hungry eyes off Eliza.

"Not at all," she muttered. She wandered back to the group and stood next to the others. Raff moved around and stood beside her, then subtly slid a hand down her backless dress and squeezed her arse. I chuckled because the rest of the group were oblivious to his sly move.

"What's funny?" Eliza asked, her eyes inquisitive.

"Beth and Raff have a thing going on and no one else knows about it."

"Poor Beth," she muttered, and I laughed.

"You know, Raff's going to be looking after you as well, once you come to live in the US."

"Are you deliberately trying to put me off?"

"Of course not, but don't worry, they mainly eat salads and burgers in Florida, not mashed potatoes or Brussel sprouts."

She laughed. "You're never going to let me live that down, are you?" she asked, patting my chest.

Grabbing both wrists I pulled her closer until I felt her breath on my face. My heart clenched, then swelled inside my chest. I looked into the gorgeous hazel eyes of the woman I had always loved and didn't dare to blink. "I can hardly believe you're really coming with me this time," I confessed.

Eliza smiled. "I'm shit scared of the change, but I don't want to live another minute without you," she admitted in a desperate whisper.

"I promise, I'll take care of you, Lizzie. You're the most precious person in the world to me."

"I still find that hard to believe. But in my heart, I know that's the truth," she admitted as we began to sway to the music.

"What do you say that we ditch these people and I take you home to bed?"

"I say, what are you waiting for? Will Brutis need to come with us?"

"You know, I think if I ask Raff to put us in a taxi, we might just get him to stay," I suggested, assessing how into Beth he appeared. "Come on, we'll be polite for five minutes since it's Levi's bachelor party, but once you've said hello, we're out of here."

By the time we reached the table where everyone sat, Levi was acting like nothing had happened while he'd been out with us.

In front of his woman and sisters, Levi was the same attentive, charismatic, and charming guy, they knew him to be. Then, I reflected upon Jude's suspicions as to why Levi had gone off the rails.

It can't have been easy for Levi to believe he had no living relatives, then to find out he had two sisters. I could see what placing his trust and committing to one person must have felt like to him, until he met a woman like Trinnie.

CHAPTER 55

ELIZA

Just as Greg predicted, for once Raff was happy to pack Greg and I off in a licensed taxicab. The ride home was extremely PG rated and nothing I envisaged Greg would be like once we were alone. But this was probably due to us being driven by a female taxi driver.

The middle-aged woman never stopped talking about Screaming Shadows and how much she loved their music. And once Greg knew she was an avid fan of the band, he concocted a whole story about the house being my brother's and how he was visiting us there.

"You've got a smooth tongue in your head," I muttered in response to his white lie, as we walked down the driveway toward his house.

"It was either that, or risk her potentially camping outside my house or spreading my address on social media," he explained, as he wrapped an arm around my shoulders and pulled me into his side.

Creeping into the hallway so as not to wake up the household, we tiptoed upstairs and into my room. The moment the door closed, Greg dipped, picked me up bride style and ran toward my bed. "Fuck," he said, flopping me onto my back, sideways on the bed. He caged me in with all four limbs as he hovered above me.

My breath hitched as I landed, but the moment I stared up at him, I was met with eyes filled with a mixture of love, lust and passion. Watching me silently as his eyes searched my face, Greg stayed perfectly still as he absorbed our first moments alone together again.

"I want you to know that leaving you earlier to go with the guys felt like a special kind of agony to me," he confessed gruffly. "Baby, it killed me not to do it, but if I'd kissed you right then, I could never have left with them. That's the only reason I have for not doing it. The fire that you ignite within me, isn't one that's easily extinguished, Lizzie. Now, I'm guessing that it's the same for you, so I wasn't going to give you a taste of me and leave you wanting either."

"Are you going to kiss me now or should I take off my coat first?" I asked, teasing him.

He rose onto his knees, bent over me, dragged his thumb across my bottom lip, and licked his own lips. Sliding his other hand up to my head, he closed the space between us and crushed my lips to his. Between us, it was a passionate kiss, full of hot, frantic tongues, as we tasted each other like it was our last meal ever.

Breaking contact, Greg's hands immediately moved from my head to beneath my dress. Then his fingers curled around the elastic waistband and roughly dragged down my panties. Leaving them at my ankles, he put his hands in mine and pulled me up on my feet, slid my coat over my shoulders and shoved me back on the bed, with my arms trapped in the sleeves.

"Look at you, lying there at my mercy," he ground out. Something caught his eye at on the floor and he grinned. "Oh, look what I found," he said in amusement, waving my silver bullet vibrator that had fallen from under my pillow.

"Greg," I warned, a little embarrassed. I'd forgotten I'd put it in there.

Switching it on, he smiled as he held it against my cheek. "Now then, what am I going to do with this?" he asked in a mock menacing tone. His gaze dropped to my mouth, and he moved my vibrator to my closed lips. The buzz against my lips from the slow vibrations made my core pulse in anticipation. I felt a trickle of fresh heat leak down my seam toward the crack of my arse.

"You're soaking my dress," I mumbled, smiling against the vibrator.

"Yeah?" he asked, grinning. "Then, I best do something about that," he ground out seductively, and dropped my vibrator next to my head. It buzzed gently against my skull as Greg dropped to his knees. Elevating my feet, still in my stilettos, he tugged off my thong and let it dangle from his teeth. His eyes dropped from my face to watch as his hands slid up my legs. "Such silky skin," he mumbled playfully around the string of my thong still in his mouth.

Once his hands reached my thighs, he slid them underneath. "Oh, shit," I gasped the moment he folded my straight legs over my body and roughly shoved my dress up to my waist. Moving back to my knees he bent my legs and spread me wide open for him.

My panties fell from his mouth when he swallowed hard. Then, the look he gave me was one of pure, carnal desire.

"Fuck, Lizzie," he muttered in a voice filled with reverence as he gently slid a finger along my seam, lifted it to his mouth, and coated both lips with that finger. I tried to wriggle free, desperate to touch him the moment I saw his lips glisten with my slick arousal.

Giving me a wicked grin, he stood, unbuttoned the top two buttons of his shirt and pulled it over his head. Reaching for his belt, he slid it through his belt loops and pulled it free. "Want to swap your coat for this?" he asked playfully.

I nodded. "Good because you're wearing far too many clothes for my liking." Helping me to my feet, he made short work on my coat, dress and bra, turned me around and pushed me down to my knees. Before I knew what was happening, he'd grabbed both wrists behind my back and tied them together with his belt.

"All right. Now where was I?" he whispered close to my ear, sending a shiver down to the base of my spine and a rash of goosebumps covered my skin. Reaching past me to pick up my discarded vibrator that was still buzzing.

Gently he pushed my chest down on the bed, and kicked my feet wider so that I was displayed from behind in front of him.

"So damn pretty, Lizzie. Fuck, I've missed this," he said as he began stroking the back of my knees and thighs with the vibrator as his other hand skated lightly over my back.

"Holy shit," I mumbled as my body trembled under his touch.

"You like that?" he asked before he moved the vibrator and ran it along my slit. "What about this?" he suggested.

"Mm, hm," I muttered as I squeezed my eyes together. My body was alight with the sensations, the low tone of his voice and the way he was playing my body.

"Tell me what you want, Lizzie," he ordered as he ran the vibrator from one side of my neck to the other, quickly followed by his hot breath.

A sharp thrill of delight made my legs buckle when he pressed a kiss at the side of my neck, licked up my neck and stuck his hot tongue in my ear. "Oh, fuck," I gasped.

"Oh, we'll be fucking alright," he warned playfully. "I want to taste you first."

Dropping to his knees behind me, Greg spread my folds open and began licking and sucking my pussy. In seconds I felt my body tighten as my legs began to shake. In that moment, Greg pulled back, denying me the moment of ecstasy I'd waited for all night.

"Not until I'm in you," he said sternly. The sound of rustling material behind me alerted me that he was taking off his jeans, then he placed his wet tip at my entrance.

"Oh, God," I gasped, because unlike the previous few times where he had gone painfully slow, Greg entered me in one long glide until he bottomed out. Then he stilled and I felt his hot, ragged breath on my neck.

"Jesusssssss," he ground out. "So, fucking tight," he muttered, his tone strained. "I'm sorry, I couldn't stop. Are you alright?" he muttered, sounding concerned.

"I'm more than alright, it's perfect."

CHAPTER 56

GREG - FIVE DAYS LATER

"No passport yet," I informed Bernadette over the phone. The band had been back in the US since Monday, but I'd stayed to accompany Eliza.

"I rang the Irish consulate and explained the circumstances to see if they could help. Apparently, they were making some calls and would get back to me."

"Maybe you'd better prepare Levi and Trinnie that we might not make it by Saturday," I replied, bummed that something as simple as a tiny, important document was holding everything up.

"I'm doing my best," Bernadette muttered, sounding almost as frustrated as I was.

"You don't need to tell me that," I agreed. "If you hear anything, please let me know."

After cutting the call, I went down to the kitchen to talk with Floyd and Ruth. The charter had been booked for Floyd, Ruth, my brother Tim and the kids to fly out that evening.

"It looks like we might not be joining you," I admitted, feeling devastated.

"Eliza's going to be upset, especially since it's her last day at work," Ruth offered. "It's an emotional time for her already since she's worked there since she left school."

"Yeah, at least that part worked out well. It was fortunate that she hadn't taken any holiday this year, so she only had to work for four days, instead of a whole month's notice," Floyd replied.

The doorbell rang and we all looked at each other. "Are you expecting a delivery?" I asked, Ruth.

Raff wandered past the kitchen, and I heard him open the door in the hallway. After a short exchange he came in with a package marked urgent. "It's for sunshine," he said casually, dropping it onto the table.

"Passport office," I said, grabbing it. I pulled out my cell phone and rang Eliza.

"There's a package here for you from the passport office. Can I open it?"

"Oh, God, of course. Please may it be here," she prayed as I ripped open the padded envelope and her passport dropped on the table.

"Guess what?" I asked, sounding flat.

"Oh, no," she whined, alarmed. "What's wrong with it?"

"Nothing, baby. Everything's wonderful from my perspective because we're all going to the US tonight." If I was ever in doubt that I'd actually get Eliza to go with me, the squeal of delight that I heard down the line put any reservations I had to bed.

MY HEART WAS BEATING like a drum as I climbed aboard the small jet at Dublin airport in the pouring rain. Eliza looked nervous as I held her hand in a death grip in case she suddenly changed her mind.

Ever since I'd left her behind, a piece of my heart had been missing, and right at that moment, I had a hidden anxiety that she might pull out at the last moment.

She'd barely had time to draw a breath once I'd met her after work with Raff, having taken her to say goodbye to her ma and mine before we were on our way.

"I'm so excited you're finally coming with me," I confessed as she sat down. I helped to buckle her in before I took the seat beside her.

"I'm excited. I've never been to America," my brother disclosed, settling into a seat beside Raff, and behind Floyd and his family. "What time will we get there?"

"About 3:00 a.m. our time, but 10:00 p.m. in Miami. It'll be perfect for a good night's sleep before all the celebrations begin tomorrow at the Bungalows, an exclusive resort near where Levi lives in Key Largo," I told him.

"This all sounds so posh. What if I don't fit in? I've hardly got a size slender body and I'm going to look pale and …" Eliza interjected, then trailed off, her fingers worrying her bottom lip.

"I love your beautiful body and skin," I interjected quickly, sliding a hand into her hair and making her face me before she could self-deprecate. Taking her hand away from her mouth, I held it firmly in mine.

"But—"

"Don't start getting a complex about how you look, baby," I ordered, cutting off any more negative comments. "You're stunning. And anyway, you don't need to please anyone else. Aren't I the one that counts? Just be yourself, Lizzie. I'd never want or expect you to change anything about yourself, to fit into someone else's idea of what is attractive. In fact, I think I'd be pissed if you tried to do that."

"Best I don't then," she mumbled, smiling.

"See, that's my girl. Please don't compare yourself to anyone else. To me you're unique, and that's what I love about you."

"How come you know all the right things to say to make me feel secure?"

"I'm not trying to do that, only speaking my truth. I want you to feel protected and loved."

For a long minute Eliza gazed into my eyes, and the love that poured from them gave me a sense of certainty in my heart to know that look was the forever kind of love.

"I'm struggling to get to grips with what's happening to me ... all these changes ... and being with you," she disclosed with a nervous smile. "I feel like I'm free-falling and I'm going to crash down to earth any minute."

"Trust me, Lizzie, I'll be right here to catch you whenever you feel that happening. I won't let you down or I'll die trying not to."

"I believe you," she said without hesitation, like her issues with trust were dissolving before my eyes. Although I was under no illusions that this might only happen by her challenging her faith in me, one incident at a time.

"Good, keep believing me, baby, because now that I've got you, I intend to do everything I can to keep you."

***

"Fuck me, that's a house for two people?" Eliza mumbled, staring in awe at Deakon and Sadie's place, once Mikey had opened the door of the full-sized van to let everyone out.

"Korry and Bernadette are spending the night at Levi's with Jude and his family," Mikey informed us just as Deakon wandered out of the house, dressed in a pair of basketball shorts.

"Tim, Levi's given you his pool house so that you have some personal space. I'll take you over there in a minute, once we get everyone else settled here," Deakon informed my brother. "You and Eliza are in the first bedroom at the top of the stairs, and Raff, you're in the room next to where Beth's sleeping at the end of the hallway."

Tim glanced toward me, and it was the first time in his life where he looked uncertain to be leaving me. "Don't worry, Levi only lives next door. You're going to bed. We will bring you back first thing tomorrow," I muttered in reassurance.

"That's right, we're leaving for the Bungalows resort at 10:00 a.m. So, Greg and I will pick you up at 9:30 a.m., and then the rest of the party from Deakon's place," Mikey confirmed.

Sadie came out of the house and headed straight for Eliza. "Hey, girl. You look like you could use a drink," she said casually, grabbing her hand and leading her into the house. I silently thanked Sadie's kind gesture, because usually she was snarkier than Eliza. In fact, her greeting toward my girl was probably the friendliest I'd ever seen Sadie.

Deakon took Sadie's lead and ushered us all inside, then took me with him while he showed Floyd and Ruth where their family were bedding down for the night. Leaving them to settle their girls, I felt touched that Deakon and Sadie had rearranged their den and the small reception room next to it, on the ground floor, to accommodate my buddy's family.

Deakon tossed an arm around me on the way back to our girls and grinned. "So, you finally got Eliza here," he said, sounding delighted for me.

I nodded, smiling because it was the happiest I'd felt in years. "Yeah," I replied, suddenly a little choked. "If I'm honest, I'm petrified that I'll fuck up."

"Relax, you won't," Deakon reassured me confidently. "Look at the strong women around her. Trinnie's been through a whole heap of shit ... as has Sadie. Those two will keep her straight. Esther and Beth too, since they know what it's like to have a shit father."

It was true. Everyone one of us had been through some

heartache or other to get to where we were in life. Even Jude with his perfect family had been hurt by missing those first crucial months of his first child's life.

"Thanks for the vote of confidence, mate," I mumbled quietly.

"Right, come on, let's get something to drink before bed, because we'll need to be on our game for the next two days, with Rick Fars, Gibson, Alfie, Flynn and the others all flying in."

"Can't wait," I replied, smiling. "No more slipups from Levi?" I asked, sounding more concerned.

"Nah, he's been as good as gold. I figure he scared himself with how easily he fucked up. He's drank nothing but water since that night. Not even coffee … says he reckons he's got a cold coming, but we know differently. Still, we'd best keep an eye on him this weekend, just in case he gets carried away."

I didn't believe for one minute that Levi would let Trinnie down at their wedding. But Deakon had experienced Levi during the lows in his life and I hadn't. So, I didn't feel qualified to challenge that comment.

CHAPTER 57

ELIZA

Waking to the strange sound of an air conditioner humming quietly and the sound of Greg's steady heartbeat in my ear made me appreciate the huge step I'd taken.

The bedroom was mostly in darkness but with slivers of sunlight attempting to creep in at the edge of the blackout drapes on the bedroom window.

Bees had been swarming in my belly for days. First with that uncomfortable feeling that my passport wouldn't arrive, then once it had, the butterflies took over, due to my anticipation of facing an unknown life ahead.

"Good morning, baby," Greg mumbled as his hand moved from his side to cradle the back of my head. "Sleep well?"

"Almost too well," I admitted. "Do we really need to get out of this ginormous bed today?"

"Ah, but alas we do, Lizzie. Unfortunately, we're going to need to have fun today. It's about time we forgot all our shit from the past and did that."

"You mentioned a resort. I don't think I've got that many suitable outfits to keep up with your rock star friends."

"Baby, they're going to be too busy looking at how beautiful you are to care what you're wearing."

I scoffed but the thrill of his compliment was a shot to my veins. "I think you might be a teeny wee bit biased in your assumption."

Greg pushed me gently off him, then rolled on top of me. He took the weight of his body on his forearms and settled his hips between my thighs. "Seriously, if Deakon wasn't with Sadie, I think I'd be worried. He always went for red, copper and auburn-haired girls. You're exactly his type."

"Ah, away with you," I said, smacking his chest softly.

He nodded. "I know you have a hard time with me saying it, but you're fucking gorgeous, Lizzie. Promise me, if any of those dirty musicians try to hit on you, you'll come and find me."

I smirked wryly because I figured Greg saw me through rose-colored glasses. "Oh, yeah, as if that's likely to happen. And what do you mean, come and find you? There's no way you're leaving me on my own today. What if I don't fit—"

"Enough," Greg whispered, placing a finger over my lips to silence me.

"Trust me. You fit. All you need to remember is most of the people you'll meet today didn't start their lives being celebrities. Apart from the few that had famous parents beforehand, they're just like you and me ... except they have money and fans now."

"Right," I replied, trying to accept what he said. "I know. It's up to me to try harder with people."

"Good girl," he said in an appreciative tone. "I envy you, Lizzie. You have a whole new start ahead of you here. People only know what you want them to know ... see what you want them to see of you. Sure, you'll be the other half of me now, but you'll also get to find out what else you can be."

"You have the patience of a saint," I mumbled. My heart clenched with love as I looked into his eyes.

"Nah, that spot in the family is already reserved for my brother." I laughed. "Speaking of my brother, as much as I'd love to slide inside and have my wicked way with you, I'd better grab Mikey, show my face at Levi's and rescue him. Why don't you grab a quick shower and meet me downstairs before I leave. I think the girls have something planned with you before we head down to the resort."

There had been no time for me to put together a suitable wardrobe of clothes for Miami. Fortunately, Esther had thought about this and had arranged for a personal shopper to call in at Sadie's at 8:00 a.m. I felt spoiled when she arrived with a truck full of clothes suitable for the weekend.

"See, I told you they'd have you," Greg cooed, as Sadie and Beth pulled one outfit after another from the racks, much to the personal shopper's annoyance.

"Right, shoo, Greg. Go get your brother." Sadie slapped her hands on his chest, shoved Greg outside and closed the door behind him.

"This will be perfect for the beach," Beth said.

I turned back from the door to see she had already searched through the rails and was holding up a two-piece bikini in a gorgeous aquamarine color.

I shook my head. "I don't do two-piece swimsuits," I muttered, feeling a little self-conscious about my body size, compared to theirs.

"Nonsense. Greg will cream his pants when he sees you in this." She held it out for me. "Go try it on … oh, wait," she mumbled, snatching it back to her chest and pulling a sheer, ivory beach cover-up from the same rack. "Put this over the bikini, if you want to feel less exposed," she concluded.

"While you're at it, try these on too," Sadie ordered, handing me three beautiful short sun dresses and two evening, maxi ones.

For the following forty minutes, Sadie and Beth encouraged me to try on most of what the woman had brought on her racks. By the time we'd finished, I owned more fancy clothes than I'd need for three days, though Sadie insisted that I'd likely change outfits more than twice in one day.

We were packing everything into garment holders as Mikey arrived to take us to the resort. My heart was pumping hard in anticipation of the weekend to come. Some of it from a little excitement, but mostly due to the anxiety of being a nobody and facing so many celebrities.

It had been dark when we'd arrived the night before, so I had my first glimpse of the beach and the view of the Atlantic Ocean directly across the road from Deakon and Sadie's place. It looked like paradise on earth. I immediately fought back the pang of regret that tightened my chest, once I realized what I'd been missing.

I'd never seen anything so pretty, except on TV programs like *A Place in The Sun*, or in movies on a cinema screen. Everywhere I looked appeared to shine, not that it did really shine, it was more that the sun made everything appear clean and bright.

As we arrived at the Bungalows resort, my heart almost beat out of my chest from the luxury of the place. I'd imagined it would consist of four or five bungalows. Don't ask me why. Nothing could have been further from my expectations because the resort consisted of row upon row of cute little bungalows, massive queen palm trees, some larger buildings—I guessed would be restaurants and bars—and an infinite view of the water.

"Nice, huh?" Greg mumbled close to my ear. He slid an arm around my shoulders and gave them a squeeze as we passed neat rows of bungalows each with a garden view.

Eventually we arrived at some bungalows where Bernadette was waiting outside. "These are the waterside bungalows that Levi has selected for the band. He's also marked off the Zen pool with cabanas for our exclusive use. It's a wise move because God knows what's going to happen once all those musicians and A-listers get drunk."

"Or high," Deakon muttered. "By the way, I made a fresh batch of cookies, Bernadette. If you need some just hit me up." Deakon winked and Bernadette chuckled, even if her face did go pink.

Ten minutes later, Bernadette had allocated everyone their accommodation.

"Come here," Greg mumbled as I opened our luggage and began unpacking. I glanced up to see him holding his hands out for me to take them. Stopping what I'd been doing, I wandered over to him and placed my hands in his. Leading me out to the patio, he sat on an Adirondack chair, curled an arm around my waist and pulled me down onto his knee.

Holding me tight in one arm, he used the other to make a panoramic sweep toward the ocean. "See that, baby?" he murmured close to my ear. It looks like paradise, right?" he said taking the thought from my head and speaking it out loud.

"It's absolutely breathtaking," I agreed, hardly believing I was living my dream with the only man I'd ever wanted. I rewarded Greg's affectionate embrace with an adoring smile.

"Lizzie, if we got in a boat and headed into the distance, the horizon would keep getting further away, right?" he asked.

"Yeah, I suppose it would," I mused, considering his comment.

"What I mean is, we can only see where it begins but not where it ends. One day it can appear as smooth as glass, like it is today, and a day later it can be stormy with waves that can cause mayhem and destruction."

"Right," I murmured, not sure why he was telling that to me.

He sighed, wrapped his other arm firmly around me, kissed my neck and placed his chin on my shoulder. "What I'm trying to say —badly, is that life is like the ocean. We can't see what's coming, only where we've been.

"Which brings me back to your issue with trust. I know you're probably scared about the decision you've made, but if you think about it, the way we've loved one another isn't that different from the ocean.

"We've faced highs and lows in our relationship, much like the tides. Yet, despite all of that, the bond we share has been unbreakable, regardless of what we've gone through. I want you to trust that my love for you won't evaporate ... just like that ocean never will."

"Wow, Greg. That's such a profound thought. I never knew you could be so romantic," I choked out, deeply moved by Greg's depth of thought in trying to make me feel secure. "I'm here, and I'm doing my best. I believe in you this time, otherwise I wouldn't be here," I replied as I turned my head and kissed him.

Greg broke the kiss. "Good, keep believing," he said, pushing me off his lap and standing up. "Now I've gotten that out of the way, let's have some fun." Taking my hand, he led me inside, let go of me, and began to undress.

"What are you doing?" I asked, frowning at him taking off his jeans.

"Water," he said, like I should know what he meant.

"Swimming, I'm going swimming, it's too fucking hot. Are you coming?"

"Greg we only just got here. Shouldn't we wait until—"

"Until what? Levi and Trinnie won't be here until this evening. I know for a fact she'll be having nails, hair and makeup done, and so will Gabrielle ... her daughter."

"Right, but still ..."

"Fuck. Please don't argue," he whined. "Put on a swimsuit and come swim with me."

"You win," I agreed, because Greg was right, a swim sounded nice, it was baking hot outside.

A few minutes later, I barely recognized the girl smiling nervously in the mirror. It had been years since I'd worn a bikini, but the girls had given me the confidence to wear it. Taking a deep breath, I huffed it out and opened the bathroom door.

"Ah, fuck. Now I can't leave the bungalow," Greg muttered as he took in the bikini and cover-up that Beth suggested I wear.

"That bad?" I asked, frowning and attempting to cover myself up.

"Jesus, woman. Quite the opposite," he said, sliding off the bed to his feet and gesturing at the tent in his swim shorts.

I chuckled, relieved he liked it. "You think it's, okay?" I asked.

"Fuck off and stop fishing for compliments," he replied, laughing. "You can be an arsehole sometimes," he teased. "Come on, what will it be, the pool or the ocean?"

"Pool! Doesn't everyone get eaten in Florida by alligators and sharks?" I asked, alarmed at that thought.

"Think, Lizzie. How many people do you suppose swim in the Atlantic Ocean every year? And how many get eaten by sharks?"

"Yeah, but this is me, Greg. You know how lucky I am," I argued, my tone laced with sarcasm.

"You are lucky, baby. Look where you are," he said holding his arms out and spinning around the room. "And most importantly, you got me," he remarked, wiggling his eyebrows suggestively and sweeping his left hand over his incredible body.

"This is true," I said, my grin wide. "I hit the jackpot."

"So come on. Fuck everyone else. This weekend is about my bandmate getting married, and us having copious amounts of sex to make up for lost time."

Greg's remark filled me with determination. He had bet on me as his future, so I figured I must do everything I could to push past my insecurities and own my coveted place by my boyfriend's side.

CHAPTER 58

ELIZA

*G*reg and I had been messing around in the water for about twenty minutes, listening to the playlist on his phone on shuffle. "All You're Dreaming Of" by Liam Gallagher played as we got out and lay cuddling in one of the beautiful cabanas around the Zen pool. We had around five minutes of total blissful peace until everyone came and joined us.

We heard Aria's excited voice before we saw her as she came running up into view and promptly flung herself into the pool. Greg's reaction was lightning quick, as he sprinted out of the cabana and dove in the water to rescue her.

"Fuck, what did I just tell her?" Floyd grumbled as he wandered slowly toward the cabana next to ours, using his stick. Greg sat Aria at the end of the pool and climbed out. He wandered over and toweled himself off.

"Thanks, Greg," Ruth said, laughing. "Floyd, your daughter is a better swimmer than you are, stop worrying."

Deakon, Sadie, Beth and Raff all arrived seconds after my brother's family. They took the last two cabanas on the same side, next to ours.

"Jesus, it's hot," Deakon remarked, wearing swim shorts.

"I bet he doesn't wear out his T-shirts often," I joked to Sadie. I'd never seen a Screaming Shadows concert where Deakon had kept a shirt on for longer than the first ten minutes of a gig.

"If you've got it, flaunt it, I say," he remarked slapping his chest. "Love that bikini," he offered, tipping his chin toward me.

Deakon's remark made me want to shrivel into a ball, but I pulled up my big girl drawers and flashed a grateful smile back. "Beth picked it out," I informed him.

"Lucky for you she kept yours modest. Not that the same can be said about hers."

I glanced past him to Beth, who was bending over, rubbing sunscreen over her legs. Raff was watching her intently, mostly due to her having her arse in the air in the thong bikini she wore. It left nothing to the imagination.

"Are you gawking at Levi's sister?" Sadie asked, glowering at Deakon.

"No, I was merely pointing out the comparison in bikinis," Deakon said innocently with a straight face. "I was only saying that I like Eliza's bikini's better," Deakon remarked, sounding amused he had wound Sadie up.

"Good answer, dude, because if I thought for one minute you were eyeing Beth with the slightest dirty thought in your head, I'd ask Eliza to take that fucking bikini off, then I'd make you wear it."

Greg and Floyd chuckled, although Floyd had the good grace to cover his up with a cough.

"Yes, Floyd ... Greg? Do either of you have something you want to say?" Sadie challenged.

"Yeah, I do," Greg said. He smiled and stole a look at me. "I agree with Deakon. My girl's bikini is much more enticing."

"Fuck, Greg, quit. You're not helping," Deakon admonished, laughing.

Fortunately, Greg's brother arrived at that moment, taking

Sadie's attention away from the boys. "Beautiful day," Tim announced, waving his arms to the sky. "Isn't God great to grant us such a vision of serenity today."

"Sure is," Ruth immediately replied. "God is great," she mumbled back, like Tim had expected a reply.

"It's pissing with rain in Ireland Ma said." He then cussed almost to himself before he headed to the opposite side of the pool from us and sat down in the cabana facing us.

Deakon chuckled and shook his head. "That's a priest?" he asked incredulously, chuckling.

"The holy one in the family," Greg replied, grinning. Over the years Greg had been the butt of many jokes about Tim's life path as a man of the cloth. I had never once seen anyone faze him regarding this.

"And you brought that pure, innocent man to a rock star's wedding?" Deakon questioned, sounding freaked out by the notion of it. "He's going to be ruined after this weekend, you know that, right? Every single woman in the resort is going to try to deflower him."

Greg flashed a wicked grin and shook his head because most of the girls in Dublin had already tried that tactic with Tim ... and failed.

"I think he's a lovely man. I think the life he's chosen can't be easy. At least some men don't only think with their dicks," Ruth, a devout Roman Catholic replied, glaring at Deakon.

Silence fell as everyone appeared to consider her remark, while we stared across the pool at Greg's brother. Then, as if he felt us all staring, he stood, and peeled off his shirt and shorts. Wandering from the cabana to the pool, he curled his toes over the edge and placed his hands firmly on his hips.

It was the whimpering noise Ruth made, that made me realize that Greg's brother was wearing a tiny pair of white, budgie smuggler speedos.

"Fuck me, Father Tim is packing," Deakon muttered, squinting his mouth and talking out of the side of it.

"No joke," Sadie agreed, her eyes fixated and wide. "And check out that body. You don't get a ripped set of abs like that by drinking holy water."

"I might need to go back to the room with the girls," Ruth mumbled, clearly flustered, while suddenly fascinated by Myra sitting happily on a sun lounger in the shade. "How the hell am I going to take communion from that man now without having impure thoughts about him."

"Suddenly, you're concerned about having impure thoughts?" Floyd asked. "When have you ever had anything else."

Greg and Floyd laughed, while Ruth continued to look shaken. She abruptly plucked Myra up from the sun lounger, who immediately screamed the place down because she had been enjoying chewing the spine of a hardback book.

"I Feel You" by Depeche Mode began to play from Greg's cell phone and Greg burst out laughing.

"Turn that the fuck off," Deakon said, barely holding it together. As he said this, Tim raised his arms above his head and dived into the pool, barely making a ripple. He then began to perfect his backstroke.

"That's it. I'm done. Are you coming, Floyd, or are you staying here?" Ruth ground out.

"No, I only just got here. Tim's speedos aren't doing anything for me," he replied deadpan.

"We'll walk back with you, Ruth," Deakon choked out. "Come on, Sadie. We need to go back to the room," he said, dragging Sadie to her feet.

Deakon took Myra off Ruth and put her up on his shoulders, instantly turning her cries of frustration to glee.

As we watched Ruth, Sadie and him leaving, Floyd distracted

us. "Levi said this morning that he and Trinnie will get here about 6:00 p.m."

"Yeah, he sent us a band WhatsApp message," Greg replied.

"As we were strolling up here, Gibson Barclay and Kane Exeter passed us in one of those golf buggy things. I felt like I was in a movie set or something," my brother said.

"I imagine there will be people arriving at all hours of the day and night. Some are flying in from all over the world for the wedding," Greg informed us.

A look of wonder passed between Floyd and me as we took this information in.

"Want to get a bit of exercise in?" Greg asked Floyd, nodding toward the water.

"That would be great. I didn't like to ask," Floyd mumbled.

I glanced toward Aria, Beth and Raff in the water. "Are Beth and Raff together?" I asked after watching the looks that passed between them.

"Shh, it's against Raff's contract to go out with any of the band's family. No one else knows yet," Greg informed me, as he helped my brother to his feet. Floyd peeled off his shirt and Greg helped him into the water.

After ten minutes, Greg could see my brother tiring. "You're doing great, keep going."

"I admire your determination not to let the accident beat you," I told my brother.

Floyd stopped and stood up in the water. "I don't have a choice. There are three girls depending on me to keep a roof over their heads and food on the table," he muttered, before he began swimming again.

It wasn't long before he became frustrated because he'd tired much quicker than he would have liked. Greg persuaded him not to push himself, reminding him we had to socialize later that evening.

Raff and Greg helped my brother out of the pool, then Greg asked Raff to get a golf buggy to escort him and Aria back to his bungalow. As Greg and I left to walk back, Tim continued to swim lengths of the pool with the same speed and stamina, like he was training for the Olympics.

"Christ, Lizzie, you're burnt to a crisp," Greg informed me, once we were back in our room. "How the hell did you manage that, you were under that canopy for most of the time. Let's get you in the shower to cool your skin down."

"I know exactly why you want to get me in that shower, and it has nothing to do with my sunburn and more to do with that boner in your shorts."

"Ah, you know me so well," Greg mumbled with a sheepish grin.

After making love in the shower, Greg gingerly patted my burned skin dry. "Come, lie on the bed and I'll rub some after sun lotion on you," Greg insisted.

"Listen to you. This is just another one of your excuses to feel me up," I teased.

Greg grinned. "A guy needs to have some perks," he joked.

Spreading a towel on the bed, he laid me down on my front, straddled me, and began to lavish my skin with a copious amount of soothing sun lotion.

The main problem with his innocent ministrations was that Greg had amazing hands and he didn't do anything with them that didn't have some sense of rhythm.

"Oh, God," I said, groaning, as Greg pressed his thumbs either side of my spine, then ran them down to the dimples at the base of my back. "How did I live without this?" I mumbled to myself aloud.

"That's exactly what I think every time I slid inside your warm, wet pussy," he whispered next to my ear. A shiver ran through me as my core pulsed with need despite making love in the shower, and goosebumps coursed over my skin.

I frowned, suddenly choked by emotion at his remark. "I wasted so much of our time being locked in that groove my da carved out for me," I admitted.

"Forget it, all that matters is that you're here now," Greg said, not breaking the pace and rhythm he'd set for himself while rubbing my lotion in. I could feel his semi-hard erection nudging at the crack of my behind.

Greg's cell phone rang, and he shifted past me to answer it. He listened to whoever was talking at the other end and nodded.

"We're coming in ten minutes," he mumbled, before cutting the call off.

Placing his hands on my hips, he nipped my arse cheek with his teeth. "Ow," I squealed, the moment he moved to lift himself off.

He chuckled. "Not sorry in the least. With an arse like this, it's a wonder it isn't covered in bite marks by now."

As he turned me over, a jolt of electricity coursed through my veins in response to the devouring look Greg gave me. Leaning back in, he pressed his whole body onto mine and took my mouth in another bone-melting, hungry kiss. It was fast, deep, and all-consuming and when he reluctantly pulled away from my lips, we were breathless.

"Fuck," he said, as he gulped in another breath. He rose to his feet and ran his hand through his hair. "That was Flynn Docherty. He's waiting up in the bar. Come on, cover yourself up or we'll never get out of here, Lizzie."

CHAPTER 59

GREG

My dick almost broke the moment Eliza came out of the bathroom dressed in a lime green and teal-colored wraparound, maxi dress. It hung on her curves to perfection. I took a moment to appreciate the vision before me and of everything else I'd achieved. But I knew being a famous musician was nothing compared to having Eliza in my life again.

I let out a low whistle and she chuckled nervously, oblivious of the effect she'd likely have on most of the men in the resort in that dress. She was a siren, a sex bomb of the most addictive kind—yet the girl had no idea.

"Is it okay?" she asked, placing her forearms to her chest like she was trying to hide herself.

"Okay?" I asked, peeling her hands away to take the sight of her in again. "Baby, I'm now wondering how I'm going to keep you to myself dressed like that. You don't look okay, you look sensational."

Nothing my girl ever did was for compliments because her lack of confidence had been ingrained in her DNA by her da. She'd been consistently told that she didn't amount to much, and I saw it as my mission to dispel that myth.

She flashed me a coy smile and I remembered what a big night this would be for her. Eliza would no doubt be nervous about meeting so many famous people.

"Let's go," I said, holding my arm out for her to place her hand in the crook of it.

The moment we stepped outside, we saw Floyd, Ruth, Deakon and Sadie climbing into a golf buggy. "Where's the kids?" I asked, wondering if Beth and Raff had volunteered to watch them.

"They're in the hands of God … or a budgie smuggler, I'm not sure which," Deakon remarked, laughing.

Sadie batted his chest with the back of her hand. "Stop it. If you keep doing that, you're going to say it to him when you're drunk," she admonished.

"I might tell him before that," I joked, to fuck with them both.

"You'd never do that. He's your brother. How many fights did you get into as a boy to save him from being battered?" Eliza remarked.

"From the ripped physique on Father Tim, I'd say he could handle himself pretty well these days," Deakon suggested.

"He takes boxing and kick boxing lessons," I admitted.

"He does what?" Ruth sputtered in a tone an octave higher than usual. "Why the heck would he do that?"

"Tim's mission in life isn't only praying, marrying, baptizing and burying people. He's involved in some community clubs as well. He spars with some of the older kids he works with. Tim supports hard to reach kids through a local gym. You know the kind, kids on the edge of criminality. He works with a boxing coach to keep them off the streets."

"Damn. The guy's a saint," Deakon muttered.

"You know, if you're looking for another charity to support, he'd gladly take your pennies. The gym is one of four charities I support through him. Anyway, enough about singing my brother's praises … no pun intended, Flynn's waiting for us in the Tiki Bar," I explained.

"Flynn?" Ruth questioned.

"Flynn Docherty," I clarified for Ruth.

"Oh. My. God. How am I going to get through this weekend still married?" she teased.

Floyd smirked. "Ruth, if one of those musicians you drool over on TV hit on you, you'd bless yourself and leave by the nearest exit. You're more Netflix than rock chick."

"Well, there's always a first for everything," she argued, sounding indignant.

Sadie chuckled. "Yeah, Floyd, there's a tiger in there just waiting to break free," Sadie said of Ruth and everyone laughed.

Floyd smiled adoringly toward his wife. "None of them have what I have … I still remember the first that counts," he remarked playfully and winked.

Ruth's face turned beet red, and she lowered her head.

"All right before we get into the story of how Ruth lost her virginity to Floyd, I think we should be a teeny bit drunk first," I said, gesturing as another golf buggy pulled up beside us.

THE SUN WAS low in the sky by the time we arrived at the Tiki bar. If I'd expected a sedate scene and a few drinks with Flynn, I was very much mistaken. Levi and Trinnie had already arrived, and the bar was buzzing with musicians from so many famous bands that we'd practically had to drag Ruth and Eliza through the door.

"Over here, Greg," Flynn called out, waving an arm in the air from his seat. As we made our way through the crowd, saying hello to men and women we knew. Eliza's hand became so sweaty that it slipped out of mine.

I stopped, held her head and stared seriously into her gorgeous eyes. "Please own this, Lizzie. We're all that matters, remember? They're just people. Forget what you see on stage. These are the people behind their performances."

Eliza nodded. "Right," she muttered, sounding calmer. Inhaling a deep breath, she nodded again. "Okay, bring it on. I'm good to go."

I smiled widely. "You're fucking adorable when you're nervous. All the fire in your belly simmers right below the surface. It's the only time you don't know how to react."

Eliza shook her head and gave me another coy smile. "Right, Flynn and Valerie Docherty are waiting," she said.

Flynn took one look at Eliza then back to me. I suspected the grin on my face said it all. "Hey, bud, what kept you?" he asked, standing up and eyeing Eliza again.

"My brother kept him. The two of them are hopeless at passing each other without having a conversation," Eliza mumbled, surprising me.

"Ah, don't you ever get jealous of that bromance? I know I do," Flynn teased. "So, you must be Eliza, right?"

For a second Eliza looked star-struck and she nodded. "How do you..." she trailed off.

"I know because this guy here can't stop talking about you... and the Irish accent kind of gave it away," Flynn disclosed. "Isn't that right, Valerie?" he asked his wife while he gestured to his seat for Eliza to sit down.

As she did this, Valerie studied my woman then nodded. "I can see why Greg was so hung up on you. What are you doing with an ugly guy like him?" she teased, smiling. She glanced up at me and her smile widened.

As Flynn and I started talking, the conversation between our two woman digressed from us to print techniques and other technical stuff to do with Valerie's photography and I could see by Eliza's enthusiasm during the conversation that she'd found common ground. And at that point, I stopped feeling concerned that Eliza would enjoy herself.

"Excuse me, but no poaching my bass player," Levi grumbled, interrupting our conversation. He stuck out a hand and Flynn shook it. "Always a pleasure, Mr. Docherty, we're glad you could make it," he told Flynn.

"Flynn grinned. "Never thought I'd see the day, so I had to come witness this union for myself."

"You've met Trinnie, right?" he asked, gesturing toward Trinnie, who broke away from another couple to give Levi her full attention.

"I did. What is it with you Screaming Shadows guys punching above your weight with all these beautiful women?" Flynn joked.

"Speak for yourself, some of us waited until our women had grown up to fall in love," Levi remarked, making a joke of how Flynn and Valerie's start together as a couple was marred by rumors about them being together while Valerie was underage. None of which was true as it turned out.

Flynn took this in good humor and shook his head. "You're going there, huh?" he asked, mulling over whether he should make reference to Levi's past with women.

"You're lucky you're getting married tomorrow, otherwise I'd have a few things to say about you."

"Now, boys, no dick whipping the night before we get married. I'm going to need Levi's to be in top form since I have some pretty, new, knockout lingerie," Trinnie informed them.

Levi grinned. "Is that right, baby? Then I'll peel them off you with these," he said flashing his perfect white teeth and chomping them together.

Trinnie threw her head back and laughed before she noticed Eliza and Valerie watching her. "Hey, Valerie, how are you doing, girl?"

"Great, thanks," Valerie said, reaching up and accepting a kiss on both cheeks. Trinnie turned her attention to Eliza. "So good to have you here, Eliza. I wanted to talk to you about where you're going to live once you're here full time."

I tuned into the conversation and replied. "We'll be in the band penthouse until I can find somewhere suitable for us," I muttered.

"Nonsense. I have a perfectly good house lying empty right here in the Kes. Eliza's going to need company in the Keys with that busy schedule you guys keep. I'd love to take you under my wing, Eliza. I know it isn't the same, but I moved from up north to here. So I know what it's like, trying to move to a different place where you don't know anyone."

"Thanks, Trinnie. We'll talk about the house, and I'll let you know once you come back from your honeymoon," I suggested.

"Sadie still has a key. Take Eliza to see it," she told her. "See what you think," she prompted us.

"Are you nervous for tomorrow?" Eliza asked, changing the subject back to the wedding.

"Not half as nervous as I was when Levi and I first got together. I expect this is a bit of a culture shock for you. Don't worry though, Eliza, you'll get used to the lifestyle."

"Well, fuck me. What do we have here?" I glanced in the direction of the unmistakable sound of Rick Fars' voice. Beside him was Rick's boyfriend, and XrAid guitarist, Lennon, and their beautiful blonde girlfriend, Coral.

"Fuck me, Levi, I thought you said this was going to be an exclusive wedding?" I joked when I saw Rick.

"Dude, you're only a groomsman because I turned him down," he replied. Eliza chuckled, drawing attention to herself.

"And who is this vision of beauty?" Rick asked, glancing from Flynn and Valerie to me. "I know he's with her," he said, wagging his finger between Flynn and his wife. "So … nah … it's highly unlikely you've caught the attention of such a beautiful, demure-looking woman."

I chuckled. "Lizzie meet Rick Fars. I'm afraid he has no filter. Rick, meet my gorgeous girlfriend, Eliza."

"Well—well—well, it's true. There really is someone for everyone," he mumbled, winking. Reaching for Eliza's hand he lifted it to his lips and hesitated when I growled. "Calm your tits, Greg. I'm only making this delicious beauty feel at home."

"Take your paws off my girl. I know your kind of feeling, Rick," I warned, regarding his womanizing reputation. Even though he was happy in his throuple relationship, no one ever knew exactly where the boundaries were with him.

"We're here," Lily Parnell called out as she swept into the bar with Alfie Black on her arm.

"Hey, gorgeous," Rick gushed immediately, pulling Lily out of Alfie's arms and spinning her round in his.

"Jesus, must I put up with this annoying fucker all weekend?" Alfie muttered, flashing Rick an annoyed look.

"Oh, Alfie. Of course Rick's going to keep winding you up if you react like that," Lily said, chuckling.

Alfie and Lily spent the following few minutes exchanging pleasantries with Levi and Trinnie, while Rick worked the room, catching up with the rest of Flynn and Alfie's bandmates.

"You doing, okay?" I whispered into Eliza's ear.

"I think so," she said, grinning. "This is a mindfuck though," she said, nodding at all the famous people in one place.

"I felt the same the first time I went to a festival. Half the time my jaw was hanging open in amazement and the rest of the time I was trying to keep my shit together."

Eliza laughed. "Really? I've never seen you act nervous around other people."

"Yeah, I think the first time I spoke to Gibson Barclay I actually stuttered."

"Good to know—Oh. My. God. Is that Cody from XrAid?"

I followed her gaze and caught Cody's eyes. "Greg!" he exclaimed, as he strode toward us. "I thought you were in Ireland. Alfie told Lily that Levi was worried you might not make it back for the wedding."

Eliza tugged my shirt and caught my attention. "Cody, meet Lizzie my girlfriend, apparently she's a fan," I said, with a raised eyebrow.

"Nice to meet you, Lizzie," he said, smiling. He leaned in and kissed her cheek.

"Eliza," I said, correcting the man for calling Eliza by my pet name for her.

"Lovely to meet you, Cody," Eliza said, breathily.

Sadie cut through the crowded bar and grabbed Eliza's wrist. "Eliza, come meet Chloe Barclay, she's an amazing woman. I've got a feeling you two are going to be good friends," she murmured.

It made my heart swell to see Eliza go with her without looking to me for reassurance.

"Fuck me. Is that the girl you left behind in Ireland?" I nodded.

"Then I can see why you were so bent out of shape for years, dude. She's stunning."

"I know," I replied, turning to seek her out in the crowd. She was talking animatedly, while Chloe and Sadie looked at her, enthralled. "And if you make a play for her, I'll snap off your dick."

Cody grinned. "What is it with you dudes and your women? Alfie Black made similar threats to me once about Lily."

"Can I have everyone's attention," Jude called out, bringing everyone to order. "We're going to leave you to enjoy the hospitality. The wedding party are all going off to dinner now. Don't get drunk and start fighting. As you all know, the wedding ceremony is at 3:00 p.m. on Coconut Beach. Please be seated by 2:50 p.m. at the latest. There will be transportation to get you there so—no excuses."

Taking their cue from Jude's speech, Mikey, Bodhi and Raff appeared and escorted us bandmates and our partners to dinner.

CHAPTER 60

GREG

Dinner was hardly what I'd call formal, although we were all on our best behavior, due to Trinnie's parents and Gabrielle being present for the meal.

After dinner, Mikey took Gabrielle to meet some of her favorite rock stars up in the Tiki bar, leaving the adults alone for a while.

Jude's parents, Barbara and Steve, snuck off to share a joint on the excuse of a beach stroll to walk off dinner.

Deakon went off to find them when they were taking too long to return, and when they came back, it became clear from the adolescent giggling that went on between all three of them, that they were all under the influence of something.

Levi and Trinnie looked amused, Trinnie's parents, Kathy and Paul—not so much.

"What's so funny? Did I miss something?" Eliza asked me.

"No, baby you haven't missed a thing," I reassured her, biting back a grin. Eliza frowned, then eyed me suspiciously before focusing back on Jude's parents.

"Mom, Dad," Gemma, Jude's sister said in a clipped tone, before she appeared to try to chastise them with a stern facial expression while widening and narrowing her eyes. This only made Barbara laugh harder, which became infectious to Deakon and Steve.

"Mom, a word," Jude said deadpan, sliding his chair back and almost dragging his mom out of hers. "Back in a minute," he mumbled, as he led her off, laughing, into the distance. "Quit laughing, or you'll piss yourself."

"Never give my wife, wine," Steve mumbled, trying to cover up for the fact that they were stoned. He rose to his feet and headed in the same direction that Jude and his wife had gone.

"What happened?" Trinnie's mom asked, sounding confused while her head spun this way and that, to look at everyone.

"I think Barbara and Steve have been smoking weed," Trinnie told Kathy.

"Weed? What are they … hippies?" her father Paul asked, sounding surprised.

"They're just liberal people. A little weed never hurt anyone," Korry remarked, glancing at Bernadette. They both chuckled together.

"That's not what they say in documentaries," Kathy argued in an indignant tone. "Apparently, it can lead to long-term mental health issues."

"I think I can speak for most people around this table when I say, everyone here has or has had emotional issues to deal with. But believe me, there have been times when my stress has been halved by the mellowing qualities of weed," Levi informed her.

"We've all been exposed to the stuff for years, and I believe we're doing fine, don't you think?" Korry asked, waving a finger in a circular motion, indicating everyone at the table.

"Trinnie, tell me you haven't smoked weed," her mom insisted, talking to her like Trinnie was a twelve-year-old child.

"Mom, this isn't the time to get into the politics of taking drugs," Trinnie suggested with a faint smile on her lips.

"Who said anything about taking drugs? Good Lord, don't tell me you've been taking drugs, Trinnie," her dad chimed in.

"Dad, Mom, please get a hold of yourselves. This is my prewedding dinner. Can't we just enjoy ourselves?" she pleaded, sounding annoyed with their protests now.

"Not if we're expected to take drugs," Kathy replied.

Deakon chuckled, glanced toward Sadie, who rolled her eyes to the ceiling as if to say, *please shut the fuck up.*

"Do you see any drugs on the table?" Trinnie challenged, frustrated now.

"Look. Why don't we dial this down a bit. This is the eve of Trinnie and Levi's big day," Korry suggested, interjecting to take the heat out of the situation. As the peacemaker of the group, he lifted one of the three coffee pots on the table. "That wine must have been stronger than we thought," he teased. "What about a nice cup of coffee and a homemade cookie to finish off the meal?"

"Great idea," Deakon agreed, grinning because he loved Korry's suggestion. Trinnie's eyes narrowed in suspicion as she looked at them both, then folded her arms and sat back in her seat.

"Sounds like an excellent idea," Trinnie agreed. "Then perhaps everyone will loosen up a little."

"That's exactly what I had in mind," Deakon agreed. The minute he produced a plastic tub with a batch of weed cookies, I almost lost my shit.

"Don't touch the cookies," I whispered to Eliza, chuckling.

"Why not, they smell delicious?" she mumbled, sounding annoyed.

"Just do as I say and watch," I demanded. Eliza stared me down for a moment, annoyed by my instruction, before she focused back on the group.

Trinnie's mom took a cookie from the tub, sniffed, and then nibbled at it. "You made these?" she asked Deakon, quizzically.

K.L. SHANDWICK

"Yeah, I love baking cookies," he said, offering Kathy a beaming smile.

She took a larger bite and began chewing it. "You must give me the recipe, the texture is perfect, and they taste wonderful," she gushed. "There's nothing like a home-made cookie," she informed the rest of us. "You honestly made these yourself?" she asked Deakon again, mumbling around another mouthful, her eyes wide with surprise.

"Sure did," he replied. Grinning widely, he then took a cookie out for himself and stuffed the whole treat into his mouth.

"Taste it, Paul," she said, offering the last of the cookie to Trinnie's father. "You know what a sweet tooth you have. This will hit the spot," Kathy coaxed him.

"You keep that one," Paul advised her. "May I get one of my own?" Deakon held the box out for Paul to take one.

While Paul was choosing a cookie from the batch, Kathy polished off the one she was eating and washed it down with some coffee. "May I sneak another?" she asked, far more amenable than we'd seen her all evening. Deakon nodded and she took another from the tub. "Now these, I could become addicted to."

"Mm, I see what you mean," Paul mumbled, covering his mouth with a hand while chewing the big bite he'd taken.

"No, Mom," Trinnie snapped quickly, making Levi chuckle.

"It's a wedding, Trinnie. Let your mom indulge," Levi argued.

"Korry ... Deakon," Bernadette warned for them to control the situation they'd created. Both of my bandmates glanced at her and grinned.

"For goodness' sake, it's only a cookie. Jude drank a whole bottle of wine with dinner, and I didn't hear anyone telling him no," Kathy insisted.

"Jude's a huge man, Mom, I doubt the alcohol in that bottle barely touched him."

"I know what's going on here," Kathy remarked in a warmer tone. "You're stressed, Trinnie. Are you having second thoughts?"

"No, Mom, I can't wait to be Levi's wife. This has nothing to do with the wedding. I just don't think you should eat more of Deakon's cookies."

"What does Deakon think?" Kathy challenged.

A warning look passed between Trinnie and Deakon. "I think Trinnie's right, to be honest. I mean, I only made one for each person," Deakon remarked, diplomatically.

"Pity, I could eat a whole box of those," she mused wistfully, and began pulling at the neck of her blouse, like she was suddenly too hot.

"You know, I think I might take an evening dip in the ocean," Paul said suddenly. He stood and stripped out of his shirt, before discarding it on the chair.

"I'll join you, feel how hot my hands are," Kathy mused, holding her hands out for her husband to hold. "Oh, wow, yours too," she remarked and began giggling.

"Mom, Dad, you are not going into the ocean. It's dark," Trinnie remarked as she began to stand. Levi laughed and tugged Trinnie's wrist, sitting her down again.

"Where's your sense of adventure, Trinnie. There's nothing as romantic as a skinny dip in the ocean with your lover," her mom questioned playfully.

Deakon and I barked out a laugh.

Eliza had been silent throughout the whole exchange, but leaned in with her hand cupped around her mouth and whispered, "Is it me, or did this whole thing with Kathy and Paul just get weird? I mean what the fuck is in those cookies? It's like they've had personality transplants," Eliza mused.

My cell phone buzzed in my pocket interrupting us. "Hang on," I said, pulling it out. I was instantly fuming when I saw the message.

Lori: I'm here in the resort as Shawn from XrAid's date. Can you meet me to talk?

"What the fuck?" I muttered out loud.

Eliza glanced down at my screen and her face instantly darkened. "Am I really going to have to deal with this here? Halfway around the world?" Eliza got out of her seat and began walking out of the restaurant.

"Baby, wait. Trust me. I had no idea someone had invited her."

"I believe you," she mumbled, but sounded hurt all the same.

"Then where are you going?"

"To sort this bitch out once and for all," she said, sounding furious.

"Eliza, you need to let me sort this out," I reasoned. "You don't know where she is."

"No, I don't. But I know what she looks like ... and Shawn from XrAid as well for that matter, so I think there's more than a reasonable chance of finding her."

As if Sadie and Beth sensed that something was wrong, they followed us out of the restaurant.

"Everything okay?" Beth asked, her worried eyes flitting from Eliza to me.

"No, but it fucking will be ... as soon as I deal with Lori Sinclair," Eliza told them.

"Lori Sinclair is here?" Sadie asked, frowning.

"Apparently, but I swear I knew nothing about it. I think she's stalking me," I replied.

I realized Eliza had left my side and was stomping down the hill in the direction of the Tiki bar. "Lizzie wait, please let me handle this," I pleaded.

"You handled it once and that was nearly the end of us. You're welcome to tag along and learn how it should have been done."

CHAPTER 61

ELIZA

By the time I reached the Tiki bar, I was so furious I could have cared less who was present. Straining my neck, I scanned the room, looking for the guys from XrAid. I recognized Digs first, with his mohawk and tattooed appearance, and next to him was Cody Vickers, who I had already been introduced to.

Weaving my way through the crowds, I eased past Lori before I realized it was her. Shawn hadn't been standing with her, and with her back to me, I missed her. But when I turned back to rescan the room, she was right in front of me.

My heart pounded as it pumped blood through my body at a rapid, unhealthy pace. The sound of the pressure as it flowed in my ears almost drowned out everything else.

"Could we have a word?" I asked, sounding inquisitive as I plastered a pleasant smile on my face.

"Sure," she beamed. "And you are?"

"Eliza McDade."

"E-Eliza?" she asked, her concerned eyes instantly searched

over my shoulder and the smile on her face froze once she saw Greg standing behind me.

"Oh, that Eliza. I've heard so much about you," she remarked in an innocent, friendly tone.

"Is that so? Then why are you insistent on following my boyfriend around and trying to hook up with him?" I asked loudly, drawing the attention of Rick Fars and Shawn, who had been talking about ten feet from where we were standing.

"Everything alright?" Shawn asked, as he placed a protective hand around Lori's waist. He frowned and I felt he tried to place me and decided I was a nobody.

"No, everything isn't alright. You don't know me, but my name is Eliza and I'm Greg Booker's girlfriend."

Shawn glanced past me to Greg, nodded in acknowledgement of Greg, and the hard lines on his face softened.

"Hey, Eliza, glad to meet you." He glanced toward Lori again before looking back at me. "I'm getting a hostile vibe here," he admitted, looking confused.

"I was just telling your date here to stop stalking my boyfriend. Greg told her we were together, but that hasn't stopped her from turning up in Dublin, then Paris and now she's here. Look, I don't know what she's told you or if it's a coincidence she's here, but Greg had a text from her ten minutes ago asking if they could talk."

"Is this true?" Shawn asked, glowering down at Lori. "And there I was, thinking how fucking cool it was that you contacted me and asked if I had a date for this weekend. So, let me get this straight, you're not here for me, you used me to get to him?"

"No, Shawn—"

"Yes, Shawn," I argued. "Now, listen, Bunny Boiler, I'm going to ask you for the last time to forget my boyfriend's number. Don't come near him again. If you do, Greg will ask his legal team to do something about this unhealthy obsession you've developed." I turned and looked at Greg. "Anything you want to add?" I asked.

I was breathing rapidly as my heart raced, the result of feeling more than a little pissed at Lori and embarrassed because everyone stared at me.

"Nope, baby, I think you've about covered it," Greg replied casually, like he was unfazed I'd confronted her in such a public way.

"I have something to say," Shawn muttered. "The music industry is like one large family, you know … lots of bitching and fighting, best friends to each other's faces, talking up a storm behind our backs. But if there's one thing we won't stand for is someone trying to humiliate us.

"So, thanks for trying to do that to me, Lori, and thank you, for bring this bitch to my attention," he said, looking at me. "Now, Ms. Sinclair, I strongly suggest you get your luggage out of my bungalow right now and get the fuck on your way, because I wouldn't screw you now if you begged me."

Shawn's bandmates applauded. "Good job," Alfie Black muttered and began clapping as well. "Shawn's like a brother to us. If you insulted him, you've insulted us all."

Lori turned, tears streaming down her face as she fought her way through the crowded room and disappeared out of view.

"Is it sick that I'm glad she contacted me now?" Greg asked.

"Huh?" I replied, still riled up, frowning angrily.

Taking my head in his hands to calm my flaring temper, Greg leaned close to my ear and whispered, "That was so fucking hot watching you fight for me."

"Jesus, Greg, two stunning hotties almost fist fighting for you. That cock of yours must be quite the attraction because the face isn't doing it for me," Rick Fars joked, interrupting our intimate moment.

I laughed. "I fucking love you, dude," Greg replied. "How do you do that?"

"That?" he asked, frowning.

"Manage to defuse any situation with humor by muttering a few, well-chosen words."

Rick laughed. "What? You don't think I'm serious?"

"Right, stop fucking with people and come finish the story you were telling," Lennon, his male partner of the throuple admonished, interrupting us. He slung an arm around his shoulder and led him back to the small group of rockers, waiting for him to finish what he'd been saying.

"I'm impressed at how you didn't let Lori's status as an A+ lister intimidate you."

"She's a kid that thinks because she has status, she can get what she wants," I replied. "That's not classy, so I can't respect someone like that. But what made the whole confrontation better than I'd expected is that you didn't try to defend her."

"Like I said, I tried to let her down gently and she didn't get the message."

"Well, I hope she got it this time, because that was a spectacular audience I had doing that."

Greg chuckled and kissed my forehead. "Right, shall we head back to Levi, Trinnie and the others?"

"Can't we just go to bed? I have a feeling it's going to be an emotional day tomorrow," I replied.

"Sure. Bed it is."

"Let me just use the loo before we walk back."

I felt eyes on me as Greg walked with me in the direction of the restroom, but by then I just didn't care. Greg and I had been apart for too long to let my self-consciousness get the better of me.

Three introductions and an invitation to a party later, Greg finally deposited me at the restroom door. Rushing into the stall, I quickly did my business, then washed my hands at the communal sinks.

"So, you're the flavor of the week?" I heard a female with a Southern American accent drawl. As there were two other celebrities washing their hands alongside me, I figured the woman was talking to one of them, regarding their career. Turning with wet hands, I came face to face with Lexi, bass guitarist in Flynn Docherty's band, RedA.

Lexi scrutinized me from head to toe, then her gaze settled back at my face. I felt self-conscious until the other two women moved past me and left, then I realized she'd been talking to me.

"Excuse me?" I challenged, eyeing her carefully after the way she'd perused me.

"I said you're Greg Booker's plaything this week," she muttered, sounding indignant about that.

"Oh, were you speaking to me?" I drawled slowly.

"Who else is here?" she asked in a snarky tone, holding her hands up to the empty restroom, like I was stupid.

"Should we start again?" I suggested deadpan. "Are you asking if I'm Greg Booker's plaything this week?"

"That's what I said," she muttered, leaning toward the mirror, and applying a ruby-red lipstick she already had in her hand.

"Oh, so it was a statement not a question? Look at me, I'm hardly a plaything," I said, chuckling and holding my hands out at my fuller figure. My curves weren't like any of the girls seen in the photographs with Greg.

Lexi nodded. "See, I was thinking the same thing. It must be a phase he's going through," she mused. "You know, Greg and I go way back."

"Oh, you do?" I asked as my heart began to beat out of my chest at being challenged by yet another conquest of Greg's. Fury began to boil my blood as I stood there, trying to appear as confident as her.

"That was some speech you gave out there. I commend you for telling Lori Sinclair where not to go. But I must warn you that she's a mere slip of a girl, compared to some of the women Greg has dated."

"Right," I said, as I felt my blood close to boiling point. "Why don't you stop dancing around me and cut straight to the punchline of this conversation, because I'm getting tired of you trying to undermine my relationship with my boyfriend."

"Ha! Boyfriend … this week maybe, but Greg doesn't do long-term relationships."

"He doesn't…. usually," I agreed, given what Greg had told me before.

"Besides, do you know I was with him the other week? I bet he didn't tell you we shared a long-distance flight to Ireland when he went to visit his sick buddy."

"Is that right?" she almost threw me for a moment, until I remembered that Greg had traveled on Flynn's private jet. Then it made sense, that as part of the band, she'd have been there as well.

"It is true. Look at your competition, lady," she remarked, sweeping a hand from her face down her body. For a second my confidence wavered because there was no doubt about it, Lexi was a stunningly beautiful woman, even if she was a manhunting bitch. "What do you have that I couldn't possibly compete with?" she suggested.

"Lizzie, what's keeping you in there. Are you okay?" Greg called impatiently, from the other side of the door.

"Yeah, I'm fine, I'll be out in a minute," I replied, before returning my attention to Lexi.

"Since this is Levi and Trinnie's wedding and we're all supposed to be getting along, I'm going to humor you," I said.

Lexi folded her arms and cocked out a hip, like she couldn't wait to hear what I had to say.

"That sick friend Greg went home to Ireland for, was Floyd

McDade. He's here by the way, no doubt you'll meet him and his wife tomorrow. Oh, and by the way, Floyd is my big brother.

"And to answer your question as to what I have that you don't ... I'd say years on you—five as his girlfriend—before he was famous to be exact. I know the real Greg Booker, not the rock star. And now that we're back together and we're serious, you can strike him off your hitlist. This woman is going nowhere this time, and as far as you are concerned, Greg Booker is taken."

"Eliza—what the fuck?" Greg asked as he pushed the door open properly and eyed both of us women together. His eyes almost bugged out of his head. Pushing open the door, he stepped inside.

"I'm coming. I was just informing another of your one-night stands that wanted to warn me off, that I've never been one of those to you."

"Lexi what the fuck did you say to her?" Greg muttered, glaring toward her with stormy eyes.

Wandering over to Greg, I placed my hand on his chest and patted it softly. "It doesn't matter now since I put her straight. Maybe Rick Fars was right about women being attracted to your dick," I mused. "I'm ready to go home to bed now. It's been an exhausting night, explaining that we're together to your one-hit wonders."

Greg glowered toward Lexi as he led me out of the restroom.

"Fuck, I'm so sor—"

"Don't," I said, holding a hand up and cutting him off. "I decided the moment I agreed to come with you that I'd need to put the past behind us. I also considered that I might face girls just like Lexi as well. But they're your past. Let's go to bed, it's going to be a long day tomorrow, and I want to enjoy myself."

CHAPTER 62

GREG

"What the fuck?" I muttered, waking to the sound of metal tapping on glass.

"Greg, it's me. Open the door."

Confused by Raff's muffled voice, I reached over in the darkness and lifted my cell phone off the nightstand. The time was 4:45 a.m. I crept out of bed and padded over to the window, then opened the front door.

"What is it? It's the middle of the fucking night," I grumbled, still naked.

"It's Levi," Raff said, and my heart sank.

"Is he drunk?"

"I wouldn't have woken you up for that. I'd have called a doctor to rehydrate him," he replied.

"Then what the fuck is it. Do I need to get Jude in here and give you a drumroll before you spit it out?"

"What's the matter?" Eliza asked, sleepily.

"Nothing, go back to sleep, it's only Raff."

"Levi's gone home," Raff said in a hushed tone.

"He's what? He's got three hundred and forty guests here."

"I know. Trinnie messaged me that Beth and Levi had an argument and Levi's gone off somewhere to think. I believe she thinks he's still at the resort, but Bodhi has texted me that they are at Levi's house."

"Fuck, get the car, where's Jude?"

"I didn't wake him. He's got Bailey and Honey in there ... and Esther is struggling with morning sickness."

"Deakon, Korry?" I suggested.

"Both stoned ... Deakon's stoned and blind drunk. He had a session with Rick Fars and Kane Exeter that only finished an hour ago. Mikey's already had a doc on speed dial to come and sober him up."

"So, I'm supposed to talk Levi down from the ledge? It would help if I knew what the problem was ... you know, to see if I'm qualified."

"I don't know, but you're it. Bodhi took him, so you'll have some support there. I need to stay here, since Mikey's taking you and Bodhi is off the grid."

"Alright, I'm getting some clothes on. Make sure Beth takes care of Lizzie."

"I got her. Don't worry," Raff murmured.

"Where are you going?" Eliza asked, sitting up in bed and turning on the nightstand light.

"Levi's gone home ... not sure what's wrong, but thanks to all the shit with Lori and Lexi last night, I'm the only one sober enough to go to his house and find out what's going on."

"You'll be back in the morning, right?" she asked, sounding concerned. I felt torn in that moment because I'd taken her out of her comfort zone, but she had Floyd, Ruth and my brother, so I didn't feel guilty about going to speak with Levi.

I went to the bed and kissed her tenderly on the lips. "Promise, I'll be back as soon as I can."

LEVI WAS SITTING out on his patio, with his head in his hands, when Bodhi let me into the house. "He's asking for a bottle of whiskey," he informed me, sounding worried.

I was out of my depth because anything to do with Levi's emotional support was usually Jude's department. "Thanks. Any idea what's going on? Is he getting cold feet?"

"All he said was that the wedding isn't going ahead."

"Fuck. Okay. Thanks, Bodhi. No alcohol, that won't help," I confirmed. "Can you make us a pot of coffee? And ask Mikey to go back and bring Sadie." How neither of the guards thought to include her, to help deal with something like this, was beyond me.

"Hey, dude. What's up?" I asked, trying to sound casual.

Levi lifted his head, gave me a sideward glance and looked down at the floor again. "What are you doing here?"

"I know … booby prize, everyone else is too drunk, stoned or dealing with morning sickness and kids to be here. So … I'm afraid you've got me." He chuckled at my attempt at humor, but I could hear the hollowness of it as well.

"Want to tell me what's got you running scared?"

"Is my fucking life ever going to be smooth or am I destined to deal with his shit for the rest of it?" he mumbled, without looking up.

"Whose shit?"

"My deadbeat, late father."

"Look you're bound to be feeling emotional … today of all days. I mean it's not every day you get married—"

"This has got nothing to do with the wedding … and everything to do with trust and family. What the fuck am I doing? What if I can't be what Trinnie needs me to be?"

"Ah, so this is a bit of cold feet? What Trinnie needs? Bullshit, that woman thinks that you hung the moon."

"No … it's the universe playing some kind of sick fucking joke on me."

"Sick joke? You've lost me, buddy." Bodhi appeared with a large pot of coffee and two mugs. He set them down on the table before he went back inside.

"DNA tests will be the death of me," Levi muttered.

"Holy shit, you've got a kid?" I asked with my eyebrows in my hairline.

Levi glanced up with irony in his gaze. "Nope."

"Mate, you need to spell it out for me. I'm not at my best between midnight and dawn," I informed him, glancing up at the sliver of light on the horizon before I filled both mugs with coffee.

"Beth uploaded her DNA result to 23andMe, and guess what? Esther, her and I have another half brother and sister."

"Brother and sister?"

"Yeah, twins—three years older than me. And here's the funniest part, they're my mom's best friend's kids. We travelled on the same school bus together. Hell, she even babysat me sometimes."

"When did Beth tell you this?"

"A couple of hours ago when she was drunk. She started talking about these twins in conversation." He shrugged. "Once I started questioning her because there were twins that I knew that had the exact same names, she couldn't hide the truth from me. You know how bad of a liar Beth is, right?" I nodded. "So, she came clean, said she'd been FaceTiming with them for over a week, and was going to tell me after the wedding."

"Fuck, Levi, that's … a lot," I mumbled. "What is Trinnie saying?"

"She doesn't know."

"You're still getting married today, aren't you?"

"That's just it. I don't know."

"Why not?" I asked, almost shrieking at his logic.

"Who can I trust? I mean, does Esther know ... anyone else. Did you know about these twins?"

"What? No, of course I didn't. And I think Beth would have told you already, had you not been getting married." I sighed. "Here, drink this coffee."

Taking the mug from me, he gulped the hot liquid down in one long gulp. Reaching over, he placed his mug back on the table. "I'm so fucking shocked ... no devastated, that these kids were my kin and none of us had any fucking idea." He snorted. "Hell, the bus driver used to make comments to the boy, Dante, that I looked more like him than his sister did."

"Dante?"

"Dante and Catelina, that's the twins' names." He inhaled deeply and blew out a breath. "You know what? This is another mindfuck from beyond the grave. Am I going to spend the rest of my life wondering if there are any more of us out there. I spent most of my life thinking I was an only child ... and now there are five of us. And if that wasn't enough, I'm the fucking middle one now."

I laughed at the note of humor in Levi's tone. "They live in Florida or New York?"

"New York," he replied.

"Do you know what they do for a living?" I asked.

"Catelina is a child therapist of some kind and Dante is a dentist."

"Your father may have been a deadbeat musician, but his kids all turned out great in spite of him," I mused.

"That's what Beth said," he agreed.

"So, what did you hope to achieve by coming home here? Your bride is waiting at the resort. The way I see it, you have two options. You tell Trinnie quickly that this isn't happening today, bearing in mind that girl needed a lot of persuasion in the first place to agree to marry you.

"Now think of the humiliation she'd have facing everyone alone if you've bailed. Can you imagine her telling all those heavy hitters you invited to be there? You're risking losing her forever," I mumbled, and paused to let that information sink in.

"The alternative is, you put your family issues aside and concentrate on the family you know and are building with Trinnie, and get your arse back there before she realizes you left and doesn't go through with the wedding."

He glanced up at me and chuckled. "Me ... taking advice from Greg Booker." He chuckled again. "That's a first." For a long minute he sat considering what to say next. "You know, I'm glad it's you here and not Jude."

"What makes you say that?"

"He knows me too well, and I think I'd have had a flair for the dramatic with him."

I laughed. "Glad to be of service. Now, what's it to be?"

"You're right. I can't do anything about these new relatives between now and the wedding, so I need to put that news to one side and get on with marrying Trinnie. Bodhi, get the car ready, we're heading back to the resort," he shouted, loudly.

CHAPTER 63

GREG

"It feels a bit odd going to a wedding with no shoes," Eliza mumbled, staring down at her feet. She looked incredible with her sun-kissed face and wild auburn hair cascading over her shoulders. She was dressed in a plain, turquoise, figure-hugging maxi dress with spaghetti straps, and it looked like it had been made for her.

"Every man apart from Levi is going to be jealous when he sees you in this," I said, wandering over to her and holding her by her hips.

Eliza pressed her lips to mine in a closed-lip kiss, then mumbled over them, "Is this really my life?"

I smiled against her mouth before I pulled my head back to look at her. "It is, and you don't know the half of it yet," I confirmed.

Her smile lit up the room and my heart clenched to acknowledge how happy she'd made me.

Sliding her hands up my back, Eliza pulled me closer and laid her cheek on my bare chest. "I love you so much, Greg. I'm so sorry I put us both through all that."

"Don't be. I probably wasn't ready to be the man you needed back then. I know I was immature and irresponsible, but I'd never have cheated on you ... I want you to know that."

"Me too, I wasn't ready for all this either. I'm still not," she said, chuckling. "But I know what I want now, and I'm ready to fight for us."

"No need to fight anymore, baby," I said, sliding one hand tighter around her back and the other into her hair. Grabbing a fistful, I kissed her leisurely. allowing us both to taste the other and feel all the sad emotions from the past ebb away.

The moment Eliza moaned, I broke our kiss and tried not to get carried away. Then I stared into her gorgeous hazel eyes and became lost for a moment, as my heart filled with love when I noticed how they glittered with a mixture of adoration and desire when she looked back at me.

"That was beautiful," I murmured, smiling, then I pressed a small kiss to her nose. "But I think we'd better get out of here or Father Tim will catch us with your knickers down and me balls deep inside you."

Eliza laughed as I let her go, then pulled on the white linen shirt and blue casual shorts that had been given to me by Bernadette, as per Levi's instructions.

"Feels strange going to a wedding dressed like this," Eliza muttered again.

"It's a beach wedding, baby. There's usually less pomp and ceremony."

"What kind of wedding do you want?" Eliza asked as we were leaving the bungalow to go meet up with the others.

"Oh, we're getting married already?" I teased, sliding a hand around her waist again.

Eliza became flustered and shook her head. "No, I didn't mean that ... I-I mean ... do you ever want to get married?"

"It's a bit late to ask me that since you've packed up and come all the way here. What if I told you no, I don't feel the need to get married."

"Oh, right. I see ..." she trailed off as we began to walk.

Eliza frowned and I felt guilty for fucking with her. "What kind of wedding do you want?" I asked, firing her question back to her.

"None if that's not what you want," she said, playing into the comment I'd made.

I stopped, swung her around in front of me and took her head in my hands. "Eliza, I'd marry you tomorrow, if that's what you wanted."

That wasn't the way I wanted to propose to her. And although it was something I had assumed we'd get to at some point, I was just happy to finally get her to come with me that I hadn't really thought much beyond that.

However, as she had brought it up in conversation, I felt it was important to address the subject with her.

Time stood still as Eliza stared into my eyes like she was afraid to blink in case what I'd said was a dream or something. "So? Has the cat finally caught your tongue? What would you say to that?"

"I'd say you're not allowed to play with my feelings like this, Greg Booker." She swallowed roughly and I realized she didn't believe me, and that I had upset her.

"Who's playing?" I dropped to my knee, right there in front of her, wearing the stupid outfit Levi had chosen for me, and grabbed her hand. "This life we're about to build between us has been years in the making, Eliza McDade.

"It has always been my intention to lay claim to you as my wife. I'm still just getting used to the thought that we're finally doing this. Lizzie, you are my heart's desire, my soul's other half, my missing piece of all that makes sense to me. Nothing makes me happier than the thought of spending the rest of my life with you."

Eliza started trembling and tears welled in her eyes as she

stared down at me, wide-eyed in disbelief. I placed my free hand on her hip to steady her.

"I know this isn't exactly the most romantic way of doing this, especially as we're going to someone else's wedding. But Lizzie, would you do me the honor of being my wife and marry me?"

"God, yes," she replied without hesitation as her hands flew to my head. She began to cry and signaled for me to stand, then she wrapped her arms around my neck and buried her face in it.

"Hey, come on," I said, smiling. I pulled back to look at her face and saw her mascara had run. Holding her head in both hands, I wiped it away with my thumbs. She gave me a watery smile and it took my breath away.

"Is that you upsetting that poor girl again?" my brother admonished as he stepped out of his bungalow in front of us.

"Happy tears, Tim," Eliza responded, wiping the frown from his face.

"Ah, well, that okay then," he mumbled. Switching his attention, he walked to the bungalow next door and knocked on the door.

Floyd, Ruth and the girls came out as if they'd been waiting for Tim to arrive.

"Are you walking, Floyd, or do you want a golf buggy?"

"Walking. I woke up this morning with pain in my legs. I'll take that over the numbness every day of the week," he replied.

"Sounds like something's healing," I mumbled, glad he was getting some feeling back, but sorry he was in pain.

He smiled. "Yeah, it's an incredible feeling in here," he said, placing a hand over his chest.

Aria rushed over to me and held onto my leg. "Hi, Uncle Greg."

"Hello, princess," I replied, smiling. I peeled her hand off me and handed her back to Ruth.

"Can you all walk ahead, and we'll catch up? I just want to talk to Eliza for a moment," I asked.

"Sure, come on, Aria, there will be plenty of time to hang with Uncle Greg after the wedding," she told her daughter.

I waited until I was sure everyone was out of earshot, then I turned to look at Eliza again. "How soon do you want to get married?"

Her breath hitched. "You mean it?"

"Absolutely, I can't wait to call you my wife."

Eliza's grin would have lit up the dark as she beamed back at me. "Erm … Ireland. I'd need to get married in Ireland … I mean our mas need to be there and …"

"All right. After the wedding what say we talk to Tim, and we can organize our wedding then?"

"Oh. My. God. I'm getting married," she gushed, then frowned in the same breath. "We can't say anything to the band guys … the last thing I want is to steal Trinnie's thunder."

I chuckled. "Of course, we'll give it a day or two. It'll give me a chance to take you ring shopping before we go back to Ireland."

"Jesus, I'm getting married … and to Greg Booker. Do you realize how unbelievable that feels to me?"

I nodded. "Ditto." I smiled. "Now hurry up, or we'll miss Trinnie and Levi's nuptials."

ROW UPON ROW of rock stars sat in front of a bamboo arch covered in fresh flowers, dressed casually in shorts and T-shirts at Levi and Trinnie's request. Jude stood by Levi, who thankfully didn't look nervous in the least. The man that stood patiently waiting was a completely different person from the one who had looked shaken to his core less than twelve hours before.

As we took our seats in the front row on the groom's side of the seating beside Beth, Levi made eye contact with me. He smiled, then winked at me as if to say, *I got this.*

Billie Idol's "White Wedding" began to play over the loud speaker system, which brought mutterings of the lyrics from the rows of rock stars that couldn't help themselves from joining in. Even Jude and Levi appeared to be mouthing the words while we waited for Trinnie to arrive.

"Fucking perfect choice," I heard Rick Fars murmur from the row behind us. "Shh, and stop cussing," Coral, the female of his throuple, chastised him. As the song finished, another started as a recording of Levi singing a cover of that old The Style Council song, "You're The Best Thing".

I turned my head and saw Gabrielle, dressed in a simple baby-pink sundress, scattering pink rose petals in front of Sadie and Esther, who wore longer versions of the same style as Gabrielle's. Once they cleared the aisle and stood on the bride's side of the seating, Trinnie and her father came into view.

A collective gasp of approval from the guests hung in the air as everyone took her in. Dressed elegantly, in an ivory silk gown, she looked sensational. I glanced toward Levi again, who had tears in his eyes as he watched her move toward him, with a simple halo of pink flowers in her hair, and a small bouquet of pink peonies in front of her.

My eyes cut to her father who looked less put together, and plenty hung over after his first encounter with Deakon's weed cookies. This instantly made me lean forward and I caught Deakon's eyes, who flashed me a toothy grin as we shared the private joke.

Cutting back to the wedding party, I was in time to see Levi take Trinnie's hand from her father, lift it to his lips and press a kiss to her knuckles. He mouthed, "Are you okay?" Trinnie smiled and nodded.

A hush descended upon the group, as the preacher stepped

forward. Then the only sound on the beach was a few gulls in the distance and the soft waves lapping against the shore.

"Wow," the wedding officiant said as he glanced toward the people congregated to watch their friends being married. "I'm afraid my performance likely won't match up to the kind you're used to," he joked to all our peers. A ripple of laughter went back toward him.

"We've gathered here today in this beautiful setting, to witness the wedding of Theresa Dixon to Levi Milligan and to join them together in marriage."

The officiant left a short pause to add weight to the proceedings.

"Before we go further, I first need to ask if anyone present knows of any lawful impediment as to why this man and this woman should not be joined in matrimony?"

Levi visibly sighed in relief when no one made a comment. Jude whispered something in his ear and both Levi and Trinnie chuckled.

"Okay, ... that's good to know. We'll crack on then," the officiant said, making everyone laugh.

"The couple have written their own vows, so we'll start with Levi."

Levi reached for Trinnie's other hand, cleared his throat and faced her. "Theresa ... Trinnie," he said, smiling. "You came into my life right as I was walking out of a dark period in it. Since then, you have continued to be my beacon of light, my compass, my eternal flame.

"You make me breathe easier, sleep sounder, laugh louder, and love deeper for having you by my side. Baby, no matter where I am in the world, when you are with me, that's my home. Your calm patience, confidence, special brand of humor and reasoning capability to cope in the mad world that I live, makes you unique. My promise to you in this married life we are facing together is to always be faithful, to protect you, love and defend you, and most importantly to treasure you, for you are my queen. In sickness and in health, my love for you will remain infinite, Trinnie, and I can't wait to grow old with you."

"Thank you, Levi," the officiant said as Trinnie who had been quietly crying, accepted a second tissue from Esther before Esther moved back, to take her place beside Sadie.

"Do you need a minute?" the officiant asked Trinnie.

She chuckled. "No. I promised myself I wouldn't cry."

"As long as that's the only promise you break today," Levi mumbled at her and winked. Everyone chuckled.

"Alright, I'm ready," she said, huffing out another breath and nodding toward the officiant. She gazed into Levi's eyes and the smile on her face fell. "Levi Milligan. I had a crush on you in middle school when you didn't even know I existed."

"I did," Levi argued, smiling.

"Alright, maybe as Gemma's geeky friend with the braces," she agreed, making everyone chuckle. "Who knew then we'd be here today, with me about to become your wife?" Levi flashed her an affectionate smile. "When we became friends, we both had scarred hearts and had become wary of the world around us.

"Perhaps it really was fate that we met on the beach that day, and why the familiarity of our past has helped lead the way for us," she suggested. "Once we morphed from friends to lovers that was an especially scary time for me. I had barely left my old life at that point, and yet, almost against my will, I fell hopelessly in love with you.

"During that time, one question burned in my mind—I have you now, but how do I keep you? Since then, you've taught me time and again that it's your job to stay. Now I can't imagine life without you. Not only did you steal my heart, but you stole my daughter's as well. And no matter what we face in the future— good, bad, happy or sad— I promise I'll always try to give you the love and support you deserve, because you are my one in a billion, Levi."

"Thank you," the wedding officiant muttered. "Now we move on to the declaration of intent and exchange of rings."

Jude pulled a small velvet pouch out of his shorts pockets and emptied it into his hands. The officiant placed them on a plinth next to Levi.

It then took less than a minute for the couple to exchange rings before the officiant finally announced them as man and wife.

Levi grabbed Trinnie, slid his hands down her back, grabbed her arse and kissed her hard, much to the pleasure of the rowdy bunch of rock stars witnessing the event.

Another cheer went up when "Signed, Sealed, Delivered I'm Yours" by Stevie Wonder began to play as Levi and Trinnie made for the aisle. Levi, ever the showman, swung Trinnie into his arms and waltzed her back past everyone. From my perspective it was the perfect song to end their nuptials.

"So, I think I missed half of the vows because I went off in a daydream trying to think what I'd say about you," Eliza confessed, still elated after my impromptu proposal right before the wedding. "Can I ask you something?" she mumbled in a serious tone, with a worried look on her face, as everyone made to leave. I held her back until it was just the two of us left.

"Shoot," I said, sensing something was bugging her.

"I need to ask you if you got carried away by the moment earlier. It's okay if you did because I never expected you to ask—"

"You to marry me?" I said, finishing her sentence. "Baby, I've been drunk as a skunk and married someone for a bet. You seriously think I'd have asked you if I wasn't serious. What I did might have felt impulsive, and maybe it was, but I have never wanted to marry you more than I do right now."

"Oh, well ... I was just checking," she said, all signs of concern instantly gone from her face.

"Don't second guess yourself, Lizzie. I felt jealous that it was Levi and Trinnie up there, and not us." The smile that lit up her face made me grin in return.

"Now come on, let's get drunk and do something stupid—like make a baby or something." Eliza chuckled, but she didn't admonish me for making such a suggestion.

"We really are going to be okay this time, aren't we, Greg," she said. One glance at her smiling face and I realized that it wasn't a question my Lizzie was asking, it was a statement of her newfound faith in us.

"You bet your arse we are."

EPILOGUE

GREG (1 YEAR LATER)

"I can't believe you got me on a plane," my ma admitted, marveling at the ocean as Raff drove Eliza's family and mine in the van, to the house Trinnie used to own in Key Largo.

"I can't believe it either … or that I'm an uncle—or that this eejit is in charge of a six-week-old baby," Tim joked, elbowing me. I grinned widely because I knew he was secretly delighted to have a baby niece to dote over.

"Eliza said you were great in the birthing room, Greg."

"I was!" I grinned. "If I wasn't a rock star, I think I would have made an amazing midwife." Raff chuckled and shook his head. "What? You don't think so?" I challenged.

"I could say something, but it wouldn't be appropriate in front of a priest, your mother and Eliza's family."

"Oh, so it would be along the lines of gynecologist jokes?" When his grin widened, I knew I'd tapped into that dirty mind of his. "Probably keep those thoughts to yourself," I said, winking.

Beth, Sadie and Deakon were at our house with Eliza when we arrived home with everyone.

"Oh, I want one, Deakon," Sadie cooed, cradling Ciara in her arms.

"Put her down, it might be catching," Deakon teased, although I saw the wistful look in his gaze when he glanced a moment too long at our daughter.

"So, she was a honeymoon baby," my brother remarked, obviously having done the math from our wedding to Ciara's birth in his head.

"Yep. We didn't waste any time. As soon as the date was set for the wedding, we got busy making a baby," Eliza informed him.

"And there was I thinking I was marrying two virgins in my chapel on your wedding day," Tim joked.

"Don't you ever wish ..." my ma asked, looking at Tim.

"No, Ma. I have enough of a flock to care for without one that pisses, shits and wants me to feed them all the time." Deakon, Floyd and I cracked up laughing.

"Tim loves sitting for our girls, don't you, Tim?"

"Aria's a delight. Myra, well, sometimes I think that one is possessed. She bit my thigh the last time I didn't give in to her wants," he remarked, laughing.

"I love kids, but we're just not ready for one, are we Raff?" After an initial blow up with Levi when he found out about Raff and Beth, Raff kept his job—and Beth. Partly because I said that I'd employ Raff myself if the band tried to get rid of him, and Beth had a bust up with Levi.

"Nah, we don't get as much time as we want together ... not that I'm complaining," Raff mumbled, glancing toward me.

"Life should get a little less crazy now you're solely on me," I remarked, smiling.

Since Eliza and I had gotten married, Raff had continued to work mainly with me. He'd been back and forth to Ireland several times since Levi's wedding, and he'd accompanied me to Eliza's maternity appointments as well. I made sure he was well compensated for the extra time.

Deakon, Korry and I had pushed for a review of security, since Korry and Bernadette lived all the way up in Coco Beach. Raff was being run ragged, trying to keep up with everyone, while Bodhi and Mikey tended to cover Levi and sometimes Deakon.

Eventually a new guy, Keith, was hired to shadow Korry and Bernadette.

The doorbell rang and Raff answered it.

Levi, his brother Dante, sister Catelina, Trinnie and Gabrielle came in. "You met my brother and sister, right?" Levi asked, not appearing to be fazed by the new additions to his family.

"Yeah, at that barbecue you had the first time you met one another after knowing you were related," I mumbled, nodding. "Nice to see you again."

"The house looks amazing. Eliza's done wonders with it," Trinnie mused as she cast her eyes around her former home.

"We can't thank you guys enough," I mumbled, humbled by her and Levi's generosity. They had gifted us Trinnie's house on our wedding day because Levi had bought another house nearby to gift Gabby when she was old enough. As Trinnie was going to put hers on the market, Levi decided to give her the money and gift the house to us.

Being the song writer in the group, Levi's wealth far exceeded the rest of us, and as I was a late edition to the group, although I had plenty of funds, I was still playing financial catch up compared to the rest of the band.

"Thanks for inviting us," Catelina said, smiling. "Congratulations, by the way," she added.

"Thanks, I did most of the work making the baby, Eliza just shoved it out," I joked. Levi, Catelina and Dante laughed. I glanced at Eliza who had obviously heard what I said. "I mean ... Eliza was incredible in the birthing room. You should have seen her."

Eliza gave me a secret smile and my heart clenched when I remembered what she went through to bring our beautiful daughter into this world.

"Oh, looks like I've lost my wife for a while," Levi muttered as Trinnie swept in, and scooped the baby out of Sadie's arms. Gabrielle peered over her mom's arms, took a tiny hand in her finger and looked completely enthralled. "Gabby, they're quiet like that for about two hours a day, the rest of the time they need tending to, so don't even think about liking babies until you're my age. It would kill my reputation if I was a grandfather."

"When is Jude getting here?"

"Anytime between now and bedtime, with the toddler version of himself Dylan is, and a wayward daughter like Honey," Levi replied.

Eliza came up and wrapped her hands around my waist from behind. I turned into her and hugged her back. "You, okay? Anytime you need to duck out, grab Ciara and I'll come and find you."

"How amazing is this, everyone under one roof?" she mused.

"Just don't let my brother take a swim while Levi's brother and sister are here. They look like pretty conservative people to me."

Eliza turned to check Dante out and chuckled. "He's a great looking man and looks like an older Levi but with short hair. Although, come on, who wears a pinstripe suit in the Keys?"

"He's a professional New Yorker," I reminded her.

"So, Tim's a priest, he hasn't turned up here wearing his cassock," she argued.

"Great place you've got here," Ruth mumbled wistfully. "Year-round sunshine too."

"Maybe you should come for the summers," Eliza suggested.

"Oh, you know what? Don't tempt me. With Floyd teaching at the university now, he's got almost three months off in summer …

although it would need to be next year now ..." she trailed off thoughtfully.

"That's it. You're coming. We're off on an eight-week tour next year, then we've got a few months off for the summer, due to Levi and Jude's commitment with the kids, then we'll be back in the studio after that to cut our next album."

"Fuck me, it's like an expedition just for a ten-minute drive," Jude mumbled as he came in the door carrying his eighteen-month-old son.

"Aw, look at you," Sadie gushed, taking Dylan from Jude's arms, while Honey wriggled her hand out from Esther's hold and made a beeline for Aria.

Dylan fussed, so Sadie set him down and he immediately toddled toward Deakon and Sadie.

"Hey, Greg," Esther said, kissing me on the cheek then doing the same to Eliza. "Things settling down now?" Esther asked Eliza.

"Yeah, for the first month we were both like headless chickens, but thanks to you and the tips you gave me about breast feeding and sleep routines, Ciara is quite the contented baby."

"That's great, glad I could help."

"Honey, put him down," Jude muttered. "Esther tell her, she's always trying to lift that kid up," Jude grumbled.

"Listen to good ol' grumpy pants," Esther mumbled, as she strode over, picked Dylan up and held him in her arms. She wandered back toward us, and Jude gave her a brooding look. "Give him here, you shouldn't lift him like that."

Esther's face grew red, and Eliza narrowed her eyes. "Why not? Are you pregnant or something?"

Esther's eyes darted to Jude's, and he let out a tired sigh. "Your fault, not mine," she muttered.

"Are you pregnant again, Esther?" Eliza prompted again.

Esther shrugged. "Five and a half months already," she

mumbled ... and don't worry, we're getting a nanny this time," she added.

"Funny you should say that," Floyd mumbled. "We were going to hold back, given that Ciara isn't even a couple of months old, but you're going to be an auntie and uncle again, Ruth's due in four months herself."

"What? You're having another one?"

Ruth nodded. "Must be something in the water ..." she mused, glancing at Esther. Both women laughed.

Gabrielle came up and wrapped her arms around Levi, "Just think, Not My Dad," she teased affectionately. "While they're all busy struggling with sleep deprivation, teaching their kids how to wipe their own butts and how to hold spoons to feed themselves, we'll be out there on the water, riding jet skis, parasailing and having fun."

"Alright, Gabrielle, you've had your fun." Trinnie muttered.

"Jesus, you're not pregnant as well, are you?" Deakon muttered, chuckling.

Trinnie and Gabrielle all looked at each other, then they both looked at Levi, "As a matter of fact, I am."

A hush fell among us because although Levi had said he didn't mind not having a kid of his own, most of us suspected it was a sacrifice he had been willing to make for Trinnie, who had figured she was too old to be a mom again.

During this quiet time, Levi stood frozen and stared at Trinnie before he spoke. "Baby, don't make jokes like that," he admonished. I heard the hurt in his tone.

"No joke—I'm pregnant."

Levi scoffed. "Pregnant?" he asked, his eyes bulging as he looked from Trinnie to me, then to Deakon.

"This might be too much information for everyone here, but you know how I began putting on weight and my period has been irregular for the past year? I figured I might have been perimenopausal, so I went to see my doctor. It turns out we're sixteen weeks pregnant."

"Sixteen weeks? That's what? Nearly halfway there, right? This isn't a stunt, is it?" Levi asked. The emotional turmoil of the news changed his wide-eyed, facial expressions from concern to confusion on his ashen faced, as he ran a hand nervously through his hair. Trinnie shook her head, smiling affectionately toward him.

"Shocking, right?" she asked, smiling.

"Seriously? I'm going to be a dad again?"

Trinnie teared up, nodded, and grabbed Gabrielle close to her chest, Levi's comment which had included Gabrielle clearly affected her.

"Holy crap," he mumbled, "We're having a baby?" he said, this time with tears in his eyes. "Baby, I ... fuck, I'm speechless," he mumbled.

Everyone clapped and congratulated them, but I could see Levi was still struggling to process the news.

"Maybe you should take Levi into the kitchen for a bit," Eliza suggested.

I slapped a hand on his back, smiled at his siblings and guided them toward the patio instead of the kitchen, figuring there would be less interruptions there.

"I can't believe you did this in front of everyone," Levi muttered, warily. "How do you feel about it ... I know you said ..."

Trinnie pressed her fingers to his lips. "Like you, I was shocked, but I couldn't be happier now that I've seen this little nugget on the scan," she mumbled, rubbing her belly. "Rock stars aren't the only ones with shock factor you know. I did toy with telling you last night, but I figured you'd have been up all night."

"A scan. Do we know what it is yet? Is it too early to tell?"

"I have an envelope from the scan in my purse with the sex of the baby. I haven't opened it yet, so although I saw the scan briefly, I asked if the sonographer could give us a picture and put the gender in an envelope. We've got to go again in a month for the proper twenty-week scan."

Trinnie handed Levi the envelope from her purse. Gabrielle bounced on her toes excitedly as I made to walk away. Levi grabbed my hand. "Stay," he muttered.

Levi began opening the envelope, stopped and glanced toward Gabrielle. "This won't change how I feel about you, Gabby," he disclosed.

Gabrielle flashed him a wicked grin. "I know. But I guess I'll need to start calling you Dad now ... I mean, we wouldn't want to confuse the new baby ... me being its sister and everything."

Levi grinned. "I'd be honored if you called me that."

"Go on then, open it. I'm dying to know what it is," Gabby prompted.

Levi pulled out the scan picture and for a long while he stared at the grainy image. He wiped away a tear and Trinnie put her hand on his forearm as a measure of silent support.

"You need to turn it over to see if it's a boy or a girl," she coaxed.

Reluctantly, he did as she said, then immediately turned it back to the picture again. "We're having a son," he choked out. The disbelief in his tone made my heart clench for him.

"Good, I wanted to be the only girl," Gabby replied.

"I'll leave you guys to it," I suggested, patting Levi on the shoulder. "Congratulations again to you all," I said before I stepped inside the house and closed the patio door.

"No Korry and Bernadette again today?" Beth asked as I passed her on the way back to find Eliza.

"It was us or a week in Bali. Go figure, Bali won."

As everyone began mingling, and settling down for the first barbecue we were hosting at our home, I went in search of Eliza and found her taking some salad bowls out of the fridge.

"Come here, Mrs. Booker, ... my beautiful, sexy, hot wife," I offered. "You were given the green light at the six week check yesterday, right?"

She smiled coyly. "Are you that desperate, Greg Booker."

"That I am. My poor dick thinks I'm in prison … solitary confinement at that. I just want to offer him a glimmer of hope that he might see some action tonight."

"Let me ask you this? Do you want another baby soon?" she asked, believing that would put me off.

"If it looks anything like Ciara and her mother …" I trailed off, raising a suggestive brow. Eliza swatted my chest. I caught her wrist and pulled her close to my chest. "Do you trust me, Eliza Booker?" I whispered.

"I do," she said without hesitation.

"Are you happy, Lizzie?" I pressed.

"You really need to ask me? Can't you tell by the look on my face."

"What about my face? What does it say to you?" I asked.

"It says, you dote on me, and despite me being a challenging, stubborn arsehole sometimes, you don't want to live without me."

"See, there you go! Now how do we get rid of this lot, so that I can take my woman to bed?"

The End

The Pulsetunes Rock Gods may be back in the future for a catch up, so follow my newsletter for details.

***

Want to know what happened to Levi when he met his siblings, Dante and Catelina? Sign up to my newsletter and receive access to the link for the bonus chapter.

https://dl.bookfunnel.com/rb7thhyqlf

UNTIL GREG PLAYLIST

Until Greg Playlist
Forever Young – Bob Dylan
How Do I Say Goodbye - Dean Lewis
Battleships - Daughtry
Dear Future Husband - Meghan Trainor
Let It Go – James Bay
Never Say Never - Justin Beiber ft Jayden Smith
The Lazy Song - Bruno Mars
Fighting my Way Back - Thin Lizzy
Iris - Goo Dolls
Thinking of You - Katy Perry
Swallowtail jig
You know I'm no good – Amy Winehouse
Always Remember Us This Way – Lady Gaga
All You're Dreaming Of" by Liam Gallagher
White Wedding - Billy Idol
You're The Best Thing -The Style Council

ALSO BY K.L. SHANDWICK

You can find more emotional stories with K.L.'a amazing rock star romances here.

The Everything Trilogy

Enough Isn't Everything

Everything She Needs

Everything I Want

Love With Every Beat

just Jack

Everything Is Yours

Last Score Series

Gibson's Legacy

Trusting Gibson

Gibson's Melody

Piper: A Last Score Spin off

Ready for Flynn Series

Ready For Flynn, Part 1

Ready For Flynn, Part 2

Ready For Flynn, Part 3

Flying Under the Radar

Other novels

Missing Beats

Exhale and Move On

Free to Breathe

Another Life

SOULED

My Way Back

Luvluck Novellas

Lucky Break

Lucky Chance

Lucky Star

Lucky Valentine

Lucky Man

PulseTunes Rock Gods

Until Jude

Until Levi

Until Deakon

Until Korry

Until Greg

KELLY SHANDWICK TITLES

WILD ROMANCE SAGA

CHASING LOVE BILLIE

CHASING LOVE SAWYER

CHASING LOVE JAMES

CHASING LOVE TRICIA

CHASING LOVE ERIN

CHASING LOVE RYDER

UNTIL JOSH

UNTIL LORNA

ACKNOWLEDGMENTS

Editor : Elizabeth Gardner
Proof Reader: Sue Noyes
Cover Design: Francesca- Wingfield Designs
Photograph: Eric Battershell (O Snap Media)
Cover Model : Ryan VanDyke
Beta Readers: Nikki Costello, Wendy Hodges, April Stacey, Coleen Walton, Serena Worker.

Special thanks to my dedicated Beta readers who do this for the love of books
& to Sue Noyes for her continued support
and to Serena for keeping me sane!

ABOUT THE AUTHOR

K.L. Shandwick writes emotional contemporary romance with angst, heart and heat.

She enjoys writing love stories that take place in America for characters who deserve second chances. These characters have flaws and real-life issues, but their stories have that element of escapism we all love in a book. When K.L. isn't writing, she's much in demand by her eight-year-old granddaughter, who insists her grandma can do anything. At the time of writing, she has requested K.L. teach her how to do the splits, juggle, and to play the violin... all of which K.L. has no particular talent for. Her granddaughter insists K.L. is her superhero and can overcome these minor hurdles.